The Weight of Snow and Regret

Elizabeth Gauffreau

Paul Stream Press, LLC ~ Nottingham, NH

Cover Image: "Sunshine on Snow," by Akseli Gallen-kallela, 1906, public domain.

ISBN (print, softcover): 979-8-9907913-2-9

ISBN (print, hardcover): 979-8-9907913-3-6

ISBN (ebook): 979-8-9907913-4-3

Library of Congress Control Number: 2024925369

Published by Paul Stream Press, Nottingham, NH

For information: contact@paulstreampress.com

https://paulstreampress.com

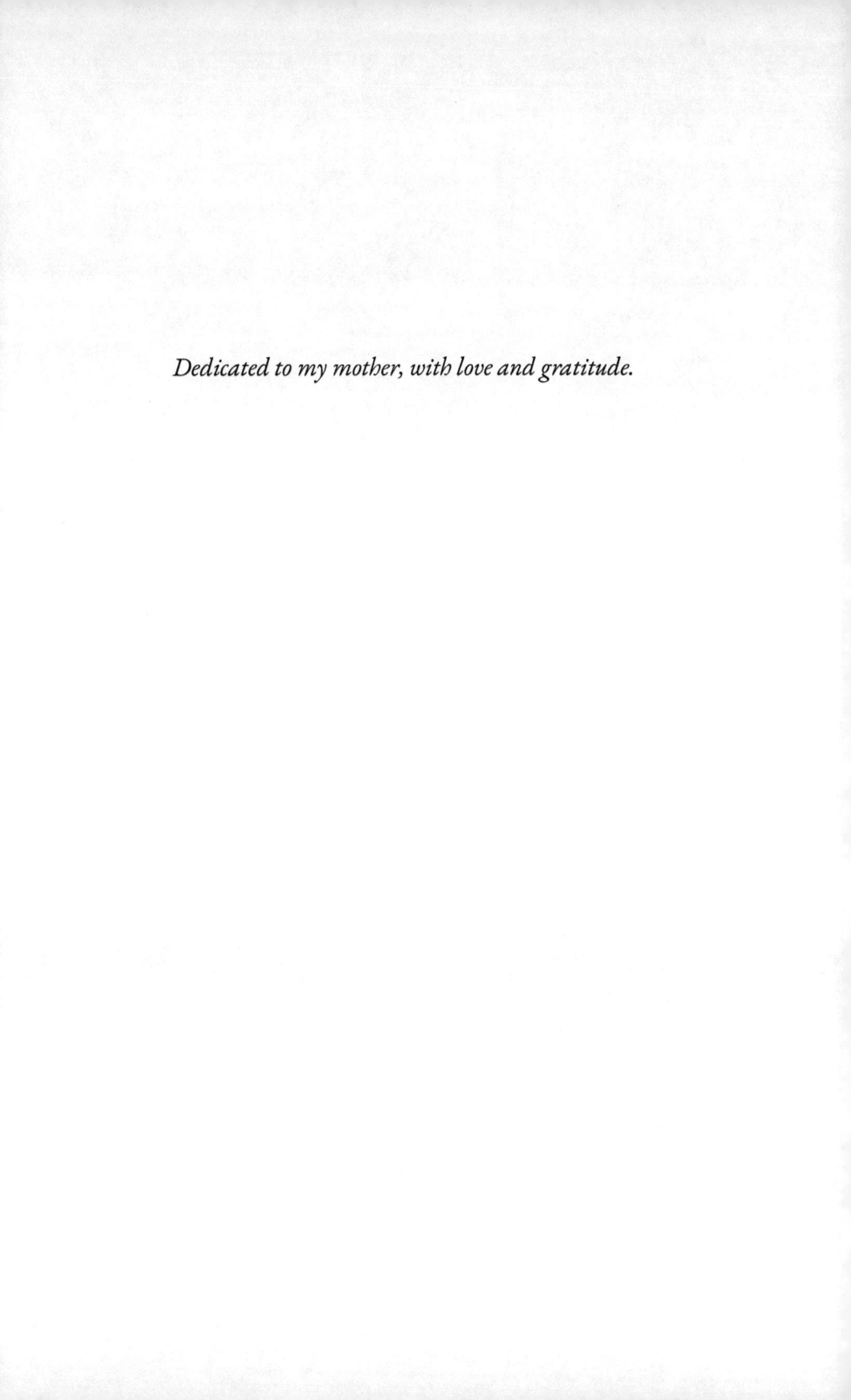

Dedicated to my mother, with love and gratitude.

DISPLACED

CLAIRE

—◦—

January 1968

As the stranger's sedan rolled through the snowy, alien landscape, Claire wondered if she might be homeless. She had not yet considered homelessness, that state of losing a house to foreclosure, a family to death or estrangement, or, worse, that pitiable state of losing a past to demons no one else can see.

The frigid air had begun its assault the night before, the skin of her face stiffening at its touch, so unlike the summer swelter of home that enveloped and caressed. The cold had driven the heat of her life's blood deep into her core, leaving the rest of her in a desperate huddle and shake trying to find it again.

Cold air eddied around her ankles, passing through the thin fabric of her slacks.

"Sorry the heater don't work," the man driving the car said around the unlit pipe clenched between his teeth. He had told her his name back in Enosburg Falls, but she couldn't remember it now. He had the oddest-looking hat on his head.

"I keep meaning to take the car into Jim Tatro to get the heater fixed, but I ain't got around to it yet. Jim takes forever. He'll keep a vehicle for weeks; you know what I mean?"

Claire shook her head.

"Nice feller and the best mechanic you're ever gonna find—but between you, me, and the lamppost, he's got a drinking problem. I never had to arrest him for it, mind, but still—"

The car turned onto a narrow road surrounded by snow-covered fields flowing from a wooded hillside.

"I got people up there." The driver—Claire still couldn't remember his name—pointed to a hillside, headstones nearly buried in snow. She quickly looked away, grateful he didn't tell her who his people were or how long they had been up there on that hillside, frozen in their graves beneath the snow.

"This here's Sheldon," he announced.

A trestle bridge, a faded brick church with faded stained glass, a small cluster of weather-beaten houses.

Before long, he turned onto an even narrower road, its surface covered in packed snow, dirt sprinkled haphazardly down the center. The car slipped, and Claire grabbed the armrest.

"Don't worry," the driver said cheerfully. "I got sandbags in the trunk."

Claire didn't loosen her grip on the armrest.

Trees lining the narrow, winding road advanced and retreated, their branches laden with snow. They might have been pines once. More snow-covered fields, dried brown skeletons of summer flowers poking through, here and there a derelict barn. They crossed a single-lane iron bridge over a snow-covered river—or a river-shaped field covered in snow. Claire could not be sure.

The car jolted and bumped.

"Sorry about that. Frost heaves. This stretch of road is terrible for 'em. I probably should get Jim to replace the shocks when he does the heater. When I get around to it."

They pulled into the driveway of a small, white house with a bell tower on top and a shed of some sort off to one side. The driver gently pumped the brakes to bring the car to a stop.

"Here we are." He turned off the engine. "This was the schoolhouse up till the '40s. The village had no use for it after they built the new school, so I got it for a song; you know what I mean?"

This time, Claire didn't bother shaking her head.

Despite the heater not working, the car was getting even colder with the engine turned off. Claire wasn't sure whether she should get out of the car on her own or wait for the man to open the door for her—or whether he meant for her to get out of the car at all.

"You sit tight, and I'll get the door for you." He walked around the car and opened the door. "You better take my arm. The driveway's slick, and your feet ain't dressed for it."

As they gingerly made their way down the driveway, a woman in a bulky sweater appeared in the doorway of the house. She pushed open the storm door and hollered, "Johnny, Dwight Demers called here after you. He said you're looking for him."

Johnny. That was his name, easy enough to remember. Deceptively so.

"Figures," Johnny said. "Now, we're gonna have to turn around and go back. Master of timing, that one. He'll be late to his own funeral. Well, come in the house while I call him back, and the wife will make you something hot to drink."

Johnny held the door open, and Claire stepped into what appeared to be the main living area of the house. She stood hesitantly on the mat, unsure what she should do. Large windows on either side of the room looked out over the snowy landscape. The room smelled strongly of wood smoke and pipe tobacco.

"Have a seat on the couch here," Johnny's wife said, "and I'll get the kettle on."

Claire was about to do as she was told when Johnny hollered from the kitchen, "Ain't time for the kettle! There's coffee in the pot."

Johnny's wife shook her head and gestured toward the couch. "First time I ever seen that one in a hurry. How do you take your coffee? Cream and sugar?"

Claire nodded. She heard the telephone dial spin as Johnny's wife proceeded to the kitchen to fetch her coffee. Claire didn't bother straining to hear what Johnny was saying about her. Hearing it wouldn't change anything. Hearing it could only serve to make the situation she found herself in even more surreal, sitting on this worn plaid couch in a country schoolhouse, about to face down a cup of coffee she didn't want. It was bound to be bitter.

"Here's your coffee," Johnny's wife said.

As Claire took the cup from her, Johnny entered the room. "We best be going before Dwight changes his mind. You know how he is."

Out the door, up the frozen driveway, back in the ungainly sedan with the broken heater, the cold air eddying around her ankles.

The ride back to Enosburg Falls was even colder than the ride over, the skeletal flowers more forlorn, the derelict barns about to collapse beneath the weight of snow and regret.

A New Arrival

Hazel

***

January 1968

THE COLD WINTER SUN hung low on the horizon, casting long shadows through the trees where once had stood clear meadow. Looking out the kitchen window as she peeled potatoes for supper, Hazel regretted the loss of the meadow—but when a meadow lost its usefulness, the forest would have its way and reclaim it.

The shadows lengthened. Hard winter had set in, a time of concern for the animals in the unheated barn and worry for her husband crossing the frozen dooryard in the dark to tend to them. Keeping up with the farm wore on him, now that he was in his sixties and there were no able-bodied men left with the wits needed to help him with the milking and the fields. Like it or not, Paul was showing his age.

As Hazel cut a bad spot from a potato, she thought she saw the bump and flash of headlights from a vehicle slowly making its way up the icy driveway. Looking more closely, she was surprised to see the Enosburg town constable's LTD.

By 1968, new arrivals at the Sheldon Poor Farm were rare, just the occasional pitiful soul too infirm or senile for their families to bother with anymore. Even the derelicts no longer appeared at their door seeking a fresh start, only to drift into drink once more after a decent meal and a good delousing.

Hazel and Paul had seen so many of those old rounders come and go over the years. Buried a few, too, in the farm's cemetery down the road. Each time Paul looked into an open grave, he pronounced its intended occupant a "poor bastard," while Hazel murmured, "No mother's son should come to such an end as this."

The only constant as the years had gone by was Philo Roy, catching a freight train south at the first sign of snow, returning with the robins in the spring. Every spring, Hazel wondered if he would be back or if he had met his preordained fate under those crushing steel wheels.

As the LTD pulled into the dooryard, she was surprised to see that the passenger huddled in the back seat didn't appear elderly. Hazel wondered what could be wrong with her.

The LTD eased to a stop, and the front doors opened. Two men got out, each in his official capacity, Dwight Demers as Overseer of the Poor for Enosburg, and Johnny Clough as Enosburg Town Constable. Such as he was.

Dwight would be expecting coffee, and Hazel got a fresh pot going on the stove as a matter of course.

Johnny opened the rear door of the car and leaned down to help the woman out. Before she could stand to her full height, her feet slid out from under her, and she went down.

Hazel rushed from the kitchen, yanked open the front door, and stepped onto the porch, holding the door open as Dwight and Johnny walked the woman to the house, the snow squeaking under their boots with each step. On either side of her, the two men struggled to hold her up as her feet slithered and slipped on the packed snow. Their breath steamed from their mouths in shallow bursts.

Paul emerged from his office across the hall. "What the hell, Dwight? You're bringing us another one?"

Hazel reached for the woman and helped her to the kitchen, easing her onto a chair at the table. "Never mind about that, Paul. Get me a blanket."

"I got the milking to do."

"Never *mind*. Get me a blanket!"

Hazel sat in the chair next to the new arrival and took her hands to warm them. The woman's dirt-smudged face was so pinched from the cold, Hazel couldn't tell how old she was or if her face held any expression. Even her eyes seemed frozen in her face, as if mere minutes ago she had witnessed a horrific event, a fatal car accident or a house fire too far gone for those trapped inside screaming to be rescued. She wore a grubby trench coat, no hat, nothing on her hands, her hair a dark, tangled mess.

Hazel could not recall ever seeing anyone look so cold, as if the marrow of her bones had seized, and she were freezing from the inside out. Her face was drained of color, and her lips were blue.

"Paul, a blanket!"

Paul's footsteps trudged down the hall as Johnny and Dwight deposited their coats on the hall tree before entering the kitchen.

"What happened to her, Johnny? Was she in some kind of accident?"

"Couldn't tell you. I got a call from Norman Lapierre's cousin over to Orchard Street. Said he had a trespasser, and she refused to leave. When I got over there, I found her in the garage, half-froze sitting on the floor under a tarp."

"Norman Lapierre's cousin on Orchard Street?" Hazel said. "Which one is that?"

"Couldn't tell you. I can't keep them Lapierres straight. Too damn many of 'em."

"Roland Lapierre," Dwight interjected. "He's not from around here."

Paul returned to the kitchen, and Hazel stood up to take the blanket from him. He'd brought the handmade quilt from the footboard of their own bed. Maybe he sensed something different about this new arrival. Or maybe not. He'd probably just grabbed the closest thing to hand.

Hazel arranged the quilt around the new arrival as she would for an invalid, gently so as not to pressure aching joints and tender skin. The woman's deep-set eyes might have registered a flicker of thanks. Hazel could not be sure, just as the woman's hazel eyes seemed unsure what color they wanted to be.

"What happened?" Paul said. "Where did she come from? I thought we weren't taking new inmates."

Hazel winced. After twenty years, would he never learn? "Residents, Paul."

Johnny took his pipe from his mouth and a packet of tobacco from his pocket, the precursor to a meandering response. Hazel pulled a face and shook her head at him. The last thing the poor woman needed was pipe smoke blown in her face, not when they didn't know what was wrong with her. She could very well be ill.

"Be quick about it, Johnny," Paul said. "I got the milking to do."

"We don't know. Like I said before, I got a call from Norman Lapierre's cousin over to Orchard Street. Said he had a trespasser, and she refused to leave. I found her in the garage. When I asked her who she was, she said she was Roland Lapierre's wife."

"If she's Roland Lapierre's wife, what was she doing in the garage?" Paul said. "Did he throw her out of the house? Did they have some kind of fight? We don't need no more trouble."

"Dunno. She clammed up when I asked her."

Hazel looked closely at the new arrival's face, wondering if bruises would rise to the surface when the skin finally warmed. The poor thing did look fragile, huddled in the quilt with her pale, pinched face and frozen eyes. She couldn't weigh much more than a hundred pounds.

"That's the peculiar thing," Johnny said. "When I took her to the house, that Lapierre feller denied even knowing her. He refused to let us in the house. Left the two of us standing on the porch, me trying to talk to him through the storm door like a damn fool."

"She didn't have ID?" Paul said. "We don't need no more trouble."

Johnny shook his head and swiped a bead of sweat from his forehead. Hazel didn't bother informing him it was his monstrosity of a trapper hat making him sweat. Come the first snowfall, that thing went on his head, and on his head it would remain until ice-out.

"What about her pocketbook?" Hazel said.

"No pocketbook, just a suitcase."

Hazel looked into the new arrival's frozen eyes to offer encouragement, even nodding a little—but the poor, pinched face gave no indication she knew where she was or why she was there.

Dwight had removed himself to the stove, hovering over the percolator as if one of the elderly women watching the four o'clock movie in the living room were going to swoop in, snatch the percolator off the stove, and go running out the door with it into the frozen twilight. "How about I serve this coffee, Hazel?"

Hazel rose from the table. "I'll get it, Dwight."

If Dwight served the coffee, he would be sure to seek out doughnuts to go with it, and there were only enough doughnuts left in the pantry for breakfast in the morning. While she didn't want to appear inhospitable, there wasn't a penny to spare in the poor farm's food budget. Dwight should know that. Since becoming treasurer of the Sheldon Home Association, it was his budget.

After Hazel served the two officials their coffee, she positioned a cup and spoon in front of the new arrival, who reached her hand from under the quilt and turned the cup upside down.

"Oh!" Hazel said. Never before had a new arrival to the farm refused a cup of coffee. "What's the matter? Is your stomach upset? I could make you some weak tea. Would that be better?"

The new arrival shook her head, then, as if thinking better of it, whispered in a cold, pinched voice, "No, thank you all the same."

Johnny indicated with two raps of his spoon against his cup that he was ready to resume his story. "So, there I was on the side porch playing is-not/is-so through the storm door and getting nowhere fast, with this poor woman standing next to me half-froze to death. I finally give up and drove her over to Doc Wetherbee to get her checked out."

"What did he say?" Hazel asked.

Johnny took a sip of his coffee, made a face, and added sugar. "Doc said she didn't appear to be hurt or sick or mental or nothing. She could name the year and the president of the United States, so he sent us on our way. I didn't know what to do with her, so I called Dwight. I weren't about to take her to St. Albans jail for sitting in Roland Lapierre's garage. Even if she did claim to be his wife when she ain't."

Dwight picked up his cup, then set it back on the table. "That puts me in a bind, approval-wise. It's obvious she's not from the county. But if we don't know where she's from, I don't know what authorities to contact." He drank from his cup and nodded gravely, agreeing with himself.

Paul's chair creaked as his leg jiggled under the table. "What did Norman Lapierre say?"

"I didn't talk to him. He weren't there."

"Well, did you call him and ask? Wouldn't Norman know who his cousin's wife is?"

"Mebbe no, mebbe so," Johnny said. "There's so many of them damn Lapierres I seriously doubt they can keep themselves straight."

Hazel could see from the set of his jaw that Paul was losing patience with Dwight and Johnny in their official capacities.

Before Paul could interject that the two officials needed to be on their way and take the troublesome woman with them, Hazel said, "You were right to bring her here. She can stay with us as long as she needs to. It's not like we don't have the room."

"That's not the point," Dwight said. "I can only authorize people from Enosburg to be provided for here."

"Hazel knows that," Paul said.

"Maybe I should go back up to Orchard Street and see if I can get him to talk." Johnny tried again to go for his tobacco. "Although them Lapierres are awful stubborn."

"There's no call for that," Dwight said. "I know we can't turn her out in the cold with no place to go. Why do you think I agreed to bring her here in the first place?" He turned to Paul. "I can give you two weeks to get her straightened out with a job."

Before Paul could respond, Hazel said, "It's not that simple, Dwight, and you know it. What kind of job is she supposed to get in Sheldon in the dead of winter with no transportation?"

"You can't expect a woman to work at the pulp mill," Johnny said, "even if somebody could give her a ride."

Hazel looked at the new arrival's face again. If she was aware that the three men, all in their official capacities, were talking about what to do with her and the problem she presented, neither her face nor her eyes gave any indication of it. Even so, it wasn't right to go on talking about her as if she weren't even there.

Hazel rose from the table, collected the two officials' cups and spoons, and set them in the sink.

Dwight and Johnny looked at each other. "I guess we best be going," said Johnny.

As the sound of Johnny Clough's LTD receded into the frozen twilight, Hazel resumed her place at the table next to their new arrival. In the twenty-odd years she and Paul had been managing the Sheldon Poor Farm, she could not recall any new arrivals who had come without their story—either already well-known or immediately relayed by an overseer of the poor in all its sorry detail.

The poor woman's teeth were chattering. She needed some food in her stomach, a hot bath, and a warm bed.

"When was the last time you ate?" Hazel said.

"I don't know." Again, that cold, barely audible whisper.

The late afternoon sounds of the living room drifted into the kitchen. The ebb and flow of voices from the television, an eddy of laughter, Lisa Thibodeau's loud splashes of disgust. Such a sad case, Lisa Thibodeau.

Reminded of her responsibility to the twelve permanent residents, Hazel reluctantly rose from the table. "Supper won't be for a while. Can I get you something to tide you over till then, maybe some toast?"

"Don't trouble yourself. Thank you all the same."

What a strange response from someone so obviously in need of help. Maybe Dwight and Johnny hadn't told her where they were taking her when they'd loaded her into the back of Johnny's LTD and set off for the poor farm. In this day and age, who would expect to be taken to the poor farm?

At the same time, Hazel didn't want to blurt out, "Do you know where you are?" as if the woman weren't in her right mind. Maybe the poor thing thought she'd been taken to Paul and Hazel's farmhouse, Paul and Hazel being a neighborly sort of couple who were willing to extend their kindness to strangers.

The smell of meatloaf cooking leaked from the oven. Hazel had to get to those potatoes.

"How about that coffee now?" Hazel turned over the new arrival's cup and picked up the percolator. "Cream and sugar are right here on the table."

The new arrival's forehead pinched. "I need to use the restroom." She fumbled with the quilt as she rose from her chair.

"Here, let me help you." Hazel draped the quilt on the back of the chair. "The bathroom is down the hall, second door on your left. Do you want me to take your coat?" But the new arrival was already out the door. Hazel hurried to the stove to get the potato water going, then back to the sink to peel the remaining potatoes as quickly as she could.

A few minutes later, the toilet flushed, and the hot water faucet squealed. Hazel gouged an eye out of the last potato. If she'd told Paul once to take care of that faucet, she'd told him a thousand times.

The new arrival reentered the kitchen with her trench coat still buttoned and belted. She resumed her seat at the table, pulling the quilt over her shoulders. The color had not yet returned to her face, although it did look a little less pinched. As warm as the kitchen was, with the oven on and the radiator gurgling and hissing steam, by now her face should have had a bright spot of pink high on each cheek.

Imagining her with rosy cheeks, Hazel could see that she appeared to be forty or so, attractive and ordinary, most likely a housewife or maybe a secretary. Her hands were curled around her coffee cup, perhaps to warm them, perhaps to stop them from shaking. Her left hand wore a wedding ring and a diamond, quite nice ones, from the look of them.

"Goodness!" Hazel said. "I didn't introduce myself. I'm Hazel Morgan. My husband Paul and I run this place."

The new arrival did not respond, staring into her coffee as if she expected something foul to rise to the surface.

Hazel hesitated. "What should I call you?"

The new arrival shook her head. "Nothing."

"Nothing?" Hazel paused to give her time to respond, but she remained silent.

"Well, that's all right. You can tell me when you're ready. You'll let me know if you need anything." This last a statement, not a question.

Going back and forth between the kitchen and the dining room to set the table, Hazel had doubts whether the new arrival would be able to manage eating with the others. To an outsider, meals in the dining room must appear pretty chaotic, what with Joey repeatedly asking Edna if her food was good, Elsie's crackling old voice asking when her daughter was coming, and Lisa's shrill voice flitting from insult to insult like some demonic pixie. And Homer. Sweet, gentle Homer, looking like a ferocious mountain man with his bushy, grizzled beard as his father patiently helped him with his food.

No, this woman was in a fragile state, the only saving grace being that Johnny Clough had sense enough to bring her here and not cart her off to St. Albans jail. Hazel had to give him credit for that.

When she returned to the kitchen, she found the new arrival slumped over with her arms on the table cradling her head. She hadn't touched her coffee. Hazel wondered if she should check for a pulse. Over the years, this was generally how she had found each female resident who had died: slumped in a chair, gone from this life with no fuss and little fanfare when she made the final, jolting journey to the cemetery down the road. The new arrival stirred, and Hazel let out the breath she didn't realize she had been holding. There was no way she was going to ask the poor woman to join the others in the dining room.

When the potatoes were almost ready, footsteps sounded on the porch. Paul back from the barn, right on time. After removing his barn boots, he went straight to the bathroom to wash. The faucet squealed, and a pipe thudded. How many times did she have to tell him he had promised to take care of that faucet?

Instead of going into his office to work on his reports, Paul came into the kitchen, the last thing Hazel needed.

"What's with her? She better not be passed out."

"She's not passed out; she's exhausted. I'm going to get a room ready for her and get her into bed."

Paul opened the oven door. "What about supper?"

"Get away from that oven, Paul. Supper's almost ready. I'll serve it after I get her settled."

"Dwight can't tell me one day to be thinking about other placements for the inmates we have and the next day bring us another one. And you didn't help none."

Hazel didn't bother to respond as Paul left the kitchen in a huff. She laid her hand gently on the new arrival's shoulder. "I'm going upstairs to get a room ready for you. I won't be long."

As she climbed the stairs, Hazel decided she had no choice but to put the new arrival on the unused third floor. There were several free sleeping rooms on the first floor, but most of the residents didn't sleep through the night, wandering the hall in search of the bathroom in a different house or moaning with ailments more easily endured in daylight. Poor Emmett still had night terrors when something on the television upset him.

Lisa Thibodeau was so unpredictable, she had the sleeping room next to the manager's suite. Beatrice and Carl were on the second floor, Beatrice on the women's side, Carl on the men's side, a locked door between them. The less said about those two, the better. Room 25, of course, was out of the question.

On the third floor, Hazel retrieved bedding, towels, and washcloths from the musty linen closet and hurried to Room 31. The room was chilly, as were all the rooms on the third floor in winter, the farthest away from the boiler in the basement. And, of course, in summer they were the hottest. But she didn't expect the new arrival to be with them that long.

Hazel quickly made up the bed and dusted the battered dresser and cigarette-scarred nightstand. The room wasn't much, but it would do for a short stay.

Returning to the kitchen, Hazel found that the new arrival hadn't moved. She spoke in a low voice, so as not to startle her. "Wake up, dear. I've made up your room."

The new arrival roused herself slowly, blinking as she raised her head. "I must have fallen asleep. I'm sorry."

"No need to apologize. Let's get you up to bed. I have you on the third floor. It's going to be chilly, I'm afraid."

The new arrival gave no response. As they left the kitchen, she looked so wobbly Hazel wondered whether she should try to help her up the stairs. Would she recoil at the touch of a strong arm around her shoulders or a firm hand at her elbow? Sometimes it was hard to tell which wound went deeper, bruised limbs or bruised dignity.

When they reached the third floor, Hazel opened the door to Room 31, watching the new arrival's face for a reaction, but there was none.

"That dresser is yours to use. You didn't bring any clothes?"

"In my suitcase."

"I didn't see a suitcase when you got here. Johnny must have forgotten about it and left it in the car."

The poor woman looked about to keel over. Dr. Wetherbee should have spent more time checking her over. Walking into his office under her own power and knowing that Lyndon Johnson was president of the United States didn't make her all right. He should have spent more time with her.

Hazel put her arm around her and led her to the bed. "Here, sit on the bed, and I'll get you a nightgown and robe. They'll be too big for you, but they should do until I can get Johnny to bring over your suitcase tomorrow."

After first scrubbing out a bathtub and running a bath, Hazel hurried down the stairs to the first floor, returning to Room 31 with one of her own flannel nightgowns, a winter robe, a new toothbrush, and an unopened tube of toothpaste.

After taking the new arrival to the bathroom, Hazel waited in the hall, knocking on the door and calling out every few minutes to make sure she hadn't slipped under the water. When she emerged from the bathroom, her face had regained some of its color. Hazel walked her back to Room 31. "Will you need anything else? I'm sorry the room is so cold."

"No, thank you. You've been very kind."

Still, Hazel hesitated on the threshold to the room, knowing full well that kindness would not be enough. "Well, good night, then."

As she descended the stairs, she couldn't help but wonder what would have happened to the nameless arrival if there had been no poor farm for Dwight and Johnny to bring her to. Johnny was right. She certainly didn't belong in jail, and she'd passed Dr. Wetherbee's psych evaluation. Such as it was. People in trouble with nowhere to live needed a place they could stay safe, warm, and fed while they took the time they needed to get back on their feet. They needed a safe haven right away, not when the government offices opened and the forms had been filled out.

Twilight had slipped into nightfall by the time Hazel got supper on the table. When she carried in the meatloaf, Paul and the residents had already taken their places in the dining room, all staring down at their empty plates in disbelief that the food was missing.

Setting the meatloaf on the table, Hazel said, "Beatrice, Carl, don't sit so close. Sit in your chairs properly, or I'm going to separate you."

She returned to the kitchen before either of them could answer her back.

When all the food was on the table, Hazel served the residents first, then Paul, last herself. "Who would like to say grace tonight?"

Joey's hand shot up. "Me, me, pick me!"

"You said grace last night. Let's give someone else a chance."

Joey pointed. "Pick Charlie!"

"Would you—"

"God-is-great-God-is-good-and-we-thank-him-for-our-food-Amen!"

"Hallelujah!" proclaimed Carmi, slamming both hands on the table.

"Praise the Lord, and pass the ammunition!" crowed Emmett, not to be outdone.

Cutting Flossie's meatloaf into small pieces, Hazel felt a measure of comfort that she had been right not to subject the new arrival to supper in the dining room—but only a small measure.

After wheeling Flossie into her room and getting her ready for bed, Hazel stole up the stairs to the third floor, pushing open the door to Room 31 as quietly as she could. She found the new arrival curled into the fetal position. "I'm so cold."

Hazel carefully covered her with an extra blanket, wondering what she could say to her that would ease the freezing at the heart of her, but she had nothing to offer.

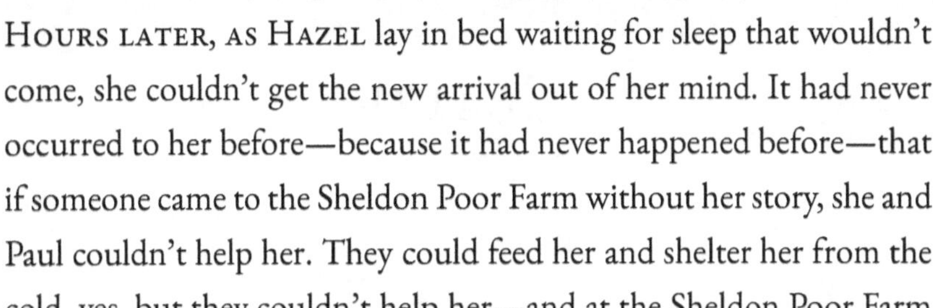

Hours later, as Hazel lay in bed waiting for sleep that wouldn't come, she couldn't get the new arrival out of her mind. It had never occurred to her before—because it had never happened before—that if someone came to the Sheldon Poor Farm without her story, she and Paul couldn't help her. They could feed her and shelter her from the cold, yes, but they couldn't help her—and at the Sheldon Poor Farm she would remain.

And what if the State made good on its threat to close them down? What then? Without the new arrival's story, the State would not be able to help her either. There would be forms filled out with spaces left blank, boxes unchecked.

In a Room Where No Music Plays

Claire

January 1968

CLAIRE AWOKE LONGING TO hear music—but none played. Something felt different, and it took her several moments to realize what it was. Although she could feel the room's chill on her face, she was no longer cold. After denying it to her for the past two days, her core had released its heat at last. She wasn't sure if this was a good sign or not.

Her body felt oddly hollow, as if it had been drained of life from sobbing all night. But she hadn't sobbed all night. She had slept all night, a begrudging sleep of constant motion, receding horizons, and no destination.

She strained to hear music. Any music would do. It didn't have to be the music she had once believed in. Any music would do, the wind singing through a live oak, the Doppler chords of a train whistle, the percussive rattling of palmetto fronds. Any music would do. Any music that would take her out of the person she had become.

The room was deathly still.

She opened her eyes to a windowed sky devoid of color, as if the world had somehow been siphoned away during the night, leaving not a trace, not a shadow of itself behind.

Distant footsteps ascended a staircase; a faint knock came at the door. After a pause, the handle turned. Claire closed her eyes and pretended to be asleep. It would be better this way.

Hazel

HAVING CONFIRMED THAT THEIR new arrival was still breathing, Hazel went back downstairs to make breakfast with the last of the farm fresh eggs until the hens started laying again in the spring.

Although Paul had initially objected, they now took all their meals with the remaining residents in the first-floor dining room, like a family—albeit a family with more than its fair share of infirm members and those not right in the head—as Paul constantly reminded her.

When she had all the food on the dining room table, including Joey's ketchup, she asked Elsie to help Flossie with her food, said grace, and turned to leave the room.

"Where are you going?" Paul said from his place at the head of the table. "Ain't you going to serve?"

"Upstairs. I need to tell the new woman breakfast is ready."

"Sit down, Hazel. We ain't running a hotel here. Joey, put down that damn ketchup. You're making a mess. Hazel, these people don't need ketchup on their eggs. My hens lay perfectly good eggs. Don't insult them with ketchup."

"You shouldn't baby us, Hazel," Joey proclaimed. "That's what Paul says."

Hazel removed the ketchup bottle from Joey's hand, set it directly in front of her husband, and left the room.

Up on the third floor, the new arrival hadn't moved since Hazel checked on her earlier, and Hazel didn't have the heart to wake her. It would be easy enough to make up a tray and take it to her when Paul went back to the barn to do his morning chores.

Returning to the dining room, Hazel noted Paul's empty chair at the head of the table. Probably for the best, the mood he was in. She scraped some scrambled eggs onto her plate and secured the last piece of toast.

Beatrice and Carl had pushed their chairs together and were whispering to each other, their foreheads touching in the manner of conspirators or lovers—neither of which bore thinking about.

Hazel put down her fork and clapped her hands. "Hey, now! Cut that out. What have we told you about sitting too close?"

"Shut up," Beatrice said. "I can talk to my boyfriend. We're getting married."

"Hah!" screeched Lisa. "When pigs fly out of my butt!"

"Language, Lisa." Hazel's fork had made it halfway to her mouth.

Carmi slammed his hand on the table. "This profanity will not stand! It will not stand, I tell you!"

"Blood pressure, Carmi."

"There oughta be a law," Emmett said.

Hazel sent up a silent prayer for patience to any saint who might be available. "Anyone finished with their breakfast is excused from the table."

Lisa wasn't finished. "Nobody's gonna let you two retards get married and have litters and litters of little retards."

"That's *enough*, Lisa. We do not call other people names in this house." Obviously, the saints were all otherwise engaged.

Joey put up his hand. "Lisa's being mean to Beatrice." He had ketchup smeared on his face, and Hazel gestured toward her own face. "Napkin, Joey."

Charlie sang out, "Ketchup face, ketchup face, Joey is a ketchup face!"

Joey scrubbed his entire face with his napkin. "Am not! See? See?"

Once again, Hazel halted the arduous journey of scrambled egg to her mouth. "Joey, have you finished your breakfast? Charlie? You're both excused from the table. Go on, now."

The two child-men pushed back their chairs with much scraping and scuffling of feet and chair legs. They left the room, Charlie still chanting, "Ketchup face, ketchup face," while Joey pounded him on the arm.

Lisa still wasn't finished. "So, who is this new woman who showed up here last night? What's her name? Who sent her? Did my mother send her? What does she want? You can't hide her from me. I know she's here."

"She's someone who needs help, Lisa. Your mother didn't send her."

Lisa sent her chair crashing to the floor and left the room, making no attempt to lower her voice. "You're lying, you're lying, I know you're all lying."

Hazel didn't have much of an appetite left for her cold scrambled eggs and soggy toast. She had to admit, Lisa was becoming harder to handle these days. She had been at the farm nearly four years, arriving mere days after she turned eighteen. Lisa was, her mother had asserted then, incorrigible—impossible to control, but not mentally ill. After Lisa's half-hearted suicide attempt, her mother had begged Dr. Wetherbee, begged him, not to pursue a judge's order to commit her to the State Hospital in Waterbury.

And who could blame her? The Sheldon Poor Farm was a working farm, and Lisa was young and able-bodied. Who wouldn't want their daughter to work outside in the fresh air and sunshine, rather than waste away in an institution? But of course poor Lisa was far from sane and far from fresh air and sunshine, confined to the house for her own safety and the safety of others.

Give Her a Tonic

Hazel

—◦—

January 1968

THE FOLLOWING DAY, JOHNNY Clough showed up as Hazel was browning onions and hamburg for sloppy joes for the noon meal. He stamped snow from his boots on the mat before entering the kitchen.

"Sorry I didn't get this suitcase to you yesterday. The wife didn't give me your message till this morning. You want me to take it upstairs?"

The wife's fault. Of course.

Hazel didn't turn around from the stove. "Thank you for bringing it, Johnny. Just set it somewhere no one will trip over it."

Johnny did as he was told, but instead of leaving and going about his business, he hovered near the stove, his parka and oversized headgear oozing cold air.

"Whatcha making there, Hazel?"

"Sloppy joes." She pushed past him to take cans of tomato sauce from the cupboard, but he made no move to leave.

"How's our little stranger this morning? She tell you her name yet? Sure is a peculiar thing, ain't it, showing up like that claiming to be a Lapierre?"

Hazel clamped the can opener on the first can of tomato sauce. "No, after you left, I put her to bed."

"Where is she?" Johnny pointed. "Living room?"

"No, she's still asleep." Hazel dumped the tomato sauce into the pot.

"Still asleep, you say?"

Hazel opened another can of tomato sauce. She tried a prayer for patience, but the saints must have been tending to other matters.

"Was there something else you wanted, Johnny? I've got mouths to feed."

"Nope, not that I can think of. I best be going. That village ain't gonna patrol itself." He continued to talk as he exited the building, as bad as Lisa in that regard, but at least he was harmless.

When the sloppy joes were ready and the table set for the noon meal, Hazel went back upstairs to Room 31. Again, the new arrival didn't respond to a light knock on her door. Hazel knocked a little harder; it was getting on to noon, after all.

She pushed the door open. The new arrival lay on her side facing the wall. As Hazel debated whether she should enter the room, she heard footsteps and sensed someone behind her. Joey, trying his best to peer around her into the room.

"What's the matter with the lady?"

"Go downstairs, Joey. You know you're not supposed to be on the third floor."

"Is the lady sick?"

"No, Joey. Go downstairs." Hazel put her finger to her lips. "Quietly."

Joey wasn't budging. "Is the lady sad?"

Hazel eased the door closed and put her hand on Joey's back. "Go downstairs, now. You know you're not supposed to be on the third floor."

"Read to her, Hazel. Read her a story. You want me to get my book?"

"No, Joey. I don't want you to get your book." The last thing the poor woman needed was a perfect stranger perched at the foot of her bed reading aloud from Joey's mangled copy of *The Wind in the Willows.* No one wants to be confronted with talking rodents when she's feeling unwell.

As if reading Hazel's mind, Joey said, "I know! Give her a tonic."

Hazel applied gentle pressure on Joey's back to move him down the hall. "It's dinnertime. Let's go downstairs and eat."

"What about the lady?"

"I'll take care of the lady after dinner. I promise."

"Okay, Hazel." Joey trotted obediently down the hall. All it took was a promise.

As Hazel scraped the dishes from the noon meal, Paul entered the kitchen. "You seen my reading glasses? I need to order more sanitizer for the bulk tank."

Hazel answered without turning around. "No, did you check your office?"

"I just come from my office. Hey, what's that suitcase doing over there?"

This time Hazel turned to face him. "Johnny brought it over this morning."

"The Lapierre woman's?"

"You don't need to bother with it. I'll take it up to her when—what are you doing?" Hazel hastily wiped her hands on her apron.

Paul heaved the suitcase onto the table. Before Hazel could stop him, he snapped the latches. She grabbed his arm as he went to flip open the lid. "Don't! You can't go into her suitcase without her permission."

Paul wrenched his arm from Hazel's grasp and flipped back the suitcase lid. A black leather pocketbook lay on top of the expected crumple of clothes.

"No!" Hazel said, grabbing for his arm again. "You can't invade her privacy!"

"Then she should have had sense enough to lock the damn thing. If that fool Johnny Clough won't do his job, I'll do it for him." He lifted the pocketbook out of the suitcase and undid the clasp. Peering inside, he retrieved a matching wallet and flipped it open. "Now, we're getting somewhere."

"Put that back, Paul!" Hazel tried to grab the wallet, but he held it above his head and took a few steps back.

"Well, she's a Lapierre, all right. According to her driver's license, anyhow. First name's Claire. Date of birth January fifth, nineteen twenty-six. She's from Vinton, Louisiana. Figures."

"What's that supposed to mean, 'figures'?"

"Just what I said. There ain't no hidden meaning. I told Johnny and Dwight yesterday we can't have no more trouble."

Paul's shoulders slumped, and Hazel took that moment to snatch the wallet from his hand. She returned the wallet to its rightful place, snapped the suitcase latches, and headed for the stairs, Paul right behind her. "Where do you think you're going with that suitcase? I ain't done with it."

"Oh, yes, you are." Hazel climbed the stairs as quickly as she could, Paul lagging behind her.

She knocked on the door of Room 31. No answer. She eased the door partway open. The new arrival—Claire—lay huddled on the bed under the blankets. Hazel set the suitcase inside the room and closed the door.

"Step aside, Hazel. I need to talk to her and find out what the hell she's running from."

Hazel positioned herself in front of the door with her hands on either side of the casing. "No, you're not. I'll stand here all afternoon if I have to. We don't know that she's running from anything, and even if she is, I'm sure she has a good reason. She'll tell us her story when she's ready."

"All right, Hazel, you stand there all afternoon. I got that sanitizer to order." Paul trudged off down the hall mumbling something about damn fool women.

As Hazel descended the stairs to the kitchen, one of the more obscure saints answered her prayer for patience. "Don't fight him," the pious voice proclaimed. "Therein lies the root of your problem."

THE USUAL MISGIVINGS

CLAIRE

<hr>

January 1968

FROST TRACED LACY PATTERNS on the window glass, but, oh, the room was cold. Frost wasn't meant for windows. It was meant to jewel the grass briefly, then melt away like morning dew. It couldn't still be morning, could it? No, it couldn't still be morning. The room was just cold.

Someone had set her suitcase by the door. Yes, it was her suitcase, a blue Samsonite, obviously meant for family vacations. Had it been there yesterday? Was she supposed to unpack now, was that it, fold her wholly inadequate clothes neatly into the displaced dresser in the corner as if they belonged there? As if she belonged here, in this place?

How strange to end up back in a boarding house. But with wallpaper. Someone had once gone to a lot of trouble to hang that wallpaper in the shabby little room she now found herself in.

Huddled under the blankets, her body still felt hollow, still missing something important inside, some vital organ she mustn't do without. She supposed she was hungry, but that wasn't it. She had no need to eat. There would be no point to it, in the end.

———◆◇◆———

SOMETIME LATER, CLAIRE WAS startled by a loud knock on the door and even more startled when it opened without her inviting whomever it was to come in. An elderly man carrying a black medical bag strolled into the room, followed by the woman who had been so kind to her when she'd arrived.

"Now, now, what is this, my girl? Still abed at three in the afternoon?"

She remembered now. He was the doctor that the man with the odd hat had taken her to when he didn't know what to do with her. The doctor who had seemed unduly elated when she told him Lyndon Johnson was the president of the United States.

The doctor perched on the edge of the bed, his weight sagging the mattress and the springs beneath it. "Can you sit up so I can talk to you? Hazel here tends to fret, and we need to put her mind at ease."

Hazel. That was her name.

Hazel looked apologetic. "You're not eating. I called Dr. Wetherbee to come and check you out in case you're ill or hurt."

Dr. Wetherbee. That was his name. There were too many new names of people she had no desire to know.

"All right, now, Claire—Hazel tells me your name is Claire—who is the current president of the United States?"

"She told you that before," Hazel said.

Claire made no attempt to sit up. Why was he asking her about the president again? He had seemed so pleased when she'd given him the answer. "Lyndon Johnson."

Dr. Wetherbee beamed. "Very good! Now, can you tell me what year it is?"

"She told you that before," Hazel said. "That's not why I called you. I called you because she's not eating. She must be ill or hurt. You're the doctor, not me."

"Quite so," Dr. Wetherbee said. "When was the last time you ate, Claire?"

Claire was surprised to realize that she didn't know the answer to his question. Even more troubling, she didn't know what day it was—but she couldn't muster the strength to lie. "I'm sorry. I don't remember."

Dr. Wetherbee frowned. "Are you sure you don't remember?"

Claire nodded.

"Well, now, we can't have that, can we?" He opened his bag and took out a blood pressure monitor and stethoscope. "Your arm, please."

When he put the blood pressure cuff around her arm and pushed up the sleeve of her nightgown for the stethoscope end, he scowled as if he were even more displeased with her. "You don't have much meat on your bones. How much do you weigh?"

"I don't know." This, too, was the truth. She couldn't remember the last time she'd weighed herself.

"I told you she's not eating." Hazel moved closer to the bed.

Dr. Wetherbee's two fingers pushed cold spots into Claire's wrist. "Pulse is a little fast."

That was odd. How could her pulse be fast when her heart was missing?

"While you're lying down, I'll go ahead and check your belly." He flipped back the covers. "Lie straight for me now. Any nausea, vomiting, diarrhea?"

Claire shook her head to all three as he proceeded to poke and prod and ask if the places he poked and prodded hurt. He used the stethoscope to listen to the places he had poked and prodded. "Well, your belly's talking to me loud and clear. Hazel, can you help her sit on the edge of the bed so I can have a listen to her heart and lungs?"

Hazel helped her up, and Dr. Wetherbee went through the motions of listening to a heart that wasn't there and lungs that must have been breathing for someone else.

"You can get back under the covers now. It's chilly in here." Dr. Wetherbee returned the stethoscope and blood pressure monitor to his bag. "Looks to me like she's suffering from nervous exhaustion. She hasn't told you where she came from or how she got here?"

Hazel tucked the covers around Claire's shoulders. "No, she hasn't."

"Let's put her on a soft diet to get her used to eating again, say, some soup to start off with. Tomorrow, oatmeal, applesauce, chicken, that sort of thing, nothing heavy, plenty of milk."

Dr. Wetherbee directed his next comment to Claire. "That should have you back on your feet in no time, my girl!"

Hazel patted the blankets covering Claire's shoulder. "I'm going to walk Dr. Wetherbee out, but I'll be right back." She left the room with Dr. Wetherbee, leaving the door open.

Claire got out of bed, put on her borrowed bathrobe, and dug a pair of socks out of her suitcase. Once she heard footsteps descending the stairs, she tiptoed down the hall to the bathroom and shut herself in one of the stalls to wait for nightfall.

Hazel

DR. WETHERBEE SET DOWN his bag and removed his hat from the hall tree. As he settled the hat securely on his head, Hazel said, "Are you sure Claire isn't ill? You didn't take very long with her."

Dr. Wetherbee smiled "Ah, Hazel, you do like to fret over your people. You would have made a good—"

Hazel's breath quickened. She knew very well what Dr. Wetherbee had been about to say before he thought better of it.

Dr. Wetherbee put on his overcoat. "I didn't see any evidence of injury. No sign of illness, physical or mental." He pulled on his gloves. "Get some food into her and give her another day to rest up. She'll be fine. You'll see." With that, Dr. Wetherbee was out the door.

Hazel hurried into the kitchen, taking a quick check of her watch. Already past four. She hadn't even begun preparations for the evening meal, and Claire needed to be fed right away. She was in no shape to come in at the tail end of the line—but at the same time, there was no denying that the residents needed their meals on time, too, the most elderly of them so terribly frail.

After dumping a can of emergency chicken noodle soup into a saucepan, she grabbed potatoes from the bin, then put them back. The shepherd's pie was simply not going to work. She yanked open the refrigerator door and poked the packages of thawing hamburg with her finger. Close enough. She could make a big pot of hamburg gravy, maybe enough for two meals if she threw in canned vegetables to stretch it. She could serve it with biscuits, dropped not rolled. She had no time to fool with rolled biscuits.

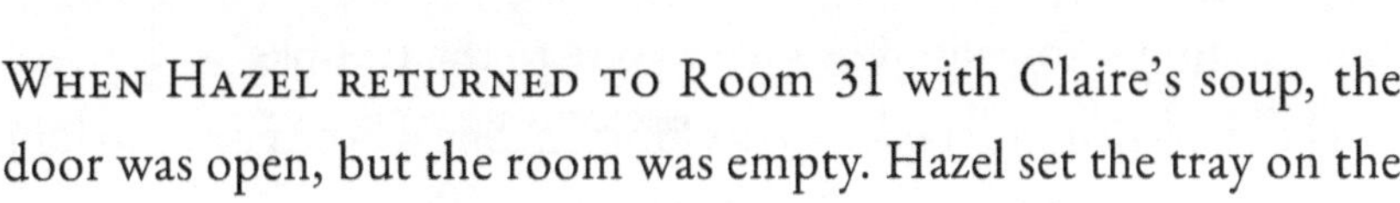

WHEN HAZEL RETURNED TO Room 31 with Claire's soup, the door was open, but the room was empty. Hazel set the tray on the dresser and, feeling only a little silly, checked under the bed. Claire must have gone to the bathroom.

Several minutes went by, and Claire did not return to the room. Hazel walked down the hall to the bathroom, calling Claire's name. When she got no response, she bent down and checked under each stall door. In the stall farthest from the door, two stockinged feet rested on the floor. "Claire?" No response. Hazel knocked on the stall door. "Claire, are you all right in there? Are you ill? Do you need help?" Still no response. Hazel knocked harder. "Claire. It's Hazel. Please answer me. Are you all right?"

Her mind's eye flashed the image of a slender woman in baggy, borrowed nightclothes sitting slumped on the toilet, the life in her body forever stilled by a fatal cardiac arrest. Hazel knelt down and reached her arm under the stall door, stretching as far up as her arm would go, but she was unable to reach the lock to slide the bolt.

She got to her feet. "Claire, if you don't come out of there, or at least answer me, I'll have to get Paul up here to take the hinges off the door." There was a faint intake of breath, followed by the bolt sliding back. Hazel stepped away from the door.

Claire's face looked as frozen and pinched as when Johnny and Dwight had brought her to the farm. She seemed steady enough on her feet, but Hazel put her arm around her shoulders anyway and led her back to her room.

Hazel settled Claire on the bed and retrieved the tray from the dresser. "Eat up, now. Your soup is cold, I'm afraid, but you need to eat." She set the tray on Claire's lap. "Doctor's orders."

Claire looked at the bowl of soup, then at Hazel, her expression unchanging. "You shouldn't have gone to the trouble."

Hazel needed to get back to the kitchen. She'd been gone too long already. The residents needed their supper. Flossie would choke if Hazel didn't break her biscuit into small pieces. "Please, Claire."

Claire ate a spoonful of broth and set the spoon back in the bowl. Before hurrying down the stairs to feed the others, Hazel waited to leave the room until Claire had taken a spoonful with chicken, chewed, and swallowed.

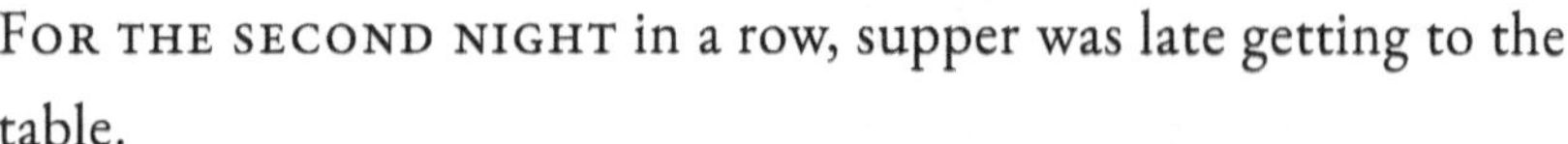

FOR THE SECOND NIGHT in a row, supper was late getting to the table.

"What is this?" Paul said, pointing to the soup tureen Hazel had brought to the table as if it were a chamber pot. "Don't we usually have shepherd's pie on Monday?"

Joey clapped his hands. "Oh, goody. I like shepherd's pie."

Charlie countered. "I like it more."

"You do not—"

Paul pointed a warning finger at them. "Don't—"

"But I like shepherd's pie," Joey said.

"Praise God from whom all blessings flow!" Carmi sang out, which sent him sputtering into a coughing fit.

"Easy, now," Homer said, patting Carmi on the back. "Don't excite yourself. It ain't good for a man your age."

Paul got up from his chair to his full height. "Hazel, serve me whatever this stuff is. I'll eat in the kitchen."

Hazel said grace and served her husband his hamburg gravy and biscuits. He left the room, muttering about peace and rights and indigestion.

When supper was over, Hazel wheeled Flossie into her room and got her ready for bed, Flossie chirping all the while about how tired Hazel looked, how hard she worked, and could a tonic be in order?

In the kitchen, Paul sat at the table looking his age, his shoulders slumped, the darns in the elbows of his baggy sweater pulling away from the surrounding yarn, his lined face as worn as his faded overalls. "Where have you been, Hazel?"

Hazel ran water into the percolator. "I was getting Flossie ready for bed."

"It don't take you that long. What were you doing? You was upstairs with that Claire. You need to quit babying these people, Hazel. How many times do I have to tell you?"

Hazel dumped fresh coffee grounds in the percolator basket. If he kept it up, she was going to start buying instant Nescafé in a jar.

"Was that Doc Wetherbee's car in the dooryard? Did you call him for somebody? Is one of the inmates sick?"

Hazel banged the percolator on the stove and turned on the burner. "I called him for Claire. She hasn't been eating, and he didn't check her properly before."

"Christ Almighty, Hazel. What did I tell you about not babying the inmates? And she ain't even one of our own."

As if the day couldn't get any worse, Beatrice wandered into the room. "Have you seen my boyfriend? I can't find my boyfriend."

"No," Paul said. "You ain't got a boyfriend. Get back to the living room."

Beatrice stamped her foot. "No! I want my boyfriend!"

Hazel adjusted the flame under the percolator and prayed for strength. "Let's get you back to the living room, Beatrice." She looked at her watch. "You don't want to miss your show."

"Where's my boyfriend?"

Hazel grasped Beatrice's upper arm and led her out of the room, taking care not to grip too hard. Beatrice was such a trial Hazel had to keep reminding herself that the girl's behavior wasn't her fault. At the same time, it was clear after Beatrice's two years at the farm that the Women's Reformatory should never have sent her here. They should have sent her to Brandon.

With the usual misgivings, Hazel reluctantly left Beatrice in the living room to interrogate the elderly about Carl's whereabouts.

When she served Paul his coffee, instead of retreating to his office to read the newspaper, he said, "Pour yourself some coffee and sit with me. You're run off your feet."

Hazel reached for a plate to scrape. "I can't. I haven't even started the dishes."

Paul got up from the table and took a cup from the cupboard. He poured coffee into the cup, stirred in cream and a scant teaspoon of sugar.

"There. I've poured your coffee. You need to sit down and drink it, so it don't go to waste."

Paul was right about one thing. She was run off her feet—run off her feet to the point of tears.

She and Paul drank their coffee in silence, the radiator gurgling, the framing of the old building creaking in the cold.

"You know, Hazel. I think this job may be getting too much for us."

Hazel had to admit—but only to herself—and only for tonight—that the thirteen-year gap between their ages was narrowing.

Furniture Emporium Blues

Claire

———◆○◆———

June 1967

Roland's new Buick sped through the flat, scrubby landscape from Vinton to Lake Charles on its way to Lapierre's Furniture Emporium. Misshapen bushes cluttered the side of the highway in a forlorn border. A tight cluster of tract homes appeared in a field, farther on, a ragged group of displaced cows.

More highway slid beneath the whitewall tires of Roland's new Buick.

Even this early in the morning, the sun streaming through the windshield was relentless. Claire flipped down the sun visor, but it didn't help. Her bouffant had already started to wilt, despite the choking cloud of hair spray she had subjected it to earlier. Before long, her makeup would start melting.

She turned on the air conditioning. Roland turned it off.

"Hey, what did you do that for?" Claire turned the air conditioning back on.

Once again, Roland turned it off. "Running the air conditioning uses too much gas. I've told you that."

"Then why did you pay extra for a car with air conditioning? What's the point if I can't turn it on? My hair is collapsing."

"Your hair looks fine to me," Roland said without looking at her.

"It's not fine. It's coming out of its set, and you're not the one who has to sleep in damn rollers every night."

"Nobody said you have to sleep in rollers every night."

"That's easy for you to say. All you have to do is slap some greasy kid stuff on your hair and forget about it."

"I never told you to sleep in rollers."

Roland ended the matter by turning on the radio, preset to a mostly news station. Local news at the top of the hour—the City of Lake Charles desirous of building a civic auditorium for which they had no funds—something about oil allowables—something about a doctor running for sheriff. Had she heard that right? A doctor running for sheriff? How irresponsible.

The inflection-flattened voice coming from the radio moved on to national news. Something about the stock market—race riots in Boston—casualties in Vietnam—more casualties in Vietnam—downed planes in Vietnam. Topped off by a brand spanking new war in the Middle East—or was it the continuation of an old war?

It was all so tiresome.

Claire turned the station dial in search of music. Any music would do, even elevator music.

"Hey, I was listening to that." Roland took his eyes off the road long enough to glare at her and stab the preset button for the mostly news station. Claire gave up on finding music. Bickering had become as tiresome as the highway and the news.

Roland put on his turn signal and passed a station wagon crammed with children who should have been in school. As to be expected, one child stuck out her tongue, and another one gave them the finger.

"I've been thinking," Roland said.

Claire didn't respond, her attention taken by a road sign that had been knocked over by someone who refused to drive straight on a straight highway.

"Did you hear me, Claire? I said I've been thinking."

"I heard you. You said, 'I've been thinking.' " Claire took a tissue from her purse and blotted the sweat on her forehead. Her makeup was melting, all right.

"I've been thinking about adding another location."

A rundown building now missing its purpose came into view, followed by a derelict house trailer and, farther on, a skeletonized billboard.

"Location for what?"

"The store. What other location would I be talking about?" Roland turned off the radio. "What's wrong with you this morning, anyway? You haven't been yourself since we got in the car. Are you not feeling well?"

"I'm feeling fine, Roland."

"I can't have you in a mood when we get to the store. We've got a sale on."

"I'm fine, Roland."

Roland nodded as if he believed her. "As I was saying, I've been thinking about adding another location. It's high time I got serious about starting that chain of stores."

He stopped speaking to pass a pickup truck with a loaded gun rack in the back window. This time, the driver gave them the finger.

"I'm not a hundred percent about the timing, though, with the economy the way it is. What do you think?"

"How many furniture stores does Lake Charles need? There's practically one on every block as it is."

"Nothing's to say they all have to be in Lake Charles. I'm looking to expand."

"I'm not moving."

"Who said anything about moving? My God, you're being contrary this morning. Are you sure you're all right?"

A tractor trailer blew past them, blasting its air horn. Claire couldn't be bothered to say, "Watch it, Roland, you're liable to get us both killed."

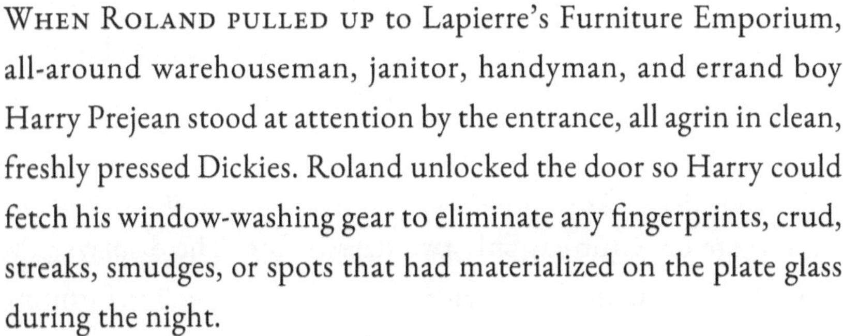

WHEN ROLAND PULLED UP to Lapierre's Furniture Emporium, all-around warehouseman, janitor, handyman, and errand boy Harry Prejean stood at attention by the entrance, all agrin in clean, freshly pressed Dickies. Roland unlocked the door so Harry could fetch his window-washing gear to eliminate any fingerprints, crud, streaks, smudges, or spots that had materialized on the plate glass during the night.

As Harry set to work, Roland studied the front window display, a cozy vignette of Mr. and Mrs. recliners separated by a floor lamp and table combination. Both recliners were upholstered in a nubby orange fabric bright enough to make one's eyes bleed.

Roland narrowed his eyes. "Do you think the front window display looks a little tired? Should we change it?"

"Tired? We just set it up last week for the sale. What's wrong with it? I chose the orange because you said you wanted something to get people's attention."

"I know. I did. I do. Orange is good—but I think we need to give the customers more choice. Nowadays, they're all about choice."

Claire took a fresh tissue from her purse and blotted her neck. "You give people too many choices, and they can't make up their minds. You've been hitting your targets for the sale so far, haven't you?"

Roland smiled and straightened his tie. "Right you are. We have. I'll see how we do today. We may not need to change the display. But be thinking about what we can do as soon as the sale's over, y'hear?"

At that point, Claire was saved from responding by Harry's announcement that all the storefront glass was spic-and-span-squeaky-clean. Pressing hard, he ran his squeegee down the door to prove it.

Out of the humidity at last, Claire found herself confronted by a ragtag band of recliners, each sporting a different brand of ugly, all set to march to their doom in a cluster of suburban tract homes. Where could they have come from?

She was struck by how different the store looked since she'd last been there on Saturday, only two days before. The displays now looked like rooms in a house where no one would ever live, furniture and decor specifically designed to make one feel ill at ease.

How could this be? She had designed all of these displays herself, working late into the night with Roland to choose just the right furniture lines, just the right accessories, based on careful analysis of customer preferences and current market trends. Roland had been so pleased with her choices. He was always pleased with her choices, escorting each husband and wife into each mock room with such pride of place. How could she have got it so wrong?

She hurried into the restroom to touch up her makeup and fix her hair, only to find that the flowered wallpaper she had chosen to give the room a homey feel had turned garish, and she could barely stand to look at herself in the mirror.

Back on the floor, she faced a pseudo-Early American living room suite that would make one's ancestors turn over in their graves if only their coffins weren't so cramped. She continued to Roland's office without looking up from the sea blue carpet now threatening storm surge.

Roland was on the telephone, and he did not look happy. That look could mean only one thing. He returned the receiver to its cradle. "I need you on the floor today. They called in sick, the both of them."

"Who?" Claire said, knowing full well whom Roland was talking about, but hoping against hope she was wrong. She couldn't go out on the floor today. She couldn't.

"Herb and Cliff. Herb sounded like he was still drunk, for Christ's sake. I could practically smell the alcohol on his breath over the phone. If I'd known he was a drinker, I never would have hired him."

"Maybe he's really sick this time?"

"If by 'sick' you mean 'hungover', yeah, he's sick." Roland took a comb from his jacket pocket and ran it through his hair. "We need to get out there to greet the customers. We can't afford to miss a sale."

"Are you sure you need me on the floor today? I haven't finished with the delinquent accounts from last week."

Roland came around the desk and put his hand on Claire's back. "We need to get out there. Now."

There were no customers on the floor that Claire could see, and she was not about to go in search of any. She watched Roland wend his way through thickets of questionable furniture choices. Textured vinyl upholstery that fooled no one? Bentwood rockers that couldn't go two years without recaning? Couches putting on airs as sofas? Claire had given her stamp of approval to every single one.

Roland returned from his reconnaissance. "No customers yet, but it's still early." He patted the pocket where he kept his breath mints. "I'll get us some coffee."

"I don't want any coffee."

Sure enough, Roland returned with two cups of coffee. Handing one to Claire, he said, "Cliff thinks he has dengue fever."

"What?"

"Dengue fever. Cliff called in sick because he thinks he has dengue fever." Roland blew across the coffee, even though the break room coffee was always lukewarm. "I swear to God, he's the worst hypochondriac I ever met. He's running out of diseases to get."

Claire hesitated, then asked the question anyway. "How long does he expect to be out?"

Roland pulled a face. "Long enough for his doctor to tell him he doesn't have dengue fever. He should be back tomorrow. You know something, if he wasn't such a good salesman, I'd have fired him a long time ago. I don't need the aggravation." He went for his comb again.

The fact that in all likelihood Cliff would return the next day to resume his rightful place as salesman of the century did little to ease Claire's rising panic.

The electric eye buzzer announced a prospective customer. Roland handed Claire his coffee cup, popped a breath mint in his mouth, and trotted off to greet the prospect in the most charming and trustworthy fashion possible. Claire walked to the break room and dumped Roland's coffee remains down the sink.

She sat at the lunch table in one of the wretched molded chairs she'd chosen when Roland had first purchased the store. Whatever body those chairs had been molded for, it certainly wasn't hers. The air conditioning came on with a clank and a whoosh, sending a blast of cold air down her neck.

"What are you doing in here?"

Claire turned to face her husband.

"I need you on the floor. I'm working with a customer, and another one just came in." He reached into his pocket and handed her the pack of breath mints. She obediently put one in her mouth and followed him onto the floor.

The customer turned out to be a teenager in a daisy print dress that might have fit a three-year-old and go-go boots. She had dragged along a woman of a certain age in a tasteful sheath and jacket combination to pay for whatever she thought she must have right that instant or she would die. Probably her grandmother.

"I want one of those ball chairs," the teenager announced.

The tastefully dressed woman grimaced, as if she wanted to tell the girl to ask politely and say "please," but refrained for fear of sparking a temper tantrum.

Claire put on her most neutral tone. Even so, she couldn't keep the edge out of her voice. "You will have to explain what you mean. I don't know what you're referring to."

The girl let loose a histrionic sigh. "You know. A ball chair. Like in the magazines."

"I'm afraid we don't stock those. Perhaps you could try Household Furniture on Ryan Street."

The girl dredged up another dramatic sigh from the depths of her wounded teenage soul. "We *tried* them already. *And* Honeycutt's. *And* Gulf Coast. They don't *have* it."

"Perhaps I could show you some other chairs that might suit?"

"I don't *need* another chair. I want a *ball* chair."

"I'm sorry. I'm afraid I can't help you. Good day." Claire turned on her heel and returned to the break room. Never before had she turned her back on a customer, but she didn't care. She wouldn't tolerate that kind of behavior from her own teenage daughter; she wasn't about to tolerate it from a stranger.

The rest of the day was more of the same. One customer after another demanding what they couldn't have. By closing time, she had a terrible headache, and she wanted to cry. Or punch her husband in the face. Or run into traffic screaming. Or something. She didn't know what she wanted.

Roland helped her into the car, started the engine, put down the front windows, and turned on the air conditioning. "It's still over ninety. I think we can afford the air conditioning this once. We've had a hard day."

He pulled smoothly into traffic. "Let me know when it's cool enough for you, and I'll put up the windows."

Once they were past the outskirts of the city, Roland turned on the radio. "How about some music? I can get the news from the afternoon paper."

Claire turned her head to the window so Roland couldn't see her tears.

That night, when they went to bed, Claire didn't immediately turn her back and feign sleep. "I'm sorry, Roland. I don't know what got into me today."

"You probably need a vacation. We haven't had a vacation in two, no, three years."

"Yes, that must be it."

Despite Roland's having the answer, she lay awake most of the night, plagued by a mockingbird unable to make up its mind whose song to sing.

When the Summer of Love Hung Heavy

Claire

<hr>

June 1967

Claire slid open the patio door and stepped outside, humidity enveloping her in its familiar nighttime embrace. A gentle breeze offered the sweet fragrance of magnolia blossoms, like a mother's kiss goodnight—but the crickets sang out of tune, and the crescent moon hung askew in the sky, too weary to hold itself in place.

Roland had gone to bed early with a sick headache after a particularly rough day at the store, starting off when Herb, in an unprecedented move, called in hungover on a Friday. When Cliff called in sick with pneumonic plague, Roland fired him, Roland's end of the conversation beginning with, "What is *wrong* with you? Why can't you be satisfied with having a cold like a normal person?" and ending with,

"You're fired—and since you're so infectious, don't come in for your final paycheck. I'll mail it to you." Bang! went the receiver.

Next, Roland dispatched Harry to repossess a bunk bed that had been bought for a set of twins. When Harry returned, he informed Roland that the lady had cried and begged him not to take the bed—her babies would have to sleep on the floor—how could he be so cruel?—and if he was forced to make another lady cry, he was quitting, no doubt about it, no sir.

As Claire contemplated the moon, so weary amid its starry neighbors, she thought she heard music, wafted on the sweet-scented breeze like a summons from a far-off land. But no, it was only the crickets, ordinary backyard crickets, followed by the sound of the patio door sliding open and her daughter's voice.

"What are you doing out here, Momma?"

Toni's hair was disheveled, her blouse rumpled and askew, but Claire didn't have the heart to scold her. "I didn't hear you come in. How was the movie?"

Toni shrugged. "I dunno. Kinda boring. I don't like James Bond. He thinks he's God's gift." She didn't move from the doorway. "What are you doing out here? You weren't waiting up for me, were you? I said I'd be home by curfew, and I am."

"I couldn't sleep."

"Daddy in bed?"

"Yes, he wasn't feeling well."

"Oh. I was hoping he would watch the eleven o'clock news with me. I need him to help me pick out my current event for history class. I don't want to mess with it over the weekend." She adjusted her blouse to properly align with her skirt. "I'm going to the lake with Curtis."

Claire also thought better of scolding her for announcing a day at the lake with Curtis instead of asking permission. The girl deserved some credit for taking responsibility for her homework.

"I don't know why we have to mess with current events in history class in the first place. It's stupid. History means it happened in the past. 'Current' means 'now.' Duh." Toni turned away without waiting for a response.

When the television came on, Claire figured she might as well go back in the house. She slid the door closed—but she didn't lock it.

Toni kicked off her shoes and flopped down on the couch. This Claire did scold her for. "Watch yourself! You'll ruin the springs." No way was she going through the agony of picking out a new couch from Lapierre's Furniture Emporium.

Toni chattered all through the local news. For someone who found James Bond boring, she had remarkable recall for preposterous spy gadgets and cheesy come-on lines.

"Didn't you say you need to watch the news for your homework?"

"Local stuff doesn't count for current events. Miss Vincent wants current events we think will go down in history. How the hell am I supposed to know that if history hasn't happened yet?"

"Watch your mouth, Toni." Claire turned her attention back to the television. The national news had come on. "How about the war in the Middle East? Israel just invaded Syria after they'd agreed to a ceasefire."

Toni drummed her pen on her notebook. "Naw, everybody will bring in that one. And don't say Vietnam either. Half the class brings in Vietnam."

At that point, Claire gave up. Toni could pester Roland to help her at the last minute on Sunday night, like she always did when homework was due on Monday. She put her hand on Toni's pen hand to still its drumming.

A commercial for a bra that promised to lift and separate a headless manikin's breasts came on the screen, immediately followed by the street sign for Haight-Ashbury in San Francisco. The camera panned to a reporter on the scene, a balding man in an ill-fitting sport coat who gripped a microphone as if he expected someone to snatch it away from him and make off with it.

Presumptive hippies littered the sidewalk behind him and drifted into the street. He announced that San Francisco authorities were concerned about an impending hippie invasion that threatened to become a "summer of love." Claire wasn't sure she heard "summer of love" correctly, as his tone of voice signaled "conflagration."

"That's the one!" Toni scribbled wildly in her notebook, as all manner of flower children danced with abandon, rolled on the grass, and blew tubular bubbles in the California sunshine to a backdrop of frenetic guitars racing to keep up with them all.

When the reporter enumerated the authorities' concerns: impeded traffic, poor hygiene, rampant drug use, infrastructure strained beyond any reasonable limit, Toni jumped up and did a little dance, her face aglow. "This is great! I bet there'll be a fight in class! The jocks hate hippies."

"You want to start a fight in class?"

"No, of course not. But history class is boring. I told you that."

Claire realized too late that all the noise had probably woken Roland. She turned off the television. "Go to bed, Toni. Just go to bed."

"What'd *I* do?" Toni stomped off down the hall.

Claire followed her and grabbed the bedroom door before Toni could slam it.

Returning to the living room, Claire knew she could forget about getting a good night's sleep, no matter how badly she needed it. Saturday was normally the busiest day of the week at the store, with husbands off work and wives looking for an excuse to get out of the house. She could only hope that Herb would show up to work with his breath fresh and his line of patter sparkling, so she could avoid the minefield the selling floor had become.

She fixed a glass of sweet tea and slipped outside to the patio to give Roland time to get back to sleep before she slid into bed to lie wakeful and restless beside him for the rest of the night.

As she sipped her tea in the shadowy darkness, she wished she hadn't watched the news. She'd become accustomed to nightly reports of war, but talk of a summer of love had unsettled her. Was it something she wanted, this freedom to dance, this freedom to love, this freedom to be? She couldn't be sure—but she didn't think so.

The crickets chirped on and on, steady as a metronome and just as tuneless. The moon still hadn't righted itself over the magnolia tree—but, in the end, wasn't Sister Moon entitled to feel weary after remaining steadfast for so many millennia, never questioning her daily obligation to gather and release the tides, her monthly obligation to do the same with Claire's own womb?

From somewhere in the distance, a train whistle blew, sounding a warning to anyone foolhardy enough not to bring their car to a full stop at a railroad crossing when the lights were flashing.

As the sound faded into the distance, Claire began to doubt she'd heard a train whistle at all. It had to have been a harmonica, not sounding a warning but beckoning her to follow the story it had to tell.

Blood Rhythm

Claire

—◆◇◆—

July 1967

As San Francisco's fevered dream of universal love hung over the sultry Louisiana summer, Claire still couldn't sleep, despite deciding never to wear rollers to bed again. She took to slipping out of bed to sit on the patio in her nightgown. When a change in the quality of the night sky signaled the coming of dawn, she slipped back into bed, with Roland none the wiser.

Although she did wonder from time to time how long a person could go without sleep, she wasn't particularly bothered by it. She had concealer to hide the dark circles under her eyes, and the lack of rest left her more calm than groggy. She now had a languid air with customers as if she couldn't care less whether they purchased that Formica dinette set or not, raised a fuss about the delivery fee or not, paid in cash, installments, or Monopoly money.

In fact, if a husband and wife had walked out the door at either end of a Thomasville triple dresser, she would have held the door for them. Poor Roland couldn't understand how the day's sales numbers were higher than before he'd fired Cliff—not that he would have believed her if she'd told him.

This night was no different than any other night that summer. On the drive home from the store—no avoiding the cost of running the air conditioning now—Roland listened to the mostly news station—a drowning here, a fatal car accident there—fighting in Vietnam, fighting at the Suez Canal.

At supper, Toni showed off her sunburn after a day at the lake with Curtis. Roland demanded to know why Curtis didn't have a summer job. Toni stormed off to her room. Claire occupied herself in the kitchen until it got late enough for her to get ready for bed without being questioned.

As Roland slept the sleep of the oblivious, Claire slid out of bed and tiptoed from the room. Sitting at the patio table, she lit a citronella candle to fool the mosquitoes into thinking she wasn't there, its lemony smell a comfort, even if it didn't really work.

She did not have to wait long before she heard the music. After a month of listening, she knew she was not imagining it, no matter how fragmented the sound became when blown by the wind.

The question was, where did this music come from, this music so unlike the bursts of psychedelia on the news that clawed at one's face and screamed, *Look at me! Look at me!* And why had she not heard it before? If the music reached her now, wending its way around rooftops and trees, it should have reached her before. She'd lived on this backwater street at the edge of town for over fifteen years.

Bought the first year Roland's store turned a profit, their house was small, four modest rooms and a tiny bathroom, but Claire had never seen the need for a move to something larger. Toni griped about having to share a bathroom and a telephone with her parents, but what teenager didn't?

But now, here was this music—unbidden, beguiling—music that could become part of her muscle memory, the warp and weft of her bones—if only she could get close enough to hear it clearly. But try as she might, she heard only fragments—guitar, voice, drum, guitar—like coming upon broken glass that could only become a vase again with a good eye, a steady hand, and strong glue.

A passing breeze guttered the citronella candle, and Claire blew it out. She rose from the table and stole into the house to change out of her nightgown, watching from the bedroom doorway as Roland lay sleeping. He stirred, and she held her breath until he settled again. Better not try to get a dress out of the closet. She tiptoed to the bathroom and pulled a shift from the dirty clothes hamper, not bothering to check if it was hers or Toni's.

Shoes. She needed shoes. Toni had kicked off her sandals by the front door. Claire wriggled her feet into them and walked out the door into the night.

At the end of the flagstone walk Roland had installed with such pride when the house was new, Claire stood poised to walk in the direction the music was coming from. The way sound traveled at night could be deceiving, though, the barking beagle next door in reality a German Shepherd five doors down. However, she had no doubt that the music had been easier to hear in the backyard. It must be coming from the direction of Williams Road, even though there was nothing but trees and vacant land out that way. She started walking.

The street's smattering of tidy postwar bungalows did not warrant any streetlights, for which she was grateful. She and Roland spent so much of their time at the store, they'd never gotten close with any of their neighbors—but still, seeing a housewife sneak out her own front door in the middle of the night would be fodder for gossip at the next ladies' luncheon.

Not long after she walked by the last house, the music became louder, but as she walked, she couldn't see any buildings, just scrubby, vacant land and trees. She kept walking. The music faded. She turned and retraced her steps. When she came to the spot where the music had played with the most clarity, when she had distinguished a man's voice imploring some nameless woman to take her hands offa him—she stopped and peered into the shadows, shading her eyes with her hand, as if that would bring light to what she couldn't see.

The music could only be coming from amid the trees, from some kind of party or club set in a clearing—but there was no road or drive to get to it. As Claire headed across the scrubby field, shaking dirt and pebbles from her daughter's sandals every few feet, the moon's hazy light revealed two dusty tracks. With bats flitting overhead, she followed the tracks and tried not to think about fire ants and snakes.

Pinpoints of light glinted through the trees. She had to be getting close. Before long, she came upon a haphazard gathering of beat-up cars and pickup trucks clustered around what looked to be some kind of shed with colored lights strung inside and out. She drew closer for a better look, taking care to stay in the shadows.

The shed appeared to be a Quonset hut that had somehow been dragged across the field and through the trees, strung with lights, and beaten with a hammer. Through the open door, she could see a few small tables and a handful of people who would not be welcome on her street of tidy postwar bungalows.

On a makeshift stage strung with white lights, a skinny old man played loud electric guitar and sang in a voice just as loud. He had the oddest-looking wig on his head, like Little Orphan Annie, only black. He stopped singing and started laughing, while a drum and bass guitar kept up a ragged rhythm until whoever was playing them gave up and hollered for beer. The place could only be a juke joint, and she had no business being there.

She was about to turn around and head home, when the old man and his backup began playing again. As she stopped to listen, she realized that the music now beat with the rhythm of her own blood.

Lightnin' Fast

Claire

—◆◉◆—

July 1967

THE WANING DAYS OF July slogged by in a muddle of avoidance. Elaborate meals requiring hours of preparation the night before and mountains of dirty dishes to wash. A frilly new nightgown. Pillow talk with Roland. Sominex.

Then one Saturday, after Claire had unloaded a behemoth of a chifforobe, Roland took it into his head that he would grill the steaks Claire had marinating in the fridge to pan-fry. And they would eat on the patio.

"It's so hot out." Claire fanned her face in the universal gesture for *It's too damn hot.* "I can grill the steaks under the broiler, if you want them grilled."

Roland pulled out the junk drawer. "Where's my apron?"

"What apron?"

Roland pushed the junk drawer back in and pulled out the one below it, which held baking utensils. "You know, my barbecue apron. It says, 'King of the Grill.' " He pulled out a third drawer and shoved it back in. "What'd you do with it?"

"I didn't do anything with it."

"You better not have thrown it away."

"For God's sake, Roland. It's in the bottom drawer with all the other aprons. As disgusting as it is, I should have thrown it out a long time ago."

Roland dropped the apron over his head and fumbled behind his back with the ties, beaming. "There, now I'm ready. I'll go out and start the grill."

Claire watched through the patio slider as he pulled the cover off the grill, dumped charcoal, squirted lighter fluid, and tossed in a lit match. The charcoal caught with a feeble flicker. Roland stood back from the grill, lighter fluid can at the ready. As Claire rapped her knuckles on the glass and shook her head at him, he unleashed a tsunami of lighter fluid. Flames shot high into the air, and he jumped back, as if completely unaware of lighter fluid's flammable properties. One of these days, he was going to set the damn house on fire.

Claire opened the slider to the reek of petroleum. "How many times do I have to tell you, Roland, not to use so much lighter fluid?"

He gave her a smile and a wave. "Not to worry! I have it all under control."

As Claire turned her attention to chopping vegetables for macaroni salad, Roland and his apron trotted into the kitchen looking for place-mats. After more drawer-pulling, he found the placemats, scooped up some silverware, and trotted back to the patio. Claire blinked away onion tears.

In no time at all, Roland had the table set, the steaks on a platter, and the macaroni salad retrieved from Claire. Toni arrived home all giddy from a day at the lake on Greg Landry's motorboat. As Claire ate her petroleum-infused steak, she refrained from demanding to know how old this Greg Landry was, whether Toni had worn a life jacket, and whether there had been a responsible adult on board. Nor did she scold Toni for talking with her mouth full. She was counting on her daughter to fill the air with happy teenage prattle and keep juke joint blues from sneaking into her happy little family's backyard.

Toni paused to gulp some tea, and Roland took that as his chance to enter the conversation. "Guess what your mother did today?"

"I dunno. What'd you do today, Momma?"

"Today, your mother sold the chifforobe!" Roland raised his sweet tea glass in an unreciprocated toast.

"What chifforobe?" Toni jerked her thumb in the general direction of her father. "Momma, what's he talking about?"

"A man came into the store this morning looking for something his wife could put her extra clothes in, so he wouldn't have to buy her a new house. I showed him the chifforobe, and he bought it."

Roland appeared not to have heard her, his glass still raised. "That thing took up valuable floor space for five years. Talk about salesmanship!" The tea in his glass sloshed. Claire clinked her glass against his, so he'd set it down before it spilled. Didn't the poor man remember it had been her idea to put the pseudo-French provincial monstrosity in their inventory to begin with, to serve as one more reminder that she really didn't know what she was doing?

Toni resumed her account of the best day of her life on Greg Landry's motorboat. When Roland didn't pick up on her cue to rush right out and purchase such a craft, she excused herself from the table.

A warm orange glow from the setting sun filtered through the magnolia tree, caressed Claire's face, and moved on. The music would not be far behind. She rose from the table and began stacking the dirty plates.

Roland also rose from the table. "I'll get the dishes. You stay here and relax."

Claire flapped a cloud of nonexistent gnats away from her face. "No, I'm going in. The bugs are coming out."

Roland didn't insist, and she followed him into the house. She might make it to bed safely after all.

However, that was not to be. After she helped Roland with the dishes, he wanted her to have coffee on the patio with him. This time, he did insist, countering her insect objection by leaving the patio light off and lighting the citronella candle.

When they were both settled at the table with their coffee, Claire turned to him, hoping he would break the silence. She truly had nothing to say to him.

Roland's face had taken on an unfamiliar expression—pensive, even wistful—as if he were about to share his innermost thoughts and feelings. "I've been thinking."

"What about?"

He looked past her into the shadowy yard, as if he didn't want whatever he was about to reveal to be overheard. "I've been thinking about opening that other store."

Claire took a gulp of coffee, but it didn't stop her from saying what she was thinking. "Why, because I sold that damn chifforobe?"

"Not just the chifforobe. I've been thinking about it for over a month. Maybe go a little more high-end with some of that Danish modern."

"Danish modern."

"Yes."

"Imported from Denmark."

"Yes. What do you think?"

Claire brushed a salty trickle from her face. "I don't know what to tell you, Roland."

"Will you think about it?"

Not trusting her voice, she nodded. What was one supposed to say to a husband whose dreams were made of wood?

They drank the rest of their coffee in silence. When Roland stood up to go to bed, Claire didn't go with him. No sooner did the patio door slide shut behind him than the music made its way to her—as she'd known it would.

She let some time pass before going into the house to use the toilet and confirm that her husband and daughter were both asleep. Then she was out the door and into the night.

As Claire walked down her darkened street, a sliver of doubt worked its way into her mind. Would she be able to find those two dusty tracks again, with the light from the moon so enfeebled by clouds? And if she did, would they be the right dusty tracks, or would they be parallel paths leading to places she didn't want to go?

She needn't have worried. Scattered words coalesced into lyrics, the clouds hiding the moon slid away, and the two dusty tracks across the field appeared before her.

Soon, the same dented Quonset hut strung with colored lights came into view amid the trees. The same skinny old man stood at the microphone playing electric guitar and singing, with the same crooked wig on his head, black curls corkscrewed every which way. This time, he was dressed in a baggy white suit and turquoise shoes.

Claire moved closer to the open door to get a better look at what sort of musicians could be keeping time so helpfully, staying in the background to let the old man shine. The drummer, dressed in chinos and a polo shirt, looked young enough to be the old man's grandson. He had the most placid look about him, tapping his sticks and smiling to himself, school out for the summer, no job to worry about. The bass player was older, a tan flat cap riding the back of his head as he nonchalantly fingered the strings.

Claire withdrew from the area in sight of the door to listen from the shadows. There seemed to be twice as many cars and pickup trucks as the first time she'd been there. A long, black Cadillac was parked some distance away from the other vehicles, out of place.

As chatter and laughter whirled in the Quonset hut, splashing out its makeshift windows, she sensed someone approaching. A man emerged from the trees, zipping up his fly. Claire quickly looked away, but he continued to walk toward her. As he passed by one of the window openings, the light revealed him to be even skinnier than the old man at the microphone, his embroidered shirt and baggy pants hanging on him like so much laundry on the line. His hair was the opposite of the old man's corkscrewed wig but no less unnatural—a stiff, black pompadour above a broad forehead and dark glasses.

"That Bilbo oughta put up a' outhouse or one of them portable johns or something. What he expect folks to do after drinking all that beer, 'specially the women?"

The man now stood directly in front of her. She kept her head down as he went right on talking.

"They take their boyfriend's automobile to the filling station to use the toilet, and they don't never come back!" He reached behind his back and retrieved a half-empty pint of liquor. "Ain't no woman gets her hands on the keys to my Cadillac, y'know what I mean?" He took a long pull from the pint and returned the bottle to his hip pocket.

Claire was sure she didn't, but she wasn't about to tell him so. She wondered if she should be afraid of him. If he had sauntered down the sidewalk in her childhood Lafayette neighborhood of manicured lawns and respectable homes, her mother would have tightened her grip on her purse, clutched Claire to her side, and crossed the street. And if Claire had asked why they must cross the street, her mother would have responded, "Do as I say."

The man dropped to one knee to lower himself to Claire's eye level. Up close, he smelled strongly of liquor, cigarette smoke, and sweat, a heady mix for Claire after the miasma of manufacturing fumes rising from the furniture swamp where she spent her days.

Above his dark glasses, his forehead was lined. Time or hard living had carved a deep groove on either side of his generous lips, which parted in a smile, a glint of gold teeth showing through.

"What you doing out here, baby? This ain't no place for a white woman."

This time, his question was not rhetorical. He was waiting for an answer. At least she didn't have to avoid meeting his eyes. She couldn't see them. She murmured, "I'm sorry."

He barked a laugh. "You sorry? What for?" He took another pull from his pint. "How'd you find the place, anyways? Bilbo got it hid pretty good out here in the damn woods. Somebody tell you about it?"

She shook her head.

He shifted to his other knee. "Say, now. You come to hear me play? How'd you know? I only set on it this morning when my Lake Charles date got canceled." He flashed his gold teeth. "Good news sure do travel fast—"

Who was this man, and why would he think she knew who he was? She tried to read his face, but his dark glasses rendered it unreadable.

"—but a juke joint ain't no place for a white woman."

How many times did he have to tell her she didn't belong there, as if her ears weren't good enough to receive the music she'd become so drawn to?

The man's tone softened. "If you wanna go out your way, I'm playing at the Vulcan over Austin next month. Be a white crowd, buncha long-haired hippies and trifling college kids—but hell, I'll take they money. Gotta warn you, though, they go in for that psychedelic shit.

Best wear shades, or the light show'll send you into a fit, y'know what I mean?"

The sudden appearance of Bilbo saved Claire from having to confess she had no idea what the man was talking about.

"You wanna get paid tonight, you best get your skinny black ass back in there. I ain't waiting around for you." Bilbo turned on the heel of his turquoise shoe and shambled off.

After informing Claire there was no rest for the wicked—and he should know—the man lurched to his feet. Then he, too, shambled off.

The time had come for Claire to go back where she belonged. Her encounter with the man in dark glasses had been so other-worldly, it wouldn't have surprised her to walk home and find that a giant sinkhole had swallowed her house without a trace, her husband and their daughter still sleeping inside. She stood up and brushed off the back of her shift.

Her departure was interrupted by Bilbo's amplified voice shooting from the Quonset hut. "Bilbo has a special treat for you folks tonight, king of the Texas blues, Mr. Lightnin' Sam Hopkins!"

A barrage of hoots, hollers, stomps, and whistles came from the Quonset hut. The folks drinking beer inside obviously knew who this man was, even if she didn't.

His voice cut through the din, as if he had just wrenched the microphone from Bilbo's hand. "Begging your pardon, Bilbo, but ole Lightnin' here's king of *all* the blues. Texas ain't the half of it."

Laughter, more hoots. Then with a shout—"Lightnin's Boogie!"—off he went—up, down, around the scale—his fingers had to be flying—drummer and bass player traipsing after him like little boys trying to follow a big brother intent on leaving them behind.

"Keep up with me, boys!"

Just when the drummer and the bass player appeared to have caught his rhythm and tempo, he shifted into another song, leaving them lying in a ditch.

"Come on, boys, don't quit on ole Lightnin' now—I'll slow it down for you."

He abruptly stopped playing. "Well, now, how do you like that?"

Much laughter from the crowd.

"Ole Lightnin' just having a bit of fun. No hard feelings, fellas?"

Long pause. A few notes and a chord.

" . . . Lemme tell you about the blues. The blues is a feelin'." Murmurs of assent from the crowd. "You don't have the blues when you happy, y'know? But say like you lose something. Your wife quit you. Your girlfriend quit you. Or maybe you want a new suit of clothes and you don't have no money to buy with. That's the blues, man. It ain't no jive. It's the blues. And when the blues be worryin' you, you just gotta sing it to the world."

And sing the blues he did. Claire sank to the ground and listened, a trespasser in the land of other people's misery. She stayed in that spot under the loblolly pine, receiving the music as best she could, until Lightnin' announced he'd best be getting on home.

Before the people who rightly belonged at Bilbo's juke joint could come straggling out, Claire left her spot, wove through the cluster of cars and pickup trucks, and ran down the two dusty tracks to the road home—only to find her home right where she'd left it, her husband and their daughter sleeping as if she'd never left them.

A Visit from the Overseer

Hazel

—◦—

February 1968

SLOW FOOTSTEPS APPROACHED AS Hazel sat at the kitchen table with the Fruitland weekly specials flyer spread open before her. When she looked up, Elsie stood before her wearing her church dress, a dainty blue print with a lace collar. That could only mean one thing.

"Did my daughter call?"

Hazel didn't need to ask her which one. None of Elsie's daughters called her. After they'd convinced the St. Albans overseer that Elsie was hopelessly senile, couldn't be trusted to live on her own, and too far gone to live with any of them, they'd delivered her to the poor farm. Once a year, one of them would arrive at the poorhouse to deliver Elsie's Christmas gift of body powder and strongly scented bath soap.

The daughter would sit with Elsie a moment or two without removing her coat, kiss her on the cheek, and be on her way.

A worried-mother expression settled on Elsie's face. "She should have been here by now. I have my suitcase all packed."

"No, I haven't heard from her today." Hazel rose from the table. "Let's get you back to your room, so you can get changed, and I'll help you unpack."

"You mean she's not coming?"

"Not today. I'm sorry."

Hazel put her arm around Elsie's shoulders and led her back to her room. As the mother of five girls, Elsie had every right to expect one of them to care for her in her old age. And she wasn't senile, just a little slow and at times befuddled. The way the world was these days, who didn't get befuddled every now and again?

When Hazel returned to the kitchen, Paul was banging cupboard doors.

"What are you doing? What do you need?"

Paul opened another cupboard. "Where have you been? You need to get a fresh pot of coffee on. Dwight Demers is on his way to see us."

"Both of us? Why?" Hazel resumed her place at the table. Chuck roast was on special for thirty-seven cents a pound. She could make a nice pot roast.

"He didn't say. About that Lapierre woman, most likely. Get a move on with that coffee, will you? You know how he is."

Yes, Hazel knew how Dwight Demers was. She rose from the table and got the coffee going, laying out cups, spoons, cream, and sugar to telegraph Paul's message: *Say what you got to say and be on your way. And be quick about it. We got work to do.*

Paul gestured toward Hazel's meal-planning paperwork. "You need to get that mess off the table."

"No, Paul. I'm going to leave this mess right where it is. Dwight needs to see how hard I'm working to keep the food bill down and still serve nourishing food."

Paul sat heavily at the table. "Pretty soon it won't matter, anyhow. Don't make no difference how much money we save the Association, State's calling the shots. Only a matter of time."

"If that's true, then why hasn't the State done anything about it? No one from the State has even been here."

"Don't be foolish, Hazel. Montpelier passed a law last year. You know they passed a law."

"Passed a law and forgot about it, you mean."

"According to Dwight, Montpelier can't figure out how to provide for the poor the way we do. They'll come up with something half-assed and then throw us all out of here."

Footsteps sounded on the porch steps.

Paul put his hand on Hazel's arm as she was about to get up and fetch the percolator. "Don't let Dwight know I told you. I got chores that need doing."

The front door opened and closed. A pause for Dwight to deposit his overcoat and hat on the hall tree. He entered the kitchen and sat at the table without being invited, but he didn't speak until Hazel poured his coffee.

"We're forecast to get some snow."

Paul didn't respond with so much as an *ayuh*. Hazel looked at Dwight to see what his next move would be.

"Could be over a foot this time."

Hazel looked back at Paul.

"If you don't have animals to tend to and roads to plow, ain't no point talking about the weather."

"Quite so, Paul. I'll come right to the point."

Dwight got to the point by going through his coffee ritual—pour in cream—stir—spoon in sugar—stir—taste—stir again—tap spoon on cup once to signal he was about to speak.

"I'm here about Claire Lapierre. You'll recall I said I would give her two weeks to get herself straightened out with a job."

"That you did, Dwight." Paul wrapped his hands around his cup, even though the kitchen was plenty warm. His arthritis must be bothering him.

Hazel took a quick gulp of her coffee. Although she'd tried to hide it from him, Paul knew full well that during those two weeks, Claire had not once left Room 31 except to use the bathroom, nor had she gotten dressed. She was eating, yes, but not nearly enough to get her strength back.

"It's been two weeks."

"That it has, Dwight." Paul kept his hands wrapped around his cup.

What did Paul think he was doing? If he let it slip that Claire had become the poor farm's resident madwoman in the attic, Dwight would have her sent to Waterbury to take up residence with the other madwomen whose only crimes were bad dreams of bad memories. Once people were committed to that place, they didn't come out except in a box.

"So, Paul, how's she doing? Has she found a job?"

"No, she—"

Hazel could stay silent no longer. "She has bronchitis. From being out in the cold. She's still recuperating."

Paul flashed her a look. She prayed he wouldn't contradict her. Just this once. Please.

"I'm sorry to hear that, of course," Dwight said, "but there's the issue of eligibility. I paid a visit to that Lapierre fellow yesterday. He said Claire is his wife all right, but he doesn't want anything to do with her. He's going to file for divorce as soon as he can get the residency situation figured out. He's already put notices in the *Standard* and the *Messenger* that he's not responsible for her debts. So that avenue is closed to us. Or, should I say, that avenue is closed to her."

Mercifully, Dwight refrained from saying, "She's not one of our own."

"What kind of trouble is she in?" Paul said. "What's she done?"

"I doubt she's done anything criminal," Dwight said. "Doesn't seem the type. Probably infidelity. Usually is."

"You're mighty quick to judge," Hazel said.

Paul's chair creaked as his leg jiggled under the table. "So, what do you need us to do, Dwight?"

"You need to level with her. She has to find another place to live. She can't stay here." He drained his coffee and pushed back his chair.

Hazel couldn't believe what she was hearing. "I said it before, and I'll say it again, what kind of job is she supposed to get in Sheldon in the dead of winter with no transportation? And she's been seriously ill! How can you be—"

"That's enough, Hazel." Paul rose from his chair and stood behind her with his hands on her shoulders.

"I can give her another week." Dwight got up from the table to leave. "But that's it. I mean it."

As the sound of Dwight's car faded into the cold, dank morning, Paul said, "I never heard you lie like that before."

Hazel turned her attention back to the Fruitland flyer. "I've never been forced to lie like that before."

COMES A RECKONING

CLAIRE

February 1968

THROUGH THE WINDOW OF Room 31, the sky looked overcast in a way Claire had never seen before, an unbroken expanse of sculpted gray, like wall-to-wall carpeting, nothing like the heaped thunderclouds she was accustomed to that quickly released their loads and moved on. The gray appeared to have taken possession of the sky, the blue having stayed away too long now to reclaim it.

The air in the room felt cold, as it usually did, but there was something different about it this morning, a certain heaviness she could not name. How long, she mused, could a person lie in bed and stare out the window all day without dying? A week? A month? A year?

She checked her watch on the nightstand for the time, but she'd neglected to wind it. Her stomach told her the time had to be getting onto noon: *You're hungry, but whether you eat or not makes no difference to me.*

She went back to staring out the window. Snow began to fall.

A knock came at the door. "Claire, I've brought your dinner."

Claire got out of bed, opened the door without relieving Hazel of the tray, and got back into bed. Hazel followed her and set the tray on her lap.

Claire looked at the plate. Some sort of casserole overrun with orange cheese. "I don't think I can eat."

"Please. You must. May I sit? I need to talk to you."

Claire nodded and picked up her fork. The last thing she needed was for someone to give her the reality of her situation—much less give it to her straight. But she couldn't refuse Hazel's kind, worried face. The least she could do to ease the woman's fretting was eat some casserole.

"Do you remember the two men who brought you here?"

Claire nodded to avoid speaking with her mouth full. Johnny's hat was memorable, even if the man beneath it had no face she could recall.

"Dwight came to see us—Paul and me—first thing this morning."

Claire forced down her mouthful of casserole, the orange cheese sticking in her gullet. "Dwight?"

Hazel's eyes seemed to be having a terrible time staying still, darting this way and that about the room. "Dwight Demers. He's Overseer of the Poor for Enosburg. Nothing special about his looks you'd remember."

"I guess so. Vaguely." Claire set down her fork. "I don't understand. He's in charge of people on welfare?"

"No, welfare's state money. Dwight approves town money to help people from Enosburg who are down on their luck. If they can't make rent, he decides if they're eligible to stay here with Paul and me until they can work again. Or if they're eligible to stay here permanently because they can't take care of themselves and their families don't want them. That happens more often than you'd think." Hazel twisted her hands in her lap. "Other people aren't—" Now she was worrying her wedding ring.

"Eligible," Claire said to stop Hazel's wedding ring from flying off her finger.

"To Dwight's way of thinking. When he brought you here, he said he'd give us two weeks to get you back on your feet and set up with a job."

It couldn't be, Claire thought. "I've been here two weeks?"

The snow falling outside the window had intensified.

"Two weeks today, not a day over. That's why Dwight came to see us. He wanted to know if you'd found a job." Hazel's wedding ring pinged onto the floor. "I told him when he brought you here, he can't expect you to go out looking for a job in the dead of winter with no car. Not that there are many jobs around here for women to begin with. I told him this morning you've not been well, and he gave us another week."

Hazel bent down and retrieved her wedding ring from the floor. "I don't think I can stall him again."

So, there it was.

Claire closed her eyes, but when she opened them again, she was still sitting on a sagging bed in a shabby room with rose-covered wallpaper on an upper floor of whatever this place was, and Hazel was frowning at her watch.

"Please," Claire said. "Go back to your work."

Hazel stood up, smoothing the front of her apron. "I'll try to think of something, Claire. I promise."

As Claire picked at her casserole, Hazel's final words bounced and pinged inside her head. Hazel had no good reason to promise her anything.

Outside the window, the falling snow thickened into an impenetrable mass indistinguishable from the clouds above it.

Slowly, slowly, the hours passed as the snow fell, while rational thought remained a distant memory. So hard to judge the time when snow negated the sky and one's watch stopped ticking. Instead of a sinkhole opening to swallow the house and everyone in it, the snow would bury it, obliterating everyone inside as surely as if they were lying in their graves.

And yet—slowly, slowly, a shift came in the light behind the snow, a subtle but sure diminution. Snow couldn't fall forever. At some point, it would stop. The air would grow warmer, and the snow would melt. After a time, bare trees would leaf, and grass would grow anew.

Claire extricated herself from the bedclothes, rummaged in her suitcase for something reasonably warm to wear, and got dressed. After brushing her hair, she unpacked her suitcase, refolding each piece of clothing and placing it neatly in its appointed drawer in the displaced dresser in the corner. She might have a home for only another week, but she would at least make an effort.

She made her bed and ventured into the dimly lit hall. She had no idea how large the building was, nor its layout, but if she checked every hall, every staircase, she was bound to smell food.

Upon reaching the dining room, she stood in the doorway, not knowing what to do. Most of the diners were elderly, a profusion of white hair and wrinkled faces under a wispy cloud of quavering voices. Silverware clattered loudly in shaky hands.

Directly across from where Claire stood, a teenage girl in a sloppy sweater gave her the evil eye, leaned toward the unshaven man sitting next to her, and cupped her hand around her mouth. She whispered to him, never taking her eyes off Claire, while he sat there slack-jawed and droopy-eyed.

Claire turned to slink away unnoticed when someone at the table shouted, "It's the lady!" She turned around to see a slight, gray-haired man standing in front of his chair pointing at her.

"The lady's here! Are you all better now, Lady? Want some tuna-wiggle?"

"Sit down, Joey," a man's voice said from the far end of the table. "There's no call for you to act the fool at the supper table."

" 'Leave the presence of a fool!' " one of the elderly men shouted, slamming his hand on the table, rattling the dishes.

"Don't you start, Carmi," the man's voice said, sounding more weary than irritated.

Hazel's familiar head rose above the clamor. She eased the man called Joey back onto his chair, informed him it was impolite to point at people, and walked around the table to where Claire stood.

"Ready for some supper, Claire? There's plenty left." She put her hand on Claire's shoulder and addressed the table. "Everyone, this is Claire. She's staying with us for a while."

No sooner had Hazel led Claire to an empty seat and served her tuna and pea casserole than a young woman with a tight little face glared at her with all the ferocity of the righteously indignant.

"Who are you? What are you doing here? Did my mother send you? I know my mother sent you. Don't you lie to me. I can tell if you're lying. Is your name even Claire? What's your real name? What are you hiding from me?"

The teenage girl hissed at Claire. "You better not steal my boyfriend. I'll kill you if you steal my boyfriend."

Claire shoved back her chair and fled to the third floor. Collapsing on the bed, she gave in to the futility of tears.

Before long, a knock came at the door. When Claire opened it, she was not surprised to see Hazel holding her abandoned plate of tuna casserole. Claire returned to the bed without saying anything or relieving Hazel of the plate.

Hazel advanced on the bed. "I am so sorry, Claire. I've reheated your supper. "

Claire made no move to take the plate. "You didn't need to do that. I'm the one who ran away from the table."

"I know. I'm sorry. I should have warned you."

Claire didn't respond, and Hazel left the room, her retreating footsteps down the hall echoing regret.

Later, when Claire had eaten as much of the tuna casserole as she could manage, she took her dirty plate and fork downstairs to find Hazel alone in the kitchen surrounded by a god-awful mess, dirty pots and dirty dishes everywhere. Was there no one to help her?

"Oh!" Hazel said, turning from the sink. "I didn't hear you come in. I could have got that."

Claire handed Hazel the plate. "No, you've been kinder to me than I deserve. I can at least help you with the dishes."

"Are you sure you feel up to it?"

"I'm sure."

Hazel wiped her hands on her apron and pulled open a drawer. "If you're sure you're up to it, I'm not going to say no." She handed Claire an apron. "You can wash, and I'll dry?"

The water was burning hot when Claire rinsed the first plate, but she couldn't drop it, not when Hazel had been so kind.

Hazel took the rinsed plate from Claire's hand. "I've been thinking. Years ago, I had a house assistant to help out with the housework, sometimes two, but not anymore. The Association doesn't see the need."

"The Association?" The word sounded a threat, like "the Mafia" or "the Klan."

"The Sheldon Poor House Association, well, they call it the Sheldon Home Association now. Paul and I work for them. What they don't understand is that even though we don't have near the number of residents now as we used to, they need more care."

Claire turned off the faucet, unsure she'd heard Hazel correctly over the running water. "Are you telling me I was sent to the poorhouse?"

"In a manner of speaking. There's no shame in it now, though, not like in the old days." Hazel retrieved several tumblers from the table. "Like I said, I've been thinking. Since the residents need so much care now, I can tell Dwight I need a house assistant, and you'll do the job for room and board. I'll go call him right now."

As Hazel left the room, a feeling of déjà vu swept over Claire so strong she nearly dropped the plate she was holding.

Hazel returned to the kitchen mere minutes later. "You would not believe what he said. He said he'd already thought of it himself; he just hadn't had a chance to stop by. That is so typical of him."

Claire allowed herself a wry smile. She was now officially pitiful.

NOT FIT FOR POLITE SOCIETY

CLAIRE

February 1968

THE NEXT DAY, AFTER barely making it through breakfast in the dining room with the other residents, Claire spent the morning with Hazel being introduced to the layout and quirks of the old building and the location of everything required to run a household of needy people.

As Hazel relayed the workings of the Sheldon Poor House, Claire drifted along in her wake, struggling to see every room, every appliance, every shelf through a haze of incredulity.

As surreal as it seemed, she had somehow managed to put herself in the poorhouse, nearly two thousand miles from home. How was that even possible? She came from a good family. She was married to a good man. She had a home in a tidy postwar bungalow on Horridge Street.

Lunch in the dining room was a repeat of the previous night's supper, a clamor of querulous voices struggling to be heard by their own deaf ears and hurled invectives from the two young women, who were obviously not in their right minds. But knowing that didn't make their vitriolic ramblings any easier to take.

Joey's voice rang out. "Claire has teardrops! Help her, Hazel."

A moment later, Claire felt a hand on her shoulder, followed by Hazel's voice. "Come with me. Take your plate."

Had Hazel at last realized that Claire was truly more trouble than she was worth, and it was time for her to go—to be trundled back into the constable's car with the broken heater and dumped on the floor of Roland's garage under a tarpaulin, never to be seen or heard from again?

But instead of heading for the stairs to fetch Claire's suitcase, Hazel steered her to the kitchen and sat her down at the table.

"Are you all right?"

Claire nodded.

"I'm sorry about Lisa and Beatrice back there. It's not their fault—but they can make other people's lives a misery. I'm thinking now that if you could help Flossie in the dining room, that would free me up to keep a better eye on the others."

"Flossie?"

"She's the little woman in the wheelchair. She's our oldest resident, turned ninety-four in December, if you can believe that."

"Does she need to be hand-fed?"

"Oh, no, nothing like that. She needs her food cut small, so she doesn't choke. And you need to watch her while she eats and stop her if she puts too much on her fork. You eat up now, and I'll come get you when Flossie's back in her room, so you can be properly introduced."

Flossie's room was set up as a sick room, with a commode chair in the corner, an overbed table holding a box of tissues and a hand bell, and a nightstand crowded with prescription medication vials and old-fashioned faces in old-fashioned frames. What must have been her wedding portrait took pride of place in front of the clutter, undoubtedly getting knocked over each time she needed to take her medication.

Flossie lay propped in a hospital bed. She didn't look sick, just extremely frail, as if her bones might crumble like so much elderly detritus if she attempted to cross a room unaided.

"Claire's come to visit me?" Flossie said in a voice like a little house sparrow.

"Yes, she'll be helping you with your meals in the dining room now."

"How delightful!" Flossie clapped her tiny, wrinkled hands, then let them drop. "One thing, though, Claire. You have to tell me when it's raining. I have a hard time seeing to the window, and my hearing's not what it used to be. And you can't tell me it's not raining when it is, just so I won't worry. I need to know when it's raining, so I can make my peace."

While Claire assumed Flossie meant make her peace with her Maker, she didn't dare ask for further explanation for fear Flossie would provide it.

SHADES OF BLUE

CLAIRE

◆○◆

July 1967

AFTER CLAIRE'S ILL-FATED NIGHT outside Bilbo's, Roland unwittingly gave her something to hold onto: the promise of a week's vacation in the Blue Ridge Mountains. When he announced the vacation, over yet another cold supper—eaten in the dining area, not on the patio—Claire didn't believe him at first.

"What about the store?"

"Herb and Harry will take care of the store while we're gone."

"Those two? You can't be serious. You keep threatening to fire Herb."

"I'm serious." Roland left the room. When he returned, he laid several glossy travel brochures and a AAA TripTik on the table with a flourish. "The route is all mapped out for us, and we have motel reservations."

"But what about the store?"

Roland reached for her hand across the table and squeezed it. "You need this vacation. *We* need this vacation. I'll phone in every day to check on the store."

"I'm not going," Toni said. "Me and Curtis have plans."

Roland gave her a look. "Oh, yes, you are, missy. There is no way we're leaving you in this house alone."

Toni turned to Claire. "Momma, do I really have to go? I can stay here and take care of myself. You *know* I can take care of myself. For God's sake, I babysit all the time. *Those* people trust me."

"If your father says you're going, you're going."

"It's not *fair*." Toni stomped off to her room, lobbing an 'I hate you!' grenade over her shoulder.

Claire started to get up from the table to go after her, but Roland put his hand on her arm. "Let her be. She'll get over it."

The following Saturday, Toni forgot all about hating her parents when Roland presented her with a new Kodak Instamatic camera, five rolls of color film, a photo album, and a scrapbook to chronicle their family trip. To protect their eyes during the long drive, he had also bought three pairs of matching Ray-Ban sunglasses.

Their departure the next day went according to Roland's plan, beginning with skipping church to get an early start. Unfortunately, it hadn't registered with Toni that getting to the Blue Ridge Parkway would take two days of driving. Instead of sitting back to enjoy bayou country and the Mississippi Delta, scenic in their own right, Toni kept up a constant stream of aggrieved sighs and groans until they stopped for the night in Alabama, and she could complain about the funny smell in their motel room.

The following day was more of the same. The only way her father could get Toni to stop was to keep adjusting the radio to play the music she liked—at full volume so she could hear it in the backseat over the road noise. As for Claire, she put on her new Ray-Bans and daydreamed behind them all the way to North Carolina, where they stopped for the night before getting an early start the next day.

As soon as Roland turned onto the Parkway, he shut off the radio and announced, "Here we are, ladies, the Blue Ridge Mountains. Toni, you keep a sharp eye out for those scenic overlooks, y'hear?"

"I will, Daddy. I've got my camera out."

Claire took off her sunglasses and put them in her purse. Nothing must filter her vision today, her first time on a winding mountain road, after a lifetime of straight and flat. There was no telling when—or if—they would ever be back.

When they scrambled out of the car at the first scenic overlook, the mountain air was so different from the air Claire was accustomed to, she had to stand still for a moment to keep from losing her balance. Missing was that swampy undercurrent of stagnant water and decay that hung over one's days, no matter how far one was from a swamp. The air of the Blue Ridge was so clean, no one else could possibly have breathed it before. She had to be the first.

Claire stretched her arms above her head and rolled her neck to get the kinks out. Spread out before her was a foregrounded study in the color, texture, and sound of green, the mountains beyond flowing to the horizon in ombré blue waves, from dark to light, the clouds above them holding the faintest tinge of lavender.

"Look at me, Momma!"

Claire turned and waved. The camera shutter clicked, and Toni advanced the film. "Now, Daddy!"

Back in the car, as Roland pulled onto the Parkway, an odd sensation swept through Claire's body, akin to nausea, but she wasn't the least bit carsick. Not until they passed a slow-moving station wagon full of kids who paid them no mind at all did she realize that she felt serene, as if whatever imp had taken possession of her earlier in the summer had grown bored with her and lit out for parts unknown, twitching his tail and snickering. She bade the imp good riddance.

Sure enough, when they stopped for the night in Blowing Rock and entered their motel room, the half-hearted attempt at Early American in wood laminate did not offend. It looked like what it was: perfectly serviceable motel furniture.

Over the next two days, Roland drove the Parkway at a leisurely pace—stopping for Toni to take photographs for the album or scoop up tourist brochures for the scrapbook—detouring to check out museums—looking for just the right restaurant for their next meal.

The third day's drive also passed at a relaxed pace, with stops for woodland strolls and more photographs. It was a Friday, when Lapierre's Furniture Emporium stayed open until nine, so they were able to have supper before checking into their motel, which turned out to be a tiny tourist cabin overlooking the mountains. Unlike the previous nights' motels, the room was all done in knotty pine, ruffled curtains at the windows. Claire expected Roland had splurged on the room. God bless him, he tried so hard.

Roland sat on the edge of the bed and called the motel office to place his nightly long-distance phone call. The call lasted barely a minute. When Roland dropped the receiver into its cradle, his brow was knotted.

Claire sat next to him on the bed. "That didn't take long. Everything all right at the store?"

"Harry answered the phone. He said Herb's on the floor with a customer and can't come to the phone." Roland's brow remained knotted. "He says everything is 'right as rain'."

"If Herb is with a customer, wouldn't it make sense for Harry to answer the phone?"

"Maybe. Not necessarily. There's something he's not telling me. Harry never answers the phone."

Roland raised his voice to address Toni, who was prancing in front of the television with her hand on the channel knob. "Will you *quit* flipping those channels, Antoinette? I'm about to jump out of my skin."

Toni stopped flipping. "Sorry, Daddy. What do you want to watch?"

"I'm trying to find out what's going on with the store. I don't need the damn television on."

"Jeez, Daddy. You don't have to get all bent out of shape. I was just asking." Toni took herself and her hurt feelings out to the porch. At least she had sense enough not to slam the door behind her.

Roland reached for the phone. Claire resisted the urge to yank the damn thing out of the wall.

"I'm going to try Herb at home." Roland called the motel office to place his call. Several minutes went by. No answer.

Claire patted his thigh. "See, he's at the store."

"Then why didn't his wife answer?"

"How should I know? Maybe she's in the bathroom."

Roland got up from the bed. "I'm going to get some air." He opened the door and stepped onto the cabin's narrow porch.

Claire leaned back on the bed and closed her eyes. This fretting about the store the night before they were to start the trip back home was pointless.

"Momma. Momma."

Claire opened her eyes.

Toni pointed at the window. "Look, the sun is setting. Daddy said I should come get you." She put out her hand.

Claire took her daughter's hand and followed her onto the porch, where the three of them could watch the sun's passage from day to night as a family.

THE MUDDY MISSISSIPPI
CLAIRE

August 1967

THE NEXT DAY, CLAIRE woke before dawn, an hour before Roland's travel alarm was set to go off. Opening her eyes, she couldn't fathom why she had awakened before the day was to begin. It wasn't as if she were eager to get home. The scenery would be just as stunning on the drive back, but with the image of LaPierre's Furniture Emporium superimposed to spoil the view.

An owl sounded a reluctant goodbye to the night. A songbird warbled. One by one, other songbirds joined in to herald the coming of the dawn.

As Roland and Toni slept, Claire got out of bed and stepped outside to wait for the sun to rise, wrapping her arms around herself against the mountain chill.

She could not remember the last time she'd gazed at a sunrise for its own sake. Lavender and gold painted the sky in broad strokes above the mountains she had come to love, a multilayered rhapsody in blue.

By the time Roland's alarm sounded through the closed door, the sun had erased the last streaks of color, revealing billows of fog nestled in the low areas between the mountain peaks. Claire remained outside, breathing in the mountain air, just breathing, until Roland opened the door and told her to come inside and get dressed. They needed to get on the road.

Roland paced and fussed as Claire and Toni took turns in the bathroom and packed their suitcases. When they were ready, he slung each suitcase into the trunk of the Buick and slammed the lid. "Come on, come on, let's go."

Toni rolled her eyes at Claire. "Jeez, Daddy, don't be so uptight."

Claire fought to keep her face impassive.

Instead of finding a restaurant for a decent breakfast, Roland stopped at the first miserable diner they came to and sent Toni inside for to-go coffee and stale doughnuts. Then he missed the turn for the Parkway.

After waiting for him to turn around, Claire said, "What are you doing? That was our turn back there."

Roland's tone sounded as if he had no idea why she would ask such a question. "I'm taking the highway."

"But why? I thought we'd be going back the same way we came."

"Did you even *look* at the TripTik? We're taking the highway. I need to get back to the store." He put on his turn signal and accelerated faster than necessary to merge into traffic. "Besides, we're all tired. We'll sleep better in our own beds."

"I won't."

"Don't start with me, Claire." His voice dropped to a mumble. "I must have had rocks in my head."

"What? What did you say?"

Roland passed a sedate blue sedan doing the speed limit. "I said, 'I must have had rocks in my head'. "

"Rocks in your head. Really."

"Yes, really. I must have had rocks in my head to take a whole week off. We should only have gone as far as Asheville." Without putting on his turn signal, he passed a GTO exceeding the speed limit, the driver blaring his horn as Roland cut back in, again, without using his turn signal.

Claire's foot punched her imaginary brake pedal. Once, twice. "Watch your *speed*, Roland."

He didn't ease up on the gas. "You don't need to backseat drive, Claire."

"I do if you're going to drive like a maniac."

Toni beat her open hand on the top of the front seat. "Will you two *quit*? You're getting on my nerves."

Without turning around, Claire said, "Sit back, Toni," silently willing her to choose petulant silence over shooting off her mouth.

Claire put on her sunglasses and turned to face the window. Hour after hour, mile after mile, another futile tear to hide, another futile tissue to staunch her nose.

As the sun neared its zenith, the car became uncomfortably hot. Roland refused to turn on the air conditioning so as not to strain the engine. Toni informed her father that he was not only mean but heartless and rolled down both her windows. As road noise roared and grit blew higgledy-piggledy through the car, Claire put both hands to her head to keep from being sucked out by her hair.

Roland white-knuckled them to a motel in Alabama, stopping only for truck stop food and begrudging bathroom breaks. Claire was relieved to see that the motel had a restaurant, so they could at least have one decent meal for the day.

As they entered the restaurant, she didn't remove her sunglasses, so of course Roland had to ask her what was wrong. She told him nothing, nothing was wrong—which was true. The tears had come for no reason, no reason at all.

On their way to the ladies' room, Toni came straight to the point and asked her why she was crying.

"I'm not crying."

"You are so. What's the matter?"

"Nothing. There must be something in the air around here I'm allergic to."

"You're lying, Momma." Toni stepped inside the toilet stall and closed the door.

When they got back to their table, Roland wasn't there.

"He must have gone to the restroom." Claire opened her menu. "We should decide what we're going to order before he comes back."

"I don't know why he has to be so uptight." Toni opened her menu and made a face. "I guess I'll have a hamburger. Again."

When Claire looked up from the menu, Roland was making his way back to the table. As he sat down, she was relieved to see that he looked a little less tense. Not relaxed, but at this point she'd take what she could get. They were still a very long way from home, highway or no highway.

"I just got off the phone with Herb. He says everything at the store is 'fine and dandy.' I'm not sure I believe him, but at least he's there. I need to get serious about finding another salesman to replace Cliff."

"You should get somebody young," Toni said. "Nobody wants to buy furniture from an old fart."

"Watch your mouth. We're in a public place." Roland opened his menu and made the same face Toni had. "Take off those dark glasses, Claire. People will think I'm a wife beater."

At breakfast the next morning, Roland was in a much better humor, slicing into his stack of pancakes and holding up the speared forkful in triumph. "We're halfway there, ladies! We should be home by eleven, midnight at the latest."

"At *night*?" Toni said, her eyes round with outrage.

"Yes, at night. I can't very well drive six hundred miles in three hours, now can I?"

Back on the highway, Roland put on the radio to keep Toni from complaining, and Claire spent the rest of the trip in a Top 40 bubble of studio-enhanced daydreams and happy togetherness until they crossed the Mississippi River, when the tears came again, flowing all brown and muddy down her face.

As the Summer of Love Waned

Claire

⊶◦⊷

August 1967

AS THE END OF August neared, Claire didn't need the nightly news to tell her that the Summer of Love would soon come to an end, the fevered dream of San Fransisco a frenzied nightmare from which innocent flower children would inevitably wake, gasping for air and crying for their mothers.

But knowing this did not keep her from Bilbo's, sitting on the ground outside the Quonset hut waiting for the next song, her legs tucked to one side, her skirt grazing her knees.

The earth beneath her held the heat from the sweltering day like a life force, the full moon glimpsed momentarily through the loblolly pines too far away for its cooling beams to reach the air below. The sounds of men and women enjoying themselves with people they knew in a place they belonged spilled from the Quonset hut's crude window openings.

The noise from the crowd shifted as a few chords teased. Then, a few more, a bit of boogie-woogie, and a challenge tossed to the crowd to watch his fingers do a thing'a work like nobody else, fingers sliding, skipping, scampering over the strings.

What a showman he must be, Claire thought. She wished she could go inside, sit at one of those little tables bathed in colored lights, and watch him play. That's all, just watch him play.

Before the crowd had stopped laughing and hooting from his display of self-proclaimed virtuosity, he slid right into a lament for a lost love who used to cook him breakfast in the early morning—the full import of that breakfast left unsung, too painful to recall.

After two more songs, Claire stood up and stretched. She then resumed what had become her spot on the ground, despite knowing it wouldn't do for her to be out too late. A yowling cat, a full bladder, a supper that didn't sit well—any of these could wake Roland to find her gone. She would stay for one more song. Only one more, then make her way back down the dusty tracks for home, Lightnin's music tucked safely in a secret drawer inside her head.

When that song was over, Lightnin' called for another break. Claire drew further into the shadows until everyone had gone back inside and she could leave without being seen.

Thoughts of the store slithered into her head. Roland had found a salesman to replace Cliff, but he was very young, barely out of high school, with a new baby prone to colic and an exhausted wife. He often arrived late to work, claiming he had slept through his alarm. When he did make it in, he gave customers the hard sell to make up for lost time—but he was too young to have perfected the art of the hard sell, sending the hapless customers fleeing out the door.

Then Claire had to hear about it all the way home—mile after mile after mile. Should Roland allow Keith more time to prove himself? Should Roland give him more training? Should Roland fire him? What to do, Claire, what to do? How the hell should I know? not an acceptable answer.

"You back," a voice said from somewhere above her head. "Couldn't keep yourself away?"

Claire looked up to see Lightnin' Hopkins standing in front of her, as surely as if she had conjured him to appear, right down to his patterned shirt, dark glasses, and cocked fedora.

He lowered himself to the ground. "I reckon I'll have me another smoke. Always keep the crowd wanting more, y'know what I mean?"

This time Claire knew exactly what he meant. She also knew enough not to tell him so.

He lit up and blew the smoke skyward. "What you doing back at Bilbo's, anyways?"

Claire waited for him to say, "This ain't no place for a white woman." When he didn't, she remained silent, her face turned away from him. The sounds of people who have had too much to drink but don't know it yet pinwheeled through the muggy air.

"Say, what's this? You crying? What you crying for?"

Claire put her hand to her cheek, surprised when her fingertips came away wet. She'd grown accustomed to crying for no reason, but never before had she cried without knowing she was crying. "I guess I am."

"What's the matter, baby? Tell ole Lightnin' what's wrong." He took off his dark glasses, the ambient light from the dented Quonset hut instantly aging his face.

She brushed away more tears. "I don't know."

"You don't know?" He blew more smoke skyward. "Gotta be something worryin' you. You lose somethin'?"

Claire shook her head. She had nothing to lose, it would seem.

"You man treatin' you mean?"

Claire answered his question without thinking. "No, my husband is very good to me."

"Ain't got sufficient money to buy with?"

She had to think about this question. Roland's constant fretting about sales numbers was normal for someone who owned a small business. It would be irresponsible of him not to. "No, I don't want for anything. . . . I want to listen to the music. That's all."

Lightnin' stubbed out his cigarette. "That's all? There's more to it than that, what's worryin' you." He didn't say anything else for several moments, as snatches of laughter and slurred conversation launched themselves into the night air and sank to the ground.

At last, he spoke again. "The reason don't make no never mind in the end, I reckon. That sad feelin' what's dwelling with you? You got the blues, baby. You got the blues. Only one thing for 'em."

Before Claire could ask what that one thing was, the bass player approached the spot where she and Lightnin' were sitting. "Bilbo says get your ass back inside. Crowd's getting restless."

"Tell 'em hold they water. I'm coming."

The bass player didn't move, and Lightnin' rumbled a laugh. "He don't trust me—do you, boy?"

Before getting to his feet, he put his dark glasses back on. "Come by here tomorrow evenin', and I'll explain it to you." He stood up, brushed off the seat of his pants, and ambled back to the Quonset hut with the bass player at his side. Claire rose from the ground and made her reluctant way home.

When she crawled into bed next to Roland, she expected to stare at the ceiling as the hours ticked by, in dread of first light. Instead, she found herself lulled to sleep on a buoyant cushion of hope. When Roland's alarm clock went off, Claire's first thought was to tell him she now had hope—for what she didn't know—but she couldn't. That buoyant cushion had room enough for only one.

How to Get Shut of the Blues

Claire

August 1967

The day at Lapierre's Furniture Emporium plodded its way around the clock as it usually did, in brief squalls of indecisive customers and ingratiating sales pitches, followed by stormy customers looking for someone to blame for the plaid couch with loosely woven upholstery their cats had clawed to pieces.

That evening, Claire served their cold supper of macaroni salad and peach cobbler on the patio. There was no reason not to now. After washing the dishes and watching the late news with Roland, she said goodnight and told him she would read for a bit in the living room, so the light wouldn't keep him awake.

When she was certain Roland and Toni were asleep, she slipped out the front door and set off for Bilbo's.

The indigo sky held no moon or stars as oppressive humidity dogged her steps. She pushed the forecast of rain from her mind. When she got to Bilbo's, it was as if she had never left the night before. The same dented blue Quonset hut festooned with sagging strings of colored lights. The same cars and pickup trucks parked in the same places around the hut, Lightnin's black Cadillac still parked some distance away. Lightnin' still stood at the microphone singing in his dark smoky voice, hint of gravel and rasp, smile on the backbeat.

She settled herself in her usual spot to listen, unconcerned that it took awhile for Lightnin' to call for a break. He soon emerged from the Quonset hut, walking toward her as he mopped his face with a white towel, his dark glasses in his other hand.

"Hey, there, baby." He draped the towel around his neck and put his dark glasses back on. "Hotter'n Hades in there." He extracted the pint bottle from his back pocket and took a long pull.

He returned the pint to its rightful place and eased himself down to sit next to her. Wincing, he removed the bottle from his pocket and set it on the ground.

"Them blues still worryin' you, baby?"

Lightnin's question hung in the air, like a wedding vow the groom intends to decline, the congregation holding its collective breath, waiting.

Claire could only answer yes.

He didn't say anything, but Claire couldn't retract the yes. She'd said it. It was the truth. She tried to read the expression on his face, but she couldn't be sure if he looked saddened by her answer or if it was a trick of the shadows on his lined and furrowed skin.

He took the towel from around his neck and mopped his face again. "Well, there's only one thing for 'em—and that's to listen to someone play the blues from his heart till it touches yours." Lightnin's hand gently touched her shoulder, and she couldn't stop herself from flinching at its warmth. "Listen to me, now—what's your name, anyways?"

"Claire."

"Listen to me, now, Claire. I ain't jiving." His hand didn't leave her shoulder. "The blues dwell with me every day—every day, y'understand?—so every day I gotta tell the world I got the blues. Folks listen to Po' Lightnin' play, and it's like he speaking what's in their heart, and after a while, it pacify their mind."

A freshet of tears coursed down Claire's face. Soon she would need to wipe her nose, and she hadn't thought to bring a handkerchief. "But how long will it take? I can't sneak out of the house to come over here every weekend. I can't."

Lightnin' removed his hand from her shoulder. "You ain't got to. Nobody got to sneak around like a' alley cat to get shut of what's worrying 'em."

Jagged lighting ripped++ the sky, the rumble of thunder not far behind. The storm was getting close.

"I don't know what you mean," Claire said. "Are you saying I should leave my family? I could never leave my family."

Lightnin' let a long silence go by. "Baby, you done left 'em already, and you knows it."

"I think I should go."

"Yeah, I need to get back inside. But before you go, I'm gonna make you a' offer, and I want you to think on it."

Oh, no, here it comes. I should have known.

"I'm staying in a boarding house over by the old train depot, and the woman what runs it got a vacant room. She looking for a girl can cook and clean for room and board, on account of her sugar diabetes don't let her get around too good no more."

What could the man be thinking? "You're telling me I should leave my family and become a maid?" This was too much. She really needed to go home.

"Wait. I ain't finished. Listen to me now. I gotta make this quick, before Leroy come out here after me. Listen. How you feel when you hear me play?"

"How do I feel?"

"That's right. How you feel when Lightnin' play the blues?" He took off his dark glasses, so she couldn't turn tail and run without giving insult.

"I don't know." She tugged at the hem of her dress, which seemed to have retreated from her knees as soon as Lightnin' had emerged from the Quonset hut and approached her.

She considered her answer carefully. "I don't feel any particular way. I guess I feel normal."

"Well, all right, then. Normal is when you get shut of what's troubling you. See what I mean? Listen here, you help Eula Mae with the cooking and cleaning, and you can come along wherever I play. Till Bilbo get sick of me, I do his place Friday and Saturday nights, but I get club dates during the week. If you with me, you can come inside and sit wherever you want, 'steada hidin' in the shadows. Nobody gonna bother you if you with Lightnin'."

Now would have been the time for Claire to jump up and run home as fast as her pasty white legs could carry her. Instead, she whispered, "What else would I have to do?"

Lightnin' rolled out a rumbling laugh. "Nothin'. I got plenty women to keep me satisfied. Too many, mosta the time."

Claire's face grew hot with embarrassment. She wanted to say, "I meant no offense," but doing so would either offend him or prompt another derisive laugh. Still whispering, as if afraid of being overheard by some unknown person who meant to do her harm, she said, "Why would you want to help me?"

"Can you cook fried chicken?"

"What?"

"Can you cook fried chicken? Yes or no?"

"Yes."

"Corn bread?"

"Yes."

"Banana puddin'?"

"Yes." Why was he asking her about such heavy food? As thin as he was, he couldn't eat more than a couple of meals a week, if he ever ate solid food at all.

"Me and the rest of the fellas getting mighty sicka Wonder Bread 'n' jam. I told you, Eula Mae don't wanna take care of her sugar diabetes, and now she cain't be on her feet hardly at all. And she half-blind."

He reached behind him for his pint. "I like livin' there. Don't nobody bother me. Back in Houston, some fool always be pullin' a knife on me."

Out of nowhere, the drummer and the bass player started up—a loud, driving beat as if they were going somewhere. Lightnin' grabbed his pint and scrambled to his feet.

"Oh, no, he ain't. None of that Bo Diddley shit he ain't. I gotta go. Think about what I said, y'hear. You wanna take a coupla months to get shut of them blues, be here next Friday with your suitcase packed."

STARRY NIGHT

CLAIRE

September 1967

HOW DOES SHE EXPLAIN to her family that she's leaving when she has no good reason to give them—and no good reason to give herself?

She doesn't.

She wakes early on the day—or did she not sleep, the music coursing through her blood not a dream at all but a vision?

She waits until her husband is in the shower, water pummeling his body, deodorant soap readying him for a busy sales day. She dashes to the garage—grabs a suitcase—dashes back to the bedroom—drops the suitcase on the bed—throws open the lid. Her heart pounds, but her breath is calm. She throws all her underwear in the suitcase, some slacks, blouses, a dress, a nightgown, a sweater for cool fall days—she'll be back home before Thanksgiving—crams in her trench coat in case of rain.

Her husband's shower has stopped. Her breath quickens. She sits on the suitcase to close it—shoves it under the bed past the dust ruffle.

She's in the kitchen now, fixing breakfast as usual. On the pretext of suntan lotion for her daughter's day at the lake, she goes into the bathroom—scoops up her toiletries—shoves them in the suitcase—shoves the suitcase back under the bed—delivers the suntan lotion.

And what of the rest of the day, this final day before she takes action to get shut of the blues, after which she will return home, equilibrium restored, the imp that has plagued her all summer gone for good?

In the car with her husband, she listens to the news—traffic fatalities—stock market down—more bombing in Tonkin Bay. She makes the appropriate concerned noises.

At the store, she drifts through the accounts, neat little numbers in neat little boxes. She thinks about leaving a note, wonders what it would say.

Back in the car with her husband, she hears him rehash the events of the day—sales made and lost—complaints made and resolved—Harry Prejean's gimpy leg troubling him again. She makes the appropriate concerned noises.

At home, the time for her to leave grows closer. She makes supper—scolds her daughter for sunburned shoulders—washes the dishes—watches the news. She thinks about a note—tells herself it's for the best—her husband loves her—her daughter loves her—they will understand. She scribbles the note on her grocery list pad—*I'm going away for a while—I don't know for how long—No need to worry—I have a safe place to stay.* She leaves the note unsigned and slides it under the breadbox before leaving the room to stash her suitcase in the linen closet.

After a while, her husband falls asleep on the couch. She wakes him gently, sends him to bed. Her daughter is already in her room. She taps lightly on her closed door and tells her good night.

The time has come. She retrieves the note—anchors it to the dining table with the sugar bowl—retrieves her suitcase—fights the urge to kiss her husband goodbye. She opens the suitcase—throws in her purse—then she's out the door into the starry night.

— ◦ —

NEVER BEFORE HAD CLAIRE seen so many stars, spread across the sky in glittering banners of light. Never before had she seen a night so clear, with no hint of haze. She didn't watch where she was walking for fear that when she looked up, the stars would be gone, never to return.

By the time she reached the end of her street, the suitcase was getting heavy, but her steps did not falter. Approaching Bilbo's, she heard Lightnin's unmistakable voice singing what sounded like "Baby, come go with me"—as if his vision extended past the doorway of the dented Quonset hut, past the trees and across the field, to her small, hunched figure making its way along the dusty tracks, suitcase in hand.

When the glimmering lights of the dented Quonset hut came into view, she sought out her spot by the loblolly pine, set the suitcase down, and settled in to listen. Lightnin' called for a break when he got part way through singing something about a shaggy dad and broke out laughing. The laugh turned into a coughing fit, followed by an announcement that he had to see a man about a dog.

She heard Lightnin' humming before she saw him. When he spotted her, he started laughing again. "Lord, have mercy. Sorry about that last number. After I cut the record, they stuck in a fool trombone. Sounds like a damn cartoon. I bust out laughing every time I try to play it."

He extracted his pint from its customary pocket and gestured toward her suitcase. "Got your suitcase, I see. I told Eula Mae not to let the room go till after tonight. You tell your man?"

"I left him a note. It didn't say where I was going."

"Much obliged." He took a quick swallow from his pint. "Time for me to get back. I reckon I'll try that shaggy dad again, just so you'll know how it's supposed to sound. How 'bout that?" Lightnin' smiled a glint of gold teeth and ambled off, the pint bottle sagging the seat of his pants.

True to his word, he immediately launched into "Shaggy Dad." He laughed his way through it, but he kept on playing—although the drummer and the bass player soon gave up trying to follow him and stopped playing.

As each song marked the passage of time, and the loblolly pine swayed against the star-strewn sky, Claire decided that her husband would not come looking for her when he discovered her gone in the morning. He had no reason to. She'd left a note. Besides, he must know that the store would be better off without a buyer who couldn't tell the difference between a serviceable living room suite and junk.

Bilbo's voice came over the microphone. "Any y'all want another beer? This be it!"

Lightnin' ended the night's performance with an instrumental so showy, if he'd done it at a school talent show, he would have been given detention and a stern talking-to by the principal, who didn't hold with such showboating.

Men and women meandered out of the Quonset hut to their vehicles, sending up an occasional burst of "Who the hell moved my vehicle?" followed by raucous laughter.

Lightnin' emerged carrying a guitar case in each hand, confirming the acuity of Claire's ear. He'd been switching between acoustic and electric.

She scrambled to her feet, picked up her suitcase, and followed him to his car. He placed the guitar cases in the trunk, along with her suitcase. She winced when he slammed the lid closed with such finality. He'd not believed his own assurance that his brand of blues would—what had he said?—"pacify her mind"—with nothing expected from her except frying some chicken?

After unlocking the driver's side door, Lightnin' slid into the Cadillac and reached over to unlatch the passenger door. "Get in, door's unlocked."

Claire got in, arranged her skirt to a modest level, and pulled the heavy door closed. The car reeked of alcohol.

Lightnin' inserted the key in the ignition, and the Cadillac bellowed to life. He revved the engine a few times, poking the snarling bear, then turned to Claire as he put the car in Reverse. "How you like my Cadillac?"

Truth be told, she didn't much like Lightnin's Cadillac. It was too big, too black, and too loud. If Lightnin's big, black Cadillac were to rumble down her street of tidy postwar bungalows, a vigilant neighbor would be sure to take down the tag number and call the police. She would try a neutral response, something noncommittal. "I've never ridden in a Cadillac before."

Lightnin' put the car in Drive. "Well, then, you in for a treat."

As the Cadillac rolled down the dusty tracks to the road, Claire couldn't help but question whether Lightnin' was fit to drive. He'd obviously been drinking, but how much?

The car bumped onto Williams Road, prompting a vision of swirling red light in the rearview, followed by a siren—*Pull over—Stop—Now.* The imposing cop, the Breathalyzer, the arrest, the demand for an explanation of her presence in the car.

But the path of the Cadillac was unwavering.

The Cadillac rumbled down her street and the surrounding streets with no one the wiser. Lightnin' put on his turn signal and turned into an unfamiliar neighborhood. From what she could see in the Cadillac's headlights, the street was a hodgepodge of different types of houses, most single-story and fairly small, some shaded by trees, others not. It was hard to tell in the dark what kind of neighborhood it was, but it didn't matter either way. Claire had never been there before, so her husband would not know of the neighborhood either.

Lightnin' stopped in front of a large, two-story wood building with double verandas. "It ain't as grand as it looks."

Was he trying to be funny? Or perhaps lowering her expectations so she wouldn't be disappointed? Even in the limited light from the car's headlights, the building appeared badly in need of paint. The dim light from a bare ceiling bulb revealed what looked to be an old car seat on the lower veranda.

Lightnin' turned the steering wheel sharply and eased the car alongside the building. "Eula Mae don't like me to park here, says I'm ruining her grass, but I don't give a rat's ass. Ain't no way I'm parking my Caddy on the street." He turned off the engine and opened his door. "All right, then, time to call it a night."

Claire got out of the car as Lightnin' opened the trunk and removed his guitar cases. She picked up her suitcase and followed him onto the veranda.

"Watch your step. That board's rotten. Can you get the door for me, darlin'? I ain't got but two hands."

"Do you have the key?"

"Naw, Eula Mae don't keep it locked. We come and go as we please."

Claire turned the knob, pushed open the door, and stepped inside to let Lightnin' pass, but he stayed on the veranda.

"Turn on the light, will you? I don't wanna trip and break my fool neck."

Claire found the switch, flipped on the light, and stepped aside, still holding her suitcase. Lightnin' entered the house and headed for the stairs. "Le'me put these guitars up. You stay put till I get back." Even as skinny as he was, every step of that staircase protested his weight.

Claire closed the front door and set her suitcase down to take stock of her new surroundings. Lightnin's Cadillac had delivered her to a narrow, wainscoted hall, made all the narrower by a high ceiling, the light provided by a dangling bare bulb that appeared to be attached to its ornate fixture with electrical tape. A clear fire hazard. And after her note had assured her family she would be staying in a safe place.

Lines of dingy yellow boards ran above the wainscoting. In the limited light, she could make out a large archway and random doors leading to several rooms. So far, the place didn't look too bad, nothing a good cleaning—and a competent electrician—couldn't fix. The place did have an odd smell to it, though, not exactly unpleasant, just odd, some combination of old wood, dust, stale smoke, and something else—dry rot, mildew, unfamiliar bodies? She couldn't be sure. The morning would bring clarity.

Creaking stair treads signaled Lightnin's return. Claire looked at her watch. Getting on to three in the morning.

Lightnin' had removed his fedora, leaving a big chunk of hair standing at a stiff angle from his head. Without the dark glasses, his face looked tired and old.

"Your room down there, commode under the stairs." He dug into one of his front pockets and handed her a key with a plastic fob attached, on which "2" was scrawled in black Magic Marker.

"See you in the morning, darlin'. Eula Mae probably get you up at the crack of dawn to fix breakfast for the fellas. I get mine at eleven. Or thereabouts. Depends when I wake up." He disappeared up the complaining staircase.

Claire took a few tentative steps down the hall and found a door with an oversized black "2" painted on the header. Above the door, an open transom window leaned into the hall. She inserted the key Lightnin' had given her in the lock and tentatively pushed the door open, passing her hand over the wall to find the light switch. This light, too, consisted of a bare bulb dangling from an ornate fixture, but at least there was no electrical tape.

The room had the same odd smell as the hall, but stronger. Claire set her suitcase down and crossed the room to open the large window for some fresh air—or, more precisely, some muggy night air, thick with the smell of plant decay. The window's dingy net curtain hung limp and still.

Before getting ready for bed, Claire took in the rest of the room to get her bearings, so she wouldn't wake up frightened in the morning after falling asleep in a strange room.

Horizontal boards painted white. Old-fashioned dresser and mirror combination. Mangy maroon armchair. Chipped iron bed. Night-stand of a sort. The mattress on the bed—a double—was bare, pillows and folded bedding at the foot. Apparently, the first task for her to earn her keep was to make up her own bed in the wee hours of the morning.

Claire's last thought before drifting off to sleep was that she had not slept in a room by herself since she was a child. In college, she'd had a roommate, and she'd married her husband right after graduation. They'd never spent a night apart. Perhaps this was what she needed, to become a child again, sitting cross-legged on the living room floor, held in thrall by her father's old dance records spinning on the Victrola.

SLIPSTREAM

CLAIRE

———◆O◆———

September 1967

CLAIRE SLAPPED THE NIGHTSTAND to turn off her husband's alarm clock. It wasn't there. She slapped again. Her hand still didn't hit the alarm clock, and the racket continued. She opened her eyes. Dingy white room, early morning light, someone rapping on her door with something other than knuckles.

"Yes, yes, I'm coming." Claire got out of bed and rummaged through her suitcase for her bathrobe. No luck. She'd forgotten to pack it.

She opened the door to an immense woman in a purple flowered muumuu, the crook of the wood cane in her hand poised to knock again.

The woman's voice, when she raised it from the depths of her massive chest, was gruff but not at all unpleasant. "You Lightnin's girl?"

Oh, no, what had Lightnin' told the woman?

"You're Eula Mae?" Claire clutched the neck of her nightgown in her fist. "I'm Claire, yes. Mr. Hopkins told me you need someone to cook and clean in exchange for room and board?"

The woman's dark eyes, small behind thick eyeglasses, gave her face a bewildered look. "You look kinda puny. I need a big, strong girl ain't afraid of hard work. I don't get around so good anymore." She lowered her cane and leaned on it.

"I can work. I just need to get dressed."

"Well, you here now. You may as well see to breakfast. I'll wait for you in the kitchen, show you where stuff is." Aided by the cane, Eula Mae slowly rotated her body to face in the direction of where the kitchen must be. "And be quick about it. You shoulda been up by now."

In the kitchen, Eula Mae stood wheezing in front of a cluttered worktable. "Get them biscuits going first. Dozen and a half. Them men don't need more'n two apiece. Flour'n stuff's right here. Lard'n milk's in the Frigidaire."

Claire knew better than to ask for a recipe. There wouldn't be one. She simply put each ingredient into a bowl until Eula Mae told her to stop. Same procedure with the grits and the coffee. As for the fried eggs, "They all gets over easy. I don't hold with no special orders."

When the food was ready, Claire loaded it onto a rusty version of the tea cart her mother used for presenting finger sandwiches and petit fours to her bridge club ladies. Claire wheeled the cart into the dining room, where a table full of men halted their talk and gaped at her. Lightnin' was not among them.

Never before had she been the only white person in a room full of people. Never before had she regretted a hem that stopped above the knee. If she'd hadn't already crossed the line, she would have fled.

Eula Mae lowered herself onto the chair at the head of the table. She started to explain how Claire was to serve, then broke off, giving the assemblage the fiercest evil eye Claire had ever seen. "Put your eyes back in your damn head! Was you brought up in a barn? This is Claire. She be helping out with the cooking and cleaning."

An elderly fellow sporting a frayed bolo tie cackled, but before he could say anything, a much younger man in a neatly pressed Esso shirt piped up, "Don't you start, Anthony, or we back to Wonder Bread 'n' jam. I cain't live on no Wonder Bread 'n' jam."

Claire managed to get the food served, then escaped from the table at Eula Mae's cue, profoundly grateful for the need to wash at least a week's worth of dirty dishes, not to mention scrub all manner of crud and grime in the neglected kitchen.

At quarter of eleven, Eula Mae appeared in the doorway to give Claire instructions for Lightnin's breakfast: two sunny side eggs on toast and a glass of sweet milk. "Take it up to him on this here tray. He be in Room 24 upstairs. You rap on the door and leave the tray. He don't like nobody seeing him when he just woke up. Oh, and if you see clothes hanging on the doorknob, he wants 'em pressed. Ironing board and iron be in the pantry."

Lightnin' didn't put in an appearance until Claire was finishing up the supper dishes, when she heard his unmistakable voice. "Well, look at you."

She turned around, and there stood Lightnin': jaunty fedora, dark glasses, freshly pressed purple shirt, freshly pressed baggy trousers, black-and-white spectator shoes.

"I'm fixing to leave for Bilbo's. You finish up them dishes and meet me on the veranda, y'hear? I ain't a man to be kept waiting." He flashed his gold teeth in a smile that appeared genuine—for the most part—and left the kitchen.

When Claire made it out to the veranda, Lightnin' was waiting for her, a lit cigarette stuck in the corner of his mouth, his guitar cases at his feet. "Get them for me, would you, darlin'?"

When they arrived at Bilbo's, Claire carried Lightnin's guitars into the Quonset hut. He introduced her to Bilbo and informed him that she would take the table directly in front of the stage. If Bilbo questioned who she really was and what she was doing there, his face under his corkscrew wig gave nothing away.

As soon as Lightnin' began to play, his music entered her like a slipstream, drawing her past all thought and reason.

OF SUSPICIOUS ORIGIN

CLAIRE

December 1967

THE SUMMER OF LOVE had reached its inevitable conclusion unnoticed, as had the mock funeral in October for the death of the hippies, both events as far from Claire's consciousness as the primacy of time.

The autumn months passed in an alternate universe of childhood—in the morning, a knock on her bedroom door, a grown-up's voice urging her to rise and ready herself for the day ahead, the hours of that day spent doing as she was told, an evening of music her reward for being a good girl.

Now, standing in the archway to the living room, she had a mess to clean up. Eula Mae couldn't abide anyone distracting her with busyness while she watched her shows. So, unlike the other rooms, which Claire cleaned weekly, she cleaned the living room once a month, when Eula Mae ventured out for her regular beauty parlor appointment.

Claire opened the windows to air out the room for a bit, dumped the ashtrays, and took them to the kitchen to be washed. Back in the living room, as she gathered scattered newspaper sections, she was stopped by a banner headline: "Lake Charles Furniture Store Burns," followed by the story headline, "Store Gutted in Pre-Dawn Blaze."

No, it couldn't be. There were plenty of furniture stores in Lake Charles that weren't Lapierre's Furniture Emporium. The photograph under the banner headline had been taken at night and showed a building in the process of burning to the ground. It could have been any downtown business. Not to wish those store owners any ill will, but the store in question had to be one of theirs.

Claire sank to the couch to read the article, the newspaper rattling in her hands. ". . . destroyed . . . a complete loss . . . of suspicious origin . . . owner Roland Lapierre . . ."

No, it couldn't be. The reporter had gotten the owner's name wrong. She reached for the telephone on the end table next to her, sending the phone crashing to the floor. So what if Eula Mae didn't allow boarders to make toll calls? This was an emergency.

Claire hauled the telephone into her lap by the receiver cord and dialed, but instead of Roland's cheery, "Lapierre's Furniture Emporium, how may I help you?" she heard, "We're sorry. The number you have dialed is not in service at this time. If you think you have reached this message in error, please dial the number again. This is a recording."

She disconnected and dialed again. Same recording. She dialed her home phone. When Roland answered, she cried, "Roland, thank God you're all right! I read—" but the call was disconnected. She dialed again. "Roland—" Dial tone. She dialed a third time and got the strident *beepbeepbeepbeep* that could only mean, *I will not speak with you. You are dead to me.*

She lowered the receiver from her ear but continued to hold it in her hand. Roland's unspoken *You are dead to me* ricocheted in her chest cavity, which had emptied itself of all her vital organs.

Oh, God, what had she done—and how could she ever make it right? She had to get home and speak with Roland, try somehow to explain the inexplicable.

Or would that make matters even worse—as if she were making excuses for herself and didn't care how much she had hurt him—and Toni—by acting like a spoiled child running away from home when she didn't get her way?

What was she going to do? What *could* she do?

She needed to think, she had to think, but something was beeping, and she couldn't think. She looked down to find the telephone receiver still in her hand. She replaced the receiver in its cradle and put the phone back on the end table. There was no point trying to call Roland now when he was so angry. It had to have been the shock of hearing her voice again with no warning—that, and the shock of losing his business to fire. It had to have been.

She would give Roland time to recover from the shock of hearing her voice before trying again to get him on the phone. What else could she do?

She looked back at the article. In her haste to read it, she hadn't thought to check the date. Three weeks ago. The fire had occurred three weeks ago. How could that be? How could she not have known her family's livelihood had been destroyed? Their Thanksgiving would have been ruined.

As she reread the article, more slowly now, to understand its full import, her eyes kept returning to the phrase "of suspicious origin."

The text of the article blurred and receded before her eyes, replaced by a dark, slow-moving sedan with two masked figures in the front seat, their tall, pointed hoods unmistakable. The sedan came to a stop in front of Roland's store, and one of the hooded figures jumped out, his long, white robe flapping around his legs.

He carried a shotgun in one hand and a bottle of some kind in the other. Setting the bottle down, he raised the shotgun and blew out the glass door. Raising the shotgun again, he blew out the plate glass window. He dashed back to the sedan, threw the shotgun onto the back seat, and grabbed two more bottles. Back at the ruined storefront, he lit the three bottles on fire and hurled them into the store. He got back into the sedan, and it drove away.

Someone had seen her riding in Lightnin's big, black Cadillac with him at the wheel. The suspicious origin of the fire that destroyed everything Roland had worked so hard for could only be herself. She alone was to blame.

Tears seemed to be wetting her face, but she didn't wipe them away. Tears were fruitless. Tears neither changed nor rectified a wrong. They would dry on her face, leaving nothing behind but salt. She must rouse herself, dispose of the newspapers, sweep the floor, wash the ashtrays clean of ash.

But she couldn't move, her brain having lost its ability to will her legs into action. All she could do was sit there, staring at the floor she needed to sweep, until she heard Eula Mae's plodding footsteps on the veranda, but even they were not enough to rouse her.

Eula Mae appeared in the archway, leaning heavily on her cane. "You ain't finished in here? I gotta watch my stories."

Claire shook her head, fresh tears following the salt tracks on her cheeks. "No, I'm sorry."

"Lord, have mercy. You look like your dog just died."

"I'm fine." Claire rose from the couch and resumed picking up the scattered newspapers. There was no way she could confide in Eula Mae. There were some lines a person could not cross.

CONFLAGRATION
CLAIRE

—◆O◆—

December 1967

LIGHTNIN' NAVIGATED HIS BIG, black Cadillac through silent streets of lighted houses with normal people inside going about their normal—and presumably happy—lives. Televisions glowed through living room windows as families gathered 'round to hear Uncle Walter deliver bad news that only happened to other people.

Lightnin' seemed in a particularly jovial mood, nattering on about cutting a record in Houston—fifty bucks for five minutes' work, cash on the barrelhead, none of that royalty shit and not a cent to them thieving tax bastards—then winning another fifty shooting dice. Or maybe he was drunk earlier than usual. It was hard to tell with him sometimes.

He broke off in the middle of a rambling story about helping a down-and-outer on the street. "You awful quiet tonight, darlin'. Them blues still dwellin' with you?"

Claire nodded. For the first time since getting into the car that evening, she turned to look at him. His fedora and dark glasses hid most of his face—but even so, the dash light cast in relief furrows and lines from a life she had never experienced and could never presume to understand—this life of cotton fields and prison time, hard times and worry, whiskey and swagger. She had no metaphorical hellhounds on her trail. Hers had been a life free from metaphor until her inner child ran away from home to join the juke joint circus.

And yet, as the lights from the Quonset hut glimmered through the trees and she heard Bilbo's rollicking guitar and ringing old man's voice, she felt the familiar stirring in her blood.

She followed Lightnin' into the Quonset hut and sat at the table he'd assigned her in front of the stage. She would lose herself in the music for a time and pretend she hadn't found the person she had become.

By the time Bilbo finished his set, the air in the Quonset hut seemed unusually warm, even though there weren't more people than usual. As Claire removed her trench coat, she caught sight of an old kerosene heater set among the tables, all ready for someone wandering around looking for another beer to knock it over and set the place ablaze.

She shrugged her trench coat back on and slipped out the door. After the heat inside, the night air felt even chillier than when she and Lightnin' had arrived. She settled under the loblolly pine to listen, resting her back against the tree and closing her eyes, her arms wrapped around her torso to either keep herself warm or protect what little was left of her insides. She couldn't be sure.

Lightnin' told the drummer and the bass player to get themselves a beer and sit this one out. Unlike his customary sets, Lightnin' played no rip-roaring numbers. Even though he'd brought both his guitars, he stayed with acoustic, no fancy fingering, no showmanship, just a dark, mournful night of the soul.

He had to be playing for her. He had to be telling her that if she would only listen, she could come out of her funk and resume her life. She had no childhood picking cotton, no prison time, no ill health, no money woes, no Mister Charlie to make her life a misery.

After the break, as if he knew his first set hadn't been enough to convince her, Lightnin' eased into his second set with a moan, crying for his baby to come back, come back to him.

Claire didn't wait for the song to end. She scrambled to her feet and took off running as fast as she could for those two dusty tracks that would lead her out of Lightnin's world and back to her own, running, running, running down Williams Road to her quiet street of tidy postwar bungalows, running, running, to her own tidy postwar bungalow, the one she'd made into a home for the two people in this world who loved her most.

Nearing her house, she paused for the briefest moment to catch her breath before smoothing her hair and proceeding up the front walk. The lights in the living room were on, which meant Roland was still up. She raised her hand and knocked on the door, in the same instant questioning why she felt a need to do that. This was her home. She should be able to walk right in.

The light over the front door came on. The door opened slowly, as if the person behind it needed to be able to slam it shut immediately if he sensed danger standing on the stoop.

Roland's face went from the natural apprehension prompted by a late-night knock at the door to the disdain of someone who has been wronged but no longer cares. "Claire. What are you doing here?"

A shout came from behind him, more a cry than a shout. "Is that Momma?" Running footsteps. "Momma, is that you?"

Roland turned his head. "Go to your room, Toni. I'll handle this."

"No! I have a right to know what's going on." Louder now, heart-piercing. "Why did you leave us, Momma? What did we do?"

"Toni, go to your room. I told you, I'll handle this."

"Momma, I miss you!"

The front door closed, which could only mean that Roland had grabbed Toni by the arm and forcibly removed her to her bedroom, Toni's response a slammed door.

The front door opened again. Roland stepped onto the stoop and pulled the door closed. "What are you doing here, Claire? Haven't you done enough already?"

"I'm sorry, Roland. I don't know what came over me. I want to come home."

"Do you, now? You run off with a colored man, and I'm supposed to take you back like nothing happened?"

"But I didn't run off with him. I needed to listen to him play. It was the music, don't you see?"

"What? That has got to be the sorriest excuse for screwing around I've ever heard. The least you could do is tell me the truth."

"But it *is* the truth!"

"Lower your voice. Toni does not need to hear this."

"I *am* telling you the truth. I did not have an affair with anybody. The furniture in the store turned so ugly on me, I couldn't trust my judgment for choosing what would sell. Don't you see?"

"Stop, Claire. Just stop." Roland moved to go back inside.

"But I'm sorry. I want to come home. You have every right to be angry with me, but I just want to come home."

"Listen to me, Claire. Don't try to contact me again—or Toni either."

"But—"

"Claire, I've lost everything. You hear me? Everything. I'm still trying to figure out what I'm going to do. One thing I know for sure is I'm filing for divorce. And just so you know, I've changed the locks. Your keys won't work."

Roland opened the door and stepped back inside. Closing the door behind him, he turned the deadbolt. But not in anger. If only he had turned it in anger.

BEWARE THE SPARROW

CLAIRE

January 1968

CLAIRE SPENT THE REST of December in a state of suspended animation, waiting, as she made up the beds or peeled potatoes, for some sign that Roland was ready to listen to what she had to tell him and, most important, believe it. But each time she saw a sign—fried eggs with unbroken yolks, grits with no lumps—when she brought Lightnin's breakfast tray up to his room and set it on the floor, she knew the sign was not to be trusted.

Christmas Day, she managed to cook the dinner, a baked ham with all the fixin's, but she couldn't bring herself to eat at the dining room table with the rest of the boarders, instead fleeing to the kitchen to choke down a piece of ham and wait for the dirty dishes.

For New Year's, all Eula Mae required of her was to cook up a big batch of Hoppin' John and leave it on the back of the stove. The boarders would help themselves as their hangovers allowed.

Her sign came the following Saturday. Instead of sleeping until Eula Mae's cane knocked on her door, Claire was awakened by a sparrow's whistle, a repeated series of long, clear notes beckoning her home.

As soon as she had a break from the day's chores, she packed her suitcase. Once she'd spoken with Roland at the house, he would drive her back to Eula Mae's to retrieve the suitcase and inform Eula Mae she was leaving. There was no need to get Lightnin' involved.

That evening, as Lightnin's big, black Cadillac rumbled down her street, the headlights swept over camellias in full bloom, up and down both sides of the street, televisions glowing through living room windows as families gathered to watch their favorite Saturday night shows together.

Her own house, however, was dark. Could Roland have gone out? Where would he have gone, with the store where he spent all his time now destroyed? Even if he had gone out, the light over the front door would be on for Toni when she got home from her date with Curtis—although she might be dating someone else by now, teenagers being the fickle creatures they were. She and Toni would have a lot of catching up to do.

At Bilbo's, Claire waited for the first break to slip out of the Quonset hut and head for home, but when she reached her house, all the lights were still off, and there was an air of something off about the place. Something appeared to have fallen over on the grass. She bent down and picked it up.

There was just enough ambient light reaching the yard for her to make out what the sign said: "House for Sale or Rent" and a number to call. The sign fell from her hands. Her family was gone.

Or were they? Maybe a gust of wind had uprooted the sign from a neighbor's yard and carried it to her front yard like so much litter.

She proceeded up the walk and tried the front door. Locked. She walked around the house to the patio slider. Also locked. When she tried her keys, she found that Roland had been as good as his word.

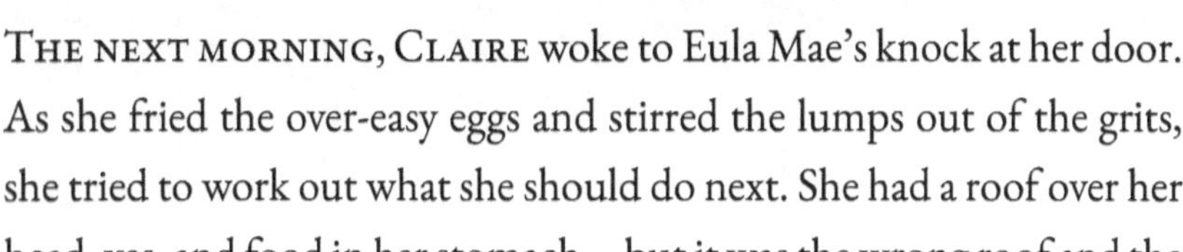

THE NEXT MORNING, CLAIRE woke to Eula Mae's knock at her door. As she fried the over-easy eggs and stirred the lumps out of the grits, she tried to work out what she should do next. She had a roof over her head, yes, and food in her stomach—but it was the wrong roof and the wrong bill of fare.

She loaded the food onto the tea cart and trundled the cart into the dining room. Roland's close family all lived in Vinton, but he would have forbidden them to tell her where he and Toni had gone. Might Roland have told one of their neighbors where he and Toni were going? The thought of canvassing the neighborhood for information about the husband she'd driven away was humiliating, but she'd do it if she had to.

Eula Mae snapped her fingers several times. "Look alive, there. I got church this morning."

"Sorry, Eula Mae." Claire served everyone at the table and slid the last egg onto her plate.

Later, as she scrubbed dried egg yolk off the breakfast plates, the answer to the question of how to find out where Roland had gone popped into her head. The post office. He would have filled out a change of address card for his mail to be forwarded. All she had to do was walk over to the post office and say her husband had sent her to check the change of address card for correctness, as he might have put down the wrong house number.

The following day, her postal subterfuge proved successful—and surprisingly easy, no questions asked. As soon as she was out the door, she scribbled the address on a memo pad and returned the memo pad to her purse. Of course, an address was of no use without a way to get there—but it was a start. She'd find a way. Somehow, she would find a way.

As it turned out, she didn't have to find a way. The way found her.

BLIND FAITH
CLAIRE

January 1968

THE FOLLOWING FRIDAY NIGHT, after Bilbo had shooed the last of his drunken patrons out the door of his battered Quonset hut, Claire sat with Lightnin' in his big, black Cadillac beneath a dusky sky, waiting for him to start the engine. He seemed to be waiting for the other vehicles to leave first.

"You got trouble on your mind."

Not a question, a statement.

Claire didn't want to divulge the details of her personal life to this man who was, for all his show of concern, a stranger. She'd already crossed a line in leaving her family for no good reason and working in a boarding house on the other side of town. She needed to cross back over the line, not leave it even farther behind.

The taillights of the last vehicle leaving Bilbo's disappeared into the night. Lightnin' started the car. "Take your time, darlin'."

Claire didn't speak until the headlights of the Cadillac illuminated the righted "For Sale or Rent" sign in her front yard. She might as well blurt it out. At this point, what had she to lose? "I need a way to get to Vermont, and I don't have any money."

"Vermont, you say? Ain't never played there. Canada, is it?"

"Not exactly. It's on the border."

"That where your man gone off to?"

"Yes, how—?"

"I know man trouble when I sees it. Caused enough of it, y'know."

Lightnin' didn't say anything else as he navigated the Cadillac through the darkened streets. At Eula Mae's, he pulled into the side yard and shut off the car but made no move to open his door. He turned to look at Claire, his face as hard to read as ever.

"You know what town?"

"What town?"

"You know what town he gone off to, your man?"

"Oh. Enosburg Falls. I'd never heard of it before."

"You got a phone number?"

"No. I suppose I could get it from the operator, but he wouldn't accept the charges anyway."

Lightnin' took off his dark glasses and made eye contact. "You sure you want to go after him, even though he quit you?"

Why was he questioning her? He had no right to question her. "Yes."

"Well, all right, then. Tell you what. You sure you want to go after him, I can spot you the money for bus fare. One way, y'understand."

"No, I couldn't—thank you all the same."

Lightnin' put his dark glasses back on, took the keys out of the ignition, and opened his door. "I'll see to that ticket in the afternoon. One way, y'understand." He staggered out of the car, trailing his offer of a way out behind him. Claire followed him inside.

Lying in bed, unable to sleep, Claire reconsidered Lightnin's offer, then chalked it up to his having had too much to drink. In all likelihood, he wouldn't even remember the conversation. Hitchhiking was an option, she supposed, but it would take days, weeks, and she still wouldn't have money for food or places to sleep. She had to find another way to get the money.

The next day, she woke to a vision of three dented brass balls suspended over a grimy storefront. Had she been dreaming? Her left hand rested on top of the covers. Of course. The diamond in her engagement ring was half a carat. Surely, she could get enough for it to purchase a bus ticket.

She jumped out of bed, hauled on her clothes, and darted into the living room to look at the phone book. She found one pawn shop listed in Vinton. All the others were in Lake Charles. She snatched paper and pencil from the end table, scribbled down the address, and tucked the paper in her pocket.

After the breakfast dishes, she left for the pawn shop. She had to ask for directions from three different people—who seemed to be wondering who had let her out of the house without her keeper—until she found the pawn shop on a grungy side street.

She hesitantly pulled the door open and stepped inside. The pawn shop smelled of mildew and rotting subfloor, as if the dingy indoor-outdoor carpeting had been lifted from some suburban patio after a passing rain shower and installed with no thought to the consequences.

A small man with a Sad Sack face perched on a stool behind a display case of disinherited estate jewelry, disavowed wedding ring sets, and handguns. Sad Sack was reading a newspaper.

"Can I help you—" Sad Sack hesitated as if unsure whether Claire was still young enough to be called "Miss" or had crossed the threshold to "Ma'am"—Ma'am."

Claire stepped up to the counter, twisted off her engagement ring, and thrust it at him.

"Aw, jeez, don't do that," Sad Sack groaned, "not while it's on your hand."

But he already had his jeweler's loupe up to his eye. He took the ring from her. "Pawning or selling?"

"Oh! I don't want to sell it. I could never sell my engagement ring."

"Half a carat. Clarity could be better. Fifty bucks." Sad Sack set the ring on the glass counter with a little clink.

Fifty bucks. That's all her life with Roland was worth. Fifty bucks.

Claire snatched up the ring, jammed it back on her finger, and ran out the door.

Back at the boarding house, she was grateful it was getting on to lunchtime. The boarders would have been happy with just the re-heated chili, but she made a batch of corn bread to go with it—and banana pudding, too. Anything to stop from thinking how she was now trapped in Eula Mae's boarding house for the rest of her life, cooking for strangers who would always remain strangers, cleaning their messes, and sleeping alone in the white room with the mangy maroon armchair, never to see Roland or Toni again.

She spent the rest of the day fighting back tears. Her tears would only prompt questions for which she had no answers.

As she was washing the supper dishes, she sensed someone behind her. She turned around to see Lightnin' saunter into the kitchen. "Got your ticket. It won't take you all the way, 'cause the greyhound, he don't run that far, but I reckon someone'll give you a ride the rest of the way." He set the ticket on the table. "Monday, you be ready with your suitcase at two. Bus leaves at four."

He sauntered out of the kitchen without waiting for a response, humming "Shaggy Dad," of all things.

There's Something Happening Here

Hazel

***

February 1968

AFTER DWIGHT AGREED TO Claire's staying on as house assistant, Hazel put off telling Paul until he got up during the night to tend to the boiler. So as not to disturb her, he never turned on his bedside lamp, and she usually didn't awake. Tonight, her conscience woke her. She turned on her bedside lamp.

"I need to tell you something."

Paul didn't respond, grimacing in the sudden light as he reached for his bathrobe. "What is it? I need to tend to that boiler before it goes out."

"I spoke to Dwight yesterday, and he agreed that Claire can stay on as house assistant for room and board. You know, till she gets back on her feet."

Paul pulled on his bathrobe. "You should have talked to me first."

"I know. I'm sorry."

Paul sat on the bed to put on his slippers. "You and Dwight have gone soft in the head, the both of you."

To her surprise, on his way out of the room, Paul stopped with his hand on the doorknob. "You really think she can be a help to you? She don't look very strong."

"She's strong enough."

"Okay, I guess I'll allow it if she really is a help to you. The minute I see you babying her, I'm calling Dwight and putting an end to it."

Then Paul was out the door to the boiler room to see to it that everyone in the house stayed safe and warm in their beds until morning.

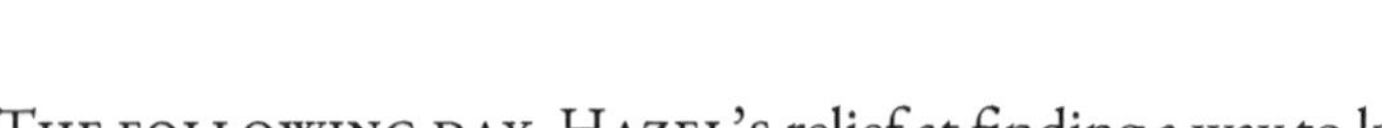

THE FOLLOWING DAY, HAZEL'S relief at finding a way to keep Claire with them until she got back on her feet was soon replaced by other worries. No sooner had Hazel and Claire begun cleaning up after the noon meal than cries sounded from down the hall.

Hazel rushed out of the kitchen, drying her hands on her apron, Claire following close behind. When they reached the living room, the residents were in various states of agitation. Hazel scanned the room. No Lisa, no Beatrice, no Carl.

Emmett sat on the couch rocking back and forth. "He shot him, he shot him, he shot him. Dear God in heaven, he shot him on television."

Joey sat next to him, patting his shoulder. "There, there, Emmett, there, there."

The television was off, but whatever had upset Emmett could only have spewed from a news anchor's mouth.

Hazel knelt in front of Emmett and took both his hands in hers, although it didn't ease his rocking much. "He shot him, Hazel, he shot him, right on television."

"Calm down, Emmett. Tell me what's happened. Whatever it is, you'll be all right. I promise."

"A general can't execute an enemy officer in the street like a goddamn dog. His hands was cuffed behind his back, for Christ's sake. There are rules of war. There are *rules*."

Hazel looked to Homer, who had his arm around his father's shoulders. "That's right. It was a terrible sight, terrible. They never should have showed it on TV to upset folks like that."

Joey left off trying to comfort Emmett and turned to Homer. "Is Lester okay? Is Lester upset?"

Homer nodded. "The old man's okay, Joey. His eyes are bad, don't forget."

Hazel held Emmett's hands for a few more moments, then released them. "Are you all right now? Can I get you some water?"

Emmett shook his head. "We cannot have this, Hazel. It will not stand. Goddamn Vietnamese." He retrieved his fallen cane from the floor and struggled to his feet. "I'm going to my room now."

Joey stood up. "I'll help you."

Hazel put her hand on Joey's arm. "No, son. Emmett needs some time to himself."

"But he's upset."

"I know. He needs time to himself, so he won't be upset anymore."

"Okay, Hazel. Can we watch TV now?"

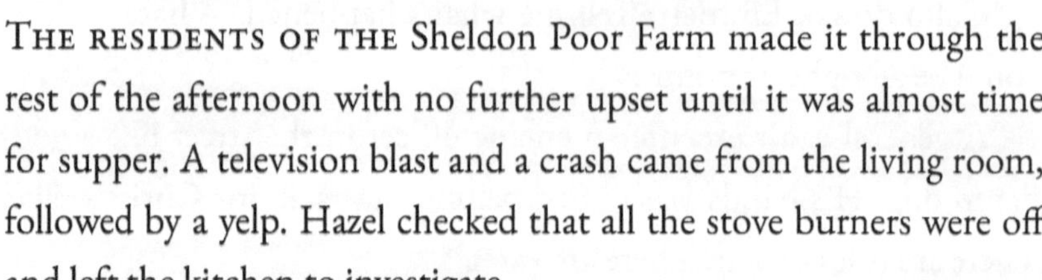

THE RESIDENTS OF THE Sheldon Poor Farm made it through the rest of the afternoon with no further upset until it was almost time for supper. A television blast and a crash came from the living room, followed by a yelp. Hazel checked that all the stove burners were off and left the kitchen to investigate.

In the living room, the television blared, and a TV tray lay overturned on the floor, along with a scattered deck of playing cards. Hazel turned the television down to a decent level and faced the residents.

"Now, what's this about?"

"Lisa knocked over my Solitaire game," Homer said.

"I was helping Homer turn the cards, and Lisa made the TV too loud," Joey said.

"Lisa?"

"He was slamming the cards too loud! I couldn't hear the friggin' TV!"

Hazel righted the TV tray and set it back in front of Homer and Joey. "Lisa, apologize to Homer and pick up his cards."

Lisa dropped to all fours, swept the scattered cards into a messy pile, and dumped them on the TV tray. "Here, take your damn cards, Homer. Sorry you don't have anything better to do than play cards with yourself."

Joey raised his hand. "Lisa said 'damn'."

"Never mind her," Lester said. "I'll play cards with you, son."

"How you gonna do that?" Lisa said. "You're blind as a bat!"

Hazel pointed to the clock above the television. "It's only fifteen minutes till supper. I know you can all wait patiently until I call you. And you don't want to miss the ending to your movie."

Not that any of them had been watching it.

AFTER AN UNEVENTFUL SUPPER and kitchen cleanup, Hazel went to the living room to tell the residents it was time for them to take turns getting ready for bed. The television was still on, still playing at a decent volume, the residents seated in their usual places watching Lawrence Welk.

Hazel scanned the room. Beatrice and Carl were huddled in a corner, whispering to each other, as usual. But no Lisa.

"Where's Lisa?"

Joey raised his hand.

"Yes, Joey?"

"Lisa left. She's mean to us."

"Where did she go?"

Joey responded with a palms-up shrug.

Hazel looked around the room a second time in vain. "Does anyone know where Lisa went?"

"Sorry, Hazel. Maybe she went to the bathroom?" Homer offered.

"No telling with that one," Emmett said. "Sorry."

"The good shepherd will find her and return her to us rejoicing," Carmi proclaimed, as only Carmi could.

God only knew where Lisa had taken it into her head to get off to this time. She was liable to freeze to death in a snowbank trying to follow the directions of whatever little people lived inside her head. Hazel prayed she hadn't left the house.

It took Hazel a good hour to search every nook and cranny of the building, right down to the vegetable cellar and the boiler room in the basement. She even checked the unused freight elevator and the inoperable dumb waiter. No Lisa. By the time she finished, the living room was dark, all the residents safely in their rooms for the night. Presumably.

Lisa had to have slipped out the back door while Hazel was occupied with putting the kitchen to rights. What with barns, sheds, and over three hundred acres of farmland and woods, she could be anywhere. It was way too cold outside to wait until morning and call the sheriff to organize a search party. She would have to wake Paul.

As expected, Paul did not take kindly to being pulled out of the sleep so essential for his running of the farm.

"Not again, Hazel. Did you check the house?"

"I just told you I checked the house."

He grabbed his overalls and pulled them over his pajamas. "What about the basement?"

"I *told* you I checked everywhere. Aren't you listening to me? She has to be outside." Hazel headed for the hall.

"No, Hazel. You stay here. I don't need the both of you out there wandering around in the dark."

"But—"

"I'll check the barns and the sheds. If I can't find her, I'll call the sheriff to organize a search. It's supposed to go below zero before morning."

Hazel spent a miserable half hour worrying that Lisa had slipped outside with no coat, mittens, or boots. If she needed hospital treatment for exposure, whatever doctor treated her would see to it she was sent to Waterbury.

Paul had returned to the bedroom. He grimly unfastened his overalls and slipped them off before crawling into bed with a groan. "Come to bed, Hazel. I don't need the damn light on all night."

"You found her?"

"She's in her room, and she damn well better stay there. I need to get some sleep before I have to get up for the milking."

Hazel let a few moments pass before asking, "Where did you find her?"

As soon as Paul answered, Hazel knew she shouldn't have asked.

"I found her in the cow barn standing by my best milker with a pitchfork. I swear to God, Hazel, I catch her in my barn one more time, I'm calling the sheriff to come and take her to Waterbury. Don't you think I won't."

"But we promised her mother!"

"No, Hazel, *you* promised her mother. Don't think I won't call them. This has gone on long enough. She's going to end up in Waterbury anyhow when the State closes us down. May as well make it sooner and save everybody a lot of grief."

Hazel snapped off her lamp. She did not want Paul to see in her face what she felt toward him at that moment. There had been too many of those moments in recent days.

When her eyes had adjusted to the darkness, Hazel left the room but not to get ready for bed. She stole down the hall to Lisa's room and pushed open the door. The dim light from the hall revealed Lisa on her back with the covers pulled up to her chin, staring at the ceiling.

Hazel approached the bed, bent down, and whispered, "Are you all right, Lisa?"

Lisa didn't move, her eyes fixed on the ceiling. "I don't know. I don't think so. My head won't quiet."

"Would you like me to stay with you until you fall asleep?"

Lisa's voice came from a faraway place she could never return to. "Yes, please."

Hazel settled herself on the floor to wait, as the waxing moon shone through the uncurtained window cold and bright and unconcerned.

TOWN MEETING DAY

HAZEL

— ◦ —

March 1968

THE WEEK OF TOWN Meeting came too soon that year. There had been no February thaw to prepare the people of the various villages to think of the new year ahead, much less to think kindly of the people who would need help.

The first week of March was no different than the last week of February: wind coming out of nowhere to rattle the windows and drift the snow that should have been melting by then, ice on the Missisquoi still entrenched, bare tree branches brittle and grasping against the sky.

Town Meeting Day dawned cold and cloudy. Or, more precisely, the day didn't dawn at all. Hazel lay awake in bed waiting for it after Paul left the bedroom for the morning milking. At five, she got up, turned on the light, and pressed Paul's suit. By the time she'd gotten dressed and headed to the kitchen to start breakfast, black of night had turned to gray of morning without her even noticing.

At breakfast, Paul gave no indication he remembered it was Town Meeting Day, that he needed to eat his breakfast in short order to have time enough to shower, shave, and get into his suit. He sat at the head of the table in his overalls, scowling at his plate as if Hazel had undercooked his sausage and burned his toast.

Then Homer piped up. "Say, Paul, it's Town Meetin' Day today, ain't it? I seen it in the *Messenger* yesterday."

"Oh, Town Meetin' Day!" Joey cried. "Can I come?"

"Me, too!" Charlie said. "I wanna go to Town Meetin'."

Paul looked up from his sausage. "You're pestering me about Town Meeting, Homer?"

"No, it's just you always go. Every year."

"Well, not this year. And don't bother asking why not. You'll find out soon enough."

"Sorry, Paul. I didn't mean nothing by it."

" 'The rich ruleth over the poor,' " Carmi said, setting down his fork and shaking his head. "And the poor man pays for all." He caught Hazel's eye. "Have we paid enough, do you think, Hazel? Will we inherit the kingdom of heaven, Hazel?"

Hazel met his gaze. "Without a doubt, Carmi."

"Bullshit!" Lisa interjected. "Don't lie to the old bastard about heaven. He's pathetic enough as it is."

Hazel didn't look up from her breakfast. "Language, Lisa." She had neglected to shine Paul's good shoes and brush his hat. She'd have to do that while he was in the bathroom. Claire was perfectly capable of handling breakfast cleanup on her own.

Paul raised his voice. "You better watch yourself, young lady. You don't know when you got it good."

"What the hell is that supposed to mean? My mother's got me held prisoner here with these loonies and retards, and you say—"

Paul shoved back his chair and left the room.

Joey put up his hand. "Lisa's being mean to Paul. Go make him feel better, Hazel."

She hesitated only a moment before going after her husband. She found him in his office standing motionless at the window staring at the cow barn, so badly in need of paint again. She tentatively put her hand on his shoulder.

"You're really not going to Town Meeting today?"

Paul put his hand on hers and squeezed it. "Leave me be, Hazel. Please. Leave me be."

With the question of Town Meeting settled, Hazel could go back to her work. Let the self-proclaimed politicians bluster and blather as they would, her work taking care would continue.

Despite a late start with the laundry the previous day, the residents' clothes were all clean, folded, and returned to their proper drawers, but the linens had been left undone. After helping Claire finish the breakfast dishes, Hazel sent her to gather towels and washcloths and strip the beds.

In the basement, as each load came out of the dryer, she and Claire grabbed a handle of either side of the clothes basket and carried the load into the residents' unused second dining room for Joey and Edna to fold, organize in stacks, and carry to the linen closets.

As silly as it seemed, Joey and Edna's folding of clean linens was a highlight of Hazel's week. They were exceedingly patient, folding sheets, towels, pillowcases, and washcloths with the utmost care, matching up the edges perfectly, doing the same when they put them away in the linen closets, the stacks all neat and orderly. How could the State close them down when the linens were clean and folded with such care and stacked so neatly in the closets? Would Brandon have linen closets like this? Would Waterbury? No, they would not.

That was her final word on the matter—and her word had to count for something.

POOR PETEY

HAZEL

April 1968

AFTER THE MISERABLE START to March, the days finally turned warm enough for the sap to run, not that it did any good. Paul had stopped sugaring two years earlier when the farm's last horse had to be put down. Even though selling the syrup brought in a tidy sum for the farm every year, he would not be swayed. The sugar bush was too dense to get tractor or truck through, the farm had no need for horses now, and that was that. No more sugaring for Paul. No more maple candy for the residents' Christmas stockings, no more maple syrup for their pancakes.

Hazel had come to dread mud season, a time of coarse, dirty snow, treacherous patches of ice, and mud, mud, mud—now with no sweet reward to follow. But mourning the loss of the residents' favorite treat and bemoaning the mud wasn't going to get the sink scrubbed, was it?

Retrieving the Comet from under the sink, Hazel thought she heard the sound of a car laboring up the muddy driveway. When she straightened up, Johnny Clough's mud-spattered LTD pulled into the dooryard. Spotting Dwight Demers in the front seat, she had to fight the urge to find Claire and tell her to hide under her bed until Hazel gave her the all clear.

A small figure barely larger than a child huddled in the back seat of the LTD. Strange that all the windows were rolled down. The air wasn't anywhere near warm enough for that. Not even a week had passed since ice-out.

Johnny and Dwight exited the car, and Johnny opened the back door for their passenger, but he didn't move. Johnny began talking to him—kindly, Hazel hoped—but he still made no move to get out of the car. Apparently, whoever it was knew he was being taken to the poor farm, and he wanted no part of it.

Johnny consulted with Dwight, and the two of them pulled the man from the car and started walking him to the house, as Hazel left the kitchen and prepared to greet them.

When they reached the porch, Johnny said, in a friendly enough voice, "Take off your boots, Petey. You can't be tracking shit all over Hazel's nice clean floors. . . . No, no, buddy, you gotta untie the laces first."

Hazel opened the door to find Johnny and Dwight holding onto the small figure, who was yelling something incoherent about a mare and struggling to get away. He smelled so bad, Hazel almost shut the door in their faces. She did not move from the doorway to let them in.

The man was in such a state he was nearly unrecognizable—face unshaven, hair wild, clothes filthy, hysterical over his missing mare—but he could only be Petey Johnson.

"What's going on?" Hazel said. "What's happened to Petey? Why have you brought him here?"

" 'Tweren't my idea," Johnny said. "Dwight here—Petey . . . Petey . . . Petey, you gotta calm down, buddy, or Hazel's not gonna let us in—Dwight here's got it in his fool head that poor Petey's better off with you and Paul than going to Brandon."

Petey twisted and jerked. "No! Save the mare!"

"But what's happened? I thought he was living with his sister."

"He stole the mare! Him! Him!"

From behind Hazel's shoulder in the hall, a chorus of voices joined the fray.

"What's going on, Hazel?"

"Help him, Hazel!"

"Don't let him in, Hazel!"

"He better not hurt my boyfriend, Hazel!"

"Quit that goddamn racket, retard!"

Hazel left Petey at the door with Johnny and Dwight and herded the resident brigade into the living room. She ordered them to sit down and take some deep breaths.

Joey put up his hand. "You want us to mind our own business, Hazel?"

"Yes, Joey. I want you to mind your own business. You can leave the worrying to Paul and me."

"Okay, Hazel." Joey turned to the others and waved his hands. "Okay, everybody. Hazel wants us to mind our own business now."

Upon returning to the kitchen, Hazel found Petey seated at the table with Dwight standing next to him. Now that Petey had stopped struggling, he looked terribly thin, as if the slightest draft could lift him off the chair to eddy to the floor like a pile of dead leaves. She should offer him something to eat, but she couldn't bear the thought of getting close enough to set a plate down in front of him.

Meanwhile, Johnny stood in front of the window above the sink pounding on the sash.

"That window doesn't open anymore," Hazel said. "It's painted shut. I'll open the front door."

The dank air didn't do much to dispel the stench that followed them out of the kitchen, but at least she no longer felt as if her lungs had collapsed. Johnny joined her at the open door for several gulps of breathable air.

"The wife's gonna kill me when I get home and she smells that car." He went for his pipe. "Maybe Jim Tatro has some of that special cleaning fluid to get bad smells out, like after there's a dead body in the trunk."

Through the open door, Hazel saw Paul advancing on the house, his face clenched with questions.

He clumped onto the porch. "Hazel, what is going on here? Get back in the house and shut the door. This coal's gotta last us till summer. Johnny? What's going on?"

Hazel and Johnny stepped away from the door as Dwight emerged from the kitchen.

"Ask Dwight," Hazel said.

" 'Tweren't my idea," Johnny said.

"Dwight?"

As Dwight said, "You, see, Paul—" Petey took that moment to bolt, pushing past the three of them to stumble down the steps and into the dooryard in his stocking feet, hollering for his mare. Johnny ran after him, grabbed hold of his jacket, and dragged him back to the house.

"Well, now look what you done. Take off your socks."

Once Petey was back in the house, standing barefoot and miserable on the kitchen linoleum, Johnny said, "Let me call the judge for a committal order for Brandon, Dwight. Petey's too much for these good folks to handle. If worse come to worse, he can spend the night in St. Albans jail."

"It's not that we don't want to help—" Hazel said.

Paul interrupted her. "What the *hell*, Dwight? You bring me another inmate after all your talk of the State closing us down? And he stinks to high heaven. You need to put him back in the car and call that judge about Brandon."

"No, Paul. Petey is not going to Brandon. He's one of our own. I went to school with his *sister*, for Christ's sake, and she's in the hospital with a stroke. Even if it's only temporary, we can take care of him a damn sight better than Brandon ever could. I am sick to death of the State thinking it knows our business better than we do. I've been doing this job for over twenty years. It's damned insulting is what it is. Besides, at town meeting this year, the good people of Enosburg elected me Overseer of the Poor for another year. Let the State put *that* in their pipe and smoke it."

Hazel had never before seen Dwight actually angry—or even annoyed. A hesitant look flickered across Paul's face before he shook his head and said, "You can't have it both ways, Dwight."

Petey was shivering, his eyes sunken and desperate in his dirt-encrusted face. In all likelihood, he had witnessed his sister's stroke, growing frightened as her face drooped and she couldn't answer him when he asked her what was wrong.

"Well," Hazel said, "maybe we could at least get him cleaned up. He's in no fit condition to be going anywhere. Paul, can you get him into the shower, find him some clean clothes to wear?"

Paul shook his head. "Take a fire hose to him, more like. Come on, Petey—and I don't want to hear another word about that damn mare."

When they were out of the room, Hazel opened the front door again. Coal or no coal, she had to prepare food in that kitchen. "I think we could all use some coffee." As it was perking on the stove, she retrieved bleach from the laundry room and wiped down the chair Petey had been sitting in, followed by the table.

After serving the coffee, Hazel sat at the table with the two men, whose official capacities now seemed beside the point.

Johnny dumped sugar in his coffee. "That's real good of Paul to get Petey cleaned up. You would not believe the mess we walked into. Worse than a murder scene."

"You've never been to a murder scene," Dwight said.

"That's beside the point, Dwight."

Hazel peered into her coffee as if something loathsome would reveal itself if she took a sip. "It's not that we don't want to help—" She looked up from her coffee. "Are you going to tell me what happened to poor Petey or not?"

Dwight tapped his spoon on the rim of his coffee cup, as if suddenly remembering he was sitting at the bleach-reeking table in his official capacity. "As you know, Hazel, Petey is feeble-minded. Well, mentally retarded's what they call it now. He managed well enough when he lived with his sister—"

Johnny interjected. "Except for keeping that horse and buggy of his off Main Street. I warn him one day to keep to the side streets, and the next day he's back on Main Street holding up traffic. Mind like a steel colander, that one."

"As I was about to tell you, Hazel," Dwight said, "Marjorie had a stroke two weeks ago, and she's still in the hospital. The neighbors were checking in on Petey once a day and bringing him food. When it became apparent that Marjorie wasn't coming home any time soon, and Petey was incapable of taking care of himself without supervision, someone called me. I didn't know what I would be walking into, so I called Johnny."

Johnny helped himself to more coffee and freshened Dwight's cup without asking him first. "When we got to Marjorie's place, first thing we seen was her two front windows busted out. We didn't know *what* could have happened, if somebody broke in and murdered poor Petey or what."

Dwight set his cup down. "Nobody wants to murder Petey. Stick to the facts for once, will you?"

"You would not *believe* what we walked in on, Hazel. There was horse shit all over the floor, garbage everywhere, half the furniture busted to pieces, that damn mare of his standing in the living room. And where's old Petey? Sitting on the floor watching cartoons on TV! Can you believe that?"

"He had the horse in the house?" Hazel said.

"He must have got lonely without his sister," Dwight said. "He's never lived alone before."

"You think *he* smells bad," Johnny said. "The house was a hundred times worse. He tried to clean up the horse shit by stuffing it down the toilet—so, you know what happened there."

"That's enough, Johnny," Dwight said. "He can't help the way he is."

"Where's the horse now, Dwight?" Hazel said.

"The best thing for all concerned would be to put her down, but that would mean lying to Petey about what happened to her. I can't do it. We put her in her stable and got her fed and watered. I'll call around tomorrow and see what farm might be willing to take her."

"Maybe Paul was able to get Petey calmed down? He should feel better once he's cleaned up. A good, hot shower can make a world of difference."

"You could be right about that, Hazel," Dwight said.

The three of them drank their coffee in silence until Paul returned to the kitchen with Petey, now dressed in worn-out overalls with the legs rolled up, a graying thermal shirt, a ratty cardigan, and somebody's castoff carpet slippers.

He immediately went to the window and pointed. "You get the mare? She in that barn?"

The four people in their right minds looked at each other. Then Johnny's face brightened. "The mare's on vacation, buddy. The hippies up to Skunk's Misery took—"

"*Skunks?*" Petey shrieked, heading for the hall. "*Skunks!*"

"No, wait. Wrong hippies. It's the hippies up to Cold Hollow. Those ones are giving the mare a nice vacation."

"I want a vacation with the mare. You take me."

"Your vacation is with Hazel and Paul. Dwight, I need to get going. No telling what kind of crime's happening . . ."

Even Johnny Clough couldn't keep a lie spinning for long. He wanted out of there before the lie hit the floor and broke.

Then Johnny and Dwight were out the door, leaving Hazel and Paul with Petey and the sound of the LTD churning mud as it made its getaway.

Hazel looked at Paul. Before she could ask, "What just happened?" he said, "I'm going out to the barn for my work gloves, so I can burn Petey's clothes."

Then Paul was out the door.

AT SUPPER THAT EVENING, Petey refused to sit down and eat, making several circuits of the table demanding each resident tell him the whereabouts of his mare until Paul got up from the table and took him into the kitchen, Hazel following behind with their two plates of food.

The only saving grace afterwards was the television. As soon as Hazel turned it on, Petey plopped himself on the floor and stared at it with his hands folded in his lap. On her way out of the room, she pulled Homer aside and told him not to let anyone change the channel to a Western—or any show with a horse in it.

In bed later, Paul didn't immediately settle into his customary position for sleeping. "You know, Hazel, we shouldn't have agreed to take Petey. Johnny was right. He's too much for us. I'll call Johnny tomorrow to see about a court order."

Hazel waited a long time before responding. "I hate to say it, but I think that would be for the best."

HAZEL WAS AWAKENED BY knocking on the bedroom door. Persistent knocking. The luminous dial on Paul's alarm clock showed twenty past one. She put on her robe and slippers and went to open the door.

Joey stood there in his pajamas. "The man is crying."

"What have I told you about needing to wear your slippers? You'll get splinters in your feet."

"I know. The man is crying."

"What man, Joey?"

"The new man. He's crying."

Hazel slipped out the door and closed it behind her.

"Okay, Joey. Let's get you back to bed."

"I want to help."

"I know you do. You've already helped a lot by coming to get me."

"But I want to help the man."

"I know. If you get a good night's sleep tonight, you can show him around tomorrow."

"You promise?"

"I promise."

When Hazel got to Petey's room, his door was open and he was sobbing, great, wracking sobs pulled from the depths of grief. Hazel entered the room but stopped short of his bedside. She didn't know how to comfort him. She couldn't comfort him with an embrace. He was a grown man lying in bed. She put her hand on his shoulder, but it didn't help. Finally, she sat on the floor and stayed with him until he had cried himself to sleep. There was nothing else she could do.

Returning to the bedroom, she was unable to sleep. Shortly before Paul's alarm went off for the morning milking, she had the answer. She shook Paul awake.

"Paul, Paul. I've got it."

"Got what? What time is it?"

"I know what to do about Petey."

Paul turned on the light and shut off his alarm. "What? Didn't I say I was calling Johnny about Brandon today?"

"Yes, but you don't need to now. Petey wants his horse. That's all. You go get his horse, and he'll be fine. We won't need to send him to Brandon, and when his sister's well enough, he can go back home."

Paul sat up, blinking against the glare of the light. "Don't be foolish."

"I'm not being foolish. Think about it. The reason we couldn't handle him yesterday was he was so upset over his mare being gone. You bring the mare here, and he won't be upset anymore. There's room in the cow barn."

Paul got out of bed. "I don't know. I'll have to think about it."

At breakfast, Petey ate half his oatmeal, then handed his bowl to Hazel. "Oats for the mare."

As Hazel and Claire stood at the sink doing the breakfast dishes, Paul left the house and went out to the storage shed. He opened the doors, maneuvered the farm's truck into position, hooked up the horse trailer, and drove off, the empty horse trailer clanking and banging behind him. When he returned several hours later, the trailer was no longer empty.

HE HAD A DREAM

HAZEL

— ◆◦◆ —

April 4, 1968

1968 HAD COME IN like a lion in January, roared through February, and gone out like a lion in March—yet Hazel had faith that the beginning of April held the promise of good days ahead for the Sheldon Poor Farm. All the signs were there.

Petey had been reunited with his beloved mare. Outbursts from Lisa, Beatrice, and Carl had become less frequent. There were no further visits from Dwight Demers in his official capacity, just a friendly drop-off of two gallons of Grade B maple syrup, which wasn't second-best because that's what the residents were accustomed to anyway. Today, Hazel had served them pancakes for breakfast, as if Paul had never stopped sugaring.

Now, as the day wound down, Hazel found herself humming as she began the task of putting the dining room and the kitchen to rights after the evening meal. Claire had settled into her new role as house assistant more easily than Hazel had expected, even assuming full responsibility for Flossie's care, which Hazel hadn't asked of her. In addition to helping Flossie in the dining room, Claire got her dressed for the day, administered her medications, bathed her, and got her on and off the commode when the need arose.

Most important, when it came time for Flossie's afternoon nap, Claire stayed at her bedside and listened to her story, which Hazel—however regrettably—did not have time for, although she knew the story well enough.

Ninety-four-year-old Flossie started out a happy young bride on the prettiest little farm overlooking the Missisquoi River. All that changed once the babies started coming. Three children dead before their sixth birthdays, one from whooping cough, one from diphtheria, the third from scarlet fever. Her eldest son survived childhood, only to be killed in the Great War, his grave somewhere in France bereft of a mother's ministrations. The defining event for the remainder of Flossie's life would come with the Great Flood of 1927. The rampaging flood waters destroyed the pretty little farm overlooking the Missisquoi River and swept her beloved husband away.

Hazel ran hot water and squeezed a shot of detergent into the dishpan. Now, it wasn't the details of her story that were most important to Flossie. The importance of her story was in the listening.

As Hazel reached for some tumblers, Joey, Charlie, and Edna appeared at her side. All three had on their winter coats.

"The man got shot," Joey announced. "I'm taking my friends outside." Before Hazel could react, he took Edna's hand and the three of them left the kitchen.

When the front door opened and closed, Paul stepped out of his office and yanked the front door open. "Where do you think you're going?"

"Outside," Joey said. "The man got shot."

"Don't you leave this porch. You hear me?"

"We won't, Paul," Joey said. "I'm in charge."

"Oh, for Christ's sake." Paul closed the door. "Can't a man finish reading the paper in peace for once? Go down there and change the damn channel, Hazel."

In the living room, the television was on, but instead of a Western or a cop show, a field reporter standing before a door with a spray of flowers on it informed viewers that "the impact had knocked him off his feet."

Cut to the news anchor: "Dr. Martin Luther King has been shot and killed in Memphis."

Carmi stood before his imaginary pulpit. " 'Vengeance is mine, saith the Lord.' "

Emmett was having none of it. "Sit down, Carmi. The only vengeance is gonna come from those Negroes. You wait and see. There'll be riots in the streets. Just you wait. Riots in the streets."

Hazel left the room at that point to inform Paul of the shooting and tell Joey, Charlie, and Edna to get back in the house before they caught their death of cold in the damp.

AFTER THE RESIDENTS WERE settled in their beds for the night, Hazel stayed up to watch the eleven o'clock news for further details of the assassination. Standing alone in the living room before the blank gray screen of the television, she felt the living pulse of the house beating, telling her that to turn on the television would surely sever an artery.

Murdering a man of God was beyond the pale. If a preacher could be murdered, who was only trying to help the poor and reviled, who would be next? And what did that say about the poor and reviled he was trying to help, that someone would commit murder to prevent them from getting what they needed to live a decent life? She reached behind the television and yanked the plug out of the wall before leaving the room to get ready for bed.

Getting into bed, Hazel fumbled to find one of Paul's hands. After lying awake for close to an hour, she fell into an uneasy sleep, still clutching Paul's hand.

◆◇◆

HAZEL STRUGGLED INTO WAKEFULNESS. Someone was knocking on the bedroom door. She put on her robe and slippers, but when she opened the door and put her finger to her lips, Elsie stood before her, not Joey.

Hazel stepped into the hall and eased the door shut behind her. "What's wrong, Elsie? Are you not feeling well?"

"Where did you put the telephone? I need to call my daughter." Elsie raised her fist to her throat with a faint rattle of rosary beads. "They killed the colored preacher. It's a terrible thing to do to a preacher, even if he was colored."

"I know. Let's get you back to bed. Do you need to use the toilet first?"

"I need to use the telephone to call my daughter."

"It's the middle of the night. Let's get you back to your room." Hazel put her arm around Elsie's shoulders and tried to move her away from the door, but she resisted, surprisingly strong for someone so elderly.

"I need to call my daughter and ask her a question."

"It's after two in the morning. You don't want to wake her up."

"Oh. I guess not. She gets grumpy when she hasn't had enough sleep. From when she was a baby. But, you see, she'd know what to do."

Hazel again tried to move Elsie down the hall.

"Can I ask you instead?"

"Let's get you back to your room, and you can ask me then. Come on, now. We need to get you back to bed. I'll sit with you, and you can ask me anything you want."

When Hazel had Elsie settled back in bed, she took Elsie's hand. "Now, what do you need to ask me?"

"Do you think it would be all right for me to pray for the colored preacher's soul?"

"Of course, why wouldn't it be?"

"He's colored, and he's not a priest. But he shouldn't go to hell. Is it a sin to pray for the soul of a colored preacher? Will the Pope be mad at me?"

"It's not a sin. The Pope is not going to be mad at you for praying for someone's soul."

"I don't think I can remember all the words."

Hazel squeezed her hand. "Just say what's in your heart."

Hazel stayed with Elsie until she fell back asleep, still clutching her rosary despite not remembering all the words.

As Hazel left Elsie's room, the pulse of the house fluttered and throbbed. She should make a circuit of all the occupied sleeping rooms. When she eased each door open, she prayed its unoiled hinges wouldn't give her away as she waited for the cloud-veiled moon to reveal each sleeping figure, alive and unharmed.

Then she unlocked the front door and headed for the cow barn, wrapping her arms around herself in the cold predawn air. Heaving the barn door open, she went inside. She found the shadowy form of Petey's mare resting on a bed of straw in her stall, blowing little horse snuffles through her nostrils.

When Hazel left the barn, a slight shift in the darkness signaled that the time must be after four—and there was Paul, coming across the dooryard for the morning milking.

Reaching her, he said, "What are you doing out here? You weren't there when I woke up."

"I needed to check on Petey's mare."

Instead of telling her how foolish she was and continuing to the barn, Paul embraced her. Before he let her go, he pushed the hair from her ear and whispered in a voice she had never heard him use before, "We're going to be okay."

Hazel put her hand to her ear to hold the heat of Paul's breath as she made her way back across the muddy dooryard in her nightclothes, ready to face the day.

Aftermath

Hazel

***

April 5, 1968

THE DAY AFTER THE assassination started off as well as could be expected, Paul in his rightful place in the cow barn, Hazel in her rightful place in the kitchen, frying sausage on the griddle while Claire rolled out biscuits.

Hazel nudged an errant sausage. "Elsie came and got me up in the middle of the night. She wanted to pray for Dr. King's soul, but she was afraid the Pope would be mad at her."

"Why would—"

Before Hazel could respond, an outraged cry blasted the kitchen.

"TV's busted!" Beatrice pointed at Hazel. "You busted the TV! You did it!"

Right behind Beatrice came Carl, dressed in dungarees, untied boots, and an unbuttoned pajama top. "I wanna watch TV now." He stamped his foot. "TV now! Now, now, now!"

Hazel put up her hands. "No. Not today. Please. Not today."

Claire made a move for the doorway. "I can see—"

"Not *you*, stupid. *Her!*" Beatrice stabbed her finger in the general direction of the stove.

Then Emmett limped into the room. "What the hell's going on in here?" He steadied himself on the back of a chair and waved his cane. "Leave these nice ladies alone. I'll fix the goddamn TV. Come on, get out of here."

"No!" stamped Beatrice's foot.

"No!" stamped Carl's foot.

Emmett made a move toward the doorway. "Either you leave this kitchen right now, or I get Paul, and he'll make you muck out the barn."

"Paul's *mean*," stamped Beatrice's other foot.

"Paul's *mean*," stamped Carl's other foot.

Emmett prodded them out of the room with his cane, while Hazel prayed for strength to get through the rest of the day.

NATURALLY, EMMETT FOUND THE cause of the malfunctioning television and immediately remedied it. By dinnertime, the residents had learned enough details of the assassination and its aftermath to create bedlam at the table. *Minding his own business, talking with his friends . . . bullet exploded in his face . . . Negroes crying, crying everywhere . . . billowing black smoke . . . city blocks in flames . . . alarms, sirens, tear gas . . . Negroes looting across the land . . .*

Joey ran out of the room with his hands over his ears. "Everybody's upset!"

Shooter in the bathtub . . . running like a rat . . .

Charlie ran out of the room. "You made my friend upset!"

Edna stumbled after them. "Don't leave me! I'm upset!"

Elsie rose from her chair and walked around the table to stand at Hazel's side. Bending down, she whispered what sounded like, "The Negroes are coming. We must board up the windows," before resuming her place at the table.

Hazel sat paralyzed before her untouched food. She did not know who to calm first, who needed comfort most. There were simply too many of them. And Lisa—all this time, Lisa had said nothing, nothing at all, staring at her grilled cheese sandwich as if it were crawling with worms.

Paul pounded his fist on the table. Once, twice. "Enough! Stop that racket right now, or so help me—"

The table went quiet.

Now that table had gone quiet, the residents spoke with a collective voice inside Hazel's head. *It's not right to kill a preacher, Hazel. It's not right. Can't you do something, Hazel? You have to do something, Hazel.*

Of course she could do something. She could turn off the television. She could send Paul up on the roof to take down the antenna. No reception, no TV. No husband either, after Paul slid off the roof and broke his neck.

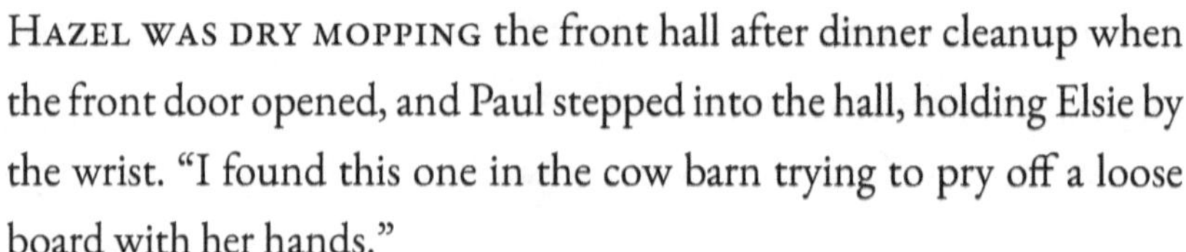

Hazel was dry mopping the front hall after dinner cleanup when the front door opened, and Paul stepped into the hall, holding Elsie by the wrist. "I found this one in the cow barn trying to pry off a loose board with her hands."

"I must board up my window before the Negroes get here."

Paul dropped Elsie's wrist. "There's no call to be boarding up any windows. You could have hurt yourself. Hazel, you need to keep a better eye on these people. Check her hands for splinters." With that, he was out the door, leaving Elsie shivering on the linoleum.

Hazel led Elsie to her bedroom and draped a blanket over her shoulders. "Let me see your hands."

"Will Paul board up my window, Hazel?"

"Nobody needs their windows boarded up. Let me see your hands."

Elsie put out her hands. "But the Negroes are coming. The TV people said so. We can't let them break in and steal everything. They'll steal my photograph album. And my clothes. My daughters will be so angry if they have to buy me new clothes."

Elsie's hands were cold, dirty, and full of splinters. She wouldn't take kindly to Hazel's probing with a needle to dig out the splinters that had broken off.

Removing the splinters from Elsie's hands was the ordeal Hazel anticipated, Elsie looking like a trapped animal, crying out and jerking her hand until Hazel had to find Claire to help hold her still. By the time all the splinters were out, tears ran down the faces of all three women.

Claire rose from her kneeling position on the floor. "Would you like me to fix Elsie some tea?"

"Please," Hazel said. "I think we could all use a cup of tea."

Elsie watched Claire leave the room. "Is she going to get Paul to board up my window now? The Negroes can't take my photograph album. They can't. It's all I have left of my Howard."

"Elsie, there is no need to board up any windows."

"But the Negroes—"

"What makes you think Negroes are coming after us?"

"They're mad at us because a white man killed the colored preacher."

"No, they're mad at the people in their own city, not us. They've never even heard of Sheldon Springs. We're quite safe here."

Hazel kept a close eye on Elsie for the rest of the day, but there were no further upsets. Elsie spent the afternoon in her room with her photo album, murmuring precious memories to her dead Howard's dear, sepia face.

THE SOUND OF SLEIGH bells woke Hazel in the middle of the night. Thank God Paul had remembered to drape the sleigh bell strap over the doorknob when he'd locked up for the night. Someone was leaving the house.

Hazel put on her robe and slippers and hurried down the hall to find the front door open and a shadowy figure standing on the porch with her hands pressed against both sides of her head. It had to be Lisa, standing there in her nightgown and bare feet, putting her head in a vise in an attempt to squeeze out whatever was in there torturing her.

Hazel could only hope Lisa was suffering from a very bad headache. She cleared her throat, so Lisa would know someone was behind her.

"Lisa? Are you all right? Do you have a headache? Let's get you back inside where it's warm, and I'll get you some aspirin."

Lisa turned around, her face cloaked in despair. "I don't know what happened to turn my mother against me. She loved me when I was little. Before my father left, they took me to the Essex Fair. I got to ride on the merry-go-round and feed the animals. How could she turn against me when she took my picture feeding the animals? She bought a frame for it and everything."

As much as Hazel wanted to reassure Lisa that of course her mother loved her and would never turn against her, she couldn't do it. Any words she said in comfort could make Lisa that much worse. She wouldn't risk it.

Lisa now had her arms wrapped around herself in the chill night air. "Every day, she tells me she wants me out of the way so she can get another man. All day long, she tells me. She's not going to stop. It's going to go on and on and on until I die. Don't you see, Hazel? I don't think I can live anymore."

Oh, no. It couldn't have come to this. Not here. Not now. Lisa had never attempted suicide in her time at the farm—or was it that she had the motivation but not the means? "Let's get back inside. It's cold out here."

Lisa did as she was told without responding, going straight to her room. She crawled under the covers and pulled them over her head. Maybe she'd sleep now, her despair gone by morning, like a will-o'-the-wisp in the night?

Hazel lay awake the rest of the night wondering what she would tell Lisa's mother the next time she called the Sheldon Poor Farm with hope in her voice.

WHERE THERE'S SMOKE

HAZEL

◆━◦━◆

April 1968

HAZEL WOKE WITH A start. Something wasn't right. She looked at the illuminated dial of Paul's alarm clock. Quarter of three. If she'd been awakened by a bad dream, it had taken hold and cast her aside too quickly for her to remember it. She reached over and touched Paul's neck to confirm his warm heartbeat beneath her fingers.

Someone was knocking on the door. She pulled on her bathrobe and slid her feet into slippers, but when she opened the door, Claire stood there, not Joey, not Elsie.

"I'm sorry to wake you, but I smell smoke. I don't know where it's coming from. It seemed to get stronger on the second-floor landing."

Hazel turned to wake Paul, but his feet had already hit the floor. All it took was the word "smoke" to rouse a farmer from a sound sleep. Hauling on his bathrobe as he hurried into the hall, he said, "I don't smell anything here. Must be on the second floor. I'll check the men's side. Hazel, you check the women's. If you find the fire, pound on the partition and yell for me. Claire, wait on the landing in case we need you to call the fire department."

When Hazel entered the women's side, the hall had begun to fill with smoke, rising in thin curls from under Beatrice's door. Hazel pounded on the partition and yelled, "Beatrice's room, Paul!" She dashed back to the second-floor landing and told Claire to call the fire department and get the residents out.

Back at Beatrice's door, Hazel pulled a handkerchief from the pocket of her robe, held it to her nose and mouth, and flung open the door. There stood Beatrice, fully dressed for a day out, watching flames slither up the wall. She held a small suitcase in her arms, her face as serene as a Madonna's.

"What have you done, Beatrice?" Hazel said from behind her handkerchief.

The blast of a fire extinguisher sounded through the wall.

"I set my room on fire. My boyfriend did, too. We're gonna get married after everybody in the house burns up. I packed my clothes."

Another blast from the fire extinguisher.

"Come on, Beatrice, you're coming with me."

"But my boyfriend—"

Hazel snatched the suitcase from Beatrice's arms and dropped it on the floor. "Move! Now!" She grabbed Beatrice's arm and half-dragged her down the stairs before shoving her out the front door, soon followed by Carl, propelled by Paul's hand on his back. Before she could stop him, Paul ran back inside and pounded up the stairs, yelling over his shoulder, "Help Claire get these people out!"

Carl joined Beatrice on the grass to wait for everybody in the house to burn up, as Claire came down the hall leading Petey and Emmett, followed by Homer and Lester. After Hazel had helped each man down the steps, Lisa emerged from the building wild-eyed.

"She's trying to kill me. I knew she would, but you wouldn't listen. Oh, you wouldn't listen, Hazel, and now she's going to kill me."

Lisa ran across the dooryard for the road, Hazel yelling after her as best she could before choking on a cough, "Get back here, Lisa!"

Next to emerge from the building was Edna, supporting Carmi with his arm around her shoulders. Hazel reached for Carmi and helped him down the steps. "You and Edna stand over there, now, where it's safe, away from the building."

Carmi looked hollow-eyed at Hazel. "Armageddon is upon us. Prepare for the end of days."

For once, Hazel didn't contradict him. For all she knew, he was right.

Claire wheeled Flossie's wheelchair onto the porch, followed by Joey and Charlie, who lifted the chair down the steps. "Be very, very, careful," Joey instructed Charlie. "Flossie is very, very old."

Behind them came Elsie, clutching her photo album to her chest looking as wild-eyed as Lisa. At least Elsie was too infirm to go running off down the road.

With Claire's help, Hazel herded the residents to a safe distance away and waited for the fire department to arrive. Paul should have been out by now.

Hazel shivered in the chilly night air as the windows of the second floor glowed and flickered with flame while Beatrice and Carl looked on. Paul should have been out by now.

She heard the first fire engine long before it arrived, siren wailing, engine roaring, air brakes hissing as it tried to rush to the scene on a narrow dirt road that was not made for rushing. She felt a tug on her sleeve.

"How long will it take for everybody to burn up, so me and my boyfriend can get married?"

Hazel yanked her sleeve away so violently she almost lost her balance. "Get out of my sight, you wicked, *wicked* girl."

As if she hadn't heard her, Beatrice went back to gazing at the fire behind the second-floor windows as she waited patiently for everybody to burn up, even though several of her fellow residents were in her direct line of sight, standing on the grass in their nightclothes.

When the fire engine arrived at last, Hazel approached the first fireman who jumped from the truck. "The second floor's on fire. My husband's up there trying to put it out with a fire extinguisher."

"How many people still in the building?"

"Just my husband. Please, hurry. He's been in there too long."

More firemen jumped from the truck, put on helmets, hauled out hose.

"Stay back now, ma'am. We'll get your husband out."

The fireman in charge barked orders. Firemen strapped on masks and tanks, entered the building. When they brought Paul out, he was coughing and gasping for air. Hazel threw her arms around him and wouldn't let him go until he wheezed, "I better sit down." She helped him to the ground and sat next to him rubbing his back.

The Swanton fire department arrived, more swarming men, more helmets, more hoses. An ambulance. Another ambulance. Several sheriffs. As the dooryard became more and more crowded, each new vehicle had to park closer to the barns, sending the cows into plaintive fits of bellowing. It would soon be getting on to four o'clock. Who would milk the cows? Would they still be able to give milk? And what of the hens? Would the hens still lay? Petey's mare whinnied. Where was her Petey? Was he all right? Why wasn't he coming for her?

The dooryard became a dizzying swirl of red and blue lights as water shot from hoses and ambulance crew hustled Paul to an ambulance and Beatrice and Carl looked on with slack-jawed delight.

As Hazel stood by the ambulance waiting for Paul to be checked out and released to her, the Sheldon sheriff approached her. "Do you have any idea how the fire started?"

Hazel didn't hesitate. "Two of the residents set fire to their rooms." She pointed. "Those two, Beatrice Budd and Carl Plouff."

"How do you know that?"

"Beatrice told me. She said she set her room on fire and Carl set his room on fire so they could get married after the building burned down. With everybody in it."

The sheriff let out a groan. "She told you that? They were trying to kill everyone in the building?"

"Yes." A twinge of unfairness pinched Hazel's innards. "They're both mentally retarded."

"I understand, but I still have to arrest them and charge them with arson. It's up to the court to decide if they're competent to stand trial."

"I'm sorry."

"Not your fault."

The sheriff proceeded to handcuff Beatrice and Carl and lead them to his car—whereupon Beatrice turned around, stuck out her tongue, and yelled, "The policeman is taking us to get married now, and you can't stop us!"

Hazel found herself trembling as she watched the car's taillights disappear around the bend, but out of regret that Beatrice and Carl would be institutionalized on her say-so or fear that when all was said and done, they would be sent back to the farm, she didn't know.

Paul was still breathing through an oxygen mask, but he appeared to be doing better. Then Johnny Clough arrived on the scene—but instead of parking by the other vehicles, he did a three-point turn and stopped, leaving the engine running. Hazel caught sight of movement in the back seat, a head jerking and weaving as if trying to avoid the vortex of red and blue light whirling around Johnny's LTD.

Johnny got out of the car and beckoned to Hazel. When she got close enough to hear him speak, he said, "I got Lisa—"

Lisa was screaming for help as if being set upon by a pack of wolves. Hazel ran to the car. Johnny ran after her, grabbing her arm as she tried to open the back passenger door.

"Don't, Hazel, come away."

"What have you done to her, Johnny? Why is she screaming like that?"

"I ain't done nothing to her. I'm taking her to St. Albans jail, so she'll be safe—"

"But she's safe here. She's not like this when she's here with me. You must have done something to upset her." Hazel again tried to get to the car, but Johnny blocked her way.

"Hazel, listen to me—"

"What are you doing here, anyway? Get out of my way. You don't need to be here."

Johnny looked over his shoulder, as if expecting to see Lisa fleeing the scene in his LTD, despite her being in the back seat with her hands cuffed behind her. "I was on my way over here after I heard about the fire on the scanner. I found Lisa walking up the middle of goddamn 105. Right up the double yellow line. I had to run my car off the road to keep from hitting her."

"It was good of you to bring her home, but you need to let her out of the car now."

"You're not listening. She's out of her mind. I need to take her to St. Albans till we can get a court order—"

"No! You can't do that. We take good care of her here. You *know* we do."

Paul was now standing at Hazel's side. "What's going on, Johnny? You got a black eye starting?"

Johnny jerked his thumb at the LTD. "I was telling Hazel here I'm taking Lisa Thibodeau into custody. I found her walking the double yellow line up 105. I nearly run her down. When I got to her, I had a devil of a time getting her off the road. She was completely out of her mind. First time I ever had to use my handcuffs."

"You'll see to a court order for Waterbury?" Paul said.

"In the morning."

"You can't *do* that, Johnny. We're taking good care of her here. I promised—"

Paul's arms went around her. "Let her go, Hazel. It's time. Let her go."

Now, the fire appeared to be out, firemen milling about, rolling up their hoses, ambulances departing, various neighbors arriving to take residents home with them to get some food and rest. The fire chief gave Paul the all clear to return to the building, with the entire second floor off-limits. Paul hurried into the building to get dressed and tend to his milking, leaving Hazel standing on the grass with Claire's arm around her shoulders as the first streaks of dawn lightened a night sky that had seen too much.

Sifting Through the Ashes

Claire

◆━◇━◆

April 1968

THE WEEK AFTER THE fire saw a parade of men, some with clipboards, some without, clucking and tutting the way men do when someone has done something exceptionally stupid.

Claire worked around them—sweeping, mopping, wiping, scrubbing—intent on doing whatever she could to rid the old building of its acrid smell of smoke, soot, and wet, charred wood, anything to ease the heartsick look on Hazel's face.

At the end of the week, the neighbors returned the residents to their rightful home. Hazel helped each person from the car with a smile and a quick embrace, while Claire stood by the steps, willing to lend a hand, yet knowing all the while that her help was not needed.

When the last resident had been led into the house, Claire slipped away and began the long walk to Enosburg Falls.

She met no vehicles to disturb her thoughts as she walked down Poor Farm Road in the mid-April sunshine, slowing her pace momentarily when she reached the overgrown, gravestone-strewn plot of land that served as the poor farm's cemetery—but she didn't linger. It was for others to mourn those poor souls.

Reaching the main road, she stopped to look both ways. From which direction had they come when the constable delivered her to the poor farm on that frigid January afternoon a lifetime ago? More traffic seemed to be coming from the right than the left, so Enosburg Falls would be in the direction from which people were leaving.

She ran across the road and resumed walking, against traffic so no one would stop to offer her a ride. The walk would take several hours, but she didn't care. The sun was warm, the air filled with the scent of damp earth reawakening, and she was certain of her destination.

Nearly three hours later, she thought she recognized the turn onto the street where Roland and Toni were staying. When she came to a downhill grade followed by a steep hill, she knew she had the right street.

Roland's car was not in the driveway or parked on the street. Claire approached the front door and knocked, but no one answered. She knocked again, a little louder, which brought footsteps thudding down the stairs.

Toni opened the door. "Momma, you're here! " She threw her arms around Claire, almost knocking her over before releasing her and taking a step back. "When did you get here? Don't just stand there. Come in!"

Claire stepped into the hall, and Toni shut the door behind her. "What are you *wearing*? And what have you done to your *hair*? You look a mess."

Never had Claire been so happy to have someone tell her she looked a mess.

"Daddy's not home now. He hasn't got back from work yet."

"When do you expect him?"

"Five-thirty. He works at Union Carbide in St. Albans. Cousin Norman got him the job. He hates it."

Claire couldn't bring herself to ask if he had an office job or if he was working on a factory line.

"We can wait for him in the living room. He should be back soon."

Claire followed her daughter into a living room wallpapered in an extravagant floral print of the same vintage as the wallpaper in the poorhouse. The tasteful gray living room suite Claire had chosen so carefully for their cozy bungalow looked lost and out of place in the large, old-fashioned room.

Settling on the couch next to Toni as the late afternoon sun slanted through the bay window, Claire noticed that the lines and planes of her daughter's face had undergone a subtle change since she'd seen her last, a little more defined, a little closer to womanhood than girlhood.

Toni had turned sixteen in November, a milestone as momentous for a girl as her first baby steps had been for her mother. And her mother had missed it. She hadn't been there to throw Toni the Sweet Sixteen Party she had looked forward to since she turned thirteen—with a lemon chiffon cake and pink streamers and all her friends from school dancing into the furniture with the hi-fi turned up as loud as they wanted.

Toni met Claire's eyes, then looked away. "Why did you leave us, Momma? You took off one night, and Daddy wouldn't tell me why. I asked and asked, but he wouldn't tell me."

Several moments went by before Claire could bring herself to speak. "Daddy didn't tell you why I left because I had no good reason to leave. I couldn't even explain it to myself."

"That's stupid. People don't up and leave for no reason. There's always a reason. Why won't you tell me? I'm not a child." Toni's voice thickened with tears. "Did I do something wrong? Did Daddy do something wrong?"

"You didn't do anything wrong, sweetheart. Daddy didn't do anything wrong either. Your daddy has always been very good to me."

"Then why? You hurt me, Momma."

Claire took Toni's hand, surprised when she didn't yank it back. "Please believe me. I didn't mean to hurt you. All I can tell you is how sorry I am."

"I *hate* it here, Momma." Toni waved her free hand to include the living room and, presumably, the entire town and everyone in it. "Curtis broke up with me, and I don't have any friends. The school is old and creaky, and it smells. I have to go to history class in a store on Main Street. Some pervert died in there, and they didn't find his rotting corpse for a week. It's horrible! Daddy's in a bad mood all the time, and I have to fix his supper every night, even when I don't know what to make. I *hate* cooking." She rested her head on Claire's shoulder. "I want to go home, Momma."

Claire stroked Toni's hair. "So do I. There is nothing in this world I want more."

They sat in silence, Claire content to hold her daughter's hand and imagine the possibility of home.

The sound of an exterior door opening and closing came from the other room, then Roland's voice. "Toni, you home?"

"In here, Daddy!"

Roland appeared in the archway, stopping short when he saw Claire.

"What is this?"

Toni's grip on Claire's hand tightened.

Roland remained in the archway, as if entering the room would expose him to something vile. "What are you doing here, Claire?"

"Momma's come back."

"Has she now? Well, she needs to leave. She's not welcome here."

Claire turned to Toni. "Could you please go to your room so your father and I can talk?"

Toni didn't let go of Claire's hand. "No. I'm staying right here. I have a right to know what's going on."

"Go to your room, Toni," Roland said. "This is between your mother and me."

"No! You can't send her away."

"Toni, do as your father says."

"But, Momma—"

Roland took a step forward. "Now!"

Toni ran from the room and stomped up the stairs. A door slammed.

Roland took another step forward. "You had no right to come here and upset Toni like that. Haven't you done enough damage already?" He sank into an armchair and put his head in his hands. "Can't you leave us alone?"

She could, but she wouldn't. She wouldn't leave her husband slumped in an armchair, sitting there in a rumpled dress shirt and crooked tie with his head in his hands. She wouldn't.

"Before you end it, I wanted to try one last time to tell you how sorry I am for hurting you and Toni. I know how much I've hurt you."

Roland lifted his head from his hands but didn't look at her. "No, Claire, I don't think you do. I did nothing to deserve this, nothing. Everything I've ever done has been for you and Toni."

"I know it has."

"You know it has. Then why did you leave me? And for a colored man? If you had to have an affair, why did it have to be with a colored man? You have no idea how humiliating that was. It was bad enough you abandoned us, without that. I couldn't show my face in town."

A creak sounded from the staircase.

Roland turned his head and yelled, "Toni, get back in your room!"

Stomping feet, slammed door.

"I lost the store, Claire. While you were off finding yourself—or whatever the hell you thought you were doing—I lost everything, everything I'd worked so hard for. I had to fire the new kid, and I couldn't get anybody decent to take his place."

Claire could see in his face the carefully written want ad, the awkward interviews, the lost cause training sessions, the complaints, the inevitable, regretful firing.

"I mean, how hard is it to show up to work on time and sell some furniture? It's not like people don't need furniture." At last, he looked up and made eye contact. "With you gone, I had to manage the store and handle all the sales on the floor by myself. It's no wonder I couldn't stop Harry from burning the place down."

"Harry? Harry set the fire? Harry Prejean?"

"He didn't do it on purpose. He left a mess of oily rags in a cardboard box in the back, and they caught on fire. I should have checked the back that day, but I just didn't think."

So, it hadn't been the Klan. No hooded night riders, no shotgun blasts, no Molotov cocktails hurled in hate. Merely a simple man who took pride in his work but needed supervision to avoid dangers he knew nothing about.

"I am so sorry."

"Yeah, well, sorry won't bring back the store or our sorry excuse for a marriage, now, will it?"

"Roland, you need to believe me. If you believe nothing else, believe this. I did not have an affair. Ever. I won't let you end it between us without knowing that I've always been faithful to you. I won't."

Several moments of silence went by, dust motes hovering along the shaft of light from the bay window as if waiting for Roland's response.

"Then why?"

Claire had considered her response to Roland's inevitable question on the long walk from Sheldon Springs. As ridiculous as it was, she would tell him the truth. Even if he didn't believe her, she owed him the truth.

When she was finished, Roland stared at her for the longest time. "That's the most ridiculous thing I've ever heard." Another long pause, the dust motes hovering. "You're telling me the truth, aren't you?"

"Yes."

"God help me, I believe you."

Claire wanted to leap from the couch and throw her arms around him, but of course she couldn't. "I've been hoping we could be a family again, but—"

Roland held up his hand. "But—"

Another creak sounded from the staircase, followed by Toni's voice. "Are you done yet? Can I come down now?"

Roland got up from his chair to answer. "Yes, we're finished. You can come down now."

Toni's expectant expression was no surprise, but before she could say anything, Roland said, "I'm driving your mother back."

Claire rose from the couch and followed him into the kitchen, Toni following close behind, until Roland stopped and said, "I'll drive your mother back. You need to stay here."

"No, I'm coming with you. I have a right—"

"Antoinette, don't argue with me. You and I can talk when I get back."

In the driveway, Claire was surprised when Roland opened her door for her as if they were still in Vinton and headed for work or a rare night out. Old habits died hard.

When they had their seat belts fastened, Roland said, "Where are you staying?"

"Sheldon Springs."

"I know where that is. I pass it on my way to work every day." He started the Buick, put it in gear, and backed out of the driveway. He didn't speak or turn on the radio, and Claire dared not break the silence until they approached Poor Farm Road.

"Turn here."

"Here?"

"Yes."

"This is a dirt road."

"It is."

"You live on a dirt road?"

"I do."

When she pointed to the turn for the poor farm, he again said, "Here?" as if he didn't believe it. He was even more incredulous when three weatherbeaten barns appeared around the bend.

Claire pointed to the house. "Right here."

Roland eased the car to a stop and put it in Park. "This is where you're staying?"

"That's right."

"What is this place? It looks pretty run-down."

"The Sheldon Poor Farm."

"What is it now?"

"It's still a poor farm."

"They still send people to the poor farm in Vermont? This place is more backward than I thought." Roland pointed through the windshield. "Was there a fire?"

"Yes, a week ago, but no one was hurt. We were able to get everyone out safely."

"I probably shouldn't ask, but—is it safe to leave you here?"

Claire opened her door. "Safer than you'll ever know." She got out of the car and ran to the house, just in time to take her place next to Flossie at the supper table.

As APRIL SLIPPED INTO May, life returned to normal at the poor farm—or as close to normal as it could with all the construction noise above their heads.

Claire knew the time was approaching when she would call her parents and ask for bus fare to Lafayette and a place to stay until she got back on her feet. There would be a divorce to contend with and custody of Toni—she knew this—but for now, she would stay right where she was—helping care for those who couldn't care for themselves, as the days became warmer, and the farmland surrounding the house took on the vibrant green of early summer, the air alive with birdsong.

Two Troublesome Priests

Hazel

May 18, 1968

THROUGH THE KITCHEN WINDOW that faced the overgrown meadow, Hazel could take in the gently rolling landscape of the farm and ruminate on the season: its beginning, its height, its passing. Sometimes she even offered up a little prayer of thanksgiving.

Today was one of those days. Spring had come to the Sheldon Poor Farm at last, the bitter cold of winter a memory easily distanced, the quagmire of mud season replaced, seemingly overnight, with leafy green trees and fresh, new grass.

Claire had taken over cleaning the bathrooms, leaving Hazel free on this balmy Saturday morning to give the kitchen cupboard doors and drawer fronts a good scrubbing.

As she rinsed out her rag, Homer appeared at her elbow, still dressed in overalls and a chambray work shirt for the farm work he could no longer perform. He hid his crippled hands in his pockets.

"Excuse me, Hazel. Have you seen Mouser?"

She wrung out the rag. "No, I haven't."

"I don't want to be a bother, but the old man ain't been himself all morning."

"What's wrong? Do I need to call the doctor?"

"No, thank you kindly. He's just going on the way he does about being a burden because he's too old and poor-sighted to work. Do you think Paul would mind if I went out to the barn to look for Mouser? I don't want to trouble him."

Of course Paul would mind. Hazel dried her hands on her apron. "I'll go, Homer. You have a seat at the table."

Hazel hurried across the dooryard to the cow barn. It would take her some time to find Lester's cat, but she needed to do it before Paul brought in the fresh eggs from the chicken coop and spotted Homer sitting forlornly at the kitchen table with his bushy mountain man beard and useless hands. God love him, Homer did his best to look out for his father, even after they lost the family farm to the Depression and ended up at the poor farm as charity cases when neither of them was able to hire out for farm work any longer.

Hazel located Mouser in the hayloft, although it took some doing, first to get the cat to come to her, then to climb down the ladder with the squirming animal under one arm.

Back at the house, she grabbed the morning paper off the porch and ducked into the kitchen—but Paul was already in the room with questions on his face. She dropped the paper on the table, set Mouser in Homer's arms, and sent him on his way.

Paul gave her a look. "Barn cats belong in the barn. You oughta know that by now."

He offered no further comment, for which Hazel was grateful. If it soothed the old man to pet the barn cat, let him have the barn cat. It was little enough to ask.

Paul picked up the paper from the table and pulled his reading glasses from the bib pocket of his overalls. Something must have caught his eye.

"What the *hell*!"

"What? What's wrong?"

Paul put up his hand. "Wait, let me read."

Hazel could not imagine what would upset him so on a bright May morning when the repairs to the fire damage on the second floor were well underway, and the time of assassinations and riots in the streets was over.

Paul held up the paper and shook it at her. "Look at this, Hazel. Look at this. How *dare* they? And they're priests for Christ's sake. It's an insult is what it is, an insult."

He left the kitchen and walked out the front door without another word, Hazel right on his heels. She stopped at the porch steps when he got into their car, watching as the dust kicked up by the retreating car drifted and settled. Since Paul took their car and not the farm's truck, she knew right where he was going. Duffy Hill. He'd been going there for years, to pull over to the side of the road and sit in the car for an hour or more, stewing, as he stared at a certain ruined barn and derelict farmhouse.

By now, the barn site must have so much vegetation growing on, around, and through it that no one would know a barn had once stood there but Paul and her. As for the farmhouse, he would bear witness as it quietly rotted away, one shingle, one clapboard, one porch post at a time. Morbid is what it was.

Hazel went back into the kitchen to find out what had upset him this time. The article title read, "9 Seize, Burn Draft Records." The accompanying photograph showed two priests, one in the act of light-ing a match, the other having just dropped a match onto the flaming objects in front of them. According to the caption, one of the priests, the Reverend Philip Berrigan, had been involved with pouring blood on draft records the previous October.

Apparently the two priests, along with seven unnamed protesters, had walked into a draft office in Maryland, grabbed a bunch of draft records, and set them on fire in the parking lot. No wonder Paul was so upset.

Of course, Vietnam War protesters didn't want to see any more young men killed—nor did she. But still, those two priests should have a care about those who had been drafted into war and served. Her husband, her father.

Screams in the Night

Hazel

January 1927

COLD AIR WOKE HAZEL in the middle of the night, seeping through the covers and her flannel nightie to goosebump her skin. The room shouldn't be this cold. She curled up as tight as she could and drew the covers up to her neck, but it didn't help. She was still cold, and the air in the room smelled funny.

Had the kerosene heater in the living room gone out? Or worse, had they run out of kerosene? That happened once. Daddy went to Ralph's instead of coming home with the kerosene. Mama borrowed some from the neighbors, but when it ran out Hazel had to wear her coat to bed.

She listened intently for stirrings from her parents' bedroom on the other side of the wall. Nothing. Neither of them was waking up to tend to that heater. She would have to check it herself. As she was getting up, she noticed that the bedroom door was closed and realized the source of the funny smell. Her stupid brother had closed the door to sneak a cigarette! He should be the one getting up to open the door, not her. She felt like smacking him, but she didn't. Instead, she tiptoed across the cold linoleum, opened the bedroom door, and dashed to the heater. It was still on, sending out blessed heat. She warmed her hands, her front, and her backside before making the dash back to her bed.

As she settled her head on the pillow, she hoped she wouldn't be sleepy in school the next day. Usually when she got woken up in the middle of the night, she was tired the following day and nodded off during arithmetic. This brought nasty remarks from Miss Manahan about the wrong side of railroad tracks. Much, much worse than a ruler across the knuckles. Well, at least she had her arithmetic homework done. No telling if it was right, but it was done. Miss Manahan couldn't punish her for not doing her arithmetic homework.

The sound of a freight train rumbled in the distance, getting louder as it approached the Junction. The engineer blew his whistle, and a fearsome scream pierced the wall next to Hazel's bed, a scream so fearsome it could only bring more screams.

They're coming, they're coming! Down, boys, down!

Oh, no, not again. Hazel put her pillow over her head.

All is lost! We're done for!

Daddy should be over the war by now. The war happened long, long ago, when Hazel was a baby. Daddy didn't need to scream in his sleep. He was home now. But still, he screamed.

We're done for, I say!

Mama was trying to wake him up, but he kept on screaming at whatever it was that wasn't there. Hazel couldn't tell from her mother's muffled voice if she had failed to wake him or if she had woken him, and whatever it was that wasn't there was now in the room with them.

Stop, stop, stop, stop, stop, stop, stop, stop!

Three thumps came from the floor and a deep, angry voice.

Cut that shit out! Goddamn it, we're trying to sleep down here!

The downstairs neighbors banging on the ceiling with a broom handle. Again. What if Daddy didn't stop, and the neighbors came thundering up the stairs and pounded on the door and cursed and pounded and cursed and pounded until the door that kept them all safe in their home crashed to the floor?

Hazel sat up, hoping the slight squeak of her bedsprings would wake her brother. "Sam, are you awake? I'm scared."

In the dim shadows of the room, she could now see that Sam was sitting on the edge of his bed. The thumping from the floor came again.

Cut that shit out, goddamn it!

"Of course, I'm awake, stupid." Sam jumped off his bed and stomped his foot on the floor. Once, twice, three times. "*You* cut that shit out, goddamn it!"

"Sam, don't! I'm scared!"

Sam grabbed his bathrobe from the foot of the bed.

"What are you doing? Where are you going?"

"I'm going to get Mama out of there. Where do you think?" Sam dragged on his robe and scrabbled his feet on the floor for his slippers.

"Daddy'll get mad if you interfere."

"I need to get her out before she gets hurt. He's going nuts in there."

"Daddy wouldn't hurt her, would he?"

Sam left the room without answering. Hazel slid out of bed and went after him, not bothering with her bathrobe. Daddy would be so mad if Sam tried to interfere. He'd yell and storm and then he'd go to Ralph's and Mama would have no money for bread and milk. Hazel reached the doorway of her parents' bedroom as Sam turned on the light. The harsh glare from the bare bulb did nothing to stop Daddy's arms and legs going every which way on the bed, an elbow hitting Mama's tender belly.

No, no, no, no!

Mama flinched from the blow. "Sammy, what are you doing? You shouldn't be in here. Go back to bed."

Sam advanced toward the bed and grabbed Mama's wrist. "You need to go in the other room. Now. Before you get hurt." He tugged on her wrist.

"Don't, Sam! You're hurting her!" Hazel said, but she didn't dare enter the room to try and stop him.

And still Daddy screamed.

Stop, stop, stop, stop, stop, stop, stop, stop!

Sam grabbed Mama's other wrist and pulled and pleaded until she stopped resisting and let him help her out of bed. When he had her steady on her feet, she said, "Hazel, go back to bed. You can't be in here."

"I'm scared."

"There's nothing to be scared of, sweetheart." She crossed the room and put her arm around Hazel's shoulders. "Daddy's having a bad dream."

"But he won't stop screaming."

"I know. He's having a very bad dream, but when he wakes up, it will be gone, like any other bad dream."

"Are you sure?"

"I'm sure. Let's get you back to bed."

Mama tucked Hazel into bed the same way as she had when Hazel was very little. "Do you want me to stay with you until you fall asleep?"

"Yes, please."

Mama sat on the edge of the bed and stroked Hazel's hair, but it didn't help.

"Shouldn't Daddy be over the war by now? It was ages ago."

Mama hesitated, and Hazel thought she wasn't going to answer. "That's not for me to say, Hazel. Or you either."

A smack and a gasp came from the other side of the wall.

What are you doing? Get off me, boy!

Mama rose from Hazel's bed as Sam entered the bedroom.

"I finally got him to wake up," Sam said.

"Is he all right?" Mama turned to leave the room.

"You know he's not." Sam put his hand on her arm. "You can take my bed. I'll sleep on the couch."

"No, Sam, I need to get back to your father."

"Mama, please—"

Daddy appeared in the doorway. "Alice? What are you doing in here? Come back to bed."

Daddy didn't seem mad or upset, just confused, and Mama followed him back to their room.

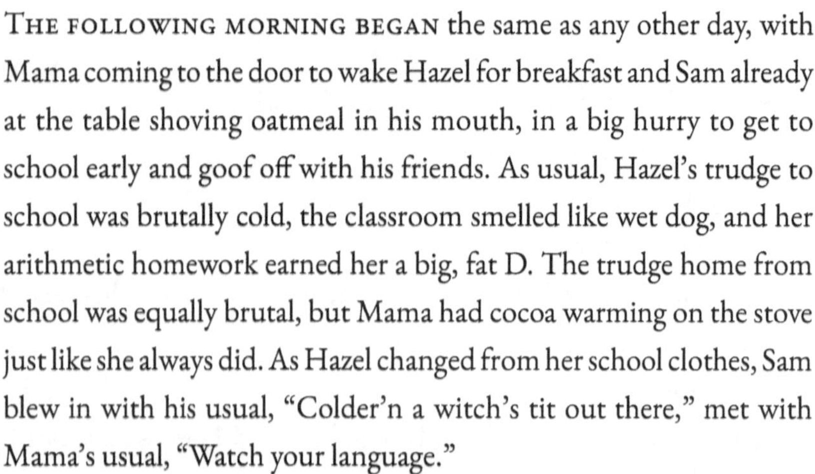

THE FOLLOWING MORNING BEGAN the same as any other day, with Mama coming to the door to wake Hazel for breakfast and Sam already at the table shoving oatmeal in his mouth, in a big hurry to get to school early and goof off with his friends. As usual, Hazel's trudge to school was brutally cold, the classroom smelled like wet dog, and her arithmetic homework earned her a big, fat D. The trudge home from school was equally brutal, but Mama had cocoa warming on the stove just like she always did. As Hazel changed from her school clothes, Sam blew in with his usual, "Colder'n a witch's tit out there," met with Mama's usual, "Watch your language."

When Hazel sat at the table for her cocoa, Sam was already sprinkling sugar on a piece of buttered bread. He took a big bite, the sugar crunching between his teeth. A sharp knock came at the door.

Sam shifted his bread-and-butter wad to his cheek. "Are we late with the rent again? We better not be late with the rent again."

Mama took off her apron. "No, we're not late with the rent. I wonder who it could be?"

She opened the door, and a man Hazel didn't recognize stood there. He was dressed the same as any other man in the wintertime, bulky wool, toque, big, clunky boots, but she couldn't read the expression on his face. Sam leaned across the table and whispered, "Sheriff."

"Can I come in?" the man said. "I'm Maynard Blouin, Sheldon sheriff. You're Alice Lumbra?"

Mama nodded and took a step back.

Sheriff Blouin closed the door behind him, stomped snow from his boots, and pulled off his toque. "I'm here about your husband."

Mama wobbled like she was going to faint. Hazel jumped up at the same time as Sam to steady her and lead her to a chair, both of them glaring at Sheriff Blouin, both of them with a protective hand on her shoulder.

"What is it?" Mama whispered. "What's happened?"

"He's not hurt or anything, but there has been an incident."

"What does that mean?" Sam said. "An incident? What kind of an incident?"

"Let him speak," Mama said. "What's happened?"

"The children don't need to hear this."

"I'm thirteen years old!" Sam said. "I am not a child."

"Please, Sheriff," Mama said, crossing her arms to grasp each child's hand. "Tell us what's happened."

"We've had to take him to Waterbury."

"Waterbury? Did something happen at the mill?" Mama said. "Was that the incident?"

"Something set him off, and he just went crazy. It took three rugged men to restrain him till Doc Wetherbee could come and give him a shot. Your husband—and a lot of other people—could have been seriously hurt."

"You've had him committed?" Mama whispered.

"The judge did—but it's just for a three-day observation."

"He had no right," Sam said.

"Actually, son, he did. We can't have someone going berserk around all that dangerous machinery. No telling what he'll do next. Needless to say, the mill won't be taking him back. I'm sorry." Sheriff Blouin opened the door and let himself out without another word, his boots thudding heavily down the stairs.

Mama rose from her chair, brushed at her eyes, and put her apron back on. She picked up Hazel's cup from the table. "I'll reheat your cocoa."

"Daddy's not allowed to come home?"

"Not for a while." Mama lit a match.

"They can't do that," Sam said.

The burner under Hazel's cocoa burst on.

"Well, they did, and we'll just have to make the best of it."

WHAT HAPPENED IN WATERBURY

HAZEL

March 1927

MAKING THE BEST OF it meant no more hot cocoa for Hazel at the end of her cold walk home from school, just half a bread-and-butter sandwich for her packed lunch, and a largely empty plate for supper. Then it meant oatmeal for breakfast and supper, just oatmeal, no bread, no milk, no packed lunch for school. It meant crying herself to sleep in the cold after the kerosene ran out, only to be awakened in the middle of the night to Sam grinding his teeth and Mama crying on the other side of the wall.

Making the best of it meant an eviction notice on the door and Mama's desperate visit to the Overseer of the Poor to plead for money for a roof over their heads, a warm bed, and food in their bellies, this after begging for a ride from the awful downstairs neighbors.

They made the best of it until the sheriff came again two months later, while Hazel and Sam were doing their homework at the table. By that time, Mama needed to keep off her feet, and Sam answered the door.

"Is your mother home? I need to speak with her."

"She's resting," Sam said. "What do you want?"

Hazel winced. He was going to get them all in trouble. "Do you want me to get our mother, Mr. Blouin?"

Before Sheriff Blouin could answer, Sam said, "Whatever you have to say, you can say to me. I'm the man of the house now."

"Now, look here, boy—"

Mama's slippers scuffed across the floor. Hazel turned from the sheriff at the door to her mother. Between the look on her mother's face and the look on Sheriff Blouin's face, something must be very, very wrong. She'd never seen a grown-up's face look like that before.

"You better sit down," Sheriff Blouin said, leaving his place on the doormat to help Mama into a chair himself. Hazel and Sam stood at her side.

For several long moments, no one spoke. Then Mama whispered in the smallest voice Hazel had ever heard, "He's dead, isn't he?"

"Yes, I'm afraid so."

"How? When? What happened?"

Sheriff Blouin retreated to the doormat, as if he wanted nothing more than to run back down the stairs and never come to the Lumbra apartment with bad news ever, ever again.

"I don't know exactly. Details from the hospital were pretty sketchy. He got into some kind of ruckus with a few of the other inmates during breakfast—"

"Ruckus!" Sam yelled. "Some kind of ruckus? What the hell! Don't lie to us!"

"Sammy, let the man speak," Mama said. "He has no reason to lie."

"You can't lock my father up and then come over here with some bullshit story about dying in a ruckus."

"Samuel, that is enough," Mama said without raising her voice. "Let the man speak. I need to know what happened."

"Like I was saying, your husband got into some kind of ruckus with the other inmates and had to be restrained. When an orderly went to check on him later, he'd stopped breathing. It was too late to revive him."

"That's it?" Sam said. "That's all you're going to tell us?"

"Son, that's all I have to tell you. I've told you everything I know." Sheriff Blouin shifted his weight on the doormat. "I hate to bring this up now, Mrs. Lumbra, but as next of kin, you will need to claim the body."

Mama didn't say a word, and the hateful sheriff kept right on talking. "Is there someone I can call for you? To help with arrangements? A relative, a friend?"

Mama shook her head. "We have no one. It's just us three."

Sam opened the door. "You can leave now."

"You have my condolences." Sheriff Blouin made his exit as Sam yelled down the stairs after him, "Your condolences don't mean *shit* to us!"

Hazel woke the next morning with the feeling she hadn't finished her arithmetic homework the day before, but she didn't know why. As much as she hated it, she always did her homework. She remembered as she was getting dressed in her school clothes. Sheriff Blouin had come to the door yesterday while she was working out long division and told them Daddy was dead. Just like that. Daddy was gone with no word of goodbye, never to return.

But, but—they only had Sheriff Blouin's word for it, and hadn't Sam said the sheriff was lying? Daddy didn't go crazy for long. He always came out of it. He wasn't crazy all the time. He had good days. Maybe the bad days outnumbered the good, but he had good days. Every year, he took them to the Sheldon Fair to look at all the animals and have a picnic with potato chips and dill pickles and jelly doughnuts. And sarsaparilla! He taught her to play cribbage, a grown-up's game—and even though he denied it, he often let her win. What Sam said was true. It wasn't right for those people to lock him up and then tell his family he was dead, so they would forget all about him. It wasn't right.

Hazel shoved her feet in her shoes without tying them and rushed into the kitchen, where Mama and Sam were already seated in front of their oatmeal bowls.

"Sam was right! Sheriff Blouin was lying. The Waterbury people still have Daddy locked up. We have to save him!"

"Tie your shoes, child," Mama said. "You'll fall and break your neck."

Hazel bent over and yanked on her shoelaces, then took her place at the table. "Did you hear what I said?"

Sam kicked her under the table. Hard. "Ow! What'd you do that for?"

"You need to shut your mouth," Sam said, as if he hadn't heard what she said either.

"Children, please, don't bicker. I can't bear it, not today."

Mama looked like she was going to cry. Hadn't she heard what Hazel said? There was no reason for Mama to cry if she would *listen* to what Hazel said.

Mama looked at her bowl of oatmeal and pushed it away. "I'll be taking the morning train to Waterbury today to see about Daddy."

Sam also pushed his bowl of oatmeal aside. "Should you be riding the train? Let me go instead."

For a moment, Hazel thought Mama was going to agree and let Sam go to Waterbury and convince them, man-to-man, to release Daddy, but Mama still wasn't listening. "No, Sammy. This is something I need to do. They're not going to release a body to a thirteen-year-old."

"Then I'll come with you in case you need help. It won't hurt anything if I miss a day of school."

"I want to come, too," Hazel said. "I can help get them to release Daddy, too. You can write us a note for school."

Mama's face looked pained, as if she had a headache. "Finish your breakfasts, or you'll be late for school. I need to get ready to go."

She hadn't listened. In her mind, Daddy was dead.

Hazel trudged to school with Sam in dank March misery, the air halfway between winter and mud season and not happy with either one. They walked in silence, their galoshes slopping in the slush, Sam's face so grim Hazel didn't dare speak to him about telling the Waterbury people they had to let Daddy come home. Sam hadn't listened to her either. In his mind, Daddy was dead.

Hazel's school day was a misery of fear and reprimands as the image of Daddy lying bruised and lifeless in his coffin entered her mind's eye and wouldn't leave—fear for Mama riding on the train to face those strangers in that strange place called Waterbury where nobody wanted to go but where they ended up anyway when they didn't behave as others wanted them to—fear for what those people had done with Daddy after he got upset at breakfast—fear that Mama would be held in Waterbury herself, chained to the wall, and not allowed to come home ever again—the ruler smacking hard on Hazel's knuckles followed by another smack for crying out.

When Hazel arrived home with Sam after school, they both looked for Mama in the apartment, but she was nowhere to be found. Hazel sat at the kitchen table with Sam to wait for her.

"What if Mama never comes back?"

"Don't be stupid."

"But what if she doesn't?"

"Then I'll get a job to take care of us."

"What about school?"

"I'll quit. Plenty of fellows quit school to go to work."

Outside, footsteps came up the stairs—but very slowly, stopping on each step. They could only belong to Mama. Hazel ran to the door to help Mama drag herself up the last few steps, Sam right behind her. When they had their mother safely in the kitchen with the door closed, she looked pale and wobbly, grabbing the back of a chair to steady herself.

"What's wrong, Mama?" Hazel said. "Are you sick? What happened in Waterbury?"

Mama closed her eyes momentarily as if the late afternoon sun coming through the kitchen window were too bright for her to bear. "I don't feel right. I think I need to lie down."

"I *knew* I should have gone with you today," Sam said. "You should have let me, the hell with school. Come on, Hazel, help me with her coat."

They got her coat off and, with a detour to the bathroom, led her to the bedroom. Hazel untied her boots, but despite her tugging, she couldn't get them off.

"Be careful!" Sam said. "You're hurting her."

Hazel stopped tugging and removed the laces. When she and Sam had a blanket tucked around Mama, Hazel said, "Do you want us to stay with you?"

"No, thank you, sweetheart. I think I'd like to sleep now."

They went back to the kitchen to do their homework, more out of habit than the intent to actually do it, the rapidly setting sun now coming through the window at just the wrong angle at just the wrong time.

"I want to know what happened in Waterbury." Hazel shifted in her chair to avoid the sun. "What do you think happened to Mama in Waterbury? Where's Daddy now? How long do you think Mama's going to sleep?"

"How the hell should I know?" Sam said. "We need to let her sleep. Do your homework. I need to think."

"I don't want to do my homework."

"Then go to your room and read a book or something. I need to think."

"I don't want to read a book. I want to know what happened with Mama in Waterbury."

Sam looked like he was about to yell then thought better of it. He hissed instead, "Will you shut *up,* for Christ's sake? We're not going to know what happened in Waterbury until Mama wakes up."

"If you're going to be nasty to me, I'm going to my room."

"You do that." Sam slapped open one of his schoolbooks. "The trip was too much for her. She should have let me go with her."

Hazel shoved back her chair, stomped to her bedroom, and threw herself on her bed, hoping the shriek of the springs would wake Mama on the other side of the wall so she could tell them what happened in Waterbury and that everything would be all right.

Two hours later, Hazel's stomach growled with hunger, and Mama still hadn't gotten up. Hazel slid off her bed, tiptoed to her parents' bedroom, and stood in the doorway watching for some sign of life from her mother. Nothing. Mama lay motionless on her side. She must still be breathing, she must. The blanket had to be hiding the rise and fall of her chest. But Hazel needed to be sure. She took a breath, approached the bed, and slowly put out her hand to touch Mama's shoulder.

Mama groaned and opened her eyes. "Hazel? What time is it?"

"Five after six."

"It's already dark. You and Sammy must be hungry."

She struggled to sit up, and Hazel put out her hands to help her. Despite the long nap, Mama looked as if she wanted nothing more than to lie back down on her empty, rumpled bed, go to sleep, and never wake up.

"Help me with my slippers, would you, Hazel?"

Hazel knelt down and gingerly eased Mama's feet into her dilapidated slippers. "Mama, your feet are all swelled up! Should they look like that?"

"It's nothing to worry about, more of a nuisance. You'll find out when you're older." She put out her hands. "Here, help me up. I need to go to the bathroom."

Hazel returned to the kitchen to sit at the table across from her brother and wait for answers. She *would* have answers. None of this "when you're older" nonsense.

Sam looked up from sharpening his pencil with a penknife. "You woke her up, didn't you? I told you to let her sleep."

"I did not!" Hazel pointed at the pile of shavings in front of Sam. "You're making a mess on the table."

"That's no concern of yours. I'll clean it up before supper."

The scuff of her slippers signaled Mama's return to the kitchen. She still didn't look right.

"Are you okay, Mama?" Hazel said.

Sam scooped the pencil shavings into his hand and got up to dump them in the wastebasket. "Shouldn't you still be in bed? I can make your supper and bring it to you on a tray."

"I can help," Hazel said.

Mama put her hand to her head. "I just have a headache. I'll make your supper."

"When are you going to tell us what happened in Waterbury?" Hazel said. "I want to know what happened with Daddy."

Sam made a threatening gesture at Hazel with his penknife.

"Let me get your supper first. I can't do two things at once."

Supper was a fried egg on toast for each of them. While Hazel and Sam soon made short work of theirs, Mama sat looking down at her plate as if never in her life had she seen anything so revolting as a fried egg and a piece of toast.

"Aren't you eating, Mama?" Sam said. "You need to eat."

"I don't seem to be hungry, but I hate to waste food. Do you want mine, Sammy?"

"Can't you eat a little bit? I'll get you the aspirin and a glass of water."

When Sam returned to the kitchen, Mama's eyes filled with tears as she choked down the aspirin. She pushed her plate away. "I can't eat this. The director at Waterbury couldn't tell me much more than Sheriff Blouin except their autopsy showed that your father died of bleeding in his brain from a blow to the head."

"It's not right," Sam said. "It's not right."

"Who hit him, Mama?" Hazel said.

"They said there was no way for them to tell. It could have happened during the fight with the other inmates or when the orderlies were restraining him. Or he could have done it to himself."

"He didn't do it to himself! They're *lying*. It's not right, I tell you, it's not *right*."

"I know, Sammy." Mama brushed tears from her face. "Your father was a good man. He wasn't always so troubled." She pulled out the handkerchief tucked in her sleeve and blew her nose. "And he loved you two kids with all his heart. Remember that."

Hazel's own tears welled up. She'd never thought of her father as a good man or a bad man. He was just Daddy, her father. He let her win at cribbage. When she caught him at it, he'd deny it and wink—a private wink, just for her. It didn't matter that he screamed in the night and went crazy sometimes. He always came back.

"What about the burial?" Sam said, as if he didn't want to ask but knew he must.

Mama's tears started again. "There's no money to bring him home. He'll be buried in the veterans' cemetery. It's the least they can do."

"Where's the veterans' cemetery?" Sam said.

"Downstate. Randolph."

"What about the funeral?"

Mama shook her head. "They'll say a few words, I suppose. At least, I hope so. It's the least they can do."

"When is it?" Sam said.

"Not till spring. The ground's frozen."

"How will we know when to go, then?"

"Sammy, please. We'll have to wait until they notify us."

"They won't, and you know it; it's not *right*!" Sam jumped up from his chair and ran out the door, slamming it behind him.

"Where's he going?" Hazel said.

"I don't know. He's upset." Mama stood up with some difficulty and began clearing the table. "He won't get far without his coat." Halfway to the sink she paused and turned to Hazel. "Have you done your homework?"

In that moment, Hazel knew it would be best for her to lie. "Yes, Mama, I have."

Then the Rains Came

Hazel

———◄○►———

June 5, 1968

EVEN AFTER TWO MONTHS, Hazel still could not get Lisa out of her mind—the sight of her handcuffed and thrashing in the back of Johnny Clough's LTD like a caged animal, screaming for help that wasn't allowed to come.

The conversation with Lisa's mother had been nearly as bad, waking the poor woman out of a sound sleep at five in the morning before Johnny Clough could get to her in his official capacity. Lisa was safe, yes, but a fire in the building had unleashed a streaming horde of demons on the poor girl, which she'd tried—and failed—to outrun. She'd been taken into custody for her own safety, soon to be committed to Waterbury for a three-day observation.

Unspoken between Lisa's mother and Hazel was the knowledge that three days would become a month, a month would become a year, and years would become decades. Once someone went into that place, they never came out. After Hazel delivered the news, the phone line went silent. When Lisa's mother could bring herself to speak, the only thing she said was, "Do you think she will want to see me?" God forgive her, Hazel had answered, "Yes."

<hr>

RAIN RAN IN LANGUID rivulets down the windows. It had been raining for three days straight, and Flossie had been in a terrible state at breakfast, instructing Hazel to boil their drinking water, warning Paul to stay out of the barns, beseeching Homer to take them all to higher ground on the mountain. Claire finally had to wheel her back to her room to calm her enough to eat.

With the kitchen put to rights, Hazel headed down the hall to check on the residents in the living room. They were sitting in their usual places to watch their morning shows, but instead of laughing and pointing at the shenanigans on "Candid Camera," they stared at two men in suits on the screen who didn't belong there.

One man appeared to be interviewing the other, alternating between asking questions, speaking to the camera, and listening to what was coming through his earpiece. This could only mean a special news report. Live coverage. The two men were discussing the state of someone's brain.

Joey turned around. "The man got shot. He's at the doctor's."

Hazel closed her eyes and sank into the nearest empty chair. Not again. She turned to Homer. "Who got shot?"

"Bobby Kennedy." Homer did not take his eyes off the screen as a blurry photograph of the stricken man appeared. His shirt was undone, and he was clutching a rosary. "The TV doc says he'll be okay. Out of the hospital in a couple weeks, most likely."

Hazel did not ask Homer for details of when, where, and how the shooting had occurred. The way these things happened, the TV people would replay the initial shocking news with accompanying shocking footage again and again and again. She scanned the residents' faces for signs of distress. The only sign of distress she could see was confusion. She could leave the television on a bit longer to find out what had happened.

The screen changed to a reporter on the scene expressing optimism—but waiting for the latest medical bulletin. There was talk of prayers.

All too soon, Frank Reynolds came on to reiterate that Senator Robert Kennedy had been shot in Los Angles at 12:15 AM Pacific Time, immediately following his victory speech after winning the California primary—sending the entire country to their televisions to wait for medical bulletins, reminding them of their own time in hospital waiting rooms, desperate for news of a loved one lying cut open and vulnerable on the operating table.

Emmett cleared his throat. "It's the Soviets behind it. They don't want another Kennedy to be president."

"Emmett, please," Hazel said. "There's no point in speculating and getting everybody upset."

Elsie gasped. "We won't have a president anymore? The country will be in chaos, Hazel. What will happen to my girls?"

"Nothing's going to happen to your girls. We still have a president, and we always will."

"No, Hazel. Somebody shot the president. They said so on television."

Hazel couldn't bring herself to tell Elsie that her age-addled brain was confusing two brothers: a dead president and a gravely wounded senator.

The live coverage continued with the capture of the shooter, bushy-haired and wild-eyed, as yet unidentified.

"At least they caught the bastard," Emmett said.

"Language, Emmett," Joey said. He cast an expectant look at Hazel. She managed a weak smile, so he wouldn't think she was upset with him.

After more reports from the scene, earlier optimism waning, Frank Reynolds came back on. He couldn't seem to look the camera in the eye while he contradicted the optimism of earlier reports as premature. His newscaster demeanor slipped, and he wrung his hands over the current state of the country, before announcing man-on-the-street interviews.

"I think it's awful. . . . I can't understand what's happening to this country. You can't run for president; you can't walk the streets. . . . You might as well barricade yourself. . . . I don't know what this world is coming to. After all, if you don't like a man, you don't have to shoot him because you don't like him."

Now, the residents showed signs of distress, brows furrowing, eyes darting. People not wearing suits, people like themselves, with crumpled brows and rumpled clothes, were upset and confused.

Hazel rose from her chair and turned off the television. "I think we've had enough television for now. We can see if your shows are on after dinner."

When the first television had been donated to the poor farm several years before, it had been a godsend. It got the residents out of their rooms for some entertainment and socializing. When the afternoon movie was a musical, they remembered the tunes, if not the words, and sang along. Now, no good could come from the television. No good at all. If only the rain would stop.

"I know!" Joey said. He jumped up and ran from the room. His feet pounded down the hall, paused for a minute or two, then pounded back to the living room. He thrust his dilapidated copy of *The Wind in the Willows* at Hazel. "Read to us."

Hazel took the book and read to them until Paul appeared in the archway wiping rain from his face with a bandana. He said nothing, and she followed him into the kitchen, where he sat at the table, the morning paper before him, still folded in its plastic delivery sleeve. "I sure could use a cup of coffee. I didn't sleep good last night."

"Your back?"

He nodded.

When the coffee was ready and Hazel joined him at the table, he said, "What was going on back there in the living room? Why was you reading to them?"

"Bobby Kennedy was shot last night."

Paul set his cup down—hard, as if he needed to knock some sense into it. "Bobby Kennedy was killed?"

"No, he's still alive—but he was shot in the head. Last I saw, he was still in surgery."

"This is too much. This country is going straight to hell. What in God's name are decent people supposed to do?"

Even though Hazel knew exactly what he meant—she felt it herself—she didn't have the heart to tell him so. She sat with him until he felt ready to resume his normal day, no more words passing between them. And still the rain fell.

GOD'S IN HIS HEAVEN

HAZEL

◆━◆○◆━◆

July 1968

AFTER THE RAINIEST JUNE on record, July felt like a gift from God to Hazel, high summer as high summer was meant to be: meadows and pastures abundant with grass, maples and oaks such a rich, leafy green she could almost believe they would never shed their leaves.

As soon as the June rains had stopped, Petey had resumed his lobbying to take the mare out until Hazel found a small horse-drawn cart long-forgotten in the back of the oldest storage shed. Paul objected at first, then gave in.

"The poor bastard may as well enjoy his mare while he can. See to it he don't go alone. He makes it to the main road, he's liable to get his fool self killed."

It had become part of Hazel's daily routine to get the cart out of the storage shed while Petey put on the mare's bridle and led her from the barn. After his fumbling with the unfamiliar harness, off they'd go, Petey in the cart holding the reins, Hazel walking alongside, her hand on the mare's neck, in case she needed to grab her bridle. They would clip-clop the length of Poor Farm Road, Hazel instructing Petey to turn back before he spotted the main road and got ideas in his head.

On this bright July morning, Hazel was on the porch taking a break from her chores. She watched from her rocking chair as Charlie rode his beloved red bicycle up, down, and around the dooryard, gleefully blowing his imaginary air horn and applying his imaginary air brakes just for the Whoosh! of them, while Joey trotted alongside, shouting, "Make way for the milk truck!" and Edna looked on from the rocking chair next to Hazel's, her face the embodiment of "God's in his heaven, all's right with the world."

Hazel could count herself content. It did her heart good to see how well Charlie had settled in since that hot summer night last year when his mother had driven her Pontiac too fast from Enosburg Center with all the windows down, she and the Pontiac plunging off the bridge to sink to the bottom of the Missisquoi River.

With no one in the house to look after Charlie while his father worked his shifts at the Union Carbide plant in St. Albans, Charlie's father had reluctantly delivered him, along with his beloved red bicycle, to the poor farm. To his credit, he never failed to take Charlie on an outing every time he had a day off.

When Charlie first arrived at the farm, he took it into his head that he could help Paul with the afternoon milking, faithfully trailing him out to the cow barn every afternoon at the appointed hour. He was hopelessly fumble-fingered with the milking machine, so Paul set him to washing udders, in the hope of saving himself a step so the milking might go a little faster—but all Charlie could do was send the cow into a frenzy of bawling and kicking.

In the end, Paul had to concede defeat in his effort to teach Charlie any part of caring for the cows and assigned him the job of cleaning out the chicken coop, which Charlie lorded over Joey every chance he got.

According to reports, Joey's family had brought him to the poor farm to avoid shipping him off to Brandon Training Center downstate, their thinking being that if he couldn't learn in elementary school, he couldn't learn at Brandon either, so what was the point? Might as well keep the boy closer to home, although none of them came to visit him or bother with sending a five-cent card on his birthday.

Edna had been born out of wedlock to a chamber maid at Congress Hall, one of the luxury hotels in Sheldon Springs. She was brought to the poor farm in 1908, at the age of eleven, after her mother perished in an arson fire at the hotel. Edna had managed to survive the deplorable conditions of the old brick building until 1913, when a woman awaiting transport to Waterbury burned the poorhouse to the ground. When a new poorhouse was built, it too slid into squalor before long. No wonder it had taken Edna years to lose her hangdog expression.

How could the State close the Sheldon Poor Farm now, with the people entrusted to their care healthy and well-fed, happy with their home and happy with each other? After dinner, Lester and Homer would join Edna on the porch so Lester could hold Mouser on his lap in the afternoon sun, Homer at his side as placid behind his mountain man beard as the Green Mountains on the horizon.

When the afternoon sun began to wane, Carmi would join them to warble his own version of "John the Revelator," the always-obliging Homer happy to sing the responses.

Carmi had been delivered to the Sheldon Poor Farm by the Franklin Overseer in 1957. A life-long bachelor, he had lived alone in an abandoned hunting camp with just his Bible for company. In his eighties, he was too frail to work, but he'd managed to get by with food orders from the town and credit at the filling station for gas to get his ancient Model-T truck to the village for provisions.

When no one had seen him in over a month, the filling station owner went over to his place and found him collapsed on the floor. After he was treated at the hospital for pneumonia and dehydration, the Franklin Overseer delivered him to the poor farm against his wishes, his ancient truck left to rust into the weeds.

Ultimately, after a week of good food, clean clothes, and a warm bed, Carmi decided that the poor farm was God's will, and there was no point in fighting the Almighty.

By the end of July, repairs to the second floor were completed to the satisfaction of whatever authorities needed to be satisfied. With Beatrice, Carl, and Lisa now committed to their respective institutions, there had been no major upsets.

There had also been no major upsets on television. No ministers or Kennedys shot and killed. No riots in the streets. No looting. No city blocks shooting flames into the night sky. Hazel thought it would be safe to let the residents watch the news again.

She was wrong.

An Ill Wind

Hazel

—◆O◆—

August 26, 1968

IN THE DAYS AFTER Claire returned to Louisiana, Hazel found resuming her previous workload took more getting used to than she would have thought. She hadn't realized how much she'd come to depend on the younger woman's help, particularly her help caring for Flossie, who now kept asking when Claire would be coming back; she had something to tell her.

Laundry day was still the busiest of the week, the task made all the more difficult, now that using the dryer was no longer an option—not since Paul had informed Hazel that the propane tank was getting low and it would be a waste to get it refilled when the State planned to swoop in with no fair warning and shut them down.

The morning started off well enough, with Hazel, Joey, and Edna carrying out their allotted tasks with little difficulty, Hazel enjoying their easy camaraderie. At the noon meal, however, the other residents seemed subdued, forking up their food as if by rote, never looking up from their plates.

As the afternoon wore on, Hazel kept getting intimations of something wrong, like a bad smell that is too faint to identify but won't go away. Had a mouse crawled inside one of the walls and died? Lord knew, there were plenty of places for mice to get into the walls of the old building and no way to get them out. At one point, she went up to the second floor to see if smoke residue from the April fire still lingered, but all she smelled was new wood and paint.

Could one of the residents be getting sick, infected by some errant virus carried on an ill wind from Montpelier, the others to succumb in turn? Maybe she was coming down with something or Paul was? She couldn't shake the feeling. It was like overhearing two people having a conversation about some calamitous event but being too far away to hear what the calamitous event actually was.

At supper, Emmett was unusually agitated, poking at his scalloped potatoes and putting down his fork without eating any. "What do these young kids think they're doing with this "Hell, no, we won't go!" bullshit? Where the hell do they get off? You think I wanted to give up my girl and leave my father to run the farm alone, so I could get all shot to shit and come home a cripple? I sure as hell didn't. I *still* got shrapnel in my back. But goddamn it, when you get called to serve, you serve. And you're damn proud of it."

Hazel looked at Paul to see how he was taking Emmett's outburst, but his face gave nothing away until Emmett struggled to his feet and pulled his shirttail from his trousers.

"Sit down, Emmett. You don't need to be showing no war wounds at the supper table."

Emmett did as he was told and sat down, but he wasn't finished. "It's all for nothing. These goddamn kids can get themselves gassed and beat to shit all they want. It ain't gonna stop them from getting drafted."

Joey put up his hand. "Emmett said a swear."

"Let me tell you something else," Emmett continued, stabbing his fork in Paul's direction. "These goddamn kids'll have night terrors from this. They'll wake up screaming in the middle of the night like Beelzebub himself is after 'em." He stabbed a piece of potato and put it in his mouth, where it appeared to turn to ash. "And they brung it on themselves."

"Armageddon is upon us," announced Carmi. Then, in a quavering whisper, "We must prepare for the end of days."

"You can prepare for the end of days, old man. I'm going to my room." Emmett got to his feet and left the room, his cane sending back a reproach every time it hit the floor.

"I need to call my daughter," Elsie said. "She'll know how to prepare for the end of days, so we don't all go to hell."

"I don't want to go to hell," Joey said.

"Me either," Charlie echoed.

Edna started to cry. "If I go to hell, I won't see my mother in heaven. I want to see my mother in heaven."

Hazel looked around the table. Once again, she couldn't begin to comfort them because she didn't know what had gone wrong. All she could manage was a weak "Nobody's going to hell," too weak to convince anyone that eternal damnation was not in their future, herself included. She watched Paul grimly fork scalloped potatoes into his mouth until he finally looked up.

"I don't know, Hazel. I was in the cow barn with the vet tending to Mabel's mastitis."

"Fine. You tend to Mabel's mastitis. I need to take Flossie to her room."

She wheeled Flossie out of the dining room without waiting for a response from Paul.

By the time Hazel had Flossie ready for the night and the kitchen put to rights, she could barely put one foot in front of the other for the dread that hung over her like a lowering sky. She took off her apron and went to the living room to check on the residents, but instead of the "Laugh-In" crew delighting the assemblage with their antics, live news coverage was on showing some kind of riot in the streets with police in helmets wielding batons and uniformed soldiers carrying rifles, bayonets at the ready.

The whole lot of them were clubbing young people across the back—in the ribs—in the stomach. Bashing the heads of young people who had already been knocked to the ground bleeding. Bashing the heads of medics rushing to their aid, as plumes of tear gas fouled the air they needed to breathe.

Emmett, Carmi, and Homer were in the living room staring at the television, Emmett's hands white-knuckled on the head of his cane. Carmi appeared resigned to Armageddon, his head bowed, his hands dangling between his knees. Homer just looked pained. Elsie, Joey, Petey, Lester, Charlie, and Edna were nowhere to be seen.

"Where are the others?" Hazel asked.

Only Homer appeared to have heard her. "I put the old man to bed after supper. He was feeling a mite punk."

"Do I need to call the doctor?"

"No, thank you kindly, Hazel. He's just old. Elsie's in her room, most likely. She didn't come in here to watch TV tonight. Joey said he was taking the others out to the barn to check on Petey's mare."

A melee of men in suits came on the screen yelling, pushing, shoving, with Dan Rather's voice the loudest—until he got belted in the stomach and hit the floor. An unseen news anchor's voice announced, "I think we got a bunch of thugs here, Dan."

Most shocking of all was the banner on the bottom of the screen identifying where the riots were taking place: 1968 Democratic Convention, Chicago.

How could this be? This was the United States of America. Where could all this violence, this hatred, this rage, have come from? Where would it end?

Homer got up and turned off the television. "I figure we've seen enough. Carmi, can you get yourself to your room okay?"

Carmi nodded, got to his feet, and shuffled off to his doom.

Homer offered Hazel his arm. "I'll take you to your room."

"But—"

"I'll see to the others. Most likely they're in the cow barn. Don't worry. I'll ask Joey to help me lock up after."

Hazel took Homer's arm and leaned on him as he led her to the manager's suite and the comfort of her sleeping husband.

Over the Hill to the Poor Farm

Hazel

***

May 1927

THE SHELDON OVERSEER OF the Poor told Mama enough was enough; the town wouldn't pay their rent any longer. It was time for them to go.

"Go where?" Hazel said when Mama gave her and Sam the news over a meager supper of boiled beans.

"Over the hill." Mama took a forkful of beans, then set the fork down.

"Where is that?" Hazel said. "What hill? Have we ever been there before?"

"She means the poor farm," Sam said. "The bastards are sending us to the poor farm."

"Watch your language, Sammy." Mama's face looked like she didn't really mean it.

Hazel looked at her plate. She would have liked a nice piece of sausage to go with her beans, the way they used to have it, but what she had on her plate was enough. She wasn't going hungry. "I don't understand."

"The son of a bitch is cutting us off," Sam said. "No more town orders for food or rent." This time, Mama didn't say, "Watch your language." She sat there looking at her abandoned forkful of beans as if she didn't know what it was or what she was supposed to do with it.

"But why?" Hazel said. "What did we do? I don't want to go to the poor farm. I want to stay here."

"We didn't do anything," Sam said, "except keep on living after those Waterbury bastards killed Daddy."

At this last from Sam, Mama seemed to come to herself. "Sammy, that's enough. I don't like it any better than you do, but we're going to have to make the best of it. The sheriff's coming for us tomorrow."

"Tomorrow?" Hazel said. "*Tomorrow?*" How could the sheriff be coming for them tomorrow when she hadn't had time to get used to the idea? Why would the sheriff be coming for them if they hadn't done anything wrong?

"He was going to come today, but I talked him into waiting until tomorrow, so your school day wouldn't be disrupted."

"Well, wasn't that big of him. What a prince." Sam leaned forward in his seat. "Listen, Mama. I told you, I can work. We don't have to go."

"Why can't we stay here?" Hazel said.

"We *can* stay here." Sam pounded his fist on the table. Mama flinched, but she didn't say anything.

"I don't want to go to the poor farm," Hazel said. "I want to stay here. Why can't we stay here?"

"You need to let me quit school and go to work. I *told* you."

Mama put up her hands. "Stop, stop. Both of you. Stop. Son, you can talk about going to work all you want. Any job around here you could get at your age wouldn't pay enough to cover rent and food for three people. Not to mention the doctor bill when the baby comes."

Sam looked as if Mama had slapped him across the face.

"What if I work, too?" Hazel said. "If I get a job after school, would that give us enough money?"

A shadow clouded Mama's face, and she closed her eyes for several moments. When she opened them again, her voice sounded tired and weak. "I'm feeling a little dizzy. I need to lie down."

"We're sorry, Mama," Hazel said. "We didn't mean to get you upset. Did we, Sam? We're sorry."

By that time, Sam was already out of his chair helping Mama get to her feet and waddle the short distance to the bedroom. When he returned to the table, he actually looked a little scared.

"Mama told me she can't eat her supper, and we should eat it."

"But Mama needs to eat," Hazel said. "She needs to eat for the baby."

"I know. I told her that. She said she's feeling sick to her stomach."

"Should we call the doctor?"

"I already asked her. She said no."

"But what if she really is sick?"

Sam had that grim look on his face again. "If she's not any better tomorrow, I *will* call the doctor to come, and the sheriff can take the poor farm and go to the devil with it. If my mother is sick, she's not going anywhere. I know I can pick up enough odd jobs after school to pay for one goddamn doctor's visit. And if she needs medicine, I'll skip school for a few days to earn more money to pay for it." He got up from the table and put Mama's plate of untouched beans in the icebox.

The next morning, Mama looked tired with dark circles under her eyes and a droop to her mouth, but more or less okay, and she managed to eat some of her oatmeal. "Sammy, can you get Daddy's duffle bag from the army out of the closet? We need to pack our clothes. I don't know what time the sheriff is coming for us."

"All my clothes? Hazel said. "Even my winter coat and galoshes?"

"Yes, all your clothes. We won't be coming back here." Mama reached across the table to collect Hazel's empty oatmeal bowl.

"Ever?" Hazel said. "We won't be coming home ever?"

Mama shook her head. "We'll find another furnished apartment once the baby comes, and I get some work I can do from home."

"Come on, Hazel," Sam said. "We may as well pack our shit. She's not going to listen to me."

So, this time when the sheriff paid them an unwelcome visit, it did not come as a surprise. As soon as Hazel heard a car pull up, she ran to the kitchen window. The sheriff emerged from his car and shoved the door closed with his hip. Before approaching the stairs, he settled his hat more firmly on his head, tugging down the brim to hide his eyes. Remaining in the car was the profile of a man with a pipe jutting from the side of his mouth. He gave no sign he was there to help, sitting there in the stupid sheriff's car smoking his stupid pipe.

The road to the poor farm was but a short ride from their apartment by the railroad tracks, with every person in the village gawking at the sheriff's car crammed full of poor people on their way to the house on the hill, never to be seen or heard from again.

The sheriff's car turned onto a dirt road—Poor Farm Road—the car jouncing and rattling over the road's rough surface, stones clattering and pinging against the bumpers, all they had left behind transformed into a roiling cloud of dust.

The car drove by a cemetery of small, tilting gravestones set out in ragged rows in a clearing of trees. Did the cemetery belong to the poor farm? There was no church nearby. This could only mean that people died at the poor farm. Hazel fumbled for her mother's hand. Mama leaned over as best she could, squeezed Hazel's hand, and whispered, "We'll be all right. I promise."

The sheriff's car labored up a small hill and around a bend. The poor farm lay before them, barns, sheds, fields, and pastures on the right, the poorhouse itself on the left. Hazel had never seen a house that big before, so much bigger than it looked from the village—three stories high and nearly as long as a row of mill houses. How many poor people must there be in Sheldon to need a building that big to put them all in?

Hazel held tight to her mother's hand as the sheriff eased the car to a stop and both men got out. With minimal help from the sheriff and the pipe-smoking man, Hazel, Mama, and Sam extricated themselves from the backseat.

Hazel stood in the bright spring sunshine trying to get her bearings. Birds offered up a ragged chorus of desperate twittering as if railing against the branches they perched on, in trees they could never call home.

The bone-jarring ride in the sheriff's car had left her queasy and a little dizzy. Mama looked sick and dizzy, too. For his part, Sam looked grim. No, not grim. Defeated. He had not been able to talk Mama out of letting the sheriff take them to the poor farm. He could have quit school and gone to work. He would have, if only Mama had let him.

On the front steps of the poorhouse sat a man smoking a cigarette, somehow maneuvering it through a big, black mustache that covered his mouth and most of his chin. He raised a hand in greeting. "New arrivals! How d'ye do? Beautiful day, eh? Just got back from Florida, m'self."

No one answered the man's greeting. The man with the pipe spoke for the first time. "Philo, don't be a nuisance. Get your ass off the steps."

Philo jumped up, laughing. "Don't be a nuisance, the man says. Move your ass, the man says. They see me coming—and it's here comes trouble! They see me going—and it's there goes trouble!" He laughed some more and poked his cigarette through his mustache.

Philo sounded so cheerful, Hazel wondered if he might not be right in the head. He dragged the duffle bag from the sheriff's car and disappeared inside the house, hollering from the doorway, "Come on in! The place ain't much, but it'll do in a pinch," followed by a gruff voice telling him to "Shut up, Philo."

The man with the pipe took it out of his mouth. "We may as well go in and get you folks settled."

Hazel followed her mother and brother up the steps, across the porch, and over the threshold. The inside of the poorhouse was a place of dark and shadows, things no one wanted to see lurking in the corners, things about to pounce crouched at the top of the stairs.

The place smelled awful, as if the entire building had begun to rot with dead rodents trapped inside the walls. Hazel looked behind her, but the man with the pipe had already closed the door, shutting off her escape. She inched closer to her mother and took her hand. Sam put his hand on Hazel's shoulder.

In front of them stood a man with a face so mean his lips had disappeared and a woman in a filthy apron who looked like she got yelled at a lot. They must be in charge—or at least the man was. The woman could be a servant or maybe the man's wife.

The man let out a groan. "Aw, no, Burton, not kids again." Hazel recognized his voice as the one that told the man Philo to shut up, when he was only trying to help.

"They better be willing and able to work." The man jerked his thumb in Sam's direction. "And this one better not think he can eat his weight in food every day. Goddamn kids."

Sam's hand tightened on Hazel's shoulder, but he held his tongue, for which she was grateful. No telling what a man with no lips would do to them if Sam mouthed off. Mama's breath was coming fast and shallow, and her hand had become clammy. Hazel inched even closer to her in case she started to wobble.

The sheriff spoke from somewhere behind them. "This is Alice Lumbra and her children, Sam and Hazel."

"I told you about them a couple days ago," the man called Burton said. "The husband got himself killed down to Waterbury a few months back."

Sam's hand left Hazel's shoulder to jab a finger at Burton. "No, my father did not 'get himself killed.' "

"I'll have none of that backtalk, boy." The lipless man turned to the sheriff. "I won't stand for it, Maynard. Goddamn kids."

Before the sheriff could respond, Philo piped up. "Take no notice of Gary, kid. He's all bark and no bite. Come on, you can bunk with me. We had to bury poor Durgan last week, poor bastard. Rotgut got him, and he weren't even forty years old."

"Get out of here, Philo." Gary's lips appeared momentarily as if he were about to spit at Philo. "You may as well take the kid with you. I don't need no more of his mouth. And cut that damn mustache before you set your fool self on fire. Goddamn bums."

Philo laughed, grabbed the duffle bag, and headed up the stairs with Sam behind him, leaving Hazel and Mama to face mean Gary alone, while the woman wearing a filthy apron stood at his side waiting to be yelled at.

DINNER IN THE DINING room with the rest of the poorhouse people turned out to be a madhouse of spoons attacking bowls, exuberant slurping, random phrases that didn't make any sense yelled at top volume, and outbursts of laughter, all with an undercurrent of urgent muttering.

The meal itself could only be described as mean—some kind of soup consisting mainly of cabbage and water. It smelled horrible and tasted worse. No bread or milk was served, and Hazel left the table hungry, concluding as she helped Mama up the stairs to the room they had been assigned that she would rather go hungry than spend another minute with those awful people eating that awful food.

Along the way, they found a bathroom and went in to use the toilet. Hazel couldn't stop herself from crying, the toilets so filthy, the sinks so filthy, the roller towel so filthy. It all smelled so, so bad.

"Mama, isn't there any other place I can go to the bathroom? I can't sit on the toilet. It's too dirty."

"I'm afraid not, sweetheart. Do like this." Mama lifted her skirt, pushed down her drawers, and squatted over the toilet seat without touching it. Hazel went to her side to hold her steady, and Mama did the same for her. At the sink to wash their hands, they found a semisolid slime pool with a dead fly stuck to it. It might have been a bar of soap once, but it certainly wasn't anymore. Hazel couldn't understand why they weren't allowed to live in a clean home. She'd always lived in a clean home. Why were they being punished when they'd done nothing wrong?

Room 25 was a mean little room with two beds, two small dressers, and a cloudy window that let in only enough light to show the room's occupants how begrimed the walls were, so begrimed their original paint color could never be known. Somebody had set the duffle bag next to the door.

The room didn't smell much better than the front hall, the main difference being that Hazel could identify it: BO and cigarettes. Mama went straight to the window and tried to open it, pounding on the sash with the heels of her hands. When she finally got the window cracked, she shoved it all the way up, the window weights inside the wall clunking as if to say that the window was not to be opened without the express permission of the horrible man in charge, and how dare they? The window wouldn't stand for it.

"There, that's better. Get some fresh air in here." Struggling with the window had set Mama off-balance, and she put her hand on the wall to steady herself. "Gracious, that's got me all out of breath. I'd better sit down before we unpack."

"I don't want to unpack." Hazel pulled out the top drawer of the dresser at the foot of the bed that must be hers now, since Mama had chosen the other bed to sit on. "I can't put my clothes in there. It's dirty." She shoved the drawer closed and yanked out the middle drawer. "This one's dirty, too." She did the same for the bottom drawer.

"That's enough Hazel. We need to make the best of it."

Not *that* again. If Mama said, "Make the best of it," one more time, Hazel would be forced to stamp her foot in protest. Her next thought was that Sam might have gotten a better room than they had. She might have to go with pitching a hissy fit instead.

"Why isn't Sam staying with us?"

Mama gestured. "There are only two beds."

"I know, but there's room for another one. He could bring in another one."

"Sam's old enough to sleep with the men."

Hazel stamped her foot. "Well, I don't like it. He should be here with us, not having fun with that Philo."

Mama closed her eyes and took a deep breath, a sure sign she was coming to the end of her patience. Hazel would hold pitching a hissy fit in reserve.

Supper in the dining room with the poorhouse people was more of the same disgusting table manners, nonsensical yelling, and deranged muttering as the noon meal. The food smelled and tasted equally horrible, some kind of boiled dinner consisting of random bits of fatty ham and hard turnips floating in a dirty dishwater broth. Never before had Hazel eaten food that was made to taste bad on purpose. It had to be punishment for having a father who couldn't take care of his family because he died in the nuthouse for being in the army and having bad dreams.

She looked around for Sam and found him sitting next to Philo at the men's table, holding up his fork and examining what was on it, with a look on his face as if one of the boys at school had dared him to eat a live worm, and he was going to do it out of spite.

As soon as they got back to their room after supper, Mama took off her shoes, lay on her bed, and closed her eyes. Hazel wondered if the boiled dinner could be sitting as uneasy in Mama's stomach as it was in her own. They would have to share the small wastebasket to throw up in; they would never make it to the bathroom in time. Maybe sitting on the floor by the window would help clear the toxic turnip fumes from her head and settle her stomach.

Kneeling on the floor in front of the open window, Hazel breathed in the fresh air scent of a May evening. She was surprised to see daylight outside, the sun glowing well above the tree line in the distance, shedding perfectly normal light on the grass. How could this be?

Feeling a little better from the fresh air, she decided to try out the bed that was supposed to be hers. Not only was it not *her* bed, with *her* pillow, it wasn't even a bed at all, just a mean little cot with a thin mattress and a graying sheet thrown over it, no bedding. She lay down on her back, folded her hands on her stomach, and stared at the water-stained ceiling. Well, wasn't that just *dandy*? In addition to food even a pig would refuse to eat, she had to worry about being drowned in her bed while she slept, waking up just in time to suffer a horrible death.

The mattress was hard and stiff, stuffed with something prickly. She flounced onto her side. The mattress was even more uncomfortable in that position, and the pillow smelled horrible, like a thousand people with dirty hair had slept on it all at once. She sat up, threw the pillow on the floor, and cried tears of rage.

When she'd cried herself out, she got off the cot to sit on the floor next to her mother's cot, thankful that Mama lay on her side facing the interior of the room and not the wall. But her face didn't look right. The dark circles around her eyes had deepened into shadows, and there was a new puffiness about her jaw.

"Are you okay, Mama?"

Mama opened her eyes. "I'll be fine. I need to rest for a bit. It's been a hard day."

Hazel settled her head on the cot next to the baby in Mama's belly. "I don't like it here."

Mama stroked Hazel's hair the way she did when Hazel was feeling sick or out of sorts. "I don't like it either, sweetheart, but it's only temporary, until the baby comes and I can find some work."

"You promise?"

"I promise."

Promises to Keep

Hazel

<hr>

June 1927

Hazel woke to a moonlit room and the desperate cries of a whip-poor-will. Whip-poor-*will*, whip-poor-*will*, whip-poor-*will*. Why was the bird crying so? There must be a reason he had alerted her and the moon had shone its light into the room for her to see Mama convulsing on her cot.

Hazel leapt off her cot and dashed across the room. "Mama, Mama, what's wrong? What's wrong?" She leaned over and put her hands on Mama's shoulders. "What's wrong? What do I do? Mama, you have to tell me what to do! Please, Mama!"

Her mother gave no answer, her rigid, jerking limbs sending Hazel's voice far, far out of reach, animal grunts coming from her mouth where words were supposed to be. Hazel tried holding Mama's arms down to stop them from jerking, but it didn't help. When she tried to grab a thrashing leg, she realized that Mama had soiled herself.

"Oh, *no,* Mama, what's happening to you? I don't know what to do."

Hazel ran to the door, jerked it open, and careened into the hall, running, running, running to the door that separated the women's sleeping rooms from the men's, but it was locked. She shook the handle and shook the handle, but the door stayed locked. She pounded on the door with both fists and screamed, "Sam, Sam, Mama's hurt! I don't know what to do—you have to help me! Sam!"

Still no answer. No urgent feet running down the hall. How could he not have heard her? Her throat was already raw from screaming. She continued to pound on the door, hard enough to splinter it from its frame and send it crashing to the floor, but it held fast. "Sam, you have to come! Sam!"

Someone had hold of her shoulders, shaking them to stop her from getting help for her mother. She jerked away from those hands and kept on calling for Sam. Still no response from the men's side. Oh, where could he be? A hand grabbed her wrist, followed by a quavering old voice. "Stop that racket, child. Stop it."

Hazel jerked her wrist from the weak claw of the old woman, who went back to shaking Hazel's shoulders. "Stop it. Stop it, I say. What's wrong?"

"It's Mama!" Hazel let the old woman turn her so they were facing each other.

"What's wrong, child? Why are you crying? Tell me what's wrong. Is the baby coming?"

"No! Mama's hurt. She won't stop jerking."

An expression Hazel couldn't read passed over the old woman's face. "Take me to her."

But the old woman set off down the hall at a shuffle not a run. Slow, old feet shuffle, shuffle, shuffling, with no sense of urgency for her mother. Hazel ran ahead, straight to Mama's bedside, where she still lay convulsing, her twisted face in the moonlight far, far out of reach.

"Mama, I'm back." Hazel lowered her voice so Mama wouldn't know she was scared. "I'll get help. You'll be okay. I promise." She tried to catch one of Mama's hands, even though she knew the effort would be in vain. Whatever had hold of her mother was too strong.

Hazel recoiled from a sudden blast of light, followed by a gasp. Blinking, she turned her head to see the old woman standing in the middle of the room, one hand covering her mouth, the other holding the string for the overhead light. Hazel turned back to her mother. The bottom half of her nightgown was soaked in blood.

"You're bleeding!"

Blood spread a widening stain on the sheet and dripped small drops of Mama's life onto the floor. Hazel turned to the old woman. "Can you help her? She's bleeding! You have to help her!"

The useless old woman only shook her head. "She needs a doctor."

"*Please!*"

"I'm sorry, honey. There's nothing I can do." The useless old woman put her hands over her face.

And still Mama convulsed under the cruel light of a bare bulb for all the world to see and do nothing.

Hazel thought she heard voices. A small clot of grotesquely wrinkled faces, sunken mouths, and wild white hair filled the doorway. Pounding feet sounded down the hall, and Sam shouldered his way through the clot.

"Get the hell out of my way! What's wrong, Hazel? What's happened? Oh, God, she's bleeding! We need a doctor. Where's the telephone? I *know* there's a telephone here. Where is it?"

One of the sunken mouths said, "In the manager's office. Downstairs."

"But we ain't allowed to use it," a wrinkled face added.

"Gary don't like it here at night, so he goes home," offered a wild head of white hair.

Philo's head appeared above the clot. "Telephone's in Gary's office. He keeps it locked, but I know where the spare key is. I'll call Doc Wetherbee and tell him we got an emergency."

Unlike the useless old woman's shuffle, Philo's feet were urgent, pounding down the hall to get help for Mama.

Sam approached the bed and put out his hand, but Mama's thrashing limbs and jerking head denied her the comfort of his hand. "Mama? It's Sam. We're calling the doctor now, okay? The doctor's coming."

Hazel wiped her nose on the sleeve of her nightgown. She whispered so Mama couldn't hear. "Is she going to be okay, Sam?"

"We need to get these people out of here." Sam pointed at the clot in the doorway. "Get out of here. Go back to your rooms. My mother has a right to privacy when she's sick, even in this hellhole."

The clot shuffled off, and the useless old woman lowered her hands from her face. She pulled a handkerchief from the pocket of her bathrobe and blew her nose. "You children shouldn't be in here. You can wait for the doctor in the living room. I'll stay with your mother until the doctor gets here."

"No, you won't," Sam said. "She's our mother, and we're not leaving her. You hear me?"

"You don't know—"

"Yes, I *do* know—"

The useless old woman shuffled off, muttering.

Sam pulled the sheet off Hazel's cot and draped it over Mama's lower half. "She doesn't want people to see her this way." The sheet immediately landed on the floor. Sam balled it up and set it on his lap. "What happened, Sis? I heard you pounding on the door, but I couldn't unlock it. I had to go all the way downstairs and back up again to get to the women's side. What happened? How long's she been like this?"

"I don't know. A whip-poor-will woke me up, and Mama was jerking. I couldn't get her to stop, and she wouldn't answer me."

"It must be something to do with the baby. She wasn't sick today, was she?"

Hazel shook her head. "Is she going to be okay?"

Sam still wouldn't answer her question. The most important question. The only question.

The minutes ticked by as Hazel sat on the floor next to Sam cradling the balled-up sheet in his lap, and they waited for the doctor to hurry, hurry, hurry, come save their mother. Hazel wanted so badly to turn off the overhead light to save Mama from its cruel glare, but if she did, the doctor wouldn't know which room she was in, and he'd turn around and go home, with no medicine for Mama.

More time ticked by. Little by little, Mama's distress lessened. Her jerking became less violent. Her grunts softened into moans. Then her body calmed completely, and she opened her eyes.

"Mama!" Hazel cried. "You're awake! Sam, she's awake!"

Sam scrambled to his feet, shook out the balled-up sheet, and arranged it over Mama's lower half. "There, that's better." He knelt and patted her hand over the sheet. "Don't worry, Mama. The doctor will be here soon."

Hazel also knelt by the cot. "Mama, I'm glad you're awake. I was so scared."

Sam shushed her with a hand on her arm. "Don't do that. We don't want to worry her."

"Why isn't she answering us?" Hazel said. "I know she's awake. Her eyes are open."

"Hush. We should let her rest."

Hazel let her mother rest until blood seeped through the sheet Sam had so carefully arranged over her, a widening stain that grew and grew, and Mama's breath came fast and shallow through her open mouth until it caught in her throat and stopped.

"She should sleep now," Sam said. "She must have had pains from the baby."

Footsteps sounded in the hall. Sam ran to the door and waved his arms. "Down here! We're down here!"

As soon as the doctor entered the room, he dropped his black bag on the floor and steered Hazel and Sam out of the room. "Philo, take these kids downstairs—and shut the door!"

Out in the hall, Sam immediately grabbed the doorknob. "I'm going back in. I don't care what he says. I'm not leaving her."

"Me, either," Hazel said.

Philo pried Sam's fingers from the doorknob. "I know you want to be with your mama, but you need to let Doc Wetherbee take care of her now. You'd only be in his way."

"It's not right. She's my mother."

"She's my mother, too," Hazel echoed. Philo may be a grown-up, but he didn't understand.

"Come on, kids, let's go downstairs. I'll keep you company while you wait."

Philo's voice sounded strange. Hazel had never heard him speak so softly before. His voice was as grim as Sam's face. "Is Mama going to be okay?" she whispered.

Sam took her hand. "We need to go with Philo now."

As they followed Philo down the shadowed hall, the shadowed stairs, and another shadowed hall, Hazel held tight to her brother's hand, but it didn't help. They were leaving Mama alone to face a strange man in the middle of the night in her bloody nightgown after she soiled herself. She would be so scared.

Philo led them into the shadowed living room and turned on a table lamp. He swept the scattered pages of a newspaper off the couch and sat in an armchair close by. Hazel and Sam sat side by side on the couch.

"What happens now?" Hazel whispered.

Sam's face was full of shadows. "We wait."

"For how long?"

Sam's shadows deepened. "I don't know, Sis."

"I could tell you a story," Philo said. "Might help pass the time."

Sam said okay; Hazel didn't want a story but said nothing, and Philo began. "So, one time me and ole Albie decided nothing would do but we leave the snow shoveling to the other poor saps and spend the winter in sunny Florida—picking oranges off the trees and sunning on the beach. Livin' a life of ease, don'cha know." The cheerfulness had returned to Philo's voice, but it sounded off, like the piano at school so badly in need of tuning.

"This was back in twenty-two, as I recall. Coulda been twenty-one. Anyways, don't matter. It was before the TB took Albie. We hopped the first freight headed south, and who should be sitting in the car with the crates of apples but Tom Mix. The one and only, big ten-gallon hat, cowhide chaps, and all!"

At this point, Hazel knew Philo was lying, and she let herself drift off to sleep. Mama would want her to get her rest.

She didn't know how long she'd been asleep when a different man's voice woke her, a voice so sad it had no time for stories. "Wake your sister," the voice was saying. Hazel opened her eyes and sat up. The doctor was kneeling on the floor in front of the couch like he was praying.

"How's Mama?" Sam whispered. "Can we go to her now?"

The doctor took Sam's hand in his, then Hazel's. Sam jerked his hand back. Hazel jerked her hand back. The doctor was at her eye level, so she couldn't look away.

"Listen to me now. Your mother has passed away."

"No, that can't be," Sam said. "She was getting better when we were with her."

"I'm very sorry. She was already gone when I got here."

"No," Hazel said. "She was getting better. Her eyes were open. She was awake."

"I'm very sorry," the doctor repeated for no good reason. He looked over at Philo, who got up from his chair and knelt next to him.

"It's a tough break, but as long as you're here, I'll do my best to look out for you. I can promise you that."

What could Philo mean by, "I'll look out for you?" Why would they need this strange man with his stupid, droopy mustache to look out for them when they had a mother upstairs resting from a bad night? "As long as you're here?" Where else were they going to go? Their apartment had disappeared into a cloud of dust behind the sheriff's car. There was nothing left.

"Sam?"

Tears ran down Sam's face. "What do we do now? I don't know what to do now."

"Sam?" Those tears could only mean one thing. Hazel buried her face on Sam's shoulder.

"You don't need to do anything, son," the doctor said. "I'll call Mr. Willard about making arrangements for your mother's burial." He put his hand on the couch and pushed himself to his feet.

Hazel lifted her head from Sam's shoulder. "Wait. Where's the baby? You shouldn't have left the baby alone."

The doctor shook his head. "The baby left this world with your mother. They're together."

But they weren't together. Each was alone—alone and forever out of reach.

In the Cemetery Down the Road

Hazel

—◇—

June 1927

The poor farm people buried Mama and the baby the following day. Mean Gary tried to make Hazel and Sam go to school, but the woman who got yelled at a lot—Marcelline—yelled at him instead and got her way. Hazel and Sam dressed in their good clothes and went outside to wait for her on the porch.

All too soon, Marcelline emerged from the house. For the first time, she wasn't wearing her filthy apron. The hat crammed on her head looked like someone had sat on it.

"Are you ready? It's time to go."

Sam scowled as he buttoned the top button of his good shirt, which had become too small for him, his wrists dangling from the sleeves. "She'll be buried in the cemetery on the road to get here?"

"Yes. It's a pretty spot under the trees. And it's plenty easy to visit."

"She should be buried with our father. Wives are supposed to be buried with their husbands. They have one headstone with both names on it. They aren't buried miles and miles apart. You can't do this."

"Sam's right," Hazel said. "Why can't she be buried with Daddy, like she's supposed to?"

"Children, please. Your parents are together in heaven. If you want to say goodbye to your mother, we need to go now." Marcelline and her squashed hat turned to leave.

Hazel looked for the car that would take them to the cemetery, but Marcelline set off walking. Hazel glanced at Sam, but he had fallen in step with Marcelline as if there were nothing wrong with a forced march to the cemetery where Daddy wasn't waiting for Mama to join him.

Their footsteps crunched too loudly on the pebbled gravel, their shoes sending up clouds of dust to choke whoever was unfortunate enough to follow behind. The midafternoon sun sent prickles of cold through the fabric of Hazel's good dress, which would never again sit right on her shoulders.

The cemetery was larger than Hazel remembered, the gravestones more numerous, the rows more ragged. A sad little car was parked in the tall grass a short distance from the entrance. Why wasn't there a sign? There should be a sign. It was like the poor farm people wanted to make sure everybody buried there was forgotten.

Sam entered the cemetery, Hazel and Marcelline following behind. He pointed and said over his shoulder, "That must be us."

"I wonder why he dug the grave all the way over there." Marcelline put her hand on Hazel's shoulder. "Watch where you're walking. Them pine needles are slippery."

As they picked their way through gravestones and clumps of weeds, Marcelline said, "I want you to know I got your mama ready myself. Cleaned her up real nice and washed her hair. I dressed her in my best nightgown to be buried in. I hope that's okay."

Sam was too far ahead to hear Marcelline, and Hazel didn't think she should answer for him.

"It was too pretty for me to wear, so it's still brand-new. It has roses embroidered on the collar. I hope that's okay."

This time, Hazel nodded. Mama didn't have a new nightgown, and none of hers had embroidered roses anywhere.

Up ahead, Sam slowed his pace and pointed in a direction Hazel didn't want to look. "This must be it."

And there it was, a Mama-sized hole in the ground—a neat hole in the ground, but still a hole in the ground. Hanging over the open grave, the smell of disturbed earth was so overpowering, Hazel's knees buckled.

"Are you okay, honey?" Marcelline said. "You've gone white."

Sam put his arm around Hazel's shoulders. "You okay, Sis?"

Hazel nodded, unable to speak, her throat clenched and aching.

Sam kept his arm around her shoulders. "You can lean on me if you want."

Mama was nowhere to be seen by the open grave, only Philo and a man in a rumpled suit holding a prayer book. Philo set the shovel he was holding on the ground and walked over to them. "I picked the best spot for your mama. Looks out over the mountains. This field here? Come August, it's full of goldenrod, far as the eye can see."

Hazel's aching throat gave way. "But if you put her in the ground, she can't see them. She always puts them on the table."

Sam squeezed her shoulders. "Okay, Sis, okay." He turned to Marcelline. "How much longer? My sister's upset."

"Should be any time now. When I came to get you, Gary and Mr. Willard was about ready to load the—about ready to go."

Hazel turned away from the grave. She would not look at it, all dark and cold and damp with death. She heard a vehicle approaching, its tires much too loud on the road's rough surface, its engine just as loud. A truck with an enclosed back parked at the entrance to the cemetery, and two men got out. As Hazel watched, the men pulled a coffin from the back of the truck and began walking with it, one on each side. That could only be Mama, stuffed in an ugly wooden box and dragged through the cemetery to be buried in the weeds.

Marcelline bent down and whispered to Hazel, "Are you okay? Do you want me to take you back to the house? You don't have to stay if you don't want to."

"I want to stay." She sniffled, and Marcelline pressed a folded handkerchief into her hand. Sam squeezed her shoulders.

Mama's coffin arrived at the graveside, Gary on one side, his face even stormier than usual, a man who must be Mr. Willard on the other. Mr. Willard reached into his jacket pocket and tossed two long straps at Philo, who arranged them on the ground. Gary and Mr. Willard set the coffin on the straps, and the storm cloud of Gary's face burst.

"Jesus H. Christ, Philo. Why the hell did you dig the grave all the way out here? I coulda broke my damn neck lugging this coffin over here."

"Shut up, Gary. These kids just lost their mother. Show some goddamn respect."

The minister looked like he was about to cry. Sam's fist was pulled back. Mr. Willard spoke in the tone of a man who needed to scrape dog crap from his shoe. "Go on, now, Gary. I'll take it from here."

Gary stormed off but not before telling Philo not to be all day about filling the damn grave in.

The minister cleared his throat. "Let us take a few moments of silence before we lay your mother to rest." He closed his eyes.

If the minister meant for Hazel to close her eyes, she didn't. She couldn't. She couldn't look away from the wooden box with Mama inside dressed in a pretty nightgown like she was asleep. She wasn't but a few feet away. How could she be so close, yet forever out of reach, the baby a secret she held inside?

The minister opened his book, said some prayers, then some words. Mr. Willard and Philo carefully lowered the coffin into the grave. The minister said some more words, bent down, and took up a fistful of dirt. Hazel cried out, "Don't!" but he dropped the fistful of dirt on the coffin anyway, spoiling it, even though Mama was all freshly bathed inside in her pretty new nightgown. Sam squeezed Hazel's shoulders. Marcelline crossed herself. The minister closed his book and trudged back through the gravestones and the weeds to his car.

Mr. Willard pulled the straps out of the grave, returned them to his pocket, and set off for his truck. As Philo bent down for his shovel, he spoke to Marcelline for the first time. "Take Hazel and Sam back to the house. They don't need to be here for this."

Neither Sam nor Hazel made a move to leave, both staring at Mama's spoiled coffin. Something wasn't right. Something was missing from Mama's gravesite. There should be more than a hole in the ground and a big pile of dirt.

"Where's Mama's gravestone?" Hazel said. "Why doesn't she have a gravestone? Why can't she have a gravestone like everybody else? It's not *fair*!"

"When will my mother get her gravestone?" Sam said. "What about her birth date? Do you know her birth date? Nobody's asked me for her birth date."

"Don't worry," Marcelline said. "Your mama will get a gravestone like everyone else. It's going to take a few days for it to be engraved. The overseer should have your mother's birth date."

"It's September first, eighteen ninety-four," Sam said. "Think you can remember that?"

Marcelline reached her hand up to her squashed hat. "We best be getting back."

"I'm staying here," Sam said. "I'm not leaving her before it's over."

"Go on back with Marcelline, son," Philo said. "See to your sister."

Hazel didn't want to leave either. She didn't need seeing to; she needed her mother. Marcelline nudged her shoulder. She really had to leave. As the three of them trudged back through the weeds and the pine needles and the ragged rows of gravestones, Hazel kept looking back, but Philo stood there holding the shovel, waiting for them to be out of sight.

Even so, the first shovelful of dirt hit the coffin so hard Hazel cried out and put her hands over her ears.

The walk from the cemetery took forever. It was all Hazel could do to put one foot in front of the other. No one spoke, not even Marcelline telling them everything would be okay when it wouldn't. About halfway up the final rise to the poorhouse, Hazel thought she smelled smoke.

"Is something burning?"

Sam's nostrils flared. "Smells like it, yeah."

"Should something be burning now?" Hazel said. "What's burning?"

Marcelline didn't answer but started walking faster, which Hazel took to mean the poorhouse was on fire. She and Sam already had no one to take care of them. If the poorhouse burned down, they would have no place to live either. Hazel tried to run ahead to see, but her feet slipped on the loose gravel, and she fell, skinning her knee and her hand as she tried to catch herself. Marcelline and Sam helped her up as the smell of smoke grew stronger.

When the poorhouse came into view at last, no flames shot through the roof, no smoke billowed from the open windows, no screams sounded from people trapped inside. Gary stood some distance from the house poking at a small fire. He was burning the mattress and sheets with Mama's blood on them.

That night, after a miserable supper of hard, half-cooked beans, Hazel was back in Room 25, the cot where Mama had lost her life now nothing more than a rusty set of springs on the other side of the room. Hazel cried herself to sleep on a bare mattress. No one had thought to replace the sheet.

Down by the Riverside

Hazel

<hr>

July 1927

THE FIRST WEEKS OF July passed in a haze of hot weather and sadness. Sam disappeared most days, leaving Hazel to get through the long, teary hours alone. He never said where he was going or what he was doing, but he always told Hazel when he was leaving—and he always came back for supper.

A smell of manure hung over the place, raised by the oppressive midsummer heat, like storm clouds set to unleash a hurricane of filth on the poorhouse and everybody in it. Inside the house, old people followed Hazel around trying to give her sympathy, the breath from their sunken mouths, the sweat and gases from their withered bodies as bad as the smell of their sympathy.

Marcelline was back to being afraid of getting yelled at, so Hazel was back to chopping mountains of wilted cabbage and washing dishes with feeble-minded Joey, who kept insisting that she smile. No matter how many times she snapped at him, he would not stop telling her to smile. As soon as she was able to escape from the kitchen, Hazel headed for the cemetery to wait for Mama's gravestone while the meadow birds chittered and fussed.

As the heat-heavy days dragged on, Sam and Philo took to collecting Hazel for a walk to the village after the supper dishes to get her away from the stench of sympathy that hung about the living room with the old people. Feeble-minded Joey was allowed to tag along if he promised Philo not to be a nuisance.

The air was cooler by the river under the covered bridge, the current barely rippling the water in the wide places. The surrounding air smelled of clean river mud and water-washed rock warmed by the sun. As the four of them sat side by side at the river's edge, Philo told them stories of his adventures riding the rails.

The stories were always the same. The bone-chilling gray of November pushes Philo to leave the snow-shoveling for the other poor saps and set out for sunny Florida. He must choose a traveling companion, someone of cheerful disposition, but no drunkards, too dangerous. He must execute five perilous freight-hopping procedures with two near misses at capture by a huge railroad "bull." He must meet and befriend a celebrity—usually a movie star, but sometimes a boxer—until at last making his triumphant entry into Florida with its blue, blue tropical waters and sweet, juicy oranges.

True to his word, feeble-minded Joey kept his mouth shut, content to bob his head and smile.

Time to Go

Hazel

August 1927

Come August, the field behind the cemetery filled with yellow goldenrod, just as Philo had promised. Hazel spent her days keeping vigil at her mother's graveside, waiting for Mama's gravestone, which still hadn't come.

One day, while all the poorhouse people were eating dinner in the dining room, Gary appeared in the doorway and announced, "I need them two." He stabbed two fingers in the air, but he didn't say which two he was talking about, so both tables kept on slopping runny boiled beans into their mouths and mumbling.

At the men's table, Joey put up his hand with the spoon in it, sending a load of beans down his arm. "I'm ready!"

"Not you, moron. Them two." Gary stabbed the air again. "God damn it, Joey, go clean yourself up. You make me sick."

Joey burst into tears and ran from the room.

Philo blotted beans from his droopy mustache with a bandana. "You had no call to hurt the boy's feelings. You know he ain't very bright."

"That's enough out of you, Philo."

Marcelline made a move to get up, but Gary yelled at her. "Where do you think you're going? Sit down!"

"But Joey—"

"Just because he's a' idiot don't mean you have to baby him. Jesus H. Christ."

Hazel eyed the doorway through which Joey had made his escape and wondered if she would get in trouble if she ran out as well. Probably. No, definitely. She raised her hand. "Marcelline, may I please be excused from the table?"

Gary unleashed a windy sigh. "Oh, for Christ's sake. Get up, girlie. You and that brother of yours are coming with me."

Hazel tried to catch Sam's eye from the women's table, but he was looking down, frowning at his bowl, as Philo whispered in his ear. Hazel looked at Marcelline, who nodded and said weakly, "Go on, now. Do as he says."

Hazel followed Sam and Gary up the stairs to the first floor. Sam's face had that grim look again, but Hazel couldn't read it. He might be angry; he might be sad. He might even be as scared as she was, following the meanest man they had ever met up the stairs with no reason given except, "You're coming with me." Gary stopped at the door to the manager's office, unlocked it, and entered the room. Hazel and Sam didn't move from their side of the threshold.

"Come on, get in here. I ain't got all day."

Hazel looked at Sam. He took her hand and whispered, "It's okay, Sis. I won't let anything bad happen to you. I promise."

Gary led them into a cluttered room stinking of cigarette smoke. Most of the room was taken up with a large desk piled with papers, binders, and assorted junk, including several overflowing ashtrays, and what looked like the greasy pieces of some kind of motor. Behind the desk, a broad shelf held more paper and binders, all piled at crazy angles, threatening to spill onto the floor. Unlike the rest of the windows in the poorhouse, the window in this room had a shade. It was pulled all the way down, as if Gary didn't want anyone looking in to see what a mess he'd made of the place.

Hazel looked at Sam, but he, too, seemed puzzled by the room and for what possible reason he could be standing in it. Gary sat himself behind the desk with an ominous creak and scrape of the chair.

"It was a tough break losing your ma, I know—I ain't a heartless man—but it's time for you two to go."

"Time for us to go?" Sam said. "Go where?"

"Go where?" Hazel echoed. "Our apartment's gone."

"Like I said, I ain't a heartless man, but the State says children can't be kept at the poor farm more'n ninety days. Your ninety days are up next week." Gary rolled himself a cigarette, lit it, and dropped the match on the floor. "Now listen, you two, we need to get down to brass tacks. I ain't gonna put you out on the street, if that's what you're worried about, and there's no point sending you to Brandon when you ain't feeble-minded. They'll just send you back."

He dragged on his cigarette as if it gave him the power over life and death, with death being his preferred option for everyone but himself. Hazel suddenly had to use the toilet.

"Lucky for you, I found a place that'll take the both of you."

Gary shot a stream of smoke in their direction, and Hazel took a step back as her need to use the toilet became urgent.

"Like I said, lucky for you, David Myott needs a new hired man after the last one got carried off by gypsies, or run away to join the circus, or wherever the hell he went. And wouldn't you know it, his wife took it into her head she needs a hired girl to do all the chores she thinks she's too good for, now that David has a whole fifty head of cows."

Gary spoke this last in a mocking tone that would have brought a swift rap on the knuckles from Miss Manahan's ruler, followed by an hour standing in a corner with his nose pressed to the wall.

"But—" Gary gestured with his cigarette. "But—they want to take a look at you first, make sure ain't nothing wrong with you and you're ready to work, no bad habits, none of that shit. And you damn well better watch your mouth when they get here."

"I have to go to work?" Hazel said.

"That's what I said, ain't it?"

A knock came at the front door, and Gary got up from the desk. "I think that's them. You two better be on your best behavior, you hear me?" He stubbed out his cigarette and left to answer the door.

Hazel ran to the bathroom and released her bowels, then dashed back to Gary's office wiping her wet hands on her dress.

Sam had just enough time to whisper, "You okay, Sis?" when Gary entered the room, followed by a man and a woman. Their faces shone with sweat, and they looked like they had smelled something bad. Which of course they had. The man was dressed in overalls, and he didn't take off his cap when he entered the room, like men were supposed to do. The woman, wearing a fussy ruffled dress and fancy shoes, looked like she belonged to a different husband.

Gary went to his desk, but he didn't sit down. He stood there like he was about to make a speech. "Them here's the two youngsters I told you about. Boy's Sam, girl's Hazel."

The rude man looked Hazel and Sam up and down. "They're kind of scrawny. They ain't sickly, are they? You told me weren't nothing wrong with 'em."

"They're healthy enough." Gary rolled himself another cigarette. "Lost their ma couple months ago. Took it hard."

Hazel's bowels twisted one way, then the other.

"I have TB," Sam announced, sounding for all the world as if he had just grabbed the brass ring on the merry-go-round.

Hazel's bowels twisted the other way around. What was Sam *doing*? He would get them into so much trouble for lying, maybe they'd have to go to *jail*. Jail would give them a place to live, but she didn't want to live in jail with the criminals. Living with the poorhouse people was bad enough.

The fussy woman yanked a handkerchief from her dainty purse and clapped it over her mouth and nose. Gary's face looked like it was about to explode into a million pieces of mean. He let out a feeble laugh instead.

"Ha, ha, he's such a kidder—ain't you, boy? He don't have TB or nothing else wrong with him, except too much time on his hands."

But Sam wasn't finished. "I'm headed for Florida to find a sanatorium for my TB. When I'm well again, I'll send for my sister."

The rude man and the fussy woman were already halfway out the door, Gary hard on their heels with excuses.

Sam grabbed Hazel's hand. "We better vamoose before Gary gets back. We can go out the basement door."

"I have to go to the toilet!"

"Well, make it snappy. We can't be here when Gary gets back."

Hazel's bowels obliged with a quick release, she rejoined Sam, and out the basement door they went at a dead run. They skidded across the grass and hotfooted it down the rutted driveway, Sam laughing the whole time, as if there were something funny about running away from the poor farm to avoid being put in jail. Ahead of them hung a massive cloud of dust from the rude man's car racing away from the poor farm to escape the boy with TB.

On the road to the village, Hazel slowed to a walk—but not before looking over her shoulder a hundred times to see if Gary's rusty old truck was bearing down on them.

When she had caught her breath, she turned to Sam. "What did you do that for? You don't have TB. Why did you tell Gary and those people you did? Gary's really mad."

Sam appeared to consider her question. "I don't know. It kinda slipped out."

Hazel was about to tell him that his answer was no answer at all and he needed to smarten up when he said, "Now that I think about it, maybe it wasn't such a bad idea—except for the sanatorium part, a'course. I need to think."

"Mama said you can't go to work till you're done with school."

"Hush, Sis, let me think."

Sam didn't speak again until the covered bridge came into view. "We can sit under the bridge. Gary'll never look for us there."

Hazel sat on the riverbank next to her stupid brother trying to think and stared at the water, which had turned murky since they'd last sat at the river's edge listening to Philo's ridiculous stories of hopping on freight trains and meeting famous people.

Sam stared at the murky water as if the answer he was after would be revealed if only he stared at it long enough. Hazel knew better. Nothing was hiding in that river except fish and maybe a few frogs.

Sam turned away from the river, his face no longer scrunched from thinking. "Do you think there's fairgrounds in Florida?"

"How should I know?" Hazel smacked a mosquito on her arm. "Stupid bugs." She flicked the bloody mosquito off her arm and wiped her finger on her dress. "What do you want to know that for? You're not going to Florida. You just said that so we won't have to go with those people next week."

"Maybe when I said it, but not now." Sam shaded his eyes with his hand and looked off in the distance. Hazel tried to follow his gaze, but all she saw was a bend in the river, which was no distance at all.

When Sam spoke again, his voice had a strange, dreamy tone Hazel had never heard him use before. "Do you remember the last time Daddy took us to the Sheldon Fair?"

She did remember. "I got a sunburn. Mama was mad at me because I forgot my hat at home."

"Not that. You always got a sunburn, and you always forgot your hat at home, accidentally-on-purpose."

"We had to leave before the fireworks so Daddy wouldn't get scared."

"Before that. You really don't remember?" Sam scrambled to his feet. "You're hopeless. Want to skip stones?"

Hazel jumped up and brushed off her dress. "The flat ones are best, right?"

"For most people, but I can skip anything." Sam picked up a misshapen stone and held it up between thumb and forefinger. "Observe." The stone skipped merrily across the murky water, leaving a pretty little ripple with each skip.

Hazel found a reasonably flat stone, assumed Sam's stone-skipping stance, cocked her arm, and let the stone fly. It hit the river with an obnoxious splash and sank. "I don't know how you do that. I did what you did."

"Here, let me show you."

After so many demonstrations and failed attempts it was a wonder the riverbank didn't run out of stones, Hazel finally got the hang of it, one time even matching Sam's throw skip for skip. After that, Sam stopped giving instructions and went back to the subject of the fair—which had the best Ferris wheel in all the land—and the best horse races ever—and the strangest gypsies loitering outside the gate to scare the ladies—until someone yelled, "Hey! You kids down there?"

Sam scrambled under the bridge and motioned for Hazel to do the same. The familiar voice came again. Philo.

"Hey, Sam! You down there?"

"Shouldn't you answer him, Sam?" Hazel whispered.

Sam shook his head and put his finger to his lips.

"But he's your friend."

"I know you're down there! You better get up here pronto. Gary's having conniptions looking for you two."

Sam didn't stop shaking his head at Hazel, his finger slamming his lips.

"Better me than the sheriff, Sam!"

If Hazel didn't say something, they were going to jail. She stood up and hollered, "We're down here, Philo!"

Sam hissed at her. "Shut *up*, Hazel!"

"I don't care what you say. I'm not going to jail." She scrambled up the bank and joined Philo.

After several minutes went by with no sign of Sam, Philo said, "Somebody needs to knock some sense into that kid," and headed for the riverbank.

Philo soon had Sam in tow, and they were back on the road to the poor farm, Philo demanding Sam tell him what in the name of Jesus, Mary, and Joseph he'd done to get Gary so het up. "He is apoplectic—apoplectic, I tell you."

"What's apoplectic?" Hazel said.

Sam smirked. "Mad enough for his head to explode."

"I ain't laughing, kid. What did you do?"

Sam's smirk turned to a grin. "I told those people he tried to pawn us off on I have TB."

"What'd you go and do a fool thing like that for? I thought you had more sense than that." Philo stopped walking, the better to scold Sam.

"I told him I was going to Florida to find a sanatorium, and when I'm well I'll send for my sister. We're not going to be slave labor for anybody."

Philo reached into his shirt pocket for tobacco and rolling papers. "That's the dumbest idea I've heard in a very long time."

"Don't worry. I won't be looking for a sanatorium. I don't really have TB. But I am going to Florida. I'll hop a freight, and when I get there, I'll find work picking oranges and get a nice little apartment, maybe even a house. Then I'll send for Hazel."

Sam smiled at Hazel, nodded his head, and raised his eyebrows, prodding her to tell Philo her brother's dumb idea was just swell.

"What kind of apartment? Will I have my own room?"

"I don't know. Philo, how much money can I make picking oranges, enough for a place with two bedrooms?"

Philo was having trouble rolling his cigarette. He finally gave up and shoved the tobacco and rolling papers back in his pocket. "I've gotta get you back before Gary has a damn cow, but first you need to listen to me. I'm serious. You need to listen to me."

"Okay," Sam said.

"You ain't going to Florida, and you sure as hell ain't hopping no freight to get there. Riding the rails is dangerous. People get killed. I saw a feller get killed that way, all mangled to a bloody pulp, he was. I never want to see that sight again."

"But you do it."

"Don't matter. You ain't doing it. You hear me?"

"I hear you."

"See that you do. We need to get a move on."

They trudged on in silence. Hazel lagged behind, batting at a cloud of gnats that wouldn't stop plaguing her. As they walked past the cemetery, she made a silent apology to her mother for thinking of leaving her to go to Florida, even if she could have her own room.

When they reached the dooryard of the poorhouse, a car was parked there.

"Oh, Christ," Philo said. "He called the doc. You're in for it now, kid."

"It's probably for one of the old people," Sam said. "Maybe one of 'em had a heart attack."

"Watch your mouth, kid, okay? Watch your mouth before he takes it out on the rest of us."

Back at the poorhouse, Philo walked them to the manager's office and knocked on the door. When Gary opened it and Hazel saw the look on his face, she was very relieved her bowels were empty.

Gary jerked his thumb behind him. "Get your asses in here. Now. The doc's gonna check you out and put an end to this TB bullshit right here, right now."

If anything, Gary's office was even more stifling than it had been a few hours before, the cloud of cigarette smoke hanging beneath the ceiling threatening to drop and smother them at any moment. The window shade was still pulled down, pinpricks of light shining through the sun-rotted fabric. The doctor who had refused to save Mama's life leaned against Gary's desk in his shirtsleeves, his black bag at his side. He took a thermometer from the bag and snapped his wrist several times to shake it down.

"Now, what's this I hear about you saying you're sick?" He gestured with the thermometer for Sam to open his mouth. "Under your tongue, and keep your mouth closed. What makes you think you have TB?"

Sam shrugged and pointed at the thermometer. The doctor picked up Sam's wrist and looked at his watch. "Have you been coughing?"

Sam gave Hazel the eye and nodded.

"Short of breath?"

Another nod.

"Tired and run-down?"

Yes again.

"I won't ask about your appetite. Poor appetite is not unusual in your living situation."

"These people get plenty to eat," Gary muttered. "I can't help it if the food ain't good enough for 'em."

The doctor ignored him. "Chills? Night sweats?"

Yes to both of those, too.

"Your pulse is a little elevated. Have you been exerting yourself?"

This time, Sam shook his head.

The doctor removed the thermometer from Sam's mouth and squinted at it. "Ninety-eight point eight. Nothing unusual there."

The sharp smell of rubbing alcohol pinched Hazel's nose as the doctor wiped the thermometer and replaced it in his black bag. "He looks fine to me, Gary." He snapped the latch on his black bag.

"What about the rest? You didn't even check his lungs! How can I tell the Myotts he don't have TB if you ain't checked his lungs!"

"If you insist. I wasn't going to charge for the visit, but a full exam's a different story."

"Just do it."

At the end of the throat-checking, neck-pressing, chest-thumping, and stethoscope-meandering, the doctor pronounced Sam in perfect health, except for being underweight. "Son, it doesn't pay to be a malingerer. Sooner or later, you get found out. Trust me."

Sam looked so defeated, Hazel felt sorry for him. He'd brought it on himself, but still, there was no need for the doctor to play the bully and snatch the brass ring out of Sam's hand after he'd only just grabbed it.

Once again, the doctor snapped the latch on his black bag and made to leave.

"Not so fast," Gary said. "Now the girl."

"No, Gary. Enough's enough. I have patients waiting for me. I'll show myself out." The doctor exited the room.

Gary gave the doctor's back the evil eye and shuffled papers on his desk, looking for something. "Get out of here. I got a phone call to make. I'll deal with you two later."

Hazel and Sam were out of there so fast, Gary didn't even have time to add, "Goddamn kids."

Out in the dooryard, Sam halted, as if he'd suddenly lost his footing. "There's nowhere to hide in this damn place."

Hazel squinted at him, the late afternoon sun bright in her face. "Mama wouldn't like you swearing, Sam."

"I know. Sorry." Sam looked behind him, as if he expected to see a horde of old people pouring out the front door to drag them both back inside. Hazel turned to look, too, but the doorway was as empty as a toothless mouth.

In the distance, the saddest cow who ever lived let out a series of mournful bellows.

"Wait," Sam said. "We can hide in the hayloft. Come on, let's go before Gary gets done with his phone call." Sam grabbed Hazel's hand, gave one last look over his shoulder for the horde of old people, and ran to the cow barn.

The inside of the barn was as shadowy as the inside of the poorhouse, only spattered with manure. A lot of manure.

"Can't we hide someplace else?" Hazel said. "It smells horrible."

"The smell won't be as bad in the hayloft. Smells mostly like hay. You go up the ladder first."

Hazel put her foot on the bottom rung and tested it with a little bounce. The rung didn't seem any too sturdy. "Is it safe?"

"Should be okay. I'll be behind you in case you start to fall."

Hazel clambered up the ladder, figuring the less time her weight was on it, the less chance one of the rungs would give way. Reaching the top, she looked for a place to sit. Sam was right about the hayloft smelling mostly like hay, not manure. Never had she seen so much hay. Those cows must get really hungry to need that much hay.

As soon as Sam reached the top of the ladder, he threw himself onto the nearest hay mountain. Hazel flopped down beside him and waited for him to say something, but he lay back on the hay gazing up at the dark, rough-hewn rafters as if watching the clouds drift by without a single worry in his head.

Hazel wiped a trickle of sweat from the side of her face. The space was very hot—but it was still better than Gary's office. "What do we do now?"

Sam folded his hands over his stomach. "We wait."

"For how long?"

"Not long, a few hours. I'll leave while it's dark, so nobody will see me."

"Leave?"

Sam turned to look at her. "I *told* you. I'm going to Florida to pick oranges, and when I save up enough money to get us a place, I'll send for you." He went back to his rafter-gazing.

Hazel smacked him on the arm. "I didn't think you were *serious*. Philo said it's a really dumb idea."

"Look, I am not going to work for those snotty people. That's who Gary's calling—I guarantee you. Once Gary gives 'em that doctor's report, they won't give a shit I lied about having TB. They're just after slave labor. They'd probably give me the worst room in the house, the one that doesn't get any heat in the winter. Maybe the attic. Or a closet."

"But what about *me*?" Hazel blinked several times to stop tears from falling, but they fell anyway. "I don't want to live in a closet."

"They'll go easier on you. You're younger. And a girl. Besides, you'll only be there two months, maybe three months, tops."

"I don't understand, Sam. Maybe we should go back now. Maybe if we go back to the house, Marcelline will help us."

"No, she won't. She's scared to death of Gary."

"Well, what about Philo? He'll stick up for us. He said so the night Mama died."

"In case you hadn't noticed, Gary has no use for Philo. . . . Aw, Sis, don't cry. I got it all worked out."

Hazel wiped her nose on her sleeve, but that didn't stop her tears. "You're really going to ride the rails to Florida? Philo told you not to. He said people get *killed*."

"Philo thinks I'm just a dumb kid. The fellow he saw killed was probably drunk and not paying attention. I won't hop a freight in the dark. I'll wait till daylight. I'm not that stupid."

As Sam went back to staring at the rafters, the thought occurred to Hazel that he might be talking big to make her feel better until next week when they both were sent to work for the rude farmer and his fussy wife. He wasn't going to Florida at all.

Before long, Gary drove the cows into the barn for milking, and Hazel knew to lie still for the next two hours, even though Sam wasn't really going to Florida. When Gary was done with the milking and left the barn, it was time for supper. Hazel knew better than to complain to Sam that she was hungry. She also didn't complain that she had to use the toilet. As soon as she was sure Gary had left the barn and wasn't coming back, she made her way to a far corner of the loft and squatted. Once Gary had the night to cool off, they'd climb down the wobbly ladder, slip into the house unnoticed, and sit down to their breakfast of runny oatmeal as if today had never happened.

As daylight waned, Sam settled into his bed on the hay mountain and told Hazel stories of times she was too young to remember. Locking herself in the bathroom on Bridge Street, laughing like an evil little troll when Daddy had to take off the doorknob with a screwdriver. An epic temper tantrum in the IGA over a box of Cracker Jack. Running up to a clown at the Sheldon Fair and kicking him in the shins.

Hazel threw a handful of hay at him. "You're making that up. I couldn't have been bad *all* the time."

"Oh, you were. Scout's honor."

"You're not in the Boy Scouts!"

"Still counts."

They both fell silent as crickets began their familiar chorus, and night birds sang their songs for anyone who wanted to listen. The hayloft filled with shadows, the way shadows filled the bedroom at home she shared with Sam after the sun went down. The air in the hayloft now felt comfortable, the way a hot bath made her want to fall asleep in her own bed, Mama tucking in the covers all warm and snug.

COMES THE MORNING

HAZEL

August 1927

HAZEL WOKE TO FIND herself alone in the dark. Gary's voice drifted up from the barn below as he instructed the cows to stand still and behave themselves. She fell back to sleep without a second thought. Sam would soon be back.

When Hazel woke again, all she could see of Sam was the hollow his body had left next to her on the hay mountain. The hayloft was no longer filled with shadows, the rafters above her head clearly visible. No sound came from the barn below. She crawled to the edge of the hayloft and looked down. All the cows were gone. Sunlight filtered through an unseen window, confirming that it was in fact daytime.

After relieving herself in the same corner she'd used the previous day, Hazel searched the hayloft for any sign of her brother, checking the corners and the spaces under the eaves before floundering through mountains and valleys of hay, as sweat and dust stung her eyes.

She dug out great armfuls of the stuff and shoved them aside, as if Sam had decided to bury himself in the hay as a prank before they returned to the house together for runny oatmeal and whatever punishment was waiting for them. Sam couldn't have gone to Florida and left her alone. He couldn't. He was her brother.

She collapsed onto the nearest pile of hay and cried sobs of panic. When the sobs subsided into sniffles, she scrubbed her face with the hem of her dress and tried to think—but it was too hard to think when she was so hungry. And thirsty. She descended the wobbly ladder and made a run for the house.

No one was in the front hall, and she ran down the stairs to the dining room. The tables were a mess of dirty dishes, so breakfast was over. She'd have to wait until dinner to eat. One of the old women inched her way around the men's table gathering up spoons. When the old woman looked up and saw Hazel standing in the doorway, the spoons clattered to the floor.

"Good Lord, child, you gave me a turn! Look at the sight of you."

"Have you seen Sam?"

"Your brother?" The old woman shook her head. "Nobody can find him. He probably ran away."

"Don't *say* that. He did *not* run away."

The old woman eased herself onto her knees with much grunting and sighing about old bones. Sensing someone behind her, Hazel turned around. Marcelline. She must have come to find out what made all the noise when the old woman dropped the spoons.

"Where have you been, child? You look a fright. And you've been crying."

"I know. Have you seen Sam?"

"Ain't he with you?"

"He was yesterday, but now I can't find him. Have you seen him?"

"Gary and Philo was out looking for the two of you yesterday. You're in big trouble with Gary."

"I know. Have you seen Sam?"

"No, I ain't seen Sam. Lucy, what are you doing?"

"Getting the spoons. Spoons don't belong on the floor."

"Neither do you. You already broke your hip once." Marcelline put out both her hands. "Come on, get up."

Marcelline was no help at all, fooling with that old woman.

"Maybe one of the old people's seen him, and they didn't tell you. I'm going to go ask them."

On her way to the living room to see if any of the old people were in there, a knock sounded at the front door. No one came to answer it. Gary must be doing chores, and Marcelline was too busy fooling with the spoon woman to bother. Hazel opened the door herself, certain that she wasn't supposed to.

The sheriff stood there, the sheriff who had brought Mama, Sam, and her to the poorhouse, all those months ago after Daddy got killed in Waterbury. He'd come back to take her away to work for those horrid people.

"I'm not going."

The sheriff had an expression on his face like something was wrong with her, but instead of telling her she looked a fright, he said, "Is Mr. Bashaw here?"

"You can't make me go."

"Is Mr. Bashaw here?"

No. Something was wrong—but not with her. "I think he's doing chores. You want me to get Marcelline?"

"If you would, please."

The sheriff was too polite to her. Something had to be wrong. Hazel ran down the stairs to the basement to fetch Marcelline.

When she returned to the hall with Marcelline, the sheriff had taken off his hat. He now held it with both hands, worrying the brim. "I need to speak with your husband. There's been an accident."

"What kind of accident?"

"A bad one."

Hazel heard footsteps approaching from the dooryard, then Gary's voice. "What's going on, Maynard? I was in the toolshed when I saw your car pull in. You got another inmate for us? It better be someone who can work for a change."

"Can I come in?" The sheriff stepped into the hall without getting an answer and stood under the hanging light. "There's been an accident on the railroad tracks at the Junction."

Hazel must have made a sound, even though she didn't know it, because Marcelline told her to go to her room.

Hazel climbed the stairs—but only to the first landing, out of sight, where she could hear what was going on at the bottom of the staircase as the three grown-ups stood under the hanging light talking about an accident. A bad one.

"What happened?"

"Looks like he was trying to jump on the moving train, and he fell. Cracked his skull and severed both legs. I identified the body as one of yours."

"Philo?"

"No, not Philo."

THE POOR FARM PEOPLE buried Sam next to Mama the following day as a gentle summer rain fell. The scent of dying wildflowers wet with rain would haunt Hazel the rest of her life.

An Ordinary Man

Hazel

***

April 1935

Hazel looked at the clock above the blackboard in eighth-period study hall. As it did every day, the minute hand advanced way too fast, set in motion by a second hand out of control. Soon the dismissal bell would clamor, setting off a stampede of chattering girls and boot-heavy boys thundering down the stairs to be first out of the building.

Not Hazel. Gone were the days of watching the clock above Miss Manahan's head, willing the minute hand to hurry up and release her from that awful woman's cutting remarks and knuckle-stinging ruler.

School was something else entirely now. In school, she could listen to lectures on her favorite subjects without being interrupted to fetch a cup of tea or clean up cat puke. She could take notes and ask questions without being sniped at. She could eat her peanut butter sandwich in the cold lunchroom with classmates who didn't tease her.

In two short months, this all would end when she walked across the Opera House stage to receive her high school diploma and become Mrs. Myott's full-time hired girl.

In the meantime, she needed to finish her American Government theme before the bell rang. Being a hired girl did not allow for homework. Any assignments she couldn't finish before the bell rang—or dash off in homeroom the next day—were submitted to her teachers incomplete. Even when a teacher looked disappointed or concerned enough to ask what had happened, she never, ever offered them the truth as an excuse.

As her pen scratched across the paper, she paused to push up her sleeves. She'd already ruined one hand-me-down dress by getting ink on the sleeve. She couldn't risk ruining another.

The dismissal bell rang, and the stampede began. Hazel kept her head down, still trying to finish her American Government theme. When she finished it at last, she capped her pen, gathered her books, and looked at the clock. Fifteen minutes past the time to start walking back to the farm.

She broke into a run, and a teacher's voice came at her from somewhere—"Hey, slow down, no running in the halls!"—but she kept on running. She threw her books in her locker, grabbed her jacket, and ran down the stairs to another unseen teacher yelling at her. "Hey, slow down, no running on the stairs!"

She ran down the walk and across Lincoln Park before getting a stitch in her side that slowed her to a walk. She paused in front of Stanley's Store to catch her breath. Across the street in Joe Bongiorno's ice cream parlor, a group of her classmates was already seated at the counter waiting for ice cream sodas after a hard day passing notes in class and sneaking cigarettes in the bathroom.

Eyes straight ahead now, Hazel resumed walking. North Main Street was on an uphill grade, and she struggled to maintain her pace, her breath hot in her throat, her leg muscles begging for mercy. When she reached the Spavin Cure Factory, she ran across the road without bothering to look both ways for cars.

West Berkshire Road stretched before her, hilly and steep. It would take her forever to reach the farm—and there would be the long driveway to navigate, Mrs. Myott lying in wait behind the living room curtains Hazel had washed and ironed the previous Saturday. Stupid woman, insisting on spring cleaning before the furnace was turned off. The curtains would only need washing again in another month's time.

Hazel heard a car come up behind her. As she jumped aside to avoid it, her ankle turned on the soft shoulder, and she went down. She cried out as the car traveled on oblivious.

Waves of pain radiated from her ankle to her brain, telling her there was no getting up now, no walking to the farm now, no going back to undo the folly of finishing her American Government theme. When the initial shock wave of pain subsided, she heard another car approaching. She turned to look as a pickup truck crested the hill behind her. Instead of traveling on, the truck slowed, pulled to the side of the road, and coasted to a stop. A man got out and hurried to her side.

"Are you all right? Are you hurt?"

Hazel looked up at him, hoping he was someone she knew, someone who might help her, but she'd never seen him or his mud-spattered green pickup truck before. He was an ordinary man in overalls and a barn jacket, who smelled faintly of manure—nonetheless, a stranger, someone she now wished she knew.

He knelt next to her, but he didn't touch her. "Are you hurt? You could get hit by a car sitting on the side of the road like that."

Up close, the man's face still looked ordinary, much like the boys in her class, only a lot older.

"I twisted my ankle."

He leaned in for a closer look but stopped short of touching her. "Do you think it might be broken? I could take you to Doc Wetherbee, if you think it might be broken."

"No, thank you. It feels better now." Hazel didn't think her ankle was broken, but in no way did it feel any better. She looked away from the man's deep brown eyes, which no longer appeared so ordinary.

Another car approached, picking up speed on the downhill grade. The man scrambled to his feet and put out his hands. "You can't stay here. Let me help you up."

Hazel looked at his outstretched hands as if she'd never seen such a thing before, a man's hands offered in an act of kindness. The seat of her dress was getting wet from the soggy ground, and the sun had gone behind a cloud. She took the man's warm, work-roughened hands.

When he had her on her feet, she stood with all her weight on her left foot, her right foot barely touching the ground to keep her from toppling over. She tried to transform her pain-grimace into a nonchalant smile. "Thank you for stopping. I'd better be going."

"I'll give you a ride home. Where do you live?"

"I don't need a ride. I can walk. Thank you all the same."

The man pushed his cap to the back of his head. "Show me."

"Show you?"

"That's right. Show me. I ain't about to leave you on the side of the road if you can't walk."

Hazel took one knee-buckling step. Before she could fall, the man caught her under the arms.

"Put your arm around my shoulders, and I'll help you to the truck."

Hazel made no move to put her arm around the stranger's shoulders.

"Come on, now, I ain't got all day. I'm trying to help you."

The stranger sounded so impatient—no, not impatient, insulted, even hurt—that Hazel put her arm around his shoulders—but gingerly, as if she could do so without touching him.

The stranger got them both into the small cab of the truck. "Okay, now. Where do you live?"

"I'm staying at the Myotts' farm."

He started the truck. "Dave Myott's place?"

Hazel nodded. As the truck bumped back onto the road and picked up speed, Hazel stared straight ahead through the grimy windshield, not daring to look at the man. Even in her peripheral vision, he appeared very much in charge, with his work-roughened hands easy on the steering wheel and his cap pushed back. Hazel almost wished he were younger, closer to her own age.

He drove at an ordinary rate of speed, not too fast, not too slow. Even so, the landscape before her didn't look right, houses skewed on their plots, barns undecided which way to lean, tree buds snapped shut. The sky carried a strange tinge impossible to describe, so strange that when the man spoke again, he gave her a fright and she let out a yelp.

"Sorry. Didn't mean to scare you. I asked what you was doing out here—if you don't mind me asking."

She probably should answer him. He had stopped to help her, after all. "I was walking home from school." Just a little white lie. Saying, "I was walking to work after school" would only have prompted questions she had no intention of answering.

"You're still in school, then." He sounded surprised, as if he'd thought she was older. Hazel didn't know whether to feel flattered or frightened.

The truck stopped to let Guy Vaillancourt, his hired man, and his cows amble across the road for the afternoon milking. The sight of such docile creatures conjured the image of Mrs. Myott—who expected Hazel to be equally docile—waiting for her behind those freshly washed curtains. Mrs. Myott had never hit her, but Hazel had never provoked her to the extent of coming back late from school in a stranger's mud-spattered pickup truck with the stranger at the wheel.

As the pickup truck left Guy Vaillancourt and his ambling cows behind, Hazel pointed vaguely at the windshield. "You can let me out here."

The man turned to look at her without slowing the truck. "What? Here? I thought you said you live at the Myott place."

"I do, but I can walk the rest of the way from here. Please stop."

The truck drove around a bend, and the driveway of the farm came into view.

"Stop! Please! You don't need to go all the way to the house. I can walk up the driveway."

The man slowed the truck and headed up the driveway as if he hadn't heard her—or as if he had heard her and he didn't care.

"Please! Stop and let me out!"

He brought the truck to a stop, still out of view of the house. "What's wrong? Are you in some kind of trouble?"

Hazel opened the truck door, jumped down, and collapsed on the ground, pain waves flooding her body once again. The stranger picked her up and plunked her back in the truck as if she were a six-year-old.

"Now, look here," he said. "It's obvious you can't walk on that ankle. What are you afraid of? If you don't tell me, I can't help you."

"She's going to be so mad at me."

"Who? Who's going to be mad at you? No, no, no, don't do that. Don't cry." He handed her a crumpled bandana. Hazel took it without thinking, swiped it across her face, and handed it back.

"Should I take you to the constable?"

"No. I just wanted to finish my American Government theme and get a good grade." The tears began anew.

The man handed over the crumpled bandana, and the truck lurched forward. When they reached the dooryard, he turned off the engine and set the hand brake. He hopped from the truck, opened Hazel's door, and put out his hands. "Come on, now. I'll help you to the house."

Hazel wanted to take his warm, work-roughened hands in hers—she did—but she couldn't, she just couldn't. The sight of Hazel with her arm around the shoulders of a strange man, her body close to his as he carried most of her weight, would send Mrs. Myott out the front door shrieking like a she-devil from hell.

The man shook his head and left her to walk to the house. Hazel watched as he knocked on the front door. If he was foolish enough to knock on the door, he should have gone to the kitchen door. Men wearing work clothes were supposed to use the kitchen door. Knocking on the front door would only make things worse.

Several moments went by before the front door opened and Mrs. Myott's head appeared. She and the stranger seemed to be talking. God only knew what Mrs. Myott was telling him—not that it mattered. Hazel was never going to see the man again. What did it matter if he now thought badly of her?

Mrs. Myott emerged from the house and walked to the truck with the stranger. The first words out of her mouth were a lie. "Hazel, I'm so glad you're safe! I was worried sick. Let's get you back to the house and put an ice pack on that ankle."

Yet, for all Mrs. Myott's expressions of concern, Hazel found her arm around the stranger's shoulders once again as he helped her across the dooryard and up the front steps.

When they reached the front door, the stranger said, "Do you want me to help you get her inside?"

"No, thank you, Mr. Morgan. You've done quite enough."

After Hazel managed to get herself into the house, Mrs. Myott closed the front door firmly.

Mr. Morgan. How could Mrs. Myott know the name of the man who had come to Hazel's aid—and she didn't? More than anything in that moment, Hazel wished she had the courage to open the front door and watch him drive away. How she longed to keep him in view just a moment longer, now that he had a name, even if it was only his last name.

A Fragile, Feathered Thing

Hazel

—◆—○—◆—

April 1935

HAZEL MISSED FOUR DAYS of school before her ankle was strong enough for her to feel confident walking any distance. Mrs. Myott gave her a note for the office, which prompted arched eyebrows and an "Oh, you poor thing" from the school secretary. When her teachers saw her limping, they let her make up the work she'd missed without her asking.

The dismissal bell rang while she was working her way through a missed English assignment. She allowed herself time to finish her sentence, then capped her pen. She lingered in the study hall only long enough to avoid getting knocked over in the rush toward the door before going to her locker to stow her books and retrieve her jacket.

She emerged from the high school to bright April sunshine and a chill in the air. Across the street, the usual gang of immature boys sat on the curb with their feet in the gutter, attempting to sing a song to which they did not know the words. She crossed the street, and they all yelled, "Doo dah, doo dah!" at her.

How she dreaded the long, limping slog back to the farm. She could walk on her ankle, but every step still hurt. She was halfway up North Main when the bell in the Masonic Temple struck the half hour. She had such a long way to go, and the sun refused to share any of its warmth. As she put her hands in her jacket pockets, she encountered bunched up cloth that shouldn't have been there.

She pulled it out to reveal Mr. Morgan's crumpled bandana. Just an ordinary red bandana, faded from washing. She must have put it in her pocket without thinking the day he gave her a ride. She had no way of returning the bandana to him, so she put it back in her pocket. She hoped he didn't think she'd kept it on purpose, as if she had no handkerchiefs of her own to catch her tears.

Reaching the Spavin Cure Factory, she stopped to look both ways for cars. She waited for a rattletrap Model-T and a green pickup truck to pass and crossed the road. She'd walked but a short distance on West Berkshire Road when a horn tootled behind her. She turned around and saw what looked like the same green pickup truck now approaching her. She stepped aside to let it go by, taking care where she placed her feet, but the truck slowed, pulled over, and stopped. The driver gave the horn another toot and motioned for her to approach the truck. As she hesitated, he rolled down his window and leaned his head out.

"Hey, there!"

Hazel took a few steps toward the truck to confirm that the man at the wheel really was Mr. Morgan. He pushed his cap to the back of his head.

"I thought that was you! I was headed to Agway when I saw you walking, so I turned around. Can I give you a ride?"

He opened his door and hopped from the truck. He was taller than she remembered even though she hadn't had any difficulty getting her arm around his shoulders that day.

He opened the passenger door. "Come on, get in. I'll give you a ride."

Hazel's ankle pulsed and throbbed with the rhythm of her heart, but whether from pain or from seeing Mr. Morgan again, she didn't know. She let him help her into the truck.

"I been wondering how you were, with that ankle. You're still limping."

"It's better now, thank you."

He smiled. She didn't remember him smiling that day either. "Glad to hear it. I was worried about you."

"You were? Why?"

"That was a bad sprain—and you was in quite a state. How about I give you a ride and drop you off at the bottom of the driveway?"

Hazel couldn't say no. She didn't want to say no. He'd remembered. "All right."

As he let out the hand brake, she said, "Do you think you could tell me your first name?"

"What's that? I didn't hear you." The truck bumped back onto the road.

"Could you tell me your first name?"

"I didn't tell you? It's Paul."

He smiled again, and Hazel couldn't stop looking at his kind, weather-roughened face.

"Now that you mention it, I don't know your name either."

A fragile feathered thing fluttered in her chest. "I'm Hazel. My mother named me Hazel."

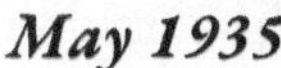

May 1935

AS THE TENDER RED maple buds of April fulfilled their promise of leafy green in May, Paul found a way to give Hazel a ride home from school at least once a week, sometimes twice. He'd located a turnout by a disused pasture where they could park undisturbed until enough time had elapsed for Hazel to have walked to the farm and he could drop her off at the bottom of the driveway with Mrs. Myott none the wiser.

The day Paul showed Hazel the turnout, he said he didn't feel right about going behind Mrs. Myott's back—but he said it only once—and Hazel loved him for it at the same time she hoped he'd never say those words again.

As the weeks went by, with May turning to June, Hazel told Paul the story of her life, turning her gaze to the lovely weed-choked pasture when Paul's deep brown eyes quickened her breath.

She told him everything, losing her father to drink and terrors in the night before the insane asylum claimed him for good—being evicted from her home to be carted off to the poor farm—how she would never, ever forget the stench of the place, the smell of lives rotting away for want of proper food and care.

She told him about Sam's losing his Florida dream to the wheels of a freight train, along with his life, all for believing in tall tales from a hobo. She even told him the cruelest cut of all, watching her mother's lifeblood leave her body right in front of her and being powerless to stop it. Compared to losing her mother, the years of servitude at the Myott farm were nothing, nothing at all.

HAZEL DREADED FINALS WEEK, not because she feared she wouldn't pass her subjects—she'd manage to get by with Cs—but because she would never again spend those golden moments with Paul.

When exam week arrived, she briefly considered failing her exams to stay in school another year. With as little time as she had to study, failing her exams wouldn't take much. As she skimmed through the exam questions for American Government, she did know the answers to most of them, and the thought of deliberately giving wrong answers was too humiliating, not to mention dishonoring Mama's memory.

Her last exam ended at two o'clock on Thursday. Hazel capped her pen, but she couldn't bring herself to get up from her desk and relinquish her exam.

"Finished?" Mr. Harvey said.

Hazel nodded and brought her exam to the front.

"See you on Tuesday at graduation?"

Hazel shook her head and left the room.

AS SHE CROSSED THE street to Lincoln Park, the immature boys sitting on the curb with their feet in the gutter shouted, "Tumble-weee-eeeeds, tumbleweee-eeeeds!" at her in a dirge of endings with no beginnings that followed her all the way to the Spavin Cure Factory.

Walking down West Berkshire Road, she was surprised by the tootling horn of Paul's truck. She turned around as he pulled over and stuck his head out the window. "Hazel! I'm glad I caught you." He leaned over and opened the passenger door.

Hazel climbed in. "How did you know when I'd be walking back to the farm? They let us out early."

He winked. "Exam schedule's in the *Standard*."

Hazel didn't know whether she should feel better or worse that Paul had sought her out when she was finished with school, never again to sit in his mud-spattered green pickup truck by the weed-choked pasture.

"How were your exams?"

"They were okay. Pretty much like regular tests, only longer."

"I plan to be at the Opera House to see you graduate."

Hazel turned away.

"What's wrong? Ain't you happy to be graduating?" He pulled into the turnout by the pasture.

Hazel didn't answer him until he'd put on the hand brake. "I can't go. I don't have a cap and gown."

"Well, you should be proud for graduating anyhow. I only made it through eighth grade before I had to quit to work on the farm full-time."

"That's what Mama wanted, for me and Sam to get our high school diplomas."

"What will you do now?"

"Work for Mrs. Myott full-time, I guess."

"You don't have to, you know," Paul said. He paused. "We could get married."

Hazel didn't think she'd heard him right. It had to be wishful thinking, her imagination running away with her. "What?"

"We could get married."

"Really?"

"Really."

"I'm not too young?"

Paul frowned. "How old are you? You're not eighteen?"

"Not yet. My birthday's next month."

"Well, there you go. Next month, you'll be old enough to get married with nobody's say-so but your own. What do you say?"

"Do you really mean it? We haven't known each other very long."

"Yes, I mean it. I ain't a man to say things I don't mean. What do you say?

"I say yes."

When they applied for the marriage license at the town clerk's office, Hazel learned for the first time that Paul was thirteen years her senior, to the day. July seventeenth. She couldn't have cared less.

Newlywed

Hazel

July 1936

Hazel opened her eyes to a small, sunlit room under the eaves. The room was papered in a charming rose pattern, delightfully faded and cracking in the corners. In the place of honor above the bed hung a Currier & Ives print, a generous basket of flowers, all water-stained and brown with age in its old-fashioned frame. The print had hung in this very spot above this very bed from the time Paul's great-grandfather built the farmhouse.

Directly across from the bed, a window overlooked the farm's small apple orchard. How Hazel had come to love that orchard, the trees twisted and gnarled with age but still blooming in the spring and bearing fruit in the fall.

Even after a year of marriage, opening her eyes to this room was a surprise and a delight. There was something about being tucked up under the eaves with Paul that brought a jolt of pleasure, as if the two of them were the only people in the world in their own little hideaway.

She hadn't become pregnant yet, but she had plenty of time to have children. How many she wanted she wasn't sure, but she understood that nature would cast the deciding vote. Her time would come soon enough.

Glancing at Paul's alarm clock, she saw that his mother—"Vera," she'd insisted on being called, not "Mrs. Morgan"—had let her sleep late again. It was terribly kind of her, but she really shouldn't have. Hazel was more than happy to get up at dawn to help with the men's breakfast and not have to wait until dinnertime to see her husband.

In fact, she enjoyed the endless chores that came with being a farmer's wife. Heating water on the massive wood stove for dishes and milk cans. Washing manure-spattered overalls. Scrubbing floors. Scrubbing woodwork. Scrubbing every last bit of soot from the kitchen walls. Vera told her nearly every day that the old farmhouse had never been so clean, while Silas, Paul's father, liked to say, "You'll make some lucky feller a good wife one day."

Hazel hopped out of the chipped iron bedstead where she and Paul lay together every night and made the bed. According to Vera, the light summer quilt had been pieced together by her grandmother out of old aprons that had outlived their usefulness as aprons but still had some usable fabric left. To think, she and Paul were sleeping under a quilt that had been made in the 1800s! In that house, it seemed everything had a family story attached to it, from the oversized rag rug in the living room to the smallest figurine on the whatnot in the parlor.

Hazel quickly dressed in her gingham housedress the color of Vera's purple lilacs in the spring. Sitting on the bed to put on her shoes and socks, she marveled that Vera had been kind (and patient!) enough to teach her how to sew: taking out the seams of the garment to be made over, pinning new seams, working the treadle, guiding the fabric to sew a straight line. So far, Hazel had made two housedresses that were every bit as pretty as the good dress she'd made for church.

When she was ready for the day, she hurried down the stairs to the kitchen, where Vera stood at the sink.

"What can I help you with?"

"Nothing at the moment, Hazel. Help yourself to a doughnut. There's fresh coffee on the stove."

As Vera busied herself with the last of the breakfast dishes, Hazel savored her doughnut and coffee. The kitchen door was open to a pristine summer morning, the kind of morning that beckoned children away from their cereal bowls into a world of infinite possibilities—and tonight, *tonight,* she would wear her good dress to her very first dance at Lake Carmi's Crystal Ballroom.

"But I don't know how to dance," she'd said when Paul asked if she would like to go to celebrate their first wedding anniversary.

"Me either. I'll just hold you in my arms while the music plays. Close enough for dancing."

Hazel spent the day all aflutter, dropping bobby pins when she put pin curls in her hair, dropping clean silverware on the floor, constantly running to the window to look for Paul when they weren't to leave for hours. A crystal ballroom sounded so very grand; could the floor be made of glass? Sterling D. Weed's Imperial Orchestra would provide the dance music—not just any orchestra, an *imperial* orchestra. She tried—and failed—to imagine what music played by an imperial orchestra could possibly sound like.

The time to leave came at last, and off they went—Hazel in her good dress, Paul in the navy blue suit he shared with his father. The ride to the lake was an anniversary celebration in itself, she and Paul sitting close in the battered green pickup truck where they had fallen in love, gravel and pebbles pinging merrily against the bumpers, the high summer scenery unrolling before them like ribbon from a spool.

Soon, the lake came into view, ringed by clusters of small, red cottages. The narrow dirt road narrowed even further, with cars parked on one side as far as the eye could see, and more cars behind them, their headlights flashing off the rearview mirror. Paul pulled over and parked, even though there was nothing resembling a crystal ballroom in sight.

"How many people come here?" Hazel said as he helped her out of the truck.

"Couldn't say. Me and the old man come up here bass fishing every now and again, but I ain't been inside the dance pavilion. Never saw the need."

He took her hand, and they set off walking, pausing to watch as each shift in the setting sun's position brought a new color to glow on the horizon.

"There it is," Paul said, pointing.

The dance pavilion seemed an unassuming structure, more in keeping with the summer cottages around the lake than a crystal ballroom where an imperial orchestra would play. An elderly gent in a rumpled summer suit greeted them at the entrance. "That's forty cents for you, young feller, and thirty-five cents for the little lady."

Paul handed over three quarters with no hesitation, seemingly unaware of the flour, the sugar that seventy-five cents could buy, the gasoline for the truck. He put his arm around Hazel's waist and bent his head to whisper, "It's okay."

The inside of the Crystal Ballroom was as grand as the promise of its name, with a huge dance floor and a soaring overhead. Views of the lake and the night sky through a series of large openings in the walls provided all the ornamentation needed.

Hazel turned her attention to the raised stage. Seated behind their music stands, the members of Weed's Imperial Orchestra wore fancy black suits and bow ties. She'd never seen anyone wear such a fancy suit before, much less a bow tie. Their shoes would be polished to a high shine, even though no one could see them. The man standing on the stage with his back to the dance floor must be Sterling D. Weed himself. When he turned to face the crowded dance floor, Hazel was surprised to see a man of about Paul's age, smooth-faced, bespectacled, and balding. Except for the fancy suit and the saxophone on a strap around his neck, he looked like her high school algebra teacher.

"Welcome, one and all! The boys and I will start you off this evening with our theme song, a little foxtrot called 'Wang Wang Blues.' If you don't know the foxtrot, don't worry. Come out on the dance floor anyway; you'll pick it up soon enough. And if you don't, there's always next week." He bent over and picked up a clarinet. "Ready, boys? A-one, a-two, a-three."

The tempo was lively, the notes tumbling from the clarinet sparkling. The melody would not be denied, despite repeated kicks from the bass drum to keep it in check—nor could it keep the crowd in check, as they stepped and glided and twirled.

Hazel looked at Paul, expecting him to get them off the dance floor and out of people's way, but he didn't move. He put his hand on her back, placed her left hand on his shoulder, and held her right hand up as the other men were doing. He stepped side to side—Hazel stepped side to side. Side to side they went, as the people who knew the foxtrot trotted around them. Paul had been right—close enough for dancing.

When the song ended, the crowd applauded and waited for the next one, which turned out to be another foxtrot, allowing Hazel to relax some and enjoy the gentle pressure of Paul's warm hand on her back, guiding her, caressing her, even though his hand didn't move from its proper position.

Sterling D. Weed announced the next song as "Sing, Sing, Sing," but instead of a sing-along, the drums pounded out a primitive beat, seemingly of their own volition. The crowd cheered, and an explosion of brass blasted from the stage as the dancers flung themselves about the floor.

Paul's eyes widened. He mouthed something, grabbed Hazel's hand, and pointed behind him.

Outside, he kept hold of her hand and led her to the edge of the lake. "Jeezum. We coulda got killed in there." He pointed to a large rock. "How about we listen from here?"

Now that she was no longer in danger of being kicked in the head or trampled to death, Hazel was perfectly content to listen to the rest of the song that seemed hell-bent on driving itself off a cliff.

Paul snapped a clean handkerchief from his pocket, arranged it on the rock, and helped Hazel settle herself, as she took care not to tear her good dress. He sat beside her and put his arm around her shoulders. "We can dance anyhow, if you want."

Hazel put her head on his shoulder. "If the right song comes along."

Light from the cottages across the lake painted narrow strokes of golden yellow on the dark surface of the water, as if reaching for the larger reflection of the crescent moon. The music from one song to the next carried clearly on the night air, as if Sterling D. Weed's Imperial Orchestra were playing for the two of them alone, accompanied by lake water lapping against the shore.

In a pause between songs, a mournful cry drifted over the water, hung suspended before it cried again. Hazel lifted her head from Paul's shoulder. "What was that?"

"Loon. You never heard one before?"

"No, what's wrong with it?"

"Nothing. That's how mates find each other in the dark."

THE OLD MAN'S DRAFT

HAZEL

◆—◦—◆

June 1943

WHEN THE LETTER FROM the draft board came, Hazel didn't think much of it. She'd walked down the driveway from the farmhouse to the mailbox the same as she did every morning, enjoying the warm summer air sweetened with birdsong and the smell of the first hay ready for cutting.

The mailbox held the monthly bill from the power company and an envelope with the return address of the draft board in St. Albans. She returned to the house and leaned both envelopes against the sugar bowl on the kitchen table so Paul would be sure to see them when he came in for dinner.

When Paul came in at noon with the hired man, he seemed to be continuing a lecture on how much care must be taken at all times to prevent mastitis. Hazel watched Paul's face closely as he talked, the hired man nodding along with unbridled enthusiasm. *Yes, Paul. Yes, Paul. You bet, Paul.*

Paul tried his best, but since the country's entry into the war and the draft, each hired man seemed more lacking than the last, this poor man included, with his mangled straw hat and missing teeth. But as Hazel listened, it became clear from Paul's even tone that this was a matter of constant repetition of information, not current infection and impending economic ruin.

"How about some more beans to go with that biscuit, Ernest?"

"Yes, Hazel. You bet, Hazel."

After putting the kitchen to rights after dinner, Hazel continued with her weekly woodwork scrubbing. If she and Paul hoped to have children, she needed to make sure they had a decent home to grow up in. Her twenty-sixth birthday was less than a month away.

At supper, Paul ignored the two envelopes leaning against the sugar bowl. Hazel passed him the plate of biscuits left over from dinner. "How's the new man working out?"

Before taking a biscuit, Paul added salt to his soup without tasting it. "Fair to middling. But at least he's reliable. I don't need to worry he won't show up."

Hazel let Paul eat the rest of his meal in peace. As they were letting their food settle before she cleared the table, he reached for the envelopes.

The power bill prompted a tight smile. "Not bad this month."

He opened the other envelope. "I hope this ain't another questionnaire. I hate them damn things." He extracted a single sheet of paper from the envelope, held it in his hand, and stared at it.

"What's the matter? What's it say?"

"What the hell."

"What?"

"I've been drafted."

"No, you haven't."

"Yes, I have."

"But you're too old."

He shook the letter at her. "Don't tell me I'm too old to be drafted. It says so right here."

"But you're nearly forty!"

"Thirty-eight ain't forty. The cut-off for this draft is forty-five. They can draft me." He pushed back his chair, but he didn't get up. "Shit."

"You must have filled out the questionnaire wrong. I remember you were in such an all-fire hurry to get through it. Did you tell them you're married?"

"Yes."

"Did you tell them you have a farm?"

"Yes."

"Did you tell them you can't get a decent hired man to help with the farm?"

He stood up. "I need to think about this."

Paul left the house to walk into the early summer twilight with his thoughts and the sweet scent of hay ready for cutting, while Hazel slopped hot water into the dishpan and scrubbed pea soup mud from their bowls.

Later, they lay together on their moonlit bed not speaking, Paul's thoughts his own, while, in the end, Hazel's thoughts were entirely dependent on his.

THE NEXT MORNING, THE letter from the draft board lay on the kitchen table where Paul had left it. Hazel picked it up and read it for herself, even though she knew it would say exactly what Paul had said it did. She folded the letter, replaced it in its envelope, and leaned the envelope against the sugar bowl. No point getting food all over the damn thing.

After cooking and serving the men's breakfast and putting the kitchen to rights, Hazel set out for the mailbox to wait for Lloyd Bingham to deliver their mail. The morning was cool and misty, the mountains veiled long after daybreak.

The sound of Lloyd's truck chugging up the road flinging gravel came muffled through the mist. He pulled to the side of the road and leaned over to speak through the open window. "Nothing for you folks today, Hazel!"

"Okay, thanks, Lloyd."

Lloyd made no motion to take the steering wheel again. "Haven't seen you in a while, Hazel. How've you been? How's Paul? I see he got a notice from the draft board yesterday. Not unwelcome news, I hope?"

"He's been drafted."

"You don't say? Well, I wouldn't worry too much about it. He should be able to get a deferment easy."

"You think so?"

"The farm's been producing right well the last couple years, I've seen in the *Messenger*. Besides, the draft board's handing out deferments right and left." Lloyd took his pipe out of his pocket and loaded it with tobacco. "A lot of people aren't happy about it. I can't tell you how many able-bodied—"

"I'm sure." Hazel headed back to the house, dismissing Lloyd to stick his nose in somebody else's business.

Dinner, of course, brought no satisfaction, Paul now onto a lecture about keeping the milk house clean and the equipment sanitized—that after needing to take Ernest to the sink to wash his hands before he sat at the table to eat in his grimy shirt and filthy overalls.

For supper, Hazel made scalloped potatoes with ham, Paul's favorite. While it baked, she picked some greens from the garden, got those washed up, then baked a pie with the apples she'd canned the previous fall. When she set the meal on the table and said grace, he looked up. "What's this, then?"

"I thought I'd make something nice." She handed Paul a full plate. "We've had a lot of pea soup lately."

"Can't argue with you there." He dug into his food without salting it.

Paul didn't come out with his decision until the meal was finished, the food put away, and the dishes washed.

Hazel sat at the table across from him, put her folded hands in front of her, and waited, the stove ticking as it cooled. Finally, Paul's chair creaked.

"I report to the draft board next Monday to get the train to Rutland."

"You'll ask for your deferment then?"

"I ain't asking for a deferment."

"What do you mean? You have to."

"I ain't happy about it, but I've made up my mind."

"But what about me? You can't expect me to run this farm with Ernest. I don't know anything about farming—and he's feeble-minded."

"Hazel—"

"You *know* he's feeble-minded. I'd have to watch him every single second, and I don't know anything about farming! Oh, why can't you go for the deferment?"

"Hazel, I thought about this. I ain't gonna shirk my duty. If I'm called to serve, I have to go."

"But what about *me*?"

"You're a grown woman, Hazel."

"What does being a grown woman have to do with anything? Being a grown woman doesn't mean I know anything about running a farm!"

"Hazel—"

"Plenty of men are getting deferments! You *know* they are. Why are you being so stubborn?"

Paul reached across the table and took her hand. "Hazel, I don't want to go any more'n you want me to. But they're calling up fathers now."

Hazel snatched her hand away and jumped up, sending her chair crashing to the floor. "And it's *my* fault we don't have children?"

She couldn't look at him. She couldn't look at him a moment longer, this husband of hers. She ran out the door and kept on running until she could run no longer, finally dropping to the ground in the apple orchard as a red-winged blackbird called for his mate in vain.

Sleep did not come for Hazel that night. Paul had no idea the risk he was taking to even *think* about leaving her responsible for the farm. If his parents had still been alive, they would have talked him out of it. But Vera and Silas weren't still alive. When an outbreak of bovine TB took his herd, Silas asked for death to take him, and a heart attack obliged. A week after his funeral, Vera suffered a stroke. Hazel tried her best to nurse her back to health and prayed hard for her recovery, but Vera wanted to join her husband in death—so she did.

That left Paul with medical bills, funeral expenses, and a dairy farm with no dairy cows—not to mention a contaminated barn. He did the only thing he could do. He mortgaged the farm for a hefty bank loan to replace the barn floor with concrete, replace all the stanchions, purchase a new herd, and modernize the milk house to increase his yield. And he'd been damned lucky to get that mortgage.

No Good Reason

Hazel

———◆○◆———

June 1943

HAZEL HAD FIVE DAYS to talk Paul into applying for his rightful deferment. She failed miserably, at one point earning herself the silent treatment.

When Monday morning came, Paul informed her on his way out the door that Cyrus Fortin's boy would be coming over to help Ernest with the chores.

"And if you pass your final physical in Rutland, I'll never see you again?"

"Don't be foolish, Hazel. I'll take the week's furlough and come home before basic training. What do you take me for?"

And off he went.

Hazel wondered how hard she might have to pray for him to fail his final physical. As she loaded his barn clothes into the washer, she told herself that her need for her husband to provide for her was a perfectly reasonable request to ask of God, and, in the grand scheme of things—even the grand scheme of a world war—a paltry request to ask of the Almighty.

Two hours later, when she caught her hand in the washing machine wringer and was barely able to extricate it, she figured God was not at all pleased with this request from her, the least of his lowly sparrows.

When Paul returned from Rutland the next day, he didn't wait until supper to give her the news. He appeared in the doorway of the small shed off the kitchen, which served as their bathroom with an old pull chain toilet, a washstand holding a basin and pitcher, and a tin bathtub.

"I passed my physical."

Hazel turned to look at him, the toilet brush dripping on the floor. He looked more tired than she expected. Could he be having second thoughts? Was it not too late for him to get out of the mess he'd put them both in?

"You'll ask for the deferment?"

"No."

She jammed the toilet brush deep into the hole where the waste entered and, more often than not, clogged. She had nothing left to say to him.

Later, as Hazel cleared the table after supper, Paul left the kitchen and returned with a notebook and several pencils. He began writing with such a fierce look of concentration on his face, Hazel returned to the sink without asking him what he was doing.

After she finished the dishes, Paul was still at it. He looked so tired, Hazel made a fresh pot of coffee. "You want some coffee, Paul?"

He set down the pencil and rotated his neck, grimacing. "Thank you kindly. I'm gonna be at this awhile. I have to write down everything Ernest needs to do."

"Does Ernest even know how to read?"

"Barely. Not enough to say so."

"Then—"

"I sure would appreciate that coffee, Hazel."

When she set the full pot on the table and poured Paul's first cup, he said, "This here is for you. Ernest needs help getting started with what needs doing." He flexed his writing hand and picked up his cup. "And when."

"And you expect me—"

"He's a hard worker and the most easy-going feller you're ever gonna find. You know he is."

"And you expect me—"

"Yes." He picked up his pencil. "I'm sorry. At least you won't have to explain why. Ernest never questions anything."

At that, Hazel left the room.

PAUL SPENT THE NEXT week getting hay cut and loaded into the barn; chopping wood for the winter; sharpening tools; preparing lye solution for the milking machine; repairing the barn; and putting more tar where the farmhouse roof was prone to leak. Ernest happily tagged along to pitch hay, stack wood, hand over tools, and hold the ladder. *Yes, Paul. Yes, Paul. You bet, Paul.*

Hazel spent the week of Paul's furlough cleaning. There would be little time for housework once she was fully responsible for the farm. As a hedge against the reduced milk yields that were sure to result once Paul left for Fort Devins, she extended the vegetable garden. For Paul to have a farm to come home to after the war, any money that came in had to pay the bank loan and the taxes. And Ernest.

The day before Paul was to leave, instead of drifting back to sleep before she had to get up and prepare breakfast, Hazel felt herself being shaken awake. "Hazel. Hazel. Get up."

She jerked her shoulder from his hand, but he kept shaking. She opened her eyes to see him standing by the bed, already dressed. "Here, put these on."

"What? Why? What are you doing?" She closed her eyes. There was no good reason for him to wake her now. No good reason for him not to stay here, producing that respectable milk yield, tending to the land he had inherited from his father, who had inherited it from his father before him. No good reason he couldn't spend each night entwined with her in the chipped iron bedstead under the eaves, facing the window that overlooked the apple orchard. No good reason at all.

Paul shook her again. "Here, put these on. I need you with me today."

She sat up. "You do?"

"Yes. I got everything wrote down, but I need to show you."

Hazel took the overalls from his outstretched hand. It was going to be a very long day.

Her tears started in the barn as Ernest fumbled with the milking machine, looking up at Paul with his head under his mangled straw hat as empty as the place where his front teeth used to be. The tears continued through the impossibly complicated procedures in the milk house—*Wait, stop, show me that again*—the preparing and serving of biscuits and sausage gravy for breakfast, the heating of beans and opening of pickles for dinner.

The tears did not ease, not even a little, through the driving of the cows to and from the pasture, Hazel stumbling along the dirt track behind the two men, the ambling cows oblivious. Then the same thing all over again for the afternoon milking—the impatient cows, the milking machine, the milk house—*Wait, stop, show me that again*—getting the cows settled for the night.

By the time they were finished, and Ernest headed to his little rattletrap truck to go home, he, *Ernest,* actually gave her a look of pity, guaranteeing more tears through the heating and serving of leftovers for Paul's supper.

Paul poked at his beans, opened a biscuit, smeared butter on it. "You got any questions? You need me to write down anything else?"

Hazel put the cover on the butter dish, took it off, buttered a biscuit for herself. "No, I don't understand any of this. There is no good reason for you to go off and leave me alone here."

"We already been over this." He reached for the saltshaker. "*Will* you stop your infernal bawling?"

"I don't think I can."

Paul pulled a bandana from his overall bib and handed it to her. "Here, blow your nose and eat your supper. No point starving yourself on account of me. It's not like they're gonna send me into combat at my age."

Later, as Hazel waited for Paul in bed, her body felt empty and drained, yet heavy at the same time, as if it were slowly sinking, losing itself in the tangled interior of the old horsehair mattress. The bed creaked as Paul lay down beside her.

"Come here."

She moved closer to him and let him take her in his arms, running her fingers over his warm, smooth skin, the muscles taut and strong beneath the surface. He stroked her hair. Deep within the apple orchard, the lone whip-poor-will sent his insistent cry into the moonless night. Before long, Hazel fell asleep, still expecting to hear an answer to his cries.

Always the Farm

Hazel

July 1943

THE DAY AFTER PAUL left for Fort Devins, cramps woke Hazel before the alarm went off. She turned on the light and got out of bed. Sure enough, she'd bled all over her nightgown and onto the sheets. A load of laundry to soak—and aspirin—before the day had even started.

Ernest knocked on the kitchen door as she was filling the washer tub with cold water, still waiting for the aspirin to take effect. She shook Oxydol into the washer tub. "Come in, Ernest."

When she looked up, Ernest was gazing about the kitchen as if he'd never seen it before.

"Paul in the army now?"

"Yes."

"Where'd he go?"

"Fort Devins."

"Where's that?"

"Massachusetts."

"Did he go on one of the big trains? I never been on one of them, just the Sheldon one."

Hazel picked up the notebook with her daily instructions and ran her finger down the first page, checking to see if the process of the morning milking involved Ernest asking a series of stupid questions. It did not.

"What you got there, Hazel?"

"Paul's instructions. He wrote down everything you need to do."

"He did? Weren't that kindly of him!"

A cow bawled from the barn, faintly, then insistently, before another and another joined in her misery.

"Ernest, please. We need to get started on the milking now."

"Yes, Hazel. You bet, Hazel." He lifted the kerosene lantern off its hook by the door and carefully lit it, smiling all the while.

As Hazel and Ernest entered the barn lugging the first of the milking equipment, twenty-four bovine heads swung in their direction with a *What the hell, Hazel?* expression on their faces.

She and Ernest set to work. Clean the udders and flanks, fit teats to teat cups, turn on the machine. Wait six minutes, no longer! Turn off the machine. Pour the milk from the machine pail into the milk can. Do the same again with the next cow. And the next one and the next one. Lug a full milk can to the milk house, heave it into the cooler. Lug another full can to the milk house. Change the udder-cleaning water. Respond to Ernest's questions about Fort Devins with, "I don't know; he just got there." Avoid the accusatory gaze of twenty-four pairs of unblinking bovine eyes. And there was still breakfast to prepare and buckets of water to heat. Heavy, heavy buckets of water.

At last, after three hours—longer than it ever took Paul, even when he was without a hired man—the morning milking was finished, and

Hazel got Ernest started on lugging the equipment back to the milk house.

When she had breakfast on the table, Ernest walked through the door and announced, "Here's the machine pails, Hazel!" as if she'd won a sweepstakes. He sat at the table and reached for a biscuit.

"Wash your hands, Ernest."

"Yes, Hazel. You bet, Hazel!"

Hazel poured them coffee and checked Paul's instructions as Ernest ate sausage and biscuits. He was to drive the cows to the pasture for the day.

"Do you think you could take the cows to the pasture on your own, so I can finish up here? Then I'll help you with the equipment in the milk house."

"You bet, Hazel. Them cows don't need me to find the pasture. They know the way in their sleep."

Hazel saw the image of Paul's entire herd trotting merrily down the road to run away from home and join the cow circus, each with a little red hobo bundle dangling from her neck. "No, Ernest!"

Ernest stopped in the midst of dumping sugar into his coffee, the same *What the hell, Hazel?* expression on his face the cows had given her earlier. "What's the matter? You know I'll take 'em." He gulped down his coffee, pushed back his chair, and left the kitchen.

As the water finished heating on the stove, Hazel took more aspirin before dealing with her bloody sheets in the washer. She washed the breakfast dishes, then tackled the machine pails and the funnel, the makeshift kitchen sink of the old farmhouse way too shallow for the job.

She plunged her arm in and out of the soapy water, scrubbing with as much force as she could muster. Never before had she been so afraid that unseen strangers, innocently enjoying a glass of cold milk with their meatloaf and mashed potatoes would get sick because she couldn't get the equipment clean enough. She doused it with a bucket of boiling water. Would unseen germs she left behind cause an outbreak? Cholera? Typhoid? Dysentery? What if milk from the Morgan farm killed someone, a child, an infant? She doused the equipment with a second bucket of boiling water.

In the milk house, there was the same worry and fret with Ernest's getting the milking machine clean enough to prevent disease and the loss of Paul's herd, in addition to preventing all those untold strangers from getting sick. But at least they had disinfectant for the milking machine. She could count on disinfectant.

At dinner, Hazel watched Ernest gobble his beans and biscuits, her own gut twisting. She took more aspirin.

"Got a headache, Hazel?"

Oh, God, why did he have to say that? Now she had a headache.

"Ain't you gonna eat?"

"Are you finished with your dinner, Ernest? It's time to water the horses."

Out in the barnyard, Hazel dutifully watched as Ernest pumped water into the trough. "Should their ribs be showing like that?"

From a distance, the two horses had always looked so strong, effortlessly pulling the plow, the mower, the hay wagon as Paul rode confidently behind.

Ernest ran his hand over the dappled gray's back, then the mare's. "Nothin' to worry about. A little swaybacked is all."

A little swaybacked is all. What did it take to break a horse's back? Would they know it was coming, a shift and creak in their bones one morning upon waking, or would it catch them unawares, like lightning striking the roof of the barn, the lightning rods bent and useless against the sky?

The rest of the afternoon brought more buckets of boiling water to clean the empty milk cans after Ernest brought them back from the creamery, the shoveling of manure out of the barn and onto the manure pile, preparations for the afternoon milking.

"Ernest, it's time to sweep the barn."

"Paul don't like a dirty barn."

"Neither do I."

Ernest looked around the manure-spattered walls of the barn as if seeing them for the first time. "Where's the broom?"

"I don't know where the broom is, Ernest. Don't you know where the broom is?"

"Can't say as I do."

Hazel turned her head away, but not in time.

"Why you crying, Hazel? Don't you worry. I'll find that broom."

When she reached the end of Paul's instructions, she could only manage tea and toast for her supper. And more aspirin. She put her dirty dishes in the sink, brushed her teeth, and climbed the narrow stairs to the bedroom Paul had abandoned, the wet bed sheets still in the washer. Sleep came crashing down before the sun had begun its descent below the horizon.

August 1943

Once a week, Llyod Bingham left a letter from Paul in the mailbox, always, always about the farm:

- How many pounds of milk this week?
- Is Ernest keeping the milk house clean?
- Is he tending to the horses?
- How's the weather holding up?

One hot August afternoon, Hazel decided to busy herself with the garden. Who knew what the winter would bring? Her hoe cutting into the rocky soil, she checked each row's vegetables for readiness as she went along, trying to figure how long it would take her to harvest them all.

She straightened up to ease her back. As she wiped the sweat from her face, she noticed a woman she had never seen before and five stair-step children at the end of the garden advancing down the row toward her. The woman wore a baggy print dress covered by an apron similar to the one Hazel herself was wearing.

As the woman drew closer, Hazel saw that she had a dilapidated pair of men's work boots on her feet, the soles held on with some kind of tape. She might have been pregnant under her baggy print dress; Hazel could not be sure. The children, three girls and two boys, were all dressed alike in patched overalls over bare, bony shoulders. All of the children were barefoot. The top stair-step, a freckle-faced boy badly in need of a haircut, looked maybe eight or nine years old. The woman carried a bushel basket, from which she handed out flour sacks to the children.

"My husband said you need some help."

"Your husband?"

"Ernest. Your hired man."

"Ernest sent you?"

They're calling up fathers now.

"Yes. He said you need help."

The shaggy-haired boy held up his sack. "Where do you want us to start, Mrs. Morgan?"

Hazel's eyes stung but from sweat or tears she couldn't tell. "Could you start with the tomatoes? Maybe the little kids could look for cucumbers?"

"You bet!"

Hazel finished the hoeing, then joined Ernest's family in gathering the rest of the vegetables that were ready to be picked, hoping the children wouldn't get too badly sunburned, but not wanting to send them away.

They're calling up fathers now.

The following morning, when Hazel came down to the kitchen and Ernest knocked on the door, his wife stood next to him. "You gonna can?"

Hazel nodded.

"You get Ernest going with the milking, and I'll start sterilizing. Where's your equipment? Down cellar?"

Hazel nodded again.

Ernest beamed. "I told Ardelle to help you."

"I'm very grateful, Ernest." Hazel hesitated. "But not if it's going to take Ardelle away from her own work." This last spoken in a whisper she almost hoped he wouldn't hear.

By late September, the two women had canned and pickled enough food to get both households through the winter, while the apples in the orchard ripened on the trees, as they had for a hundred years.

The Weight of Snow and Regret

Hazel

◆━━━●━━━◆

January 1944

SNOW HAD BEEN FALLING for days, gently sifting from calm, white clouds; tumbling in great masses from a lowering sky; blowing sideways on a bitter wind. No sooner did one storm move out, than another one moved in. Snow obscured the mountains in the distance and the hills in the foreground, obliterated the hollows and valleys below. The apple orchard lay buried in snow, weak protestations of old, brittle branches unheeded.

At night, no light from moon or stars made its way to the bedroom window, just darkness thickened by snow. No night sounds reached the farmhouse. No wind, no lone dog barking, no distant straining of a snowplow. All had been deadened by snow. Even the night sounds of the house itself were deadened, no beams cracking in the cold, no wood shifting in the furnace.

Hazel woke with a start. Something wasn't right. She looked at the illuminated dial of Paul's alarm clock on her nightstand. Quarter past one. She sat up and looked around the room, strained to listen in the deadened silence. Something wasn't right.

She searched her mind for the remnants of a bad dream—but found only the usual fragmented images of working in her sleep: kitchen, barnyard, milk house, barn. She switched on her bedside lamp. The power hadn't gone out. Even so, something wasn't right. She put on her robe and slippers and tiptoed downstairs.

She walked through each room in turn. Nothing was amiss. In the kitchen, she opened the door and peered out. Nothing amiss on the porch either. Nothing knocked over, nothing on the floor that shouldn't be there, except patches of snow blown by the wind. She peered past the porch posts into the night and saw nothing but snow-thickened darkness.

There was nothing for it but go back to bed and try to get some sleep before she had to get up for the morning milking.

She woke again an hour later to an unfamiliar creaking. She sat up and peered into the darkness once more, unable to tell if the sound came from the house settling, from somewhere outside the house, or from inside her own head.

The creaking intensified, then seemed to hesitate, like an old door straining against rusty hinges—until an ungodly rumble reverberated, followed by a crash that shook the house to its foundations and a scream which had to have come from her, even though she knew she hadn't screamed, but who else could it be when she was alone in the house?

She ran down the stairs to the kitchen in her nightgown and bare feet and flung open the door, expecting to see a heap of snow and splintered wood where her clothesline and snow shovel used to be, but the porch was intact, her barn boots standing by the door.

Maybe the crash had been the small roof over the front steps? Paul had been meaning to tear the rickety thing off, but too many day-to-day matters had come first. Once the snow melted, clearing away the rotten, splintered boards would be a nuisance, but there would be no harm done. No one had entered or left the house by the front door in years.

Hazel yanked the door open, only to find snow blowing in her face unimpeded. And something else blew in, that scream she thought must have come from inside her. She shoved the door closed, ran back to the kitchen, and threw open the door. There was no mistaking that scream now and the direction it had come from. Something had happened in the barn, and the screams were from swaybacked plow horses who were beyond help.

Hazel ran back upstairs and dressed as fast as she could, wobbling and teetering through the series of woolly layers and running down the stairs. Nearing the bottom, she lost her footing and fell. When she reached the porch and stomped on her boots, the path leading from the steps had gained another foot of snow since Ernest had finished his chores at the end of the day and headed home. She grabbed the shovel and started clearing a path while the horses whinnied and shrieked and sent great, shuddering groans into the merciless night.

It was no good. Shoveling all that snow would take her forever. She hurled the shovel toward the porch. She'd have to heave her way through it, blowing snow hitting her in the face, thigh muscles aching, toes already numb.

As she neared the barnyard, a shadowy, white-shrouded scene revealed what had happened. The barn roof had collapsed under the weight of the snow.

The horses whinnied and shrieked and groaned under the rubble—but she heard nothing from the cows. They couldn't all have been killed. Couldn't some of them have managed to get out when the rafters had signaled they were about to fall? Animals were intuitive; they had a sixth sense. She turned to look behind her—but there was no circle of cows staring back at her with a *What the hell Hazel?* expression on their faces. They had all been safely tucked away in their stalls with the barn doors closed against the cold when the warning creak came.

Now that she had made it to the collapsed barn, she didn't know what she could do. The farmhouse didn't have a phone, so she couldn't call for help, and Paul's truck was of no use to her. This far out in the country, the roads would be treacherous, if not impassable—and he'd never taught her how to drive. And still the horses screamed and sent great, shuddering groans into the snow-whirled night.

She wasn't strong enough to free the trapped horses, but she could at least sit with them until it was time for Ernest to come for the morning milking, and she could send him for help. She could comfort them, hold their heads in her lap, stroke their foreheads, somehow, somehow ease their pain.

She stepped closer to the rubble and searched for any sign of where the horses might be. In the area where the cries seemed loudest, she bent over and tried to shift a beam. It moved, and when it did, the horses' screams ascended to a whole new level of agony. Oh, God, what had she done?

Her trudge back to the house through the snow was interminable, her feet numb, her woolly layers turning cold and wet. Paul's shotgun was in the hall closet behind his winter overcoat. She found the box of shells on the shelf and shoved the box in her coat pocket.

When she got back to the barn, she yanked off her mittens, loaded the shotgun, and shot into that pile of snow and pieces of roof and broken beams and twisted stanchions until the screaming stopped. She dropped the shotgun, fell to the snow, and wept. Paul would never, ever forgive her.

When Hazel raised her head from where she had fallen, a waxing moon glowed through remnants of clouds. Inexplicably and without warning, the snow that had been falling for so long had stopped.

Hazel got to her feet, retrieved the shotgun from the snow, and trudged back to the house to find the kitchen door open. She closed it and crossed the room to build up the fire in the stove. As she struggled out of her wet clothes, she saw that a bruise from the recoil of the gun had already started to form on her shoulder. She went upstairs to get into the warmest of Paul's clothes she could find: long johns, thermal shirt, sweater, overalls, another sweater, thick wool socks.

Back downstairs, she got a pot of coffee going, returned the shotgun and shells to the hall closet, and dragged a chair to the stove. She huddled next to the stove, trying to figure out how in God's name she was ever going to tell Paul what had happened. How do you put something like that in a letter, slap a stamp on it, and stick it in the mailbox for Lloyd Bingham to send on its way to some poor, old soldier thinking he was getting a letter from home telling him all was well?

Destroying a man's livelihood was much, much worse than any Dear John letter. Wives came and went. When an inherited farm was gone, it was gone. There would never be another to take its place.

Maybe she shouldn't tell him in a letter. Maybe she could wait until he got home. But if she did, then how would she answer his next letter with its questions of milk yield and tending to the horses?

Before long, Ernest burst into the kitchen without knocking. "Hazel, the barn roof caved in!"

She nodded, unable to speak.

"Where's the cows? Where's the horses?"

She shook her head.

"They're dead, ain't they?"

"I couldn't get them out, Ernest. It happened too fast."

"Them was the best cows I ever worked with. They never kicked me. Not once. Not a one of 'em."

Hazel checked the coffee on the stove and brought the pot to the table. "I made coffee. I thought you might need some coffee."

"Thank you kindly, Hazel." He sat at the table and swiped off his toque. "Can I take off my jacket?"

"Please do. I was so cold when I got back from the barn, I built up the fire."

Ernest took off his jacket and arranged it on the back of his chair. He looked at the sugar bowl. "I guess there ain't no work for me now?"

No, Ernest, there is no work for you now. There is no money for you or Ardelle or the five stair-step children, not even a little bit for the bottom stairstep born at the end of December. There is no money for any of you.

"I'm afraid not." Hazel handed him the sugar bowl. "Not without any money coming in from the creamery. Paul's allotment from the army has to pay the bank." She handed Ernest a spoon. He dumped sugar in his coffee and agitated it with the spoon before gulping from the cup.

"I have more canned food down cellar than I can ever eat. You and Ardelle are welcome to take what you need."

"We ain't gonna take food out of your mouth, Hazel. We'll get by. We always do."

"Please—"

"I'll finish my coffee and be on my way."

After the door closed behind Ernest, Hazel poured herself a second cup of coffee, retrieved her writing materials from the cabinet in the parlor, and arranged them on the table before her. She picked up her pen, checked the ink, flexed her hand to stop it from shaking. Then she wrote the letter to her husband telling him the barn roof had collapsed under the weight of snow and killed his herd. And his horses.

Outside the kitchen window, a pink and lavender sunrise spread across the winter sky. Hazel still did not understand how the snow could have stopped falling.

SHE WHO SITS AND WAITS

HAZEL

—◆—

June 1945

A MONTH AFTER GERMANY surrendered, Lloyd Bingham delivered a telegram to the Morgan farm. *COMING HOME 3 JUN PAUL.* The army had discharged him before the war ended.

"What's wrong, Hazel? Is it Paul?"

"Paul's fine." Hazel turned and started walking back to the house. Lloyd called after her, "Your mail, Hazel!" She made a dismissive gesture behind her to leave the damn mail in the box.

She sat at the kitchen table with the telegram in front of her on the worn oilcloth. 3 JUN was tomorrow. Paul would be home tomorrow.

After the barn roof collapsed, she did not receive another letter from Paul for the rest of the war, although he did send a drugstore card for their ninth wedding anniversary. No message, just an acknowledgment of the day.

He would be home tomorrow.

She should make preparations of some kind, clean the house, prepare a celebratory meal, cut a profusion of hydrangeas for the table. She should iron her good dress, curl her hair.

But the house was clean. She'd spent the last year and a half cleaning, right down to stripping every last inch of wallpaper from the farmhouse walls, leaving cracked, mottled plaster and areas of lath exposed where plaster had come away with the wallpaper.

There was nothing left to clean.

With no meat, she did not know what kind of celebratory meal she could prepare. Pickled beets followed by a sunken one-egg cake? That certainly wouldn't warrant a profusion of pink hydrangeas on the table. As for her best dress and her hair, there seemed little point in getting all dolled up for a husband who wouldn't be able to look her in the face when he walked through the door.

Hazel picked up the telegram and leaned it against the sugar bowl. Paul would be coming home tomorrow. No matter her thoughts racing pell-mell in the wrong direction, she had to get ready for him.

She opened the screen door and stepped onto the porch. How could the air be so warm and redolent with early summer, the mountains in the distance so serenely green? She stepped off the porch and headed for the barnyard, hoping to find something she could do to ease Paul's first sight of what was left. Her first sight of the devastation had been shielded by darkness and swirling snow. Paul would be looking at what was left of his great-grandfather's legacy in the bright June sunshine.

Reaching the barnyard, she stood looking at the site where the barn had once stood silhouetted against the sky. The adjacent milk house was still intact, which made the splintered beams, pieces of roof, broken glass, and twisted stanchions look all the worse. Two of the barn walls tilted toward the rubble, on the verge of giving up and joining their splintered fellows.

Weeds and small saplings encroached on the rubble, while trumpet vines staked their claim on the twisted stanchions. Sparrows twittered witlessly from the hayfield, where the first hay of the season would go uncut.

At least there would be no animal carcasses for Paul to find under the wreckage. As soon as the weather turned warm enough, a group of volunteers, including Ernest, had showed up early one morning with heavy equipment to bury the rotting animals in the north pasture, the ruinous smell clogging Hazel's small kitchen as she rolled out biscuits for the men's dinner.

On 3 JUN, Hazel washed her hair and put it in pin curls. She ironed her good dress and set out her good shoes. Paul would have enough to contend with when he arrived at the farm, without being faced with a slovenly wife who didn't love her husband enough to make herself presentable after he'd been away serving his country for two years.

When she changed the bedding on the iron bedstead in their cozy bedroom under the eaves, she couldn't help but wonder as she smoothed the wind-fragrant sheets over the uneven mattress if a child was now out of the question. There were two clean, fully furnished spare bedrooms Paul could claim as his own.

Even so, she baked the one-egg cake and set it on her mother-in-law's fancy cake plate. Her final preparation before changing her clothes and fixing her hair was to make a potato and onion casserole to heat up for Paul's dinner—or supper—depending on when he arrived. His telegram hadn't said.

Hair curled, dressed in her good dress, Hazel opened the kitchen door and sat at the table to wait. Dinnertime came and went, but still she sat and waited, constantly checking her watch in a futile gesture to hold back time.

A little past three, the sound of Lloyd Bingham's truck came through the open door. Hazel watched as Lloyd pulled up to the house and Paul stepped out.

She rose from the table. If she couldn't run off the porch and throw her arms around Paul, she could at least not remain seated as if she hadn't noticed—or cared—that her husband was home after two years away.

Paul dragged his duffle bag from the back of Lloyd's truck and dumped it on the porch. He headed straight for the barnyard to survey the damage, not even stepping foot on the porch to call out for his wife.

Hazel resumed her seat at the table, her cheeks burning. When he returned from the barnyard, would he refuse to eat the food she'd cooked if she offered it? Regardless of whether he would refuse it or not, she should at least have it warm and ready.

She built up the fire in the stove, put Paul's supper in the oven, and set the table with her mother-in-law's best china. She resumed her place at the table.

Paul didn't return to the house for another hour. He grabbed his duffle bag, and Hazel rushed to open the screen door for him.

As he heaved the duffle bag to his shoulder, he said, "I gotta get out of this goddamn uniform."

Each of Paul's footfalls on the steep, narrow stairs landed heavy, and when his duffle bag hit the floor, the thud sent bits of loosened paint and plaster drifting from the ceiling. Hazel took the casserole out of the oven and resumed her place at the table.

When Paul joined Hazel at the table at last, he was dressed in his usual barn clothes of overalls and a buttoned summer shirt. He had some gray at his temples and another line or two where his eyes were accustomed to squinting against the sun, but otherwise he looked the same. Maybe things between them could still be the same, after all?

Hazel served him his casserole and said grace. He immediately went for the saltshaker. "That roof over the front door's got a bush growing out of it. How did that happen?"

She had no response to that, and they ate Paul's homecoming meal in silence.

He refused a piece of homecoming cake but accepted the offer of coffee. He now drank it black. "I need to figure out what I'm gonna do. I can put the equipment in the milk house to rights, but the bank will never set me a loan to rebuild the barn and replace the herd. I ain't paid off the last loan. And that old truck ain't gonna hold together much longer."

He picked up his cup and took it into the parlor where he kept all his paperwork for the farm and their household expenses, leaving Hazel alone in the kitchen to wash the supper dishes and figure out what she was going to do. The only solution she could think of was to change out of her good dress, crawl into bed, and cry herself to sleep in the warm summer twilight.

She didn't know how long she'd been asleep when a creaking jounce woke her. Night had fallen, the moonlight through the window casting shadows in the room. Paul lay motionless and silent beside her.

She had to say it. Even if the faintest of whispers, she had to say it. "I'm sorry, Paul."

"For what?"

"The barn, the animals."

Paul remained silent, staring into the shadowy eaves, his profile sharp in the moonlight. If he stayed like that all night, Hazel didn't think she could bear it. Her heart would race and thunder like a runaway horse until her chest collapsed and she stopped breathing.

Finally, he spoke. "It weren't your fault, Hazel. I shoulda asked for that deferment. If I'd been here, I would have shoveled the roof."

He took her in his arms and kissed her. Before dawn lightened the leafy trees in the old apple orchard, he had given her hope for a child.

LAST CHANCE

HAZEL

August 1945

HAZEL AND PAUL JOLTED into St. Albans in Paul's beat-up old truck. Two months after the army, he had been unable to find a job, and his muster-out pay was about to run out. The new Employment Services Office in St. Albans seemed his last chance.

He parked in front of the Employment Services Office, helped Hazel from the truck, and started up the walk. "Ain't you coming with me?"

Hazel took a step toward him. The inside of the Employment Services Office would be a haze of smoke as the men waited their turn to sit before a man with slicked-back hair and government forms waiting for the wrong answers. She couldn't bear the thought of Paul's face when the man told him no.

"Would it be all right if I wait for you in the park? I'm afraid I'd be in the way."

"Oh. I guess I can come find you when I'm done. Don't go too far."

"I won't."

Hazel hurried across the street to sit by the fountain in hopes the sound of splashing water would provide a brief respite from worrying about Paul. She reached the fountain, only to find that the source of the water was a small jug held much too carelessly by a bored young woman in barely-there clothing. Didn't this foolish young woman understand how easily a supply of clear, fresh water could run out or become contaminated?

Hazel didn't know how long she'd been sitting by the fountain when she thought she heard someone call her name. She looked around but didn't see anyone, so she stayed as she was.

When she heard her name again and looked up, Paul was advancing toward the fountain with a man she had never seen before at his side. The man was in shirt sleeves and a tie, his suit jacket slung over one shoulder. She scrambled to her feet, smoothed the front of her dress, and walked toward her husband.

When they got within speaking distance, Paul called out, "Look who I run into at the Employment Office."

The man Paul had run into at the Employment Office beamed at Hazel as if they were old friends. He looked pleasant enough, but she had no idea who he was or why both he and Paul would think that she knew him—or should know him.

The man stuck out his hand. "Dwight Demers. Paul and me go way back. I was a hauler for the creamery when he first started bringing in the milk for his dad."

"Pleased to meet you, Mr. Demers."

"Likewise. Call me Dwight."

"Dwight was elected the new Overseer of the Poor for Enosburg at town meetin' this year," Paul announced, as if being Overseer of the Poor were something for Paul to be impressed by and Dwight to be proud of. He'd undoubtedly run unopposed. What person in his right mind would want that kind of responsibility over other people's lives?

Obviously, it had been a mistake for her not to accompany Paul into the Employment Services Office. She made a show of looking at her watch. "Paul, I think we'd better start heading back now. I have a washing to do. And your dinner. It's getting on to noon."

"Dwight has something he needs to talk to us about," Paul said.

"Tell you what, Hazel. I'll run over to Ted's across the street there and get us some sandwiches." Dwight tossed his jacket at Paul. "Here, find us a bench."

"Paul, what is going on? I thought you were going to the Employment Office to see about a job."

"Hazel, I just bumped into him. He's an old buddy."

"We have plenty of food left down cellar. We don't need a town order for food. Why is he buying us sandwiches?"

"I didn't ask him for a handout, if that's what you're thinking. I told you, Dwight's a buddy."

"Then why is he buying us sandwiches? He didn't even ask us what kind we wanted!"

"Will you calm down and stop getting yourself all riled up, for once?" Paul put a firm hand on her back and steered her to one of the long benches facing Main Street. "Sit down and let me explain."

Hazel was already fighting back tears, but she did as she was told and sat on the bench.

"The Employment Services Office is new, and Dwight was in there to see about sending able-bodied indigents to register for work instead of sending them to the poor farm. When the two of us got to talking, he told me he heard about the barn and the herd."

Of course, this Dwight Demers would have heard about the collapse of the barn and the death of Paul's herd at her hands. Everyone in

Franklin County had heard about the collapse of the barn and the death of Paul's herd.

"There's a job open at the Sheldon Poor Farm, and he said he'd put in a good word for me. The job involves you, so we wanted to talk to you before we went any further with it."

"No. No poor farm. No." How could Paul suggest such a thing? How could he even *consider* it? Hazel wanted to jump up, run back to the farm, and hide in the hayloft. But she couldn't run back to the farm because her feet hurt in her good shoes, and she couldn't hide in the hayloft because it was gone.

Someone was running across the street holding a paper bag aloft and shouting about sandwiches.

"Here we are," Dwight said, plopping himself onto the bench between Hazel and Paul. "Three ham and cheese." He handed them over like he was hosting a party, dipped his hand back into the bag, and held up something wet and green wrapped in waxed paper.

"Pickle?"

"No!"

"Fair enough, Hazel. Dill pickles aren't to everyone's taste. I prefer a good bread-and-butter myself. Although watermelon are mighty tasty, too."

Hazel unwrapped the sandwich, lifted the top slice of bread to check what might be smeared there, and took a bite. If Paul's friend paid for a sandwich, she was obliged to eat it. Eat it and be grateful.

"I know you have a washing to do, Hazel, so I'll get to the point. Paul needs a job to get back on his feet, and Sheldon Poor Farm needs a new manager. The job went out for bid today, and I think Paul should apply. I can't guarantee it, a'course, but I'm on very good terms with the Association."

Dwight took a bite of the pickle, made a face, and tossed it in the general direction of some birds, who apparently also preferred a good bread-and-butter.

"We need to get somebody reliable in there who knows what he's doing. The last one left the place in a god-awful mess. He was hired to live in, but he went back to his place in Highgate every night and left the house in charge an inmate who couldn't pound sand in a rathole with the rat helping him."

"I am *not* living in a place with rats."

"No, no, it's filthy, but no rats. Maybe in the barns. I don't know. I wouldn't want to mislead you about that, Hazel. There may be rats in the barns." Dwight took a bite of his sandwich. "In any event, the bid is for two jobs: a manager and a matron. The manager takes care of the farm, obviously, animals, fields, supplies, paperwork, and so on. The matron takes care of the cooking, cleaning, laundry, and whatever else, helps the feeble-minded get dressed, that sort of thing. Some of the folks are bedridden, so there's nursing involved."

"Hazel nursed my mother before she passed," Paul said.

"The contract is for one year. There will be no obligation to apply for renewal."

Before Hazel could say anything, Paul said, "I need to go home and talk it over with Hazel. Can you stop by our place tomorrow evening, and I'll give you my answer?"

GONE TOO FAR

HAZEL

August 1945

WHEN DWIGHT DEMERS LEFT Hazel's kitchen the following evening, he wore the self-satisfied look of a man who had received not only the answer he was looking for but fresh-brewed coffee and a plate of homemade doughnuts to go with it.

Two weeks later, Lloyd Bingham delivered Paul's acceptance letter from the Sheldon Poor House Association. This envelope spent no time leaning against the sugar bowl waiting to be opened.

"Well, I guess that's that," Hazel said. "Time to start packing."

"You don't need to start packing right this second. Job don't start for another two weeks."

She pushed back her chair. "I'm going to the big shed to look for some boxes."

"You don't need to start packing right this second. Why don't you make me some coffee?"

Hazel went to the stove and tilted back the lid of the coffeepot. "There's still some from breakfast." She set the pot on the table just out of Paul's reach. "I'm going to the big shed for some boxes."

Returning from the shed, she threw four prewar grocery boxes on the floor. "These are the only ones I could find that weren't already full of crap."

Paul looked up from his coffee. "You better watch your mouth, Hazel. You're acting like a child."

"No, Paul, I'm not. I'm being practical. If we have to move, I need to pack. What are we supposed to be taking with us?"

"Our clothes and personal things. I told you, you don't need to start packing right now. It won't take you long." Paul fished something out of his coffee with his little finger. "We should probably bring our own bedstead and bedding. The last inspection found bedbugs in a couple rooms. Maybe taking our own dresser wouldn't be a bad idea either."

"Bedbugs! No, Paul. No. I am telling you no."

Paul's chair creaked as his leg jiggled under the table. "There ain't no need to get yourself all riled up. I'll have the place fumigated."

"And where are all those bedridden old people supposed to go while the place is being fumigated? The fumes will kill them. You can't very well haul them outside and dump them in the yard."

"The Association can replace all the mattresses, then. They said they was serious about cleaning the place up."

"You believed them?"

"I did. The state of the place already made the *Messenger*. The Sheldon Poor House Association don't want to make themselves look bad."

"Looking bad never seemed to bother them before." Hazel took the empty coffee pot to the sink, rinsed it out, and set it back on the stove. "So, we'll be taking the bedstead and the dresser for furniture and our clothes. What about everything else?"

"That'll stay here."

"What do you mean? We're going to leave everything?" Her voice rose. "We're going to abandon the house and everything we own to go to the poor farm?"

"The house ain't going nowhere. And we ain't being sent to the poor farm, for Christ's sake. We're taking a job."

"You couldn't get any other kind of job? The Employment Services Office couldn't get you any other kind of job besides the poor farm?"

"Look, Hazel, it's honest work, and my muster-out pay is about gone. Who knows how long it would take the employment services people to find me something we could live on? I ain't getting any younger. I was in there with a room full of vets in their twenties. Besides, the Association's in a bind with needing somebody they can trust to put the place to rights."

"And that would have to be you. It always has to be you. You know what, Paul? If the roof of this house collapses next winter, you can't blame it on me."

Paul got up from the table and grabbed her wrist. "You've gone too far, Hazel." He flung her wrist aside and walked out the door.

Hazel knew she had gone too far. She knew with the same certainty the sun would rise and set each day whether she had a husband to provide for her or not that she had gone too far.

She ran onto the porch and down the steps. Paul was nowhere in sight. She didn't dare call out for him. She had gone too far for that. She made a circuit of the farmhouse, stopping to fling open the splintered bulkhead doors and peer into the cellar, even though Paul was not one to hide in a cellar like a rat.

He was most likely standing like the wrath of God in front of the pile of rubble that had once been his barn, cursing her name. But at least his truck was still in the dooryard. He hadn't driven off and left her.

She stood sweating in the midday sun and picked at a splinter in her finger before retrieving the prewar grocery boxes from the kitchen, descending into the cool, damp cellar, and lighting the lantern.

She would pack up as many of her remaining canned goods as would fit in the boxes to take with them to the poor farm. No point in letting good food go to waste.

Suppertime came and went with no sign of Paul. Hazel set his place at the table, left a covered skillet of hash on the back of the stove, and went upstairs to bed.

When Paul returned to the house two hours later and joined her in their bedroom under the eaves, he smelled of summer twilight and a day spent in the shadows of the woods. He lay heavy beside her until dawn lightened the window overlooking the old apple orchard, and she finally dropped off to sleep.

Fresh Start

Hazel

September 1945

THE DAY OF THE move, Paul loaded the truck with the few belongings they would need at the poorhouse, secured the load, and covered it with a tarpaulin. As the truck rattled down the driveway, Hazel turned around for one last look at the farmhouse, the rickety roof over the front door still clinging to the house, the bush still growing from it, the piece of gutter still hanging down. "What's going to happen to the farm?"

"Nothing."

"Will you sell it?"

"Don't be foolish."

Hazel knew better than to take it any further. Paul would do with the farm as he saw fit, when he saw fit to do it, and not a moment before. Halfway to Sheldon, she realized too late she'd forgotten to ask Paul to bring up the canned goods from the cellar.

All too soon, Paul turned onto Poor Farm Road, its rutted dirt surface jostling the load in the back, setting Hazel's teeth on edge.

He slowed the truck to avoid a pothole, allowing her a clear view of the cemetery under the trees, dappled sunlight playing over ragged rows of small, tilting gravestones, each simple stone large enough for names and dates. Nothing more.

The truck labored up a small rise, and the Sheldon Poor Farm came into view, barns and sheds on the right, poorhouse on the left. The poorhouse was as Hazel remembered it: a long, three-story warehouse of a building that looked exactly like what it was: not a house at all but a collection of rooms with numbers on the doors to contain abandoned people with no place else to go.

On the porch, two women of about Hazel's own age slumped in rocking chairs, as if whatever misfortune had befallen them had knocked the stuffing right out of them. A cluster of bedraggled children gathered at their feet, staring at Paul's truck in a silent entreaty to take them away from this awful place, back to the homes where they belonged. Off to the side, a morose infant surveyed the scene from its apple crate prison.

Paul brought the truck to a stop next to a sedan covered in a fresh coating of road dust. "Barns could use some paint." He turned off the engine, opened his door, and hopped from the truck. "May as well get started."

A man in a suit emerged from the poorhouse and approached the truck. Hazel recognized him as the director of the Sheldon Poor House Association, one of several men in suits who had launched questions at Paul and her through clenched teeth the day of the interview. She couldn't remember his name, just that she hadn't liked him.

He shook Paul's hand, then looked at Hazel through the windshield of the truck. When Hazel obeyed his unspoken order and got out of the truck to stand at Paul's side, the Association man pulled a face. So what if she'd arrived at the poor farm dressed in her husband's overalls, with her hair tied up in a bandana? She'd come dressed to work. That's what they wanted, wasn't it?

"You remember my wife Hazel," Paul said.

The man gave Hazel a half-nod. "Mrs. Morgan."

Hazel gave a half-nod in return.

"All right, then." The Association man headed for the front door of the poorhouse. "I'll show you the manager's suite and be on my way."

For a moment, Hazel wished they had been met instead by Dwight Demers. Dwight at least was cheerful—probably to a fault, but still. The Association man opened the door and motioned for Hazel to enter first.

It was hard to make anything out in the darkened front hall—a staircase, a radiator, a narrow table of sorts—but there was no mistaking the smell, a stench of unwashed bodies, dirty clothes, soiled linens, urine, stale cigarette smoke, and garbage.

Hazel took a step back. There was no way. There was no way she was going to spend a single night in that place. Paul would have to find another job. That's all there was to it. His arm went around her shoulders in a way that carried no comfort.

"As you can see," the Sheldon Poor House Association man said, "the place is a pigsty. There is no excuse for the place to look like this, no excuse whatsoever, not when we pay a manager and a matron good money to look after things."

Now that her eyes had adjusted to the dim light, Hazel could see that the front hall was full of trash, tossed into random boxes and strewn on the floor.

The Association man pointed to a door to the right of the front door. "This here's the office to do your paperwork. The farm reports are in order, more or less, but the household accounts haven't been kept up. Mrs. Morgan, I am going to insist that you itemize the household expenses, most especially what you're spending on food."

Paul's arm stayed around Hazel's shoulders. "I'll make sure all the accounts are in order."

"See that you do. We're talking taxpayer money. Which reminds me, you don't need to call the doctor out here for every little sniffle."

The Association man set off down the hall, Paul following behind. Hazel trailed her husband, sweeping pieces of trash aside with her foot, each sweep sending up yet another vile odor. The Association man stopped, unlocked a door, and handed the key to Paul. "Here's the manager's suite. Helpers' rooms are on this floor. You'll have to make do for the time being. I fired the lot of them last week. Inmates' sleeping rooms are on the second and third floor. You'll want to keep this door locked."

He pushed the door open and took a step inside what looked like a sitting room outfitted with a forlorn tufted couch, two mismatched armchairs, a table or two, and a tiny kitchen. The room didn't actually look too bad, plenty dusty but not dirty, the net curtains needing to be washed, but not ripped down and dumped in the trash.

"Bedroom's through there. Any questions? I need to get going."

"We'll be fine," Paul said.

Hazel knew better than to tell the Association man they were not going to be fine. Far from it.

AFTER PAUL ABANDONED HER for the barn, Hazel wandered into the bedroom. To her surprise, it was larger than their bedroom at home, with two windows overlooking an expansive field bordered by dense woods. The bedroom even came with its own bathroom, including a bathtub with two faucets.

She turned the faucet on the left, waited, and put her hand under it. The water was hot! She wouldn't have to heat water. She had the worst mess in her life to clean up, but at the end of each day, there would be a hot bath at the twist of a faucet.

She wiped her hand on her overalls. She would start with the trash in the front hall. It was bad enough for a person to be hauled off to the poorhouse without rubbing her nose in it as soon as she walked through the front door.

Back in the hall, Hazel was once again assaulted by the smell of so many unwashed bodies, so much spoiled food, so much soiled linen, so much filthy clothing not fit to touch human skin. As much as she didn't want to, she knew she was obligated to seek out the human sources of those smells. But not now.

As she was on her knees tossing trash into one of the boxes, a figure appeared at the end of the hall, a small man not much larger than a thirteen-year-old boy.

As he drew closer, Hazel saw that he was dressed very neatly, in trousers and a plaid shirt buttoned all the way up. His shirt was tucked into his trousers, which were held up with a belt. His clothes were filthy, his hands and face were filthy, and the hair on his abnormally large head was matted and shaggy. He had such a happy expression on his face it was hard to gauge how old he was, possibly her own age, possibly a few years older?

Hazel scrambled to her feet and dusted off her hands on her overalls. "Can I help you?"

"I'm Joey. I live here."

Joey? Surely not. It couldn't be. Hazel hesitated. "Pleased to meet you, Joey. I'm Mrs. Morgan."

"Are you here to take care of us?"

"I—yes, I guess I am." Somehow, in all of the back-and-forth with Paul about returning to the poor farm, she hadn't thought about that. Cooking, cleaning, and seeing to the feeble-minded and infirm wasn't a job one could take or leave. People needed clean clothes, healthful meals, and a clean bed to sleep in at night to live a decent life, even in a place like this.

Joey's face had gone from happy to beaming. "Can I help? I know how to pick up trash. See?" He bent down, picked up a piece of newspaper, and set it in the nearest box.

He was Joey, all right, still at the poor farm after nearly twenty years, still oblivious to the squalor and despair that surrounded him.

"Thank you, Joey. Do you think you could pick up some of this trash on your own? I have to go see to the others."

"You bet! I like to pick up trash."

Hazel began to ascend the first flight of stairs, which were also strewn with trash. That would be all she and Paul needed their first day on the job, a series of elderly bodies tumbling down the stairs to land with a sickening thump at the bottom, their dead eyes staring at the dead flies in the light fixture. She retrieved one of the boxes from the front hall and picked up the trash as she went along.

On the second floor, she found four bedridden women whose rooms reeked of urine. They appeared to be asleep. Or dead. She waited in each doorway until she saw evidence of breathing. They were going to need a great deal of care.

The rest of the women's side yielded a dozen or so elderly women, most of whom had gotten dressed and combed their hair, each sitting on her bed staring out the window. When Hazel knocked on the open door of each room, its occupant turned her head, asked, "Who are you?" then went back to staring out the window. To her question, "Do you need anything?" they gave no response. The rooms hadn't been cleaned in quite a while, but they were reasonably tidy and hadn't reached the level of squalor that the smell in the front hall suggested.

The squalor was reserved for the men's side: overflowing ash trays, newspapers and trash strewn about, men's drawers so dirty they looked as if they had never been washed. Ever. All overlaid with a pall of sweat and other body odor she didn't want to think about.

Without exception, the window in each room was closed, despite the warm day. Most of the dozen or so elderly men sat on their beds smoking. She would have to ask Paul to speak to them about smoking in bed; it wouldn't take much to send the whole building up in flames. She would also insist that the men carry down their own dirty drawers and put them in the washer. As each man spotted her, he invited her into his room, an invitation she promptly declined.

Eight more people were on the third floor in the same situation as those on the second floor. At least none were bedridden. How could these people bear to sit on the bed and stare out the window all day? If all she had to do was sit and stare out the window, she'd go out of her mind.

Maybe their minds were already gone, with nothing left to think about, not even memories, and nothing to live for, just the color of the sky, the shape of the clouds, and the occasional bird flitting past on its way to someplace else.

In the front hall, Joey had made quick work of the mess. All the trash had been picked up and the boxes taken away somewhere. Joey stood at attention by the newel post. When Hazel reached the bottom of the stairs, he announced, "Edna knows how to sweep. I'll go get her." He bustled off and returned a few moments later holding the hand of a dumpy woman wearing a grimy dress and a hangdog expression. She stood in front of Hazel with her head down, looking at the floor.

"This is Edna," Joey said. "She knows how to sweep. Her mother showed her. Her mother's in heaven now."

"Where's my broom?" Edna said.

"I'll go get it." Once again, Joey bustled off down the hall.

Hazel thought she should say something to the poor woman, who looked as if she were expecting someone to box her ears.

"Do you like to sweep, Edna? You don't have to sweep if you don't want to."

"I like to sweep. I swept after dinner once."

Dinner. Hazel had to make dinner—and supper after that and breakfast after that—for how many people had Dwight told her? Twenty-five, thirty? She'd never cooked for that many people before. If the kitchen was as filthy as the front hall, she would have to clean it before she could even think about preparing food there. She looked at her watch. Ten-thirty.

"What time do you eat dinner, Edna?"

"When I'm hungry."

Joey arrived with the broom and dustpan. He handed Edna the broom. "Edna sweeps. I do the dustpan."

"Joey, could you tell me what time you eat dinner?"

"When the big hand and the little hand are straight up."

"Do you think you and Edna could work here on your own so I can get dinner for everybody?"

"You bet!" Joey said. "Kitchen's right there."

The kitchen was as filthy as she'd expected, every surface covered in grease, including the ceiling and the floor. The teetering pile of dirty dishes in the sink went without saying. She opened the refrigerator to find mildew and a bowl of something brown dotted with mold. Both ovens had enough baked-on crud to set them ablaze if someone attempted a batch of biscuits.

There was no way she could get the room clean and prepare dinner in time to serve when the big hand and the little hand pointed straight up. She was thankful she'd thought to borrow a pair of Paul's overalls.

Cleaning this much crud would ruin a house dress, even with an apron covering it.

God help her, sandwiches were the only option. Was there any bread? She found several loaves of store-bought bread in the pantry and a five-gallon tub of peanut butter, along with a large box of oatmeal. Peanut butter sandwiches would have to do.

There was a large table in the middle of the room, and she set about scrubbing it to make a clean workspace for preparing the sandwiches. As she stood at the sink rinsing out her rag, a voice behind her demanded coffee. She smelled the voice's owner before turning around to find a man in dungarees and a ripped flannel shirt who looked as if he had been locked in a closet for a month. Her stomach lurched, and she opened the window above the sink.

"Who're you?" the man said. "I want my coffee."

"I'm Mrs. Morgan, the new matron. My husband is the new manager. Who are you?"

"Carl. I want my coffee. Now."

"Carl—"

"I want my coffee now!" He stamped his foot. "Now, now, now!"

Hazel put the table between herself and Carl. "You need to calm down, Carl. I'll make a pot of coffee to go with your dinner. But first I need to *make* dinner."

Carl pounded his fist on the table. "Coffee! Now, now, now!"

She was about to shove the table at Carl to give herself a second or two to run past him and make her escape when a skinny man with a walrus mustache rushed into the room and grabbed Carl's arm. "Cut the shit, Carl. You leave this nice lady alone. You already had your coffee at breakfast. You don't get coffee again till dinner. Come on, let's go." He led Carl from the kitchen.

Hazel wiped the table again, paying particular attention to the spots where Carl's fist had landed, all the while willing her hands to stop shaking. When she returned from the pantry with the bread and peanut butter, the man with the walrus mustache was standing in the kitchen. He looked somehow familiar.

"You okay, miss? I thought I best come back and check on you. Carl ain't dangerous, but he sure is a pain in the ass. When God was handing out the brains, he heard *train* and run t'other way."

"I'm okay. Thank you for rescuing me."

"T'weren't nothin'. Happens all the time."

"It does? Are you sure he's not dangerous?"

"Like I said, he's a pain in the ass, but he ain't dangerous. You the new matron?"

Hazel nodded.

"Kinda young for the job, ain't ya?"

"My husband is the new manager," Hazel said, as if being married to Paul were sufficient qualification for the job.

"Well, I hope he's better'n the last one. He was about as useless as Carl. I'd give you a hand with them sandwiches, but I best keep an eye on Carl. No telling what he'll do when he gets himself all het up like that. Sing out if you need anything. I'm Philo, Philo Roy."

Before she could say, "Don't you remember me?" Philo Roy was gone, leaving behind a faint scent of dirty gabardine.

Hazel made the sandwiches, found two platters that seemed clean, and descended the stairs to the inmates' dining room in the basement. While she was there, she found what must have been a vegetable cellar, which contained bushel baskets of cabbage, shriveled potatoes, wilted carrots, and lumps that had to have been turnips at one point. She'd see what she could salvage tomorrow. Maybe make a pot of soup. She'd have to ask Paul to retrieve the canned goods from Duffy Hill.

She set the sandwich platters on the table and returned to the kitchen to make a pot of coffee. When the coffee was ready, she located a trivet and took the pot to the dining room. Then she went upstairs to call the second and third floor inmates to dinner.

Back downstairs, she informed the two mothers on the porch that dinner was ready, before finding a room that looked like a living room, down the hall from the manager's suite. Joey and Edna sat side by side on a couch looking as content as two cows in clover. Philo Roy perched on the arm of an overstuffed armchair as he smoked a cigarette. In the chair itself sat Carl, with a pout on his face a cantankerous six-year-old would have found hard to beat. As soon as he caught sight of Hazel, he started hollering about his coffee.

Philo Roy smacked the side of his head. "Will you shut *up*, Carl? Jesus H. Christ."

"The big hand and the little hand are straight up!" Joey shouted, pointing at the clock on the wall. He jumped up and grabbed Edna's hand. "Come on, Edna! Time for dinner!" Joey went running out the door, dragging Edna behind him.

"You best go after him," Philo Roy said. "He likes to put his hands all over the food. Me and Carl here will round up the others."

Sure enough, in the inmates' dining room, Joey was holding two sandwich halves, discussing the merits of each with Edna. He put both back on the platter and took two more.

"No, no," Hazel said. "We don't handle the food. You need to eat the sandwich you're holding. That one's yours."

"I want the best one."

"You have the best one. I made the sandwiches myself, so I know which one is best."

When all the inmates had straggled in and seated themselves at what Hazel guessed were their regular places at the table, the men at one table, the women at a separate table, she asked if they needed anything. They all looked at her with mouths agape, as if no one had ever asked them that question before.

When no one responded, Hazel ran up two flights of stairs to tend to the bedridden women. She spent the rest of the day getting them fed, bathed, and into clean nightclothes and clean bedding—after she'd called Dr. Wetherbee to come out and treat their bedsores, the Association man be damned.

The first night in their new bedroom, with a cool evening breeze drifting through the open windows, Hazel turned to Paul and said, "The people staying here shouldn't be called 'inmates.' Being old or down on your luck or feeble-minded doesn't make you a criminal."

Already asleep, Paul gave no response.

The next month was a blur of scrubbing walls, scrubbing floors, scrubbing toilets, scrubbing sinks, scrubbing tile, ferreting out spoiled food to throw away, and washing load after load after load of laundry. If she hadn't had Joey and Edna to hang the clothes and linens on the line and bring them back in when they were dry, Hazel didn't know what she would have done.

Then one day, while Hazel and Paul were eating their supper in the manager's suite, a knock came at the door. When Paul answered it, there stood Dwight Demers holding an armload of paper rolls of some kind, grinning from ear to ear. Paul stepped back to let Dwight enter.

"You folks up for hanging some wallpaper, Paul?" Dwight said.

"What?"

"You up for hanging some wallpaper? Look what I've got! I cleaned out Harold Stanley's entire stock of discontinued wallpaper. Hazel's done such a good job of getting the house all nice and clean, I thought some wallpaper might brighten up the place for the next inspection."

"How'd you manage that?" Paul said. "You told me the Association wouldn't approve money to paint the barns this year—and the barns need paint more'n this house needs wallpaper."

"Harold's a Lions' buddy of mine. We got to talking one night, and I asked him if he had any discontinued wallpaper he needed to unload.

We went to take a look at it, and I convinced him it was too shopworn and ugly for anyone to buy, even at a sidewalk sale, and I'd be happy to take it off his hands."

Hazel turned to Paul. "What do you think?"

"Up to you. I ain't got time to fool with no wallpaper."

Hazel got the wallpaper hung barely in time for the next inspection, the Sheldon Poor House Association man showing up unannounced. She was finishing the dinner dishes when she spotted his sedan through the kitchen window. She wiped her hands on her apron and went to meet him at the door.

"Wipe your feet."

The Association man looked as if she'd slapped him across the face. "I beg your pardon?"

She pointed to the new doormat. "Wipe your feet. I won't have you tracking dirt all over my nice, clean floors."

HOMECOMING DAY

HAZEL

⬦

January 1956

HAZEL LIFTED EACH PIECE of Alice's homecoming outfit from the open suitcase and laid it out on the bed: sweater, leggings, booties, bonnet, even teeny, tiny, little mittens, all in yellow, with a thick double knit carriage blanket to keep Alice warm and cozy on the car ride home. Despite Hazel's best efforts to hide her pregnancy from the poorhouse residents, four months in, Mildred had asked for yarn, needles, and a pattern book. There was no fooling an old woman who had birthed nine babies.

Hazel looked for the nurse through the open doorway of her hospital room, then at her watch. Five minutes past their checkout time, and there was no sign of the nurse. Why was it taking so long to bring Alice to her? There couldn't be anything wrong. Alice had been a little jaundiced at birth, but it had been properly treated and cleared right up. Oh, there mustn't be anything wrong.

What else could be wrong? A baby wouldn't get sick in the hospital. They didn't allow germs to reach the babies, not in a hospital. Hazel eased herself onto the chair by the bed, her stitches aching, the hospital pad bulky between her legs. What if Alice didn't want Paul and Hazel Morgan for her parents, had no use for the makeshift nursery in the manager's suite at the poorhouse, and decided to go to sleep in the hospital and never wake up, lying in her bassinet all gray and still under the harsh fluorescent lights?

If they would bring Alice to the room, she could reassure her. She could explain in her tender new maternal voice that the poorhouse would not be her home. It was only temporary until Daddy got another job and they moved to a proper house where she would have her very own bedroom and a backyard where she could run and play as she grew.

Still no sign of the nurse. Hazel looked at her watch. Paul should have been here by now. What could be keeping him? There couldn't be a crisis with one of the animals. There couldn't be, not on Alice's homecoming day. Maybe Carl was having one of his fits, and Paul had to call the sheriff, Philo Roy having hopped a freight to Florida after the first hard frost.

Maybe Paul had decided, after all their years of trying, that at age fifty, he couldn't face becoming a father. He was too old. Or, maybe, maybe, the car's fuel line had frozen, and he was unable to start it?

Only after seeing Paul sitting in their car in her mind's eye did it occur to Hazel that the roads might be bad, and that was what had delayed him. She rose from her chair and went to the window, which overlooked the hospital parking lot. Snow was falling faster and thicker than she had ever seen snow fall before, the cars in the parking lot mere distant white shadows.

How could she not have known it was snowing? The window was right there, and every afternoon when Paul had come for visiting hours, he had given her the weather conditions for that day and the forecast for the following day. How could she have missed the fact that a bad storm was coming? How could she have been so careless?

The squeak of wet boots on linoleum came down the corridor, and Hazel turned toward the doorway. Paul's head and shoulders were covered in snow after the short walk from the car to the front entrance of the hospital.

"Paul! I was worried when you didn't come."

"I paid the bill soon as I got here. You about ready? The roads are getting bad. I had a devil of a time getting off Poor Farm Road."

"It's not plowed?"

He shook his head and loosened the scarf around his neck, flicking melting snow from his fingers. "Village ain't got to us yet."

"Do you think it'll be plowed by the time we get there?"

"Doubt it. They need to take care of the village roads first. No telling when they'll get to us." He looked around the room. "Where's Alice?"

"The nurse hasn't brought her yet."

"We need to get going. I followed a snowplow on the way in, but that was dumb luck. I best go see what the holdup is."

Paul's boots squeaked down the corridor. After a few minutes, the squeak of the nurse's rubber soles joined the squeak of Paul's boots, and the nurse appeared in the doorway, Alice riding her shoulder like the Queen of Sheba, her eyes open and alert.

"Here she is!" the nurse said, crossing the room to place the Alice bundle in Hazel's arms. "Sorry it took so long. We needed to get your paperwork in order. Do you need help getting her dressed? You can leave what she's wearing on the bed."

"No, thank you," Hazel said. "I can manage." Paul quickly came to her side and helped her up. He stayed at her side all the while Hazel awkwardly got Alice out of her hospital garments and into her homecoming outfit, fragile elbows and knees going every which way.

"She's so small," Paul said. He put out his index finger, as if—despite the urgent need to get her dressed—he wanted Alice to take it. When Alice wrapped her hand around his finger, he looked at Hazel and smiled. She had never seen him smile that way before, and she would never see him smile that way again.

As HAZEL WAITED IN the lobby for Paul to bring the car around, all the talk was of the storm. "Haven't seen the like since the blizzard of '44. . . first time I had to use chains in near two years. . . damn fool idea to come out in this weather, but the wife couldn't go a day without seeing her mother."

Hazel feared that talk of the storm, as loud as it was, would frighten Alice. Why did these people have to talk so loudly? Wasn't there some rule that in a hospital one had to whisper, like in a library? Hazel looked down at her little bundle, adjusting the blanket so she could see her face. Alice was asleep, protected from the intrusive voices of strangers by her blanket cocoon and bonnet.

Hazel turned her attention back to the lobby door. A man dressed in red plaid wool from head to toe was shoveling the entrance walk in a frantic attempt to keep up with the snow, his shovel scraping against concrete only now and then. Paul should have the dooryard plowed, but if Poor Farm Road hadn't been plowed, there would be no clear path to get to the dooryard for Alice's homecoming.

A car with its headlights on pulled up to the entrance and stopped. Paul got out of the car, leaving the engine running, the tailpipe sending feeble wisps of exhaust into the whirling snow. He stopped to say something to the man with the shovel. The man jammed the shovel in the snow and opened the lobby door. As soon as Hazel stepped a tentative foot on the walk, Paul put his arm around her and helped her to the car. "Careful, careful."

Once Hazel was settled in the car with Alice cradled in her arms, she said, "How long do you think it will take us to get home?"

"No telling, depends on the plows." Paul put the car in gear and eased out the clutch. The car rolled forward inch by inch until it reached the parking lot exit, snow creaking under the tires. Paul put on his turn signal and started to make the turn onto Fairfield Street, then stopped and moved the steering wheel back and forth.

"Why are we stopping?"

Paul set the emergency brake and opened his door. "I need to clear the wheel wells." He spent the next several minutes kicking at the packed snow to dislodge it, the car jouncing with every kick.

"Is it going to be like this all the way home?" Hazel said as Paul made another left turn.

"Could be, depends on the plows."

The snow came at the windshield in a dizzying stream, the wipers failing to keep up with it. When they reached the intersection for the main road, Paul applied the brakes, but the car didn't respond. He corrected the steering to avoid the ditch and oncoming traffic and kept going.

"Paul, I'm scared."

He didn't respond.

"Paul, I'm scared."

"You need to let me drive, Hazel. Don't distract me."

"I think we should turn back. The roads are too dangerous."

"It's only a few more miles. I got sandbags in the trunk."

"Couldn't we pull over until the snow lets up?"

"Please, Hazel. You need to let me drive."

Hazel looked down at Alice. She was asleep, unaware that her father had taken her life in his hands and refused to relinquish it to her mother. Hazel looked up, just as the air went out of her lungs in a crush of smashing metal and her head slammed into the windshield.

When the car stopped moving and the world stopped spinning, all was silent, the snow still falling, in front of them whatever they had hit no longer recognizable as anything that would have people in it.

Alice was still safely cradled in Hazel's arms. She wasn't even crying. But there was blood on her blanket, blood on her bonnet. Something sticky trickled down Hazel's face. She put her hand to her forehead. Blood. What a shame the blanket and bonnet Mildred had worked so hard to knit were ruined.

Paul slumped over the steering wheel, blood coming from his head. Hazel wondered how long it would take for help to arrive. The interior of the car was starting to get cold. And still, Alice did not cry.

As Hazel sat in the smashed car waiting for help, she watched the color seep from Alice's face as the blood stilled beneath her delicate skin. She lifted Alice and held her close to her chest to warm her and get her blood moving again, get her lungs breathing again with the rising and falling of her mother's chest. And still the snow kept falling.

Paul groaned and stirred. She would never, ever forgive him.

A Visit from the Association

Hazel

—◆○◆—

August 1968

SWEEPING THE FRONT PORCH after breakfast cleanup, Hazel kept an ear out for any sound from the living room indicating someone had found the plug she'd duct-taped to the back of the television and managed to get the layers of tape off, the plug inserted into the outlet, and the television turned on for more news of discontent, bloodshed, and violence in the streets.

Looking up, she saw Paul advancing toward the house looking grim. Maybe his back was bothering him again, and he needed aspirin?

Reaching the porch steps, he said, "Put that broom down. I need to talk to you."

She shooed one last pile of dirt off the porch and opened the front door to go back inside. "What about? I need to get back."

Paul followed her into the kitchen as she put the broom away. "Get back where? I told you I need to talk to you. What is your problem today? You look about ready to jump out of your skin."

"I need to make sure the residents don't turn on the television." Hazel pushed past him on her way to the hall, but Paul called her back.

"Hazel, sit down. I need to talk to you."

She halted but didn't approach the table. "I can't. I have to get back."

"No. You don't. You need to sit here and tell me what the hell is going on with you."

Hazel looked at her watch. It wasn't time for the news, so maybe she could stay for a moment or two.

No. People didn't get assassinated or beaten bloody by the police on a schedule—and the television people wasted no time in getting cameras on the scene to bedevil innocent people and set off nightmares and memories best left buried.

"I'm sorry, Paul. I have to go."

"Get back here, Hazel. Now."

Something in Paul's voice compelled her to sit at the table to hear him out, however much she didn't want to.

Paul let a full minute go by before he spoke, and when he did speak, he made no mention of needing to know what the hell was going on with her. "Harland Kane called. He's coming over at two to meet with us."

"Doesn't Dwight meet with you about the accounts?"

"It ain't about the accounts. Harland—"

"He needs to meet with Dwight. Dwight knows how hard we've been working to keep expenses down. Dwight will tell him I only buy meat when it's on special. I only buy canned goods when they're on special. I buy the cheapest bread."

"No, Hazel, it ain't the food. He's coming—"

"I don't use the dryer when the weather's warm."

"Hazel, please—"

"Maybe you could start sugaring again next year. That used to bring in good money. We have Petey's mare now to pull the sledge. I'm sure Petey won't mind. He'll want to come along and make sure no harm comes to the mare, but he won't get in your way. Maybe he can help with the buckets."

"Hazel, please—" Paul rubbed his forehead as if whatever he didn't want to tell her had been written there by someone else's hand. "Harland's coming to tell us there ain't gonna be a next year."

"No, he isn't. The Association—"

Paul stopped rubbing his forehead. "It ain't the Association. I been trying to tell you for months. It's the State."

"I don't have to listen to this." Hazel rose from her chair and went to the pantry to check her supply of nonperishables, closing the door behind her. If she could have walked out the front door and driven away, she would have. But she couldn't. She had chicken croquettes to make for ten trusting souls who counted on her to keep them well-nourished and safe from harm.

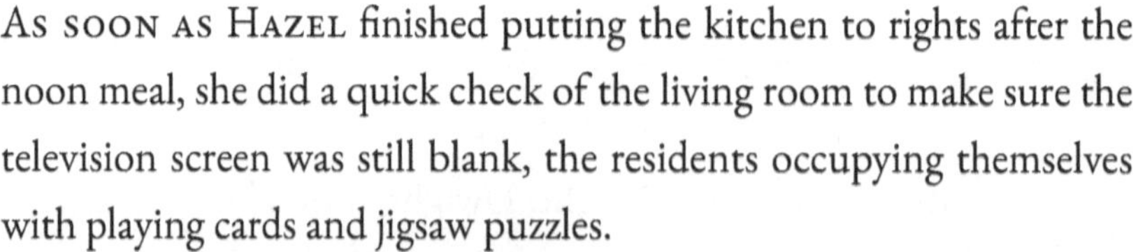

As soon as Hazel finished putting the kitchen to rights after the noon meal, she did a quick check of the living room to make sure the television screen was still blank, the residents occupying themselves with playing cards and jigsaw puzzles.

She changed into her good dress for appearances' sake, got a fresh pot of coffee going, and rummaged through the cupboards to find the cream pitcher that matched the sugar bowl. When Harland Kane arrived in his official capacity, she would be ready for him.

At the appointed hour, Harland's two-tone sedan pulled into the dooryard and parked. Dressed in a suit and tie, Harland got out, bending to retrieve something from the front seat.

The car door slammed. Footsteps up the steps and across the porch. Hearty greeting for Paul, no mention of Hazel. Paul must have been mistaken in thinking Harland wanted to talk to both of them.

Hazel was about to leave the kitchen to change out of her good dress when Paul entered the room. He had not changed out of his barn clothes. "We're in my office. Never mind about coffee. He won't be here long enough for that."

Hazel smoothed her hair and followed him across the hall. Paul's office looked the same as it always did. The same large, battered desk, the same shelves of neatly organized ledgers and report binders, the same sun-rotted window shade. Paul's office couldn't be the setting for bad news. Nothing had changed.

When Hazel entered the room, Harlan got up from his chair and remained standing until she took her seat. He had come prepared for a reckoning, with an officious look on his face, a clipboard, and a stack of file folders he set on Paul's desk.

"Well, Paul, Hazel," Harland said, looking from one to the other, "it's been a long time coming, but the State finally made up its mind. October first they're closing us down for good. I'm just on my way to deliver the overseers' files and the inmates' medical records—"

"Residents, Mr. Kane. Our residents are not criminals." Even to her own ears, her voice sounded loud and harsh.

Before she could say anything else, Paul interjected, "What do you need us to do?"

"To start, I need you to look over these records, make sure no one's missing."

Paul put on his reading glasses, reached for the files, and gestured for Hazel to come around the desk so they could review them together.

Standing at her husband's side, she bore witness to eleven people, eleven lifetimes reduced to a few sheets of paper with notes and random numbers scribbled on them.

"You can't do this," she said, her voice no longer loud or harsh. If only Paul had changed out of his barn clothes.

Paul straightened the small stack of file folders and pushed them back across the desk as Hazel resumed her seat. "That's everybody. What else?"

"Make sure the farm and the household records are in order, particularly expenses. And we'll need you to make a written inventory of everything here—"

"You can't do this," Hazel said.

"—so we can put it all up for auction. Animals, machinery, contents of the outbuildings, contents of the house, everything—"

Harland Kane was paying her no attention at all.

"You can't *do* this to them. This is their home. We promised them they'd always have a home here. Who's going to tell them their home's been taken away?"

Paul shifted noisily in his chair. "Hazel—"

"Where are they supposed to go? Tell me. Where? If they had some place to go, they wouldn't be here, now, would they?"

Paul's chair gave a mighty creak as he came around the desk to stand behind Hazel's chair and put firm hands on her shoulders. "That's enough, Hazel. It ain't his fault."

Harland Kane spoke quickly now. "I've made a list of the farm and household records we'll need. And forms for the inventory." He handed over the clipboard to Paul and reached for the file folders.

"Where are you going with those?" Hazel said.

Harland rose from his chair and scooped up the folders. "I told you. St. Albans Family Services."

"No, you didn't. We need them. A month doesn't give us much time to make other arrangements for the residents. And we'll need to notify their families—those that have any left."

Harland shook his head. "We're out of it now. State's seeing to the arrangements."

Then Harland Kane hightailed it out of there, leaving behind the stuffy room equivalent of a cloud of dust.

Paul's grip on Hazel's shoulders didn't loosen. "You need to get hold of yourself, Hazel."

She shrugged off his hands. "What are we going to do? Who's going to tell the residents? They won't understand what they've done wrong—and we can't even tell them where they'll be going."

"You need to get hold of yourself. We knew this day was coming."

"*You* did. I didn't. I tried to make it work. I tried so hard." Her voice had come out thick with tears as futile as the preacher's striving after wind.

Paul lowered himself onto the chair Harland Kane had vacated. "You can't fall apart on me now." He pulled a clean bandana from the pocket of his overalls and handed it to her. "I need you."

Hazel dried her face, blew her nose, and left the room. She had bathrooms to clean and sanitize.

AFTER SPENDING THE REST of the afternoon listening to the conversation with Harland Kane play on an endless loop inside her head, knocking over an open bottle of Pine-Sol, grating her knuckles on the cheese grater, and lying to the residents every time she opened her miserable mouth, Hazel was just as glad to go to bed early with Paul.

Instead of turning off his bedside lamp as usual after Hazel settled in beside him, he left it on as though he wanted to talk. But he remained silent as he lay there with his closed eyes facing the ceiling, the lamplight casting harsh shadows on his face, deeply lined and creased from years in the unforgiving sun.

Advancing age and a lifetime of hard, manual farm labor had already taken their toll on his body. Before long, he would be truly elderly, and she would need to take care of him the way she took care of the others, monitoring his medications, helping him manage the stairs, calling the doctor when his heart acted up. Would he even let her? And now, did she dare risk a caress to his face?

Dwight Takes Charge

Hazel

September 1968

The following Monday, while Joey and Edna hung bedsheets on the line, Hazel sat at the kitchen table with the unopened Fruitland flyer before her. The table, scarred with knife cuts, disfigured with stains and burn marks, would be auctioned off to the highest bidder in another month's time, with no regard to the intimate conversations over coffee it had witnessed or the meals it had hosted for those who arrived at the door hungry and in need of a kind word. The table would undoubtedly end up in someone's garage with his unwanted junk piled on it, not even worthy of workbench status.

She opened the flyer. Come October first, no one would be taken from this place hungry or malnourished. Not if she had anything to say about it.

But the food was all wrong. The remaining provisions in the pantry didn't go with the Fruitland specials. The Fruitland specials didn't go with each other. Tomato soup stained when eaten with shaky hands. Kidney beans were out of the question. The cheapest meats—pork livers and tripe—weren't fit for human consumption—and why was she worrying about the cost of food in the first place?

Outside, the hens sent up a squawking distress signal as a vehicle pulled into the dooryard. Hazel didn't look up. Whoever it was could turn his vehicle around and drive it straight to the devil.

Whoever it was did not oblige. His vehicle door slammed. His feet crunched gravel, climbed the front steps, and crossed the porch to appear in her kitchen as Dwight Demers in shirtsleeves and loosened necktie, stripped of his official capacity. Despite his lack of official status, he held a small stack of file folders.

"Afternoon, Hazel."

"Afternoon, Dwight."

"Paul around?"

"Out mending fences."

"Good man." Dwight sat at the table, setting the stack of folders in front of him with a little flourish. "You'll tell him I stopped by?"

"Of course." Hazel wondered why Dwight didn't ask for coffee. Did he think he was no longer entitled to it? She rose from the table. "Let me make you some coffee."

"Why, thank you, Hazel. That's very kind."

When the coffee was ready, Hazel served it, and Dwight completed his coffee ritual—pour in cream—stir—spoon in sugar—stir—taste—stir again—tap spoon on cup once to signal he was about to speak. At least that hadn't changed.

"You've been informed of the news, then."

Hazel poured coffee for herself, even though she was jittery enough as it was. "Harland Kane came by yesterday to tell Paul and me the State's shutting us down October first—and we have nothing to say about it. 'We're out of it.' His exact words."

"And the devil take the hindmost," Dwight said. "Those incompetent fools in Montpelier don't know from Shinola. It's not like they haven't proved it time and time again." Dwight picked up his cup, set it down without drinking from it, and gestured with a righteously indignant forefinger. "Mark my words, Hazel, they will end up paying four times the amount we do to keep the same person housed, fed, and doctored. And the care won't be anywhere near as good as what you give them here, not that the State gives a rat's—you know—"

"I know."

"—as long as they get to throw taxpayer money around and pat themselves on the back while our people get dumped in institutions and forgotten."

Dwight stopped speaking and picked up his coffee cup, his face now a mottled red mask. Hazel almost asked him if he was all right, but she feared it would set him off again. He actually looked damaged, as if the State had slammed into him with an anonymous government sedan and kept right on driving, oblivious to the man they'd left bleeding into the pavement.

"I have doughnuts . . ."

Dwight didn't respond. Hazel went to get him one anyway. When she set the doughnut in front of him, he seemed to come to himself as soon as he took his first bite. He patted the stack of folders in front of him. "I'd say it's about time I told you why I'm here. When Harland stopped by my place with the news, I could not believe you and Paul would have no say whatsoever about where your people would go. The State doesn't know these people. You and Paul do. You've been taking care of them for years. That should count for something."

"That's what I've been saying."

"As soon as Harland slunk out of my house like a damn weasel, I got on the horn with the other overseers and talked 'em into making photocopies of their records for me."

Hazel could not imagine what Dwight had said to the other overseers to talk them into giving him copies of their records, and she wasn't about to ask. Say what you would about Dwight Demers, he knew how to call in a favor, and he wouldn't hesitate to do it.

Dwight tapped the stack. "We've got names and phone numbers of the families. Those that have any left. It's not much, but it's something."

"I'll start calling later this afternoon."

"That's the spirit." Dwight drained the rest of his coffee and got up from the table. "I'd better be on my way. I don't want to keep you from your work."

Before he reached the hall, Hazel called him back. "No, wait."

"What is it, Hazel?"

"If their families won't take them, and for those who don't have any family, how will we know where they're going? Harland said Paul and I are out of it. The State will do everything. Will they tell the residents? Can we count on them to drive all the way up here and tell our people where they're going to live? In person? It's the only *decent* thing to do."

Dwight raised an index finger. "Give me a few minutes." He trotted across the hall into Paul's office, which hadn't been kept locked in years. Hazel heard him dial the telephone and speak to someone, seemingly in the official capacity he no longer had.

After no more than a minute or two, he returned to the kitchen, tore the page off a small memo pad and handed it to Hazel. "Here's the name and phone number for the Family Services District Supervisor in St. Albans. She won't be doing any of the work herself, a'course, but she's responsible for the placements. My advice to you, Hazel, is give that woman a week to assign the work to her snotty social workers and then you call her every day for a status on each of those placements.

Every day. Don't let up. She stonewalls you, call me, and I'll go after her myself."

Hazel was about to ask him if he would get in trouble for going after a District Supervisor when Elsie wandered into the kitchen wearing her best dress.

Dwight stood up as soon as she entered the room. "Hello, Elsie. How are you today?"

"I'm well, thank you." Elsie looked from Dwight to Hazel, then back again to Dwight. "Did my daughter send you to get me? I thought she'd come herself."

"No, I'm sorry, Elsie. I don't hear from your daughter."

Elsie plucked at the lace edging of her sleeve. "Has my daughter called, Hazel? I'm worried." She turned her attention to the other sleeve. "She's supposed to come and get me today, but she's late. I'm worried. Do you think she got in an accident?"

Hazel looked at Dwight, who said, "You tend to Elsie, while I help myself to more of your fine coffee."

Hazel shepherded Elsie to her room, helped her change into an everyday dress, and got her settled on her bed with the photograph album of the life she once had.

On her way back to the kitchen, Hazel popped her head into the living room and confirmed that the television screen was still blank. "Everybody all right in here?"

Joey waved. "I'm helping Homer turn the cards. He's winning!"

"I beat Joey at cards once," Charlie said.

"You did not!"

"We're fine, dear!" Flossie trilled. "Not a cloud in the sky!"

Hazel waited until she got an "okay" from Edna, a "yup" from Emmett, and three "ayuhs" from Carmi, Homer, and Lester. At some point, she'd need to check on Petey in the cow barn, but that could wait.

Returning to the kitchen, she found Dwight seated at the table with his shirt sleeves rolled up, scribbling notes on his memo pad, the file folders no longer in a neat stack. He reached across the table and freshened Hazel's coffee without being asked.

"All right, Hazel. Here's what I'm thinking." He tapped his finger on each folder as he called out the name. "Edna Goodhue, Carmi Delude, Flossie Kimball, and the two Shovers don't have any family, so you'll need to keep after that Family Services woman."

"Homer and Lester need to stay together."

"Obviously, the Family Services people should know better than to separate an elderly father and his son who have no one but each other, but I wouldn't put it past 'em. Too much like work to keep them together." Dwight's righteously indignant finger came out again. "They try it, you call me right away, and I'll get the Fairfield overseer down there to demand a 'Come to Jesus' meeting. Hell, I'll even go with him for moral support." He swallowed the last of his doughnut. "You don't need to worry about Charlie and Petey. I'll take care of them, same as I always have. Before those snotty social workers get around to picking up the files, I'll have the arrangements done."

"Won't you get in trouble?"

"Hardly. By the time I finish telling 'em the money the State will save by not sending them to Brandon, they'll think it was their idea and take credit for it to boot." He unrolled his shirtsleeves and buttoned the cuffs. "I'll be on my way now. You'll tell Paul I stopped by?"

As soon as Dwight left, Hazel called Elsie's eldest daughter, who informed her that she would have to talk it over with her sisters, but Hazel must understand they all had families of their own to care for.

"She's your *mother*!"

"Let me talk to the others. I'll get back to you." Click, dial tone.

When Hazel called the East Berkshire number for Emmett's brother, the man who answered the phone informed her that Emmett's brother was dead, and whatever she was selling, he wasn't buying. Click, dial tone. She immediately tried again in case she'd gotten the wrong number. She hadn't, Emmett's nephew surprised the useless old bastard was still alive. Click, dial tone.

Hands shaking, Hazel dialed the number for Joey's sister, whose response was, "Then send him to Brandon," when her family were the ones who had objected to Brandon in the first place. This time, Hazel disconnected first.

Later, when she and Paul were settled in bed for the night, Hazel told him what had transpired that day. His response was not what she expected. "Don't let it get to you. You know how you are when you let things get to you." Then he actually chuckled. "Those State people will soon learn it don't pay to get on the bad side of Dwight Demers."

Hazel couldn't remember the last time Paul had chuckled.

DUFFY HILL

HAZEL

———◆◇◆———

September 1968

To Hazel's surprise, Elsie's eldest daughter called the next day to inform her that she and her sisters would take on the care of their mother—at great inconvenience to themselves and their families—but they would do it. She was their mother, after all.

Hazel spent the week she had to wait before calling the Family Services woman about the residents' placements wondering if the same shaming tactic she'd used on Elsie's daughter might also work with the Family Services woman.

When she was finally able to make the call, the District Supervisor's response to her asking for a status of the placements for the Sheldon Poor Farm's residents—"Who is that, now?"—offered little hope that she would take Hazel's concerns on behalf of the residents seriously.

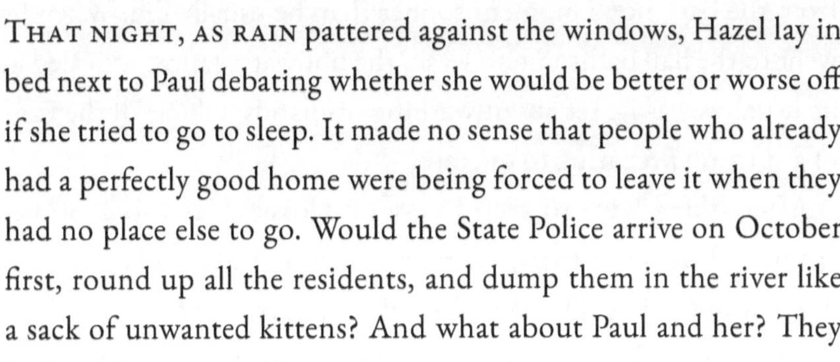

THAT NIGHT, AS RAIN pattered against the windows, Hazel lay in bed next to Paul debating whether she would be better or worse off if she tried to go to sleep. It made no sense that people who already had a perfectly good home were being forced to leave it when they had no place else to go. Would the State Police arrive on October first, round up all the residents, and dump them in the river like a sack of unwanted kittens? And what about Paul and her? They had no place to go either.

She whispered into the space between them that should have held sleep. "What are we going to do, Paul?"

"About what?"

"What's going to happen to us? Where will we go?"

"I'll take you over there tomorrow."

Hazel raised up on one elbow. "You have a place for us? Where?"

"Go to sleep, Hazel. There's no call to stay up half the night going on about it. I'll take you over there tomorrow."

Paul had spoken his final word on the matter, and that was that. She might as well go to sleep.

SOMETIME DURING THE NIGHT, the rain stopped, for which Hazel was grateful. Going to see their new place in the rain would be too depressing. She hurried through the breakfast cleanup with little more than a lick and a promise, as a parade of blank apartment windows above grimy Main Street storefronts paraded before her eyes. She wished Paul would tell her where their new place was and get it over with. He was acting as if she already knew.

She needn't have hurried through the cleanup. Paul returned from the barn not a moment sooner than he usually did. When he went to the hall bathroom to wash, the hot water faucet squealed in its usual way as he set about washing his hands, taking all the time of a surgeon preparing to operate.

After asking Edna to keep an eye on Flossie, Hazel took off her apron and went out to the car to wait before Paul could change his mind about going. The minutes ticked by. As she was about to go see what was taking him so long, he emerged from the house and moseyed across the dooryard to the car.

Fastening her seatbelt, Hazel couldn't remember the last time she and Paul had ridden in the car together. For the longest time, there had been no need. Paul started the car, put it in gear, and coasted down the winding driveway. They were on their way. More or less.

The cemetery on Poor Farm Road had begun to fill with leaves, yet the trees along the roadside were only beginning to turn color. Hazel looked at Paul, his hands relaxed and easy on the steering wheel, his face showing no hint of worry or frown. "Was it hard to find us a place?"

"Nope."

He turned right onto 105. Expanses of goldenrod, Queen Anne's Lace, milkweed, fields of corn waiting for the sharp, whirling blades of the combine. Telephone poles rushed by, carrying mile after mile of wire with news of other people's lives she would soon no longer need to concern herself with.

They traveled in silence until Paul turned onto a familiar dirt road, the landscape gently rolling, the mountains serene in the distance.

"Duffy Hill?" Hazel said. "You found us a place on Duffy Hill?"

A hint of a smile hovered about his lips. "Ayuh."

Coming to a battered old mailbox, the "Morgan" all but weathered away, Paul slowed the car and bounced onto a long, weed-filled driveway.

The farmhouse came into view. A farmhouse still standing, with windows intact and a sound roof. A farmhouse that had not fallen to ruin, the only changes a missing roof over the front door and missing front steps.

Paul parked the car and got out, as naturally as if they had returned home from a church potluck. When Hazel didn't move, he opened her door. "You getting out?"

She continued to stare at the house in disbelief.

Paul put out his hand. "Come on. I ain't got all day."

"But how—?" Hazel took Paul's hand and let him help her from the car.

"Where else would we go?"

"But how—?"

"You think I wouldn't pay the mortgage or the taxes? I knew we'd be coming back." Paul stepped onto the porch and unlocked the kitchen door. "You coming in or not?"

Hazel stepped into the kitchen, unsure of what she would find. The kitchen was as she'd left it twenty long years before, except for a lot of dust and old house chaff shed by the ceiling and the walls—the same with the living room, the dining room, the parlor, and the bedrooms.

As she followed Paul back down the stairs, he said, "Power's turned on. Plumber's coming next week to put in a hot water heater and some decent plumbing. You don't need to be lugging no damn buckets."

Hazel could not imagine how much a hot water heater would cost, never mind new plumbing. "I don't mind heating water for the two of us. I really don't."

Paul pointed at the bathroom door. "I got a real bathtub for in there. For free. Don't make no sense to me, but some flatlander is foolish enough to throw out a perfectly good bathtub, I'll take it. I should be able to pick up a decent kitchen sink for you before too long." Paul held the kitchen door open for her and locked it behind them.

Hazel stood on the porch looking at the yard overgrown with wildflowers, the untended fields, the clumps of vegetation where the barn used to be. "So, we're really coming back here? To live? You'll get a new herd and rebuild the barn?"

"Nope. I ain't never mortgaging this place again. When my time comes to go, you stay in this house free and clear."

"But—"

"I can hire out for farm work till I put in for my Social Security next year. It should be enough for us to get by if we don't go hog wild on the spending." He stepped off the porch, and Hazel followed him to the car.

When he started the car and bumped down the driveway, Hazel couldn't stop herself from twisting in her seat to look back at the farmhouse until it was out of sight.

On the ride back to Sheldon Springs, she resolved not to say another word about returning to the Duffy Hill farm. Paul wanted her to trust him; she would trust him. On the other hand, she wouldn't give herself over to daydreams of a large vegetable garden, abundant flower beds, new curtains, or chairs for the porch. Not yet.

Come Tomorrow

Hazel

September 1968

In the weeks that followed, Hazel called the State every day without fail, the Family Services woman giving up the placement information in distracted dribs and drabs—Carmi to a woman in Highgate who provided care in her home for the infirm and the demented, his calls for "John the Revelator" to go unanswered—Flossie to the nursing home in St. Albans, the blinds in her room never opened to daylight, the old woman such a nuisance when it rained—Edna to Brandon, where she would cry for her long-dead mother in an unfamiliar bed in an unfamiliar room that would always remain so.

Emmett would be dispatched to the place he least wanted to go: the Soldiers' Home in Bennington, where he would be heavily medicated at night the first time his trench was shelled in his sleep.

The battle to keep Homer and Lester together had been hard-fought, first with phone calls to the District Supervisor from

Hazel, then, when Homer and Lester were assigned to different nursing homes anyway, from Dwight. "Figures I'd have to do their goddamn job for 'em. I found a place in St. Johnsbury for both of them. Only took me a couple hours."

Dwight had been as good as his word about Charlie and Petey. Charlie would be back home with his father and a state-funded companion during the day. "No way those bastards are going to put that boy in a home because his father has to work for a living."

Unbelievably, Dwight had talked Johnny Clough—who had talked his wife—into taking Petey and the mare. "Marjorie can't take care of him anymore; she's in a nursing home, for Christ's sake. Petey gets sent to Brandon, he'd be dead in six months."

That left Joey. Hazel wanted so badly to ask Paul if they could take Joey with them to Duffy Hill, convinced she could talk Paul into it. Joey was such a cheerful sort and always willing to help out. But each time she decided to have that conversation, something had stopped her. Joey would be sent to Brandon.

WHEN PAUL'S ALARM CLOCK went off for the morning milking, Hazel jolted awake. Through the windows, not a hint of dawn lightened the night sky as Paul roused himself with an old man's groan to dress in the dark.

In the preceding weeks, no phone calls had come from the Family Services woman to arrange for a visit. In all those weeks, no one from the State had darkened the doorway of the Sheldon Poor House to inform the residents that, come October first, they would be removed from their home and taken elsewhere to live, with as little to say about it as a child who doesn't ask to be born.

Paul pulled on his overalls. "Not going back to sleep?"

"I can't. I have to tell the residents today."

Paul sat on the edge of the bed to put on his socks. "You don't need to tell them right now. Go back to sleep."

"I don't think I can do it."

But he was already halfway down the hall.

Hazel lay back down and ran doomsday scenarios in her head for delivering bad news to people who lacked the mental wherewithal to understand the news they were being given—or the physical strength to accept it—still not understanding what was happening when a social worker trundled them into the backseat of a generic sedan and drove them away, their cries of "What the hell, Hazel?" roiling with the cloud of road dust left by the car as it sped away.

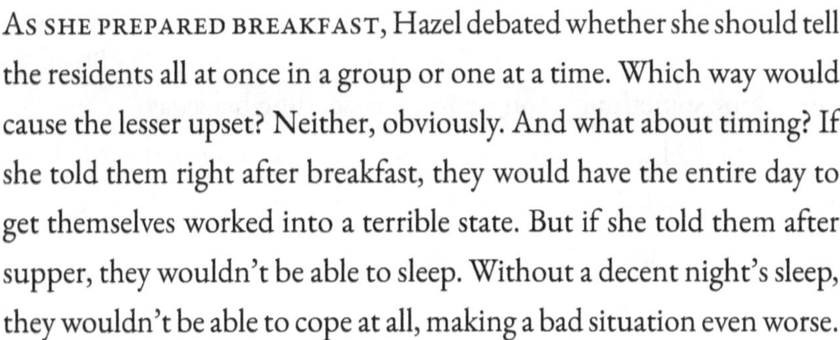

As she prepared breakfast, Hazel debated whether she should tell the residents all at once in a group or one at a time. Which way would cause the lesser upset? Neither, obviously. And what about timing? If she told them right after breakfast, they would have the entire day to get themselves worked into a terrible state. But if she told them after supper, they wouldn't be able to sleep. Without a decent night's sleep, they wouldn't be able to cope at all, making a bad situation even worse.

Consulting with Paul after breakfast, she decided to split the difference and tell them individually after cleanup for the noon meal. She told Charlie and Elsie first, in hopes their joyful reactions as they set about packing their clothes *right now* would see her through the rest.

She told Flossie next, after she'd gotten her settled on her bed for her afternoon nap.

"What do you mean?" Flossie said, her face a wrinkled cascade of confusion. "My family's all gone. There's no one left to take me in." She threw her arm over her eyes, as if to block Hazel's bad news from her sight and Hazel right along with it. "Oh, why did I have to live so long?"

"You didn't let me finish. The State's found a place—"

"But I don't want to go to a nursing home." Flossie moved her arm and looked Hazel in the eye. "I want to stay here with you and the others. Why are you sending me away? What did I do wrong?"

Hazel flinched, but she held Flossie's gaze. It was the least she could do.

"Oh, no, look what I've done. I've made you cry." Flossie picked up the box of tissues from her overbed table and held it out to Hazel, who took one look at the proffered comfort and bolted from the room. Cries of "But where am I going?" followed her down the hall and out the front door as she went in search of her husband.

She found him in the toolshed with a clipboard in his hand, working on yet another inventory. When she came within shouting distance of him, she said, "Well, I told Flossie. I told you she'd be upset. She thinks she's done something wrong, and we're sending her away."

Paul picked up a rusted coffee can of something that rattled and slammed it back down. "I should just heave all this shit in the back of the truck and haul it to the dump."

Obviously, Paul wasn't going to be any help at all. Hazel went back to the house to tell Flossie she would be going to the nursing home in St. Albans, where they would take good care of her.

LATER, AS HAZEL WASHED the supper dishes, Paul came into the kitchen. "How did it go when you told the others?"

She answered him without turning around. "I haven't told them yet."

"I thought we agreed—"

Hazel gave her full attention to the dinner plate in her hand. It had acquired a chip from somewhere. "I'll tell them."

"When? Tomorrow after the State gets here?"

She rinsed the chipped dinner plate. "I said I'll do it."

"Fine. We'll do it together."

"I'll *do* it, Paul. Stop badgering me."

Paul pushed a dish towel at her. "Dry your hands. We're telling them now."

"I'm not finished with the dishes."

"Now, Hazel."

Paul's voice had taken on that edge. Time for her to do as she was told and follow him to the living room.

When the residents looked up from their playing cards and jigsaw puzzles, their furrowed brows and darting eyes telegraphed confusion that Paul was in the living room. Regardless of the state of their wits, they knew something bad was about to happen.

Paul took Hazel's hand, but she was so startled by the unexpected gesture, she reflexively yanked her hand from his.

"Hazel has something to tell you."

Joey clapped his hands together. "Is it a surprise?"

"I like surprises," Charlie said.

"I like them more," Joey said.

Carmi got himself to his feet to stand at his imaginary pulpit. " 'Do not be surprised, brethren, if the world hates you.' The truth about us is finally known. The world hates us."

"That's enough, Carmi," Paul said. "Hazel has something important to say, and you need to be quiet and listen."

Petey scrambled up from his position on the floor in front of the blank television screen and made for the archway.

Paul grabbed him by the back of his shirt. "Where do you think you're going?"

"See the mare."

"Sit down, Petey. The mare's fine. I checked on her when I did the milking."

"What's the surprise, Hazel?" Joey said.

Elsie beamed. "I got a surprise this morning. My daughter's coming to get me tomorrow. I'm going to live with her."

The other residents paid no attention to her. They'd heard that story before.

Paul took Hazel's hand and squeezed it, the gesture saying, "Get on with it," as clearly as if he had said it out loud.

Hazel fixed her gaze on a crack in the wallpaper well above the residents' heads. "The State has decided it would be best if people didn't go to the poor farm anymore."

"They're closing us down?" Emmett said.

"Yes."

"They're gonna stick me in the old soldiers' home, ain't they?"

"I'm afraid so. The State thinks it's best for you to be looked after by the VA."

"The State don't know shit about what's best for me and neither does the goddamn VA." Emmett stabbed his cane on the floor, heaved himself to his feet, and left the room.

"Emmett's upset," Joey said.

"I don't want to be looked after by the VA," Charlie said.

"You won't be looked after by the VA. That's for veterans. Don't you remember what I told you this morning about going back home to live with your father? You'll have a companion to look after you while he's at work."

"My father's coming to get me? I gotta pack." Charlie ran from the room and pounded down the hall, even though he'd already packed his clothes earlier in the day.

"I'm staying here, Hazel, right, with you and Paul, right?" Joey said.

Hazel shook her head. *No, Joey. You will be going to Brandon.*

Never would she speak those words aloud. Her eyes blurred, and she stumbled from the room. Fleeing to the manager's suite, she collapsed on the bed.

She didn't know how many minutes had gone by when Paul entered the room and sat on the edge of the bed. "I told the others, Hazel." He rubbed her shoulder. "You're too softhearted. You did everything you could. More'n anybody else would have."

SOMEHOW, HAZEL MADE IT through the rest of the evening, putting the kitchen to rights and getting the residents ready for the night.

When she and Paul went to bed, she said, "I don't know how I'm going to get through the day tomorrow."

"You want to take the car and go to the farm? You'll have power and running water. I need to use the truck anyhow to move our bedroom furniture back."

As badly as she wanted to accept Paul's offer, she couldn't do it. Denying the residents a proper goodbye would be like refusing to sit at the bedside of a dying loved one because her own pain would be too much to bear.

OCTOBER 1, 1968

HAZEL

———◄◦►———

THE FINAL DAY OF the Sheldon Poor Farm dawned cloudy and un-seasonably warm. Hazel prepared one last breakfast of farm fresh eggs and made sure the residents were dressed neatly in clean clothes with their hair combed. She arranged their packed belongings in suitcases and grocery boxes, labeled and arranged in alphabetical order by last name in the front hall.

Charlie's father arrived first, right after breakfast, beaming as he carried his son's belongings to the truck and followed him into the storage shed to retrieve his beloved red bicycle. Before he and Charlie drove off, he told Hazel, "Thank you for finding a way to bring my boy back home." Before she could respond that it was all Dwight Demers's doing, he and Charlie were already on their way home.

Elsie was next to go, her eldest daughter pulling into the dooryard in a large station wagon with grocery bags in the back. When Hazel met her at the front door, her greeting was cordial enough, but her response to Elsie's arms open for an embrace was, "Come, come, Mother. I have frozen food in the car. We need to get going."

As Hazel helped Elsie down the front steps, the happiness on Elsie's face was more painful to see than tears ever would have been. Helping Elsie into the station wagon, Hazel tried—and failed—to erase from her mind the image of Elsie sitting alone day after day in a room she shared with the sewing machine and the ironing board, as the bustle and laughter of family life went on without her.

Hazel embraced her, kissed her cheek, and buckled her seatbelt. As the buckle clicked into place, Elsie said, "Thank you for being so kind to me, Hazel, like I was your own mother." Elsie's rare moment of lucidity couldn't have come at a worse time. Hazel acknowledged it with another kiss on Elsie's cheek before stumbling back to the house in tears.

Hazel spent a few minutes alone in the bathroom to collect herself for the next departure, which came all too soon in the form of a white passenger van from the Soldiers' Home. Emmett's response to the impossibly young social worker's introducing herself and trying to help him to the van was, "Get the hell away from me, kid. I may be crippled, but I ain't dead yet, and I don't need no help from the likes of you." The social worker dissolved in tears, and Hazel had to take her into the kitchen to get her calmed down enough to drive. If she somehow could have managed it, Hazel would have driven the two of them to Bennington herself. Neither was in any fit state for a long drive.

As the Soldiers' Home van made its unsteady way out of the dooryard, Paul emerged from the cow barn. When he reached her, he put his hand on her shoulder. "How you holdin' up?"

"Okay, I guess."

"If it gets too much, you come and get me."

Once again, Hazel stumbled to the house in tears.

Another car pulled into the dooryard. Hazel brushed the tears from her face and hurried to the porch to see who it was. A skinny kid in blue Dickies exited the car. Had whatever place he was from sent the janitor? He stood next to the car looking around as if he had no idea where he was, who had sent him there, or for what possible purpose. Catching sight of Hazel, he drifted over to the porch.

"I think I'm supposed to pick somebody up?"

Hazel waited for him to tell her where he was from and which person he needed to pick up, but he didn't. "Where do you work?"

"Uh, nursing home on 105?"

"That would be Flossie. I'll bring her out."

The kid shook his head. "Uh uh." He dug into his pants pocket and pulled out a scrap of paper. "Says here Florence Kimball."

Lord, give me strength. "Flossie is a nickname for Florence."

"Oh. You sure about that?"

Hazel had half a mind to drive Flossie to the damn nursing home herself. It wasn't but a few miles away. She retrieved Flossie's belongings from the front hall, put them on the back seat of the car, and went to Flossie's room.

Flossie's eyes were wet, and she was worrying her hands hard enough to fracture the tiny, hollow bones inside. "They've come for me?"

Hazel maneuvered the wheelchair into position by the bed and set the brake. "It's time to go, yes."

"I don't want to go." Flossie's voice quavered and broke. "I want to stay here. Please don't send me away, Hazel. I won't be a bother."

When Hazel wheeled Flossie onto the porch, the nursing home kid's eyes widened. "What am I supposed to do with her? She's in a wheelchair. And she's crying. Nobody told me she'd be crying."

"Do you want me to call your employer to send someone?"

Before he could answer, Joey's voice piped up from behind her. "I can help the man."

"Thank you, Joey," Hazel said. "You and I will move Flossie."

As they got into position on either side of the wheelchair, Joey said, "Be very, very careful, Hazel. Flossie is very, very old."

Hazel got Flossie settled in the front seat of the car, buckled her seat belt, and shortened it to hold Flossie's tiny frame securely. When Hazel released her from a quick embrace, Flossie grabbed her hand. "Look at the clouds, Hazel. It's going to rain. You and Paul have to get to higher ground. Please. Before the bridge—"

The kid got in the car and started it up. Then Flossie, too, was gone.

After a dinner of reheated beef stew at the half-empty dining room table, Paul and Petey returned to the cow barn, Hazel to the kitchen, and the five remaining residents to the front porch rocking chairs to wait for what came next.

What came next was a wheezing old Studebaker that disgorged a sturdy older woman so exceedingly cheerful, she reminded Hazel of Philo Roy, of all people.

"Sorry I'm late. The old jalopy wouldn't start, and I had to get a jump from the neighbors. That took some doing, let me tell you. Who keeps their jumper cables down cellar under a pile of junk?" She strode to the porch. "Now, which one of you fine folks is Carmi Delude?"

Carmi handed his Bible to Lester and put his hands on the arms of the rocking chair. Ignoring Homer's offer of a steady arm, he heaved himself to his feet. The Highgate woman waved Hazel off and helped Carmi down the steps herself, Hazel trailing them to the car with Carmi's belongings. As the Studebaker groaned its way out of the dooryard, Hazel noticed that the exhaust pipe was held on with a coat hanger. Poor Carmi was liable to be asphyxiated before he ever got to Highgate to evangelize the other poor souls one faltering heartbeat from meeting their Maker.

Several minutes went by as Hazel and the remaining four residents sat in silence on the porch, watching as the mountains on the horizon receded under the lowering sky.

"Looks like rain," Homer offered.

"Ayuh, feels like it," Lester agreed.

"Flossie's afraid of the rain," Joey said. "Edna's not afraid of the rain. Edna's brave."

Hazel looked at her watch. Three o'clock. What could be keeping the other two places? Had they forgotten to send someone? Or did they assume that four disabled people who couldn't live by themselves would get there of their own accord? What were they supposed to do? Shuffle their way across the state in their bedroom slippers?

As if the State had heard her thoughts and didn't like them one little bit, a generic white sedan pulled into the dooryard.

"A lady's here!" Joey announced.

The young woman who got out of the car looked as tired from driving as Lester looked from waiting for so long. Hazel left the porch to greet her. "Who are you here for?"

"Homer and Lester Shover. May I use your bathroom?"

Hazel escorted the social worker to the bathroom and went back to the porch to inform Lester and Homer it was their turn to leave.

"I surely wish we could stay here," Homer said. "The old man don't take kindly to change." He lowered his voice. "Do you think we could bring Mouser with us? Mouser's such a comfort to the old man. I don't think Paul would mind, seeing as the farm's being shut down."

"You'll have to ask the social worker."

"Ask me what?"

"Can we bring my father's cat with us?"

The social worker seemed to hesitate before giving the answer Hazel knew she would give. "No, I'm sorry. The facility doesn't allow patients to have pets." She sounded genuinely sorry.

When they were ready to go, Hazel gave Lester and Homer the best sendoff she could with an embrace, a rallied smile, and a murmured "God bless." Even so, as the car began the long drive back to St.

Johnsbury, they looked as if they were being carted off to jail, huddled together in the back seat of that generic white sedan, their heads hung in shame.

Hazel looked at her watch again. Nearly quarter of four.

"What we waiting for, Hazel?" Joey said.

"We're waiting for your ride to Brandon."

"How come?"

"That's where you and Edna will be living now, remember?"

"Okay, Hazel." Joey turned to Edna. "I bet they let you sweep. You're a good sweeper."

"I'm a good sweeper," Edna confirmed. "I hope they like me."

"They have to like you. You're Edna!" Joey set his rocking chair going fast enough to catapult him over the porch railing. "We can fold the towels, and Hazel will come visit us, and we'll eat sandwiches."

Fifteen minutes later, when the social worker arrived and got out of the car, every rumpled inch of her telegraphed that she was not happy to be the one stuck with driving all the way up from Brandon for a couple of poorhouse refugees and driving them all the way back. Her supervisor owed her one.

Joey jumped up. "The lady's here!"

As the social worker approached the porch, Hazel gestured toward the open doorway. "Bathroom's down the hall, second door on your left."

Returning to the porch, the social worker pointed with the index and middle fingers of one hand. "These two?"

"I beg your pardon," Hazel said. "They have names. And you haven't told me who you are."

"Oh, yeah. Been a long day. I've come from Brandon to collect Edna Goodhue and Joey Clapper."

Before Hazel could object to "collect," Joey interjected. "I'm Joey. This is Edna. Edna is my friend."

"That's nice. Where are their things?"

Joey dashed into the hall and emerged with Edna's box of belongings. "The men help the ladies. Ladies go first."

The social worker rolled her eyes and grabbed Joey's suitcase.

When Joey returned from the car to get Edna, Hazel said her goodbyes on the porch. As cowardly as it was, she didn't have the strength to walk to that car and watch it drive away.

Joey patted her arm. "There, there, Hazel. Don't cry. You can come visit us. Paul, too. We'll eat lots and lots of sandwiches."

JOHNNY CLOUGH DIDN'T COME for Petey until close to suppertime, and Hazel was afraid that he—or more likely—his wife had changed their minds, and she would have to turn his fate over to the Family Services woman. But no, Johnny had just taken his own sweet time about it, strolling into the kitchen, where Petey now sat at the table, ostensibly keeping Hazel company while she figured out what she should do about supper.

"Come on, buddy. The wife has your room ready for you, and she's making spaghetti and meatballs for our supper."

"The mare—"

"Don't you worry about the mare. She's coming with us."

Sure enough, Paul emerged from the storage barn, hooked up the horse trailer to the farm's truck, loaded the mare into it, and drove off.

After Johnny drove Petey away, Hazel prowled the house, as if expecting to find an elderly man hiding under his bed, an elderly woman curled up on a couch fast asleep. Not a trace of them remained, not even a mangled copy of *The Wind in the Willows*.

The Last Poor Farm

Hazel

—◦—

THE DAY AFTER THE State took all the residents away, Hazel continued the work of shutting down the last poorhouse in Vermont by laundering linens, surprised at how tiresome the task seemed without Joey and Edna to help. Shoving a load of wet towels into the dryer, she thought she heard someone call her name. She paused to listen, but the only sound she heard was the washer agitating another load of towels.

The voice didn't call out again, and she chalked it up to hearing things in a recently vacated house. The Sheldon Poor House held a lot of voices within its old walls, not surprising it would choose to release them now. Vacant-eyed families whose homes had caught fire and burned to the ground. Mothers with small children evicted from their homes after the father lost his life to the spinning blade of a mill saw. The temporarily despondent man who slashed his arm with a razor blade, only to change his mind and scream for help when a pint of his blood poured onto the floor. The permanently despondent man Paul had found swinging by his neck from a beam in the cow barn one morning before sunrise.

Footsteps sounded faintly on the stairs at the other end of the basement, stopped. "Hazel, you down there?" A few more steps. "Hazel, Paul, you down here?"

Hazel left the laundry room and walked down the hall to the front of the basement to find Dwight Demers holding a small white box.

"Ah, there you are, Hazel. I thought I'd stop by, see how things are coming along for the auction. You think Paul could join us for a cup of coffee?" He waggled the box. "I brought doughnuts." He waggled the box again. "Jelly. "

Will wonders never cease? Hazel looked at her watch as footsteps sounded above their heads. "That must be Paul." As Hazel followed Dwight up the stairs, the faucet Paul never did fix let out a final squeal.

When the three of them were seated at the kitchen table waiting for the coffee to perk, Dwight said, "I wanted to stop by and let you both know all our residents arrived safely at their destinations. You wouldn't believe how many downright unpleasant people I had to talk to before I could get a straight answer to a yes or no question."

"Figures," Paul said.

"I should have come yesterday, you know, for moral support, but I was afraid I wouldn't be able to hold my tongue, seeing those poor souls ripped from their home. Makes my blood boil even thinking about it."

"Mine, too," Hazel said.

"Hazel was a real trooper." Paul reached across the table and squeezed her hand. "I'm proud of her."

Hazel blushed from her neck to her hairline and back again as she jumped up from the table. "Oh! I didn't get plates for the doughnuts."

"Never mind about plates," Dwight said. "No need to stand on ceremony with me."

As Hazel opened the cupboard for plates anyway, a car pulled into the dooryard. Johnny Clough's LTD. She should have known Johnny would feel the need to put in an appearance.

"Well, lookee here, having coffee and doughnuts without me. What's a man to think?" Johnny plopped himself down on his usual chair and reached for the percolator with one hand, the doughnut box with the other. His coffee and doughnut at the ready, he said, "I come over to ask about that old horse cart Petey's been using. Totally slipped my mind yesterday. Didn't slip Petey's, though. He's been going on about it ever since he woke up at the crack of dawn this morning." Johnny plucked another doughnut from the box. "Don't mind if I do! I drove down to Marjorie's, but when I checked in the stable, Petey's old buggy was missing. Can't imagine who coulda made off with it. It's not like they could pawn it for drug money, although I hear tell them Tibbetts boys been known to fence stolen goods." He took a gulp of coffee. "Long story short, I surely could use that old cart. Think the Association would miss it at the auction?"

Dwight grabbed a napkin and wiped a bit of escaped jelly from his chin. "Cart? What cart?"

Johnny stuffed the rest of his doughnut into his mouth. "Be over tomorrow in the forenoon with my boy's flatbed."

Dwight and Johnny took their leave when the percolator and the doughnut box were empty, Hazel and Paul walking them to the dooryard to see them off. Paul put his arm around Hazel's shoulders as they watched the cars disappear around the bend.

"You know, Hazel, I do believe I'm gonna miss them two."

WHEN THE DAY OF the auction arrived, Paul suggested at breakfast that Hazel go on ahead to Duffy Hill. "I won't be able to leave till tomorrow. Soon as the animals are collected, I'll load up the truck and head for the farm. You can follow me when I take the truck to whoever buys it."

As much as she didn't want to bear witness to the estate sale of the Sheldon Poor Farm, in fairness to Paul, she had to ask. "You're sure?"

He pulled his key ring out of his overalls and eased off one of the keys. "Just get our clothes and things packed." He got up from the table. "Leave me a set of clean drawers."

An hour and a half later, Hazel slid into the front seat of their car and rolled out of the dooryard for the last time. She needed one final glimpse of the house in the rearview mirror, but only one and only a glimpse.

When she reached the cemetery, which still had no sign and now never would, she parked the car and got out, buttoning her sweater against the crisp autumn chill. In the cemetery, pine needles and newly fallen leaves cushioned the ground beneath her feet, releasing their early autumn scent with each step. At the back of the cemetery, she paused to look out at the field of goldenrod which stretched to the tree line. The goldenrod had gone by, drying in the sun to prepare for its winter dormancy beneath the snow.

She knelt before three gravestones, two of them discolored from forty years in the weather, the inscriptions wholly inadequate to tell the story of those two lives, Mama's and Sam's. The third gravestone, less discolored than the other two, marked the first and final resting place of Baby Alice. Paul had strongly objected to her being buried in a pauper's grave, only giving in when Hazel insisted that being buried with her grandmother and her uncle might ease the sting of the way she died.

Hazel ran her fingers over the face of each stone. Mama. Sam. Baby Alice. And Daddy, his final resting place unseen but never forgotten.

Back in the car, she turned on the radio. Someone singing about how blue her world had become since her love went away. Hazel hoped that at some point whatever Claire had done to drive her husband from their home could be forgiven, if not forgotten. At the very least, Claire should be able to reach some measure of peace staying with her parents.

Hazel shut the radio off and turned onto 105. The stubbled corn fields and changing foliage signaled that the cold weather would soon be upon them. Paul had a lot of wood-chopping ahead of him.

The car bumped over a set of railroad tracks. Philo Roy never had made it back to Sheldon this year. In all likelihood—if he hadn't met his fate under the wheels of a freight train—he had finally conceded defeat to Father Time, who had been telling him for years he was too old to be hopping freight trains. But what if next year the lure of his home state proved too much to resist and he managed to make his way back, bumming rides on long stretches of highway in exchange for a series of ridiculous tall tales? She could see him sauntering down Poor Farm Road, ragged knapsack slung over one shoulder, cigarette poking through that silly mustache of his—only to find the fields overgrown, the barns empty, and the house abandoned.

Arriving at the Morgan mailbox, Hazel bumped up the overgrown driveway, parked in front of the house, and set her grocery box of necessary items on the porch. Instead of unlocking the door to her own domain of the kitchen—so easily reclaimed with a hot stove and a new broom—she pushed her way through the burdock, weeds, and fists of Queen Anne's Lace to the ruins of the old barn. Vegetation completely covered what remained of the collapse, not as if the barn had never been there, but as the land simply returning to what it had once been.

Plucking the odd burr from her skirt as she walked back to the house, Hazel realized why her tearful goodbye to Joey the previous day had been so unsettling. Joey would remember her if he saw her again; of that she was certain. Yet, if she never visited him—and in all likelihood she wouldn't—the clear path in his mind leading to "Hazel" would become overgrown and disappear, just as the forest reclaimed its own in the natural order of things.

When she reached the porch, she paused for a moment before entering the house. Tomorrow, Paul would return to their farm and stand by her side on the porch, gazing out at the mountains, those steadfast, sheltering mountains. Next year, when summer waned, she would fill the house with goldenrod gathered from the overgrown meadow. Later, when the dark clouds came—as they must—she would open a window to the scent of dying wildflowers wet with rain.

OCTOBER 1, 2025

Autumn rain patters softly on the leaves nestled against the gravestones in the cemetery on Poor Farm Road. The surrounding maples glisten yellow through the rain, bearing silent witness to all those stories left untold. The Sheldon Poor House burned to the ground one last time in 1978.

A Note from the Author

The Inspiration

After finishing my debut novel, *Telling Sonny,* I didn't intend to write another novel right away. I fully intended to return to the short story collection I'd been working on.

Then I read an article in the Spring 1990 issue of *Vermont Life Magazine:* "Over the Hill to the Poor Farm: How an Era Ended Quietly on a Back Road in Sheldon Springs" by Steve Young.

Seeing the photographs and reading the history of the place, I was struck by the fact that while I was growing up, I'd lived only seven miles from the Sheldon Poor Farm—yet I knew nothing about it. I'd been by the poorhouse building once in the early 1970s, but it didn't register with me that it had ceased being a poorhouse only a few short years before. I had to know more.

Around the time I read the *Vermont Life* article, I'd also been toying with the idea of a woman running away from her family with a blues musician, so I thought I'd combine the two ideas. It would be a lark, something fun before I went back to the short story collection. Little did I know where this idea would lead me!

History & Poetic License

Finding the right balance between fact and fiction in a historical novel can be tricky, so for clarity's sake I'm letting you know where the two diverge.

You may have noticed two different spellings of "poorhouse." I used the dictionary spelling for references to the poorhouse. The Sheldon Poor House Association used two words, and I've kept that spelling when referring to the Assocation.

I've adhered to the basic historical facts of the Sheldon Poor Farm's history and the 1968 closure precipitated by the Vermont Social Welfare Act of 1967. I've taken some poetic license with minor details. All of the scenes are fictional.

Details of the living conditions in the poorhouse building at various times from 1913 through 1968 are taken from newspaper reports. I've also adhered to the facts of the social unrest in the United States in 1967 and 1968, which are taken from recorded television newscasts.

All of the characters in the book are fictional, with the exception of Lightnin' Hopkins, Bilbo Walker, and Sterling D. Weed. I listened to a lot of Hopkins's music to get a sense of what Claire was drawn to, and I used the actual song titles. I read two biographies of Lightnin' Hopkins to get a sense of his character quirks. I also watched recorded interviews to get a sense of the dialect he spoke, (without trying to transcribe it). While Hopkins was from Houston, Texas, his life and times in Vinton, Louisiana are completely fictional.

Bilbo Walker was also an actual blues musician, but I moved his juke joint from Mississippi to Louisiana. His actions are also completely fictional.

Sterling D. Weed was a famous big bandleader in Vermont, leading Weed's Imperial Orchestra until his death at 104 in 2005. (He'd gotten his start as a musician performing in public at age 11 in 1912.) Weed led the Enosburg Falls Town Band for many years. My brother played saxophone in the town band under Weed when he was in high school, and he played with Weed's Imperial Orchestra to earn pocket money when he went to college.

Social Justice

By the time I neared completion of the book, I was surprised by how relevant the themes are to social conditions in the United States at the present time, something I hadn't intended. Nevertheless, I believe that these characters have something to teach us about social justice and the worth of the individual.

In closing, thank you for reading *The Weight of Snow and Regret*. I hope the story of these characters has found a small place in your heart.

In Peace & Love,
Liz Gauffreau
January 2025

ACKNOWLEDGMENTS

I am eternally grateful to my husband for his infinite patience and good humor. Every time I took it into my head that I needed to take inspiration photos, experience the scent of the air each time the season changed, or clock mileages from place to place in Franklin County, Vermont, he was right there with the car keys and a packed lunch.

Thank you to Audrey Driscoll for introducing me to the one-page-a-day method of writing a first draft. (It really works!)

Thank you to Charles French's writing group for listening to my drafts and helping me work through some sticky wickets. A special thanks to Charles French for beta reading.

I am grateful to Robbie Cheadle for suggesting that my working title for the novel didn't align well with the content of the book. (She was right.)

The Woven Tale Press Prose Critique Group helped me work through some structural challenges.

Harold Smith of the Sheldon Historical Society answered my questions about the Poor Farm's history and provided me with newspaper articles for additional information. His recorded presentation on behalf of the Osher Lifelong Learning Institutes, "Poverty and The Sheldon Poor Farm History," was very helpful as well.

Prudence Doherty, Public Services Librarian in the Silver Special Collections Library at the University of Vermont photographed the original 1913 Sheldon poorhouse blueprints and emailed them to me. Not knowing the layout of the building had become a big impediment to revising my rough draft.

Sources Consulted

Books & Articles

Govenar, Alan. *Lightnin' Hopkins: His Life and Blues*, 2010. https://openlibrary.org/books/OL24324386M/Lightnin'_Hopkins.

O'Brien, Timothy J., and David Ensminger. *Mojo Hand: The Life and Music of Lightnin' Hopkins*. University of Texas Press, 2013.

Snider, Clyde F. "Town Government in Vermont. By Andrew E. Nuquist. (Burlington: Government Research Center, University of Vermont, 1964. Pp. Xiv, 276. $5.25.)." *American Political Science Review* 58, no. 4 (December 1, 1964): 1006–7. https://doi.org/10.1017/s0003055400291545.

Sullivan, Ellen. *A Vermont Scrapbook: Fifty Vermonters Remember*, 1991.

Young, Steve. "Over the Hill: The Last Poor Farm." Vermont Life, season-01 1990. https://archive.org/details/rbmsbk_ap2-v4_1990_V44N3/page/n15/mode/2up.

Newscasts

CBS. "1968 King Assassination Report (CBS News)," April 3, 2008. https://www.youtube.com/watch?v=cmOBbxgxKvo.

"NBC Flashback: The Assassination of Martin Luther King, Jr.," October 10, 2023. https://www.nbcnews.com/video/nbc-flashback-the-assassination-of-martin-luther-king-jr-658575939695.

C-Span. "[Martin Luther King - Assassination and Aftermath]." *C-S PAN.Org*, April 5, 1968. https://www.c-span.org/program/reel-america/martin-luther-king---assassination-and-aftermath/499928.

Newz Reels. "ABC News Coverage on the Assassination of Martin Luther King (1968)," April 7, 2022. https://www.youtube.com/watch?v=ks02PQiJGmQ.

———. "[Martin Luther King - Assassination and Aftermath]." *C-S PAN.Org*, April 5, 1968. https://www.c-span.org/program/reel-america/martin-luther-king---assassination-and-aftermath/499928.

"Dan Rather Convention Floor Fight, CBS News," August 28, 1968. https://www.youtube.com/watch?v=wItUjFU1i4M.

"Days of Rage: Timeline of the 1968 Democratic National Convention," August 28, 1968," August 28, 1968. https://abcnews.go.com/Politics/video/archival-video-protests-turn-violent-1968-democratic-national-37639406.

Video

The Blues Accordin' to Lightnin' Hopkins, 1967. https://www.youtube.com/watch?v=BcVbNaiBZCU.Les Blank, Director

Livin' the Blues. "Lightnin' Hopkins Story Live," April 15, 2020. https://www.youtube.com/watch?v=Yey2Nh5qrr0.

"The Mississippi Juke Joint Keeping the Blues Alive." Uploaded by Great Big Story, July 6, 2017. https://www.youtube.com/watch?v=hwt4Ng3egUc.

Northwest Access TV. "OLLI Lecture | Poverty and the Sheldon Poor Farm History With Harold Smith | 03/29/2023," April 5, 2023. https://www.youtube.com/watch?v=uo7gsQ-Uwa8.

About the Author

Elizabeth Gauffreau writes fiction and poetry with a strong connection to family and place. She holds a BA in English/Writing from Old Dominion University and an MA in English/Fiction Writing from the University of New Hampshire. Her fiction and poetry have been widely published in literary magazines and several themed anthologies. Her short story "Henrietta's Saving Grace" was awarded the 2022 Ben Nyberg prize for fiction by Choeofpleirn Press.

Liz's professional background is in nontraditional higher education, including academic advising, classroom and online teaching, assessment of prior experiential learning, curriculum development, and program administration. She received the Granite State College Distinguished Faculty Award for Excellence in Teaching in 2018. Liz lives in Nottingham, New Hampshire with her husband. Their daughter has flown the nest to sunny California.

Find Liz online at https://lizgauffreau.com.

ALSO BY ELIZABETH GAUFFREAU

Simple Pleasures: Haiku from the Place Just Right

In this collection of 53 haiku, each paired with a nature photograph, poet Elizabeth Gauffreau invites readers to join her on a poetic journey through the picturesque landscapes of Vermont, New Hampshire, and Maine. Each poem captures a moment of clarity and serenity, offering a window into the tranquil beauty of northern New England and the profound feelings these places evoke. Through her blend of poignant haiku and vivid imagery, Gauffreau creates a relatable and uplifting experience that resonates with anyone who cherishes nature's gifts and the memories made with loved ones in these serene settings.

Buy *Simple Pleasures* for Kindle or tablet:
https://books2read.com/SimplePleasures

Buy *Simple Pleasures* in PDF Ebook for any device:
https://buy.bookfunnel.com/3j53rra5k5

Telling Sonny

Telling Sonny is a coming-of-age novel set in the 1920s, when much of vaudeville had devolved into the Small Time. Not so for Faby Gauthier, a naïve girl from the small village of Enosburg Falls, Vermont. For Faby, the annual vaudeville show that comes to the village is worthy of the Great White Way itself. Little does she know that in a few short months, she will learn the true meaning of Small Time, setting her life on a path she never imagined.

Buy *Telling Sonny*: https://books2read.com/TellingSonny

Grief Songs: Poems of Love & Remembrance

When a loved one dies, the family will often turn to their photograph albums as an act of solace, to keep their loved one with them just a little while longer. *Grief Songs: Poems of Love & Remembrance* arose from that experience. The collection opens with three free verse expressions of raw grief, followed by a series of photographs from the author's family album, each paired with a poem written in tanka. Taken together, they tell the story of a loving family lost.

Buy *Grief Songs*: https://books2read.com/GriefSongs

www.ingramcontent.com/pod-product-compliance
Lightning Source LLC
Chambersburg PA
CBHW022300310726
48973CB00001B/141